HAIKA
SORU

PHANTASM JAPAN

PHANTASM JAPAN

JAPAN

FANTASIES LIGHT AND DARK FROM AND ABOUT JAPAN

EDITED BY NICK MAMATAS AND MASUMI WASHINGTON

HAIKA
SORU

SAN FRANCISCO

PHANTASM JAPAN
© 2014 VIZ Media
See Copyright Acknowledgements for individual story copyrights.

Cover art by YUKO SHIMIZU
Design by FAWN LAU

HAIKASORU
Published by
VIZ Media, LLC
1355 Market Street, Suite 200
San Francisco, CA 94103

www.haikasoru.com

Library of Congress Cataloging-in-Publication Data

Phantasm Japan : fantasies light and dark, from and about
Japan / edited by Nick Mamatas and Masumi Washington.
     pages   cm
  ISBN 978-1-4215-7174-4 (paperback)
  1. Japan—Fiction. 2. Fantasy fiction, American. 3. Fantasy
fiction, English. 4. Fantasy fiction, Japanese. 5. Ghost stories,
Japanese. I. Mamatas, Nick, editor. II. Washington, Masumi,
editor.
  PS648.J29P48   2014
  813'.0108952—dc23
                        2014024324

Printed in the U.S.A.
First printing, September 2014

CONTENTS

Introduction—The Eight Millionth and First Spirit
By Nick Mamatas

It is said that Japan is the home of *ya-o-yorozu no kami*—eight million spirits. Of course, such a thing is often said by Westerners, who simply just heard the phrase somewhere. Even after decades of globalization and cultural exchange—my mother watched *Astro Boy* on TV as a kid, I grew up with *Battle of the Planets,* and there are adults in the United States today that have never known life without some kind of Power Ranger—Japan remains a mystery to too many. Lafcadio Hearn, the famed writer and popularizer of Japanese ghost stories, said of the Japanese language after learning it and becoming a naturalized Japanese citizen over a century ago, "Experience in the acquisition of European languages can help you to learn Japanese about as much as it could help you to acquire the language spoken by the inhabitants of Mars."

Of course, Japan is no more mysterious than the haunted cornfields of Iowa or the strange and twisting labyrinths of the New York City subway system. Everything human is ultimately comprehendible, and no nation is ever mysterious to its own population. Hearn published his *Japan, An Attempt at Interpretation* in 1904, so perhaps could be forgiven for his crack about mutual incomprehensibility.

One hundred and ten years later, one of Hearn's statements from the book still holds true: "Any true comprehension of social conditions requires more than a superficial acquaintance with religious conditions." Not just for Japan, but for anywhere. Study the local religious beliefs—and this includes folk beliefs about the supernatural and the acknowledged fictions about the supernatural that any society creates—and you'll gain some insights into that society.

Phantasm Japan seeks to use the fantastic not to mystify, but to demystify, to bring to the English-speaking world not only traditional stories of *tanuki* (raccoon dogs) and *kitsune* (foxes), of ghosts and yokai, but the bleeding edge of the Japanese fantastic. Japanese fantasy is in a dialogue not only with Japan's spiritual traditions and modern experience, but with Western ghost stories and science fiction. Japanese fantasy is in dialogue with virtually everything, from the New Weird to the real-life horror of the Fukushima nuclear disaster, which spawned several new ghost stories in the evacuee camps.

So a Japanese author can write of the occult truth behind the long career of James Bond, an American author can rewrite several ancient tales from Japan, and an author from the United Kingdom can wonder aloud if Japan had ever existed, or if it was just a dream—and then subvert that notion. We even have a story about a samurai, and a long, illustrated tale from Japan that just may change everything you think you know about fantasy…and the workplace.

Fantasy is more than just an escape; it is a way of communicating about real life and across cultures. You don't need to know Japanese, or Martian for that matter, to know something about Japan. Take a look at a culture's fantasy, and you may learn some of its deepest secrets.

Foreword By Masumi Washington

When we finished editing the translation for "Sisyphean," the longest story in this anthology, I sent the text to Tetsuya Kohama, the story's original editor, who told me of the enormous amount of time he spent editing the novella before publishing it. I thought he should be the first reader to see how the translation went because people in Japan—including me, initially—thought that would be too difficult, complicated, and perplexing to be translated.

Kohama-san first congratulated us on actually managing it, then said, "The English translation reminded me of what this story actually is—besides all those neologisms, the composition itself is structurally very clear. What perplexed us is that the text is too complex to see what's what."

Translating Japanese into English involves more than just replacing words and sentences between the two very different languages. The translator has to dive into the story, sometimes deeper than the author did, to find what things it has shown. That is a series of processes for interpretation. The translator has to determine how he or she interprets what they read in Japanese. In the end, the efforts open up a door to show to English-speaking audiences what's what in the story—they are not just letters or words anymore.

The theme of *Phantasm Japan* involves a similar process for the English-writing authors, who interpret themes and stories that don't belong in their own cultural backgrounds. They dove into the sea and grabbed something with which to tell their own stories. It amazed me what they were actually bringing from the sea. Yes, I was afraid we would receive a ton of *kappa* or *bakeneko* stories. Instead, who could imagine that we'd have Kairakutei Black and US internment camps in fantasy stories? I just took my hat off.

This is our second anthology, and I am glad to have such interesting stories, not only from Western countries and Japan, as the first one was, but also from other areas in Asia. Thank you very much to the all contributors who participated and our internal staff that helped with the production. This time, I am especially grateful to Haikasoru's fabulous translators, Jocelyne Allen, Nathan Collins, Jim Hubbert, and Daniel Huddleston. We would not be able to publish a single word without you.

A Tale of Japan: In His Wake By Zachary Mason

Soon after dying, the warrior Suzano found himself before the gate of the heaven of storms. There appeared a guardian of fiercely leonine aspect who said, "Your life was a righteous one, your courage indefatigable, and your discipline relentless. If you had a flaw, it was in your unyielding harshness, but you were harder with yourself than any other." Suzano nodded, and the guardian said, "You will be reborn as a protector spirit of the first class, but until your next incarnation the gates of this heaven swing wide for you."

"Is my father here, though dead these thirty years?" asked Suzano.

"Ah," said the guardian. "No. I'm afraid he was not quite…"

"No," said Suzano. "Where, may I ask, is he?"

The guardian met his eyes with an effort and said, "The hell of tar and shadow."

"I must postpone my acceptance of your gracious hospitality," Suzano said, "until I have retrieved him."

"Filial piety has a term," said the guardian. "You performed his funeral rites, you mourned for a year, you sacrificed before his tomb. What is right, you have done. You are finished."

"I would be grateful if you would tell me how to find the hell of tar and shadow."

"He was an evil man," said the guardian, but then he saw Suzano's face and pointed out the long road.

The gate of that hell was a hundred feet high and carved of bone but burst open when Suzano struck it with his fist. Iron corridors fell away before him, branching and multiplying into red heat and darkness, and he plunged forward without a thought. He called his father's name, but the only response was a door creaking open and then a demon rushing out, its talons like scythes, but Suzano found to his relief that even there his sword was at his side, and his rage was incandescent as he made the one cut that sent the demon's spiked head rolling to the floor, and hell echoed with his battle-cry. The noise roused the pit and legions of demons seethed from the shadows, but their numbers and savagery availed them nothing, for his swordsmanship was flawless and his will immovable, and soon hell was quiet but for Suzano calling his father's name.

That was long ago, but he is there to this day and still bent on his task. Some nights the worst sinners dream of the ruin in his wake. The demons have learned to avoid him and to imitate his father's voice.

Shikata Ga Nai: The Bag Lady's Tale
By Gary A. Braunbeck

We find her, as expected, in her favorite place: the iron bench on the courthouse lawn, the one with the sculpted bronze figures of two old women doing cross-stitch sitting on it. It's fortunate that it's a big bench, because the old lady needs a good deal of room, she does, for her bags and blankets and such. Judging by her face, she's not a day over fifty, yet she claims to be in her early eighties. No one knows her name, or where she lives, or if she has a home at all. But we know her, in a way. As a neutrino has no mass or electrical charge and can pass through the planet in a blink, so this bag lady's existence can pass through this world; she, like the neutrino, is a ghost, yet both are real, both exist and have presence, even if that presence is unseen or ignored.

We take a place near the little garden a few yards behind the bench and watch as she begins to unfold the quilt; we listen as she tells the story to her still bronze companions, who never seem to tire of hearing it:

"Gene got himself shot overseas during the war and it did something to the bones in his leg, and the doctors, they had to insert all these pins and build him a new kneecap and calf bone—it was awful.

Thing is, when this happened, he only had ten months of service left. He was disabled bad enough that he couldn't return to combat but not so bad that they'd give him an early discharge, so they sent him back home and assigned him guard duty at one of them camps they set up here in the states to hold all those Jap-Americans.

"Gene guarded the gate at the south end of the camp, and I guess it was a pretty big camp, kind of triangle-shaped, with watch-towers and searchlights and barbed wire, the whole shebang. There was this old Jap tailor being held there with his family and this guy, he started talking to Gene during his watch every night. This guy was working on a quilt, you see, and since a needle was considered a weapon he could only work on the thing while a guard watched him, and when he was done for the night he'd have to give the needle back. Well, Gene, he was the guy who pulled 'Needle Patrol.'

"The old guy told Gene that this thing he was working on was a 'memory quilt' that he was making from all the pieces of his family's history. I guess he'd been working on the thing section by section for most of his life—'cording to what he told Gene, it'd been started by his great-great-great-great-grandfather. The tailor—this fella in the camp with Gene, that is—he had part of the blanket his own mother had used to wrap him in when he was born, plus he had his son's first sleeping gown, the tea dress his daughter had worn when she was four, and a piece of a velvet slipper worn by his wife the night she gave birth to their son.

"What he'd do, see, is he'd cut the material into a certain shape and then use stuff like paint or other pieces of cloth stuffed with cotton in order to make pictures or symbols on each of the patches. Gene said this old Jap'd start at one corner of the quilt with the first patch and tell him who it had belonged to, what they'd done for a living, where they'd lived, what they'd looked like, how many kids they'd had, the names of their kids and their kids' kids, describe the house *they* had lived in, the countryside where the house'd been… I guess it was really something, all right. Gene said it made him feel good, listening to this old guy's stories, 'cause the guy trusted him enough to tell him these things, you see? Even though he was a prisoner of war and Gene was his guard, he told him these things. Gene said it also made him feel kind of sad, 'cause he'd get to thinking about how most people don't even know their great-grandma's maiden name, let alone the story of her whole life. But this old Jap— 'scuse me, I guess I really oughtn't use that word, should I? Don't show the proper respect for the man or his culture—but you gotta understand, back then, the Japs was the enemy, what with bombing Pear Harbor and all...

"Where was I? Oh yeah—this old tailor, he knew the history of every last member of his family. He'd finish talking about the first patch, then he'd keep going, talking on about what all the paintings and symbols and shapes meant, and by the time he came round to the last completed patch in the quilt, I guess he'd covered something like six hundred years of his family's history. 'Every patch has one hundred-hundred stories.' That's what the old guy said.

"The idea was that the quilt represented all the memories of your life—not just your own, but them ones that was passed down to you from your ancestors too. The deal was, at the end of your life, you were supposed to give the quilt to a younger member of your family and it'd be up to them to keeping adding to it; that way, the spirit never really died because there'd always be someone and something to remember that you'd existed, that your life'd meant something. This old tailor was really concerned about that. He said that a person dies twice when others forget that you had lived.

"Well, Gene, he starts noticing that this tailor, he seemed really... I don't know...scared of something all the time. These camps, they weren't nearly as bad as them ones the Nazis built for the Jews, but that ain't saying much. Some of 'em was filthy and cramped and stank to high heaven, but this camp Gene was at—I can't remember its name, dammit—it had this sign tacked up over the entrance gate, and this sign was on the inside of the gate so everyone in the

camp could read it, and it said, 'Shikata ga nai.' It was this old tailor that had made the sign and hung it up, you see. He told Gene
that it meant, 'It cannot be helped.' I guess a lot of them poor folks
jammed into them camps felt that way, y'know? Like there wasn't
nothing they could do about it and never would be.

"Gene finally got around to asking the tailor what his name
was. The guards weren't supposed to get too familiar with the prisoners, I guess, and asking one for their name was against the rules
something terrible, but Gene was a decorated war hero and figured,
what the hell are they gonna try and do to me, anyway? So when he
notices that the tailor has been acting real scared, he tries to talk
with him, calm him down, right? The tailor tells Gene he needs to
tell him a story first, before he tells his name, and then he says—get
this—he says that he's older than any piece of land anywhere on
Earth. He's crazy, right?

"And then he tells Gene this story. He says that when a child
dies its soul has to cross the Sanzu River; that when a person dies,
they can cross the river at three different spots—depending on how
they lived their lives. Since children ain't lived long enough to have
done something with their lives, they can't cross the thing. At the
edge of the river, these children's souls are met by this hag named
Datsueba, and she takes their clothes and tells them to build a pile
of pebbles so they can climb up it to reach paradise. But before the
pile can get high enough for the children to reach paradise, the hag
and her gang of demons knock it down. If the soul is an adult's,
Datsueba makes them take off their clothes, and the old man Keneo
hangs these clothes on a riverside branch, and that branch, it bends
against the weight of that soul's sins. If the sinner doesn't have no
clothes, Datsueba strips them of their skin.

"That's when the old tailor, he told Gene that his name was
Keneo, that he'd escaped the underworld and Datsueba because
he couldn't take part in her behavior no more. He couldn't watch
them poor kids trying to climb their piles of pebbles or them adults

stripped of their skin. He said that when he escaped the under-world, he stole every piece of clothing that had ever been left by the Sanzu River, because if he could find a way to make a quilt with one section of cloth from each piece of clothing, them souls would be released and there wouldn't be nothing Datsueba could do about it. But in order to give the quilt this power, the clothes from them souls in the underworld had to be stitched alongside pieces of clothes from the living, and that's why it was taking the tailor so long to finish it. The guy, it turns out, didn't have any grandfather, or great-grandfather, or great-great-great-grandfather. They was all him! Gene, he thought the old guy had himself quite the imagina-tion, so he just smiled and handed him his needle and watched him do his work.

"'Bout ten months after Gene started Needle Patrol the old tai-lor came down with a bad case of hepatitis and had to be isolated from everyone else. While this guy was in the infirmary the camp got orders to transfer a hundred or so prisoners, and the old guy's family was in the transfer group. Gene tried to stop it, but nobody'd lift a finger to help—one sergeant even threatened to have Gene brought up on charges if he didn't let it drop. In the meantime, the tailor developed a whole damn slew of secondary infections and kept getting worse, feverish and hallucinating, trying to get out of bed and babbling in his sleep. He lingered for about a week, then he died. My Gene, he almost cried when he heard the news.

"The day after the tailor died Gene was typing up all the guards' weekly reports—you know, them hour-by-hour, night-by-night deals. Turned out that the three watchtower guards—and mind you, these towers was quite a distance from each other—but all three of them reported seeing this old tailor at the same time, at exactly 3:47 in the morning. And all three of them said he was carrying his quilt. Gene said he read that and got cold all over, so he called the infirmary to check on what time the tailor had died. He died at 3:47 in the morning, all right, but he died the night *after* the guards reported seeing him—up till then, he'd been in a coma for most of the week.

"Gene tried to track down the tailor's family but didn't have any luck. It wouldn't have mattered much anyway, 'cause the quilt come up missing.

"He didn't tell me about any of this till our twenty-fifth wedding anniversary. He took me to New York City so's I could see a real Broadway show. On our last day there we started wandering around Manhattan, stopping at all these little shops. We came across this one antique store that had all this 'Early Pioneer' stuff displayed in its window. I stopped to take a look at this big ol' ottoman and I asked Gene if he thought there were people fool enough to pay six hundred dollars for a footstool. He didn't answer me right away so I asked him again, and when he didn't answer this time I turned around to see him all white in the face. He let go of my hand and goes running into this store, climbs over some tables and such to get in the window, and he rips this dusty old blanket off a rocking chair.

"It was the quilt that Japanese tailor'd been working on in the camp. They only wanted a hundred dollars for it, so you bet your butt my Gene slapped down the cash. We took it back to our hotel room and spread it out on the bed—oh, it was such a beautiful thing. All the colors and pictures, the craftsmanship...I got teary-eyed when Gene told me the story. But the thing that really got to both of us was that down in the right-hand corner of the quilt was this one patch that had these figures stitched into it. Four figures. Three of them was positioned way up high above the fourth one, and they formed a triangle. The fourth figure was down below, walking kind of all stooped over and carrying what you'd think was a bunch of clothes. But Gene, he took one look and knew what it was—it was a picture of that tailor's soul carrying his quilt, walking around the camp for the last time, looking around for someone to pass his memories on to because he couldn't find his family and he couldn't go back to the underworld on account of what Datsueba would do to him. He was lost forever, and there wasn't nothing he could do about it. It couldn't be helped. Shikata ga nai. Isn't that sad?

"See here, this's the quilt. And this here needle? Gene gave it to me. It was the one that old tailor used. I been adding things to it, 'cause it seemed to me that's what my Gene would want me to do if he was here. See this? This is part of the suit Gene wore when we got married. And this here come off the baby gown that my mom made for Cindy when I had her. Them things there?—those're the dog tags that the army sent to us after Jimmy was killed over in Vietnam. The way I figure it, Gene was like family to the tailor, so it's only right that I do this. It's only right.

"Thing is, I'm not as sprightly as I used to be, and except for Cindy all my family's gone—she don't much want to have anything to do with me. I'm not even sure where it is she and her husband are livin' these days. And if—oh, Lord, look at me, will you? Getting all teary-eyed again.

"I don't know what's gonna happen to this after I'm gone, you see? And I don't know where any of them souls' clothes was stored. I can keep adding things from people living in this world, but I got no way to get them souls' clothes. I don't know how I'll know when this quilt is finished, and if it ain't finished and I die and don't pass it on to someone, then them souls will be trapped in the under-world forever. And that scares me something powerful, it does. Right down to the ground."

Scissors or Claws, and Holes By Yusaku Kitano
Translated by Nathan Collins

Um, well, the first thing I have to tell you is that when the time comes, don't waver. Be well sure that you make your mind up beforehand.

Yes, yes, that's right, you should make up your mind about what you want to learn, but more than that, be mentally prepared. You have to go into it ready and with resolve.

I mean, letting them into you, that takes a bit of courage, right? So when the time comes, more than a few lose their nerve. If you start hemming and hawing, you'll just ruin it for everyone else.

Exactly. Time is important. Time is money, they say. You don't want to get all the way here only to have time run out before you learn anything, do you?

Oh, and there's one more thing I have to tell you. I'm sure you're all aware, but just in case, yeah?

If you want them to show you the future, you have to give them the past. Got it?

Oh, is that too vague?

Yes, right, right, that's it. Memories, memories. I'm talking about your memories. Pleasant memories and painful memories. They'll be gone from your head. In exchange for a vision of the future.

Well, to really simplify it, in order to know the future, you have to lose an equal or greater amount of memories. That's how it seems to go, at least.

Of course, there's not a contract or any such thing, nor is it some written rule. It's just an inference, based on previous examples, that that's likely the way it goes. Lay out the long list of all the many things gained and lost by the previous participants, and that seems to be the only reasonable conclusion. It's the tidiest explanation.

As for why it's like that, well, there are many opinions. Of course all of them are no more than hypothesis or conjecture.

Sure, I can give you an example.

Maybe it's what we have and they don't. They don't have a past. What's past to us is future to them, and like how we can recollect the past, they can see the future. Therefore, we exchange the past we hold for the future they see. That kind of thing.

Yes, you're right. Certainly there are other explanations. Instead of an exchange, it could be something simpler, like that they use the memories in your brain to perform a sort of calculation that derives the future. And since it's not a reversible process, those memories are inevitably destroyed. There are many other explanations, but, well, that just indicates that nobody knows for sure. The only thing clear to us is that nobody knows.

Since we don't even know what happens, we certainly don't understand their intentions. How could we? We don't even know if they have any in the first place.

Oh, no, no, don't get me wrong. We understand the basic phenomenon, in terms of what happens. A lot of people have been through it, and with plenty of witnesses.

Since you've all come here, I'm sure you know this much, but again, I'll explain it just in case. When the time comes, I don't want to have to hear any of you going, "But I didn't hear about *thaaaat*."

Here, I'll draw it for you. Though I'm no artist, so it might be more confusing this way, *ha ha ha!*

Okay, so this here is someone's body. And this teeming bunch are them.

They have scissors for hands and many legs, so they kind of look like crabs, don't they?

Right, as far as their shape goes, they're like crabs.

Oh, and while I'm on the subject, those things at the end of crabs' arms—in the West, they don't think of them as scissors. Japanese people, on the other hand, perceive them as scissors. There's even that nursery rhyme "Crab Barber." Tell a Japanese person "crab" and they'll think "scissors." See someone making a V sign with their hand, joining and separating the two fingers, clip, clip, and anyone would recognize that as an impression of a crab.

But apparently not so with Westerners. That gesture doesn't look like a crab to them.

So, in the West, what do they call those things?

They call them not scissors, but—would you believe it?—claws. You see, according to a person's culture, things can take on entirely different meanings.

But if you think about it, crabs don't cut, they pinch, so functionally they are closer to claws than scissors. It's true. Maybe Japanese people attach more importance to form rather than function.

Either way, for our purposes, we'll be calling them scissors. We are Japanese, after all.

Since I've drawn these scissors on each of their hands, they look just like crabs, don't they? So these crablike things swarm toward the humans.

And then what do they do next?

Right, they go into us.

Yes, right, right, right, through our holes.

They enter through our holes.

They come in through our holes.

They swarm in.

Yes, right, right, you're right. We have more than one hole.

They come in through all kinds of holes. The human species has many different holes. Nostrils, ear canals. Of course, our mouths are holes too.

Yes, right, right, our pores are holes too. We have all kinds. There are holes in, and there are holes out, and there are holes that go in and out. Suffice it to say, humans have many holes.

And not just humans. Animals are all like that. We creatures live among holes. You may as well say we are holes.

And no, I'm not entirely joking. Some say that that might be how they perceive us.

Holes.

And perfect holes. To them, our holes are just right.

How are we just right, you ask?

First of all, we have the proper moistness. And our body temperature is stable, just at the right warmth. Our salinity is ideal. Oh, and also, we have plenty for them to eat. That's very important.

In other words, we maintain a steady, desirable environment. As long as we're still living, that is.

Yes, that's important. That's why they keep us from dying. Our deaths would inconvenience them.

Oh, and I can't forget, we're soft. Not only do our holes not close over, we're soft enough for them to burrow deeper and deeper within.

They like that kind of hole. They're like crabs in that way too. Well, we don't know if they "like" anything, but they seem eager to go in.

Oh, if you want to know what it is they do, well then, they use those scissors to come in.

First, they close their scissors—that is, they form the tips of their scissors into a point and push them in. Once their scissors are far enough inside, they open them. After that, there's no easy way to get the crabs out. They spread open the ends of their scissors far wider than the hole's opening. And their scissors are covered in tiny barbs that dig into our flesh, so if you try to pull them out, there'll be blood everywhere. And you still won't get them out. All pain and no gain. Well, more like all blood and no gain, *ha ha ha*!

Then, when you give up trying to pull them out, they'll close their scissors and stick them deeper inside. Once they've extended their arm out all the way, they open the scissors again.

And just like that, they force their way deeper and deeper.

They come in many sizes, and each one finds a hole the size for them.

And they enter.

Anyway, there are many sizes.

The largest are about as big as us. But ones that big are quite rare. On the small end, we don't really know. We've discovered some a few microns large. There might be some even smaller, like on the nano scale.

Regardless, each of them, of their respective sizes, goes in each hole as far as they can. Then they use their scissors.

The ones that share a hole use their scissors to join together. From the largest to the smallest, in a smooth gradation.

They join together into a single form.

To tell you the truth, we don't know why they do it.

They wouldn't tell us if we asked.

Anyway, they go into the holes, where they join together. And the result, the providers of the holes can see their own future.

That's what we call it.

Right. That's right, it does feel less like seeing it than suddenly remembering something they always knew.

And yet of course, we can't know if it's really the future.

You know how you can stimulate certain parts of your brain

with electric impulses and see something from your past, or suddenly hear a sound you'd once heard, or see a vision you interpret as the afterlife? It might be something like that.

It's like that in that you feel like what you see is your future. Maybe that's one of the functions of our brains.

But even if it is a part of our brains, it might just exist for them to come inside. Perhaps we live in a symbiotic relationship with them.

Some people say that they don't show us the future. Instead, they program us to work toward the future they showed us.

But even if that's the case, to that person, that future comes true. By that meaning, they did see the future.

At least to that person, there's no difference.

And it's not just something the person is commanded to do. What they see always comes true. It's not like they merely want something to happen. It really happens.

That said, we don't perform a follow-up survey on each and every person, and even if we did, we can't be certain that everyone reports the truth. Even if everyone honestly answers that it went well, and nobody says it didn't, some of them could be lying to themselves.

But what we can say for sure is…

Everyone who experiences it has a very contented expression.

If I could show you a movie of it, I think you'd understand what I mean—and yes, you can find them all over the Web—but anyway, their faces look satisfied, or how should I put it, they have really nice expressions.

Yes, nice expressions.

People come back with nice expressions. No doubt about it, they are content to their core. That's the kind of expression it is.

Yes, mine too.

This expression.

Ha ha ha! You're all making me embarrassed now, looking at me like that. But seriously, I can't see for myself if my expression is a nice one. I know my looks aren't nice. That much I know. But it's true that I'm content. I'm satisfied with myself right now. It's the truth. I can say it with complete confidence.

Yes, they showed me my future.

It was at a time I was most unsure of where my life was headed.

I went on a journey.

I wanted to discover my true self.

I wanted to find myself.

Yes, yes, one of those journeys of self-discovery.

And at the end of it, I arrived here.

I'd heard they would show me my future.

So why not let them, I thought.

I was lost, completely adrift. If I actually had a future, I wanted them to show it to me.

Yes, right, I came here in more of a roundabout fashion.

And then I went to them.

Well, the result is right here. You can see my face.

Yes, I saw it. I saw my own future.

They provided me the clear future—something I'd never had before. In exchange, I gave up memories from my hazy past.

Yes, yes, right, this is it now.

This is that future.

I saw myself here, talking to people like you, guiding them along. This is that very future. I saw myself just like this.

And yes, that's right. The prediction came true completely. Right?

I'm proof.

Well, I can say that, but since only I know if I'm telling the truth, it's not much proof at all.

In the end, you all will have to experience it for yourself to really know.

What's that? You're right, I'm not the only one.

Most of the guides—nearly all of us, I think—saw themselves working here in their futures, and then came here to work. Just like me.

Yes, of course I was happy.

In one instant, I realized this was what I was meant to do, and this was the path I must take. And I saw my expression as I worked here—my contented look.

Yeah, in the past, it was more gloomy and miserable.

Oh no, no, I'm not trying to make you believe what I'm telling you. You have to experience it for yourself.

I have nothing else to say to you now.

So, shall we go?

Follow after me, and don't wander off.

All right, everyone stop. Okay, let's all stop here for a moment. Is everyone here? Could everyone please look around yourselves and make sure?

What's that? There's someone being pinched, and they can't move?

Are they part of our group? Oh, they're not. Well, leave them. We can't do anything about it. I'll explain what's going on there.

Oh, and don't get too close to anyone who's being pinched like that.

No one in our group is experiencing that, right? You're all fine? All right then, listen up.

Ah, see, we're about to enter their territory, so before we do, I need you to be mindful of this one thing. Right, I know you want to say, "Enough, enough, we know already."

You already had to listen to me pester you all about it. But even though they know better, we humans will always end up doing something we're not supposed to without thinking it through. Reflexive actions—well, deeply ingrained habits, that is—are frightful things. So that's why I'm going to make this perfectly clear one more time. In short, whatever you do, don't do that.

You all got it? One hand is bad enough, but if you do it with two, they will get you 100 percent of the time.

Hey, hey! No, no, no, no, no, noooooo. You there. You just started to do it, didn't you. I'm telling you you can't.

You didn't mean to, you say? That's precisely my point. There's a lot of people like you.

It might be a simple, careless act, but you'll bring upon yourself an irrevocable fate. If things go wrong, you could get all of us sucked in.

No, I'm completely serious. I mean it.

Look, to them, nothing is more important.

What you have to understand is the weight of it is different. The significance of the meaning.

Yes, right, I'm talking about their scissors. They perceive that outline as scissors.

And if you do that with both hands...no ifs, ands, or buts about it, they will perceive you as something with two scissors for hands.

That's their nature. To them, that's everything, their entire world. It's their computational unit. And they're always computing.

Yes, always and everywhere, they're computing.

We don't know what they're computing. But we do know they are.

What we do in our brains, they do in great number, within this whole muddy expanse. From what we've been able to observe, they seem to be performing complex computations. Some say that if that's the case, then what they show us is no mere illusion, but rather a calculated projection of the future.

Yes, a computation.

They are always computing.

I'm sure that to them, the computations they make together are very important.

How do they perform computations together, you ask? Well...

Well, they have those two crab-claw scissors, right? Yes, the ones that open and close. This "open" and "close" is like a computer's "0" and "1."

They use combinations of these to perform computations.

That's what we think.

Like I just said, with one scissor, they can express 0 and 1, right?

And each of them has two scissors.

Let's call them "Scissor A" and "Scissor B."

When they pinch something between both A and B, they can open up either A or B, as long as the other remains closed, and the state of the pinched object doesn't change. In other words, they can express a state of "A or B."

Now, imagine A and B connected to each other, two closed scissors touching at the tip. In this case, if either A or B opens, the state is lost. In other words, they can express a state of "A and B."

Through combinations of these simple states, you can construct logic. Just like computers, right?

That's only the simplified version. In reality, they have many more factors at play: differences in the sizes of each scissor, differences in pinching strength, and it's not limited to the scissors themselves. For example, pinching something by the torso, or the reverse, being pinched by your torso, and so on.

In that way, by pinching each other's scissors, and pinching things that aren't scissors, they construct a giant spatial structure.

You could call it a giant thought.

A thought translated into form.

And this structure of infinite, many-sized scissors doesn't simply remain motionless.

They alter the states of their scissors to respond to input. As the structure changes, it loses stability. To regain balance, the form shifts, and the stability is lost again, and so on.

The entire structure continues to react in this manner, and a new equilibrium is found.

This is happening all around us in every part of this muddy expanse.

And the new structure birthed from this balance of various powers is the answer to the inputted value.

In other words, they performed a computation.

No, each crab isn't thinking about doing all that. Just like how each electrical element in a computer doesn't have an intent to compute.

That's just the result of their system.

To begin, they construct a giant structure within the soft mud.

This structure has a delicate balance, and then, following a new input, they alter their configuration, introducing instability, and they form yet another new state to eliminate that instability.

None can see all of the movements, and none are in control of the entire structure.

All they do is respond to the introduced forces with their scissors. But some researchers say the way their vast parallel processes converge into a single system are like quantum computers the likes of which humans have not yet attained.

Whether or not that's an overly grandiose comparison, the fact that they perform incredibly powerful computations is indisputable. On that point, the experts are in agreement.

So, with that, what do you think would happen if they mistake you for one of them? Obviously, they would respond. They would try to make calculations with you. In other words, you'll get sucked into their computations.

And what that means is this: you'll become part of their calculation formulae.

What specifically, you ask?

You'll get pinched.

In their scissors, yeah?

They'll pinch you tight.

Just like that pinched person over there.

No, no, it's not an attack. It's not like that. They don't even know what we are. All they recognize is another individual's scissors.

So why do they pinch you, you ask?

That's right. You got it!

Computations. They pinch as part of their calculations. They don't mean harm. They pinch as a fellow constituent of the computations.

That's right, that's why you need to be careful. That brings us back to my warning.

That's what I mean.

If you want them to show you the future…

If you want them to compute the future…

They have to enter inside you, right?

You don't need them to calculate with you, you need them to calculate for you. They have to perceive you as having the perfect kind of holes.

Wait quiet and still until they enter you. And when that time comes, and you do that…

Right. Anyone who does that, they'll believe is one of them.

When they see the hands in that shape.

That's right. They perceive the V sign as scissors. And they'll pinch you. Yes, exactly. A Westerner doesn't think the double-V sign looks like a crab, but they do.

Yes, I suppose that could mean that Japanese culture is closer to theirs than Western culture is.

Well, anyway, that's what happened to that person. They saw the two scissor-hands as belonging to one of their number. So they pinched, just like they do to each other. That's all it is. And once you're pinched like that, you become a part of their structure. You're forced to. You become a part of their immense numerical formula.

What you want has no relevance. Right, obviously they wouldn't let you escape just because you wanted to. They don't have any wants themselves.

You have no choice but to fulfill the same role as them.

And then what, you ask?

Once the calculation begins, most people are crushed. Our bodies aren't as strong as theirs, you see. But it doesn't seem to hinder their calculations. We're just treated as random noise. It's a pointless death. And who wants that?

So, in order to avoid that happening to us, let's please refrain from any potentially ambiguous behavior, all right? No, I don't mind if you take a picture for this occasion. It'll make for a nice memory. I don't mind it, but just be absolutely careful not to do that.

Even now that I've said all this, some people will still do it. When you point a camera at a Japanese person, they do it without any thought.

That pose.

That person doing it over there probably did it reflexively when someone pointed a camera their way.

That's what can happen.

But that's how it is. It's not something unique to here. The place and the particulars might change, but it's all the same.

It doesn't matter if you're only a tourist. When somebody points a camera at you, you shouldn't thoughtlessly flash the V sign.

What meaning does that pose hold for the people around you? How will it be taken in the place where you are?

Even among your fellow men, some will see it as an impression of a crab, and some won't.

What will you be communicating?

You have to think about that. For cultural exchange.

Right?

Okay, that's enough pictures, it's time to become holes and accept them in.

For the future.

Her Last Appearance By Lauren Naturale

The curtain opens to the sound of clapping: wooden clapping, not hands. The air smells like sugar and you're not sure why. Kairakutei, the Hypnotist, sits in the center of the platform, serene and fluffy as an enormous white cloud, a real Englishman in old Yokohama—which, in the year 1900, is New Yokohama still, a city that only recently bubbled up out of the swamp, dripping mud and slime from its outstretched arms like an undead Venus. Something smells fishy. The city spreads its legs. The curtain is all the way open.

"Volunteers?"

Raise your hand and a black-clad *kuroko* leads you to the stage, though you must pretend not to see him. This part is easy. If you've seen one stage hypnotist, you know what to expect. Instances of Victorian stage mesmerism fade one into another, variations on a theme; the English Hypnotist, who hates England, sees no need to trifle with the form, not when it is him they come to see. The public pays to watch a blue-eyed foreigner speak Japanese like a native (and why shouldn't he, when he has lived in this country since the age of seven? Kairakutei, *né* Henry James Black—no getting famous with *that* name, no wonder he changed it—was raised in the same city as the rest of you, behind the moat that closes off the Foreign District; he is amphibious).

His voice is as rich and cold as the ice cream that made you sick last week. A phantom hand caresses the back of your neck, though that, compared to the voice of the Hypnotist, is warm. Caught between extremes, you drift. The audience whispers. A woman in the front row eats sugar stars.

The Hypnotist puts dreams in your head.

I. Shizuko

Run to sea? But I'm a creature of water, I was born among boats; the entry of our house flooded when the rains came. I stepped out to work and into water; the sailors yelled, *"Hey, mermaid!"*

In the last decade of the last century, the *rakugoka* suggested we grow a third eye in the back of our heads: "That's how you keep up with progress." I touched the bump at the back of my head and waited for an eye to sprout like breasts. My friend Kazumi's brother Shôgetsu, who worked on a steamer, said he met an island girl in Honolulu with eyes on her tits, "One where each nipple ought to be—more purple than brown, aubergine, *knowwhatImean?*"

I didn't.

"It was intimidating," Shôgetsu told me, "all those eyes staring at me. Puts pressure on a guy. I never knew where to look." Would I take a walk with him, so he could tell me more about his travels? I was twelve.

By the time my body completed its changes—by the time I learned to see through people—Kazumi and her brother were both gone, Kazumi to tuberculosis (with her mother, with her father, with her father's concubine and both half brothers) and Shôgetsu to, where? He was canning pineapples in Oahu, then doing something unmentionable in San Francisco, and then no one heard from him again. I like to believe he kept going, crossed east over the Sierra Nevada like a cannibal who wants second helpings and rode the

Overland clear through to Chicago, where he buried himself deep in the Levee District like a famished bedbug until winter cleared and he emerged, bloated fat with the blood of the unwitting, to finish his travels.

This is my favorite game, this *What-is-Shôgetsu-up-to?* I revisit it when I'm bored, but more often when I'm lonely. *Shôgetsu is rolling drunks on the Bowery. Shôgetsu joined a traveling carnival that worked its way up the coastline until a mill girl in Maine nearly made an honest man of him. Shôgetsu is hunting whales off the coast of Greenland and bunking with a seven-foot-tall Maori.* I'm not sure where one goes after the Arctic; I'm not sure what's left.

It's a useful thing, looking both ways, and not only because it allows me to believe in ghosts and the Union Pacific railroad simultaneously. Consider my father, who only made one journey, from his parents' farm to the city, and that before the railroad existed, before we had steamers and factories and fire insurance. Now he could take the train, which must be why he's never been back. My father moved to the city just as the city he dreamed of ceased to exist. My father is an invisible man.

I'm not sure what sort of woman my father expected me to be, but then, neither did he. He learned life from *rakugo,* from *kabuki.* The stage was his school and his guide to the metropolis.

Once, I screamed, "You want me to be a man in drag, is that it?"

No, I would be no suicidal concubine, no tragic geisha. If anyone wrote me a love poem, I'd run in the other direction.

The question was, run *where?* And run *how?* How to run, when every step was a misstep, when every joke I told, every nut I cracked with my teeth, every night I came home late and smelling like Namiko's cigarette smoke cut fresh wounds in my father's heart? How to run away, when already I walked on knives?

II. Namiko

Close your eyes, Namiko. You're getting very sleepy.

You *should* be sleepy; you've been up since sunrise, not because the café opens then—they're French, or Francophiliac, anyway; they sleep in. The café, the Pantheon, is run by a Russian Jew from Geneva. You get coffee and croissants for free, but you won't get them until nine, when the doors open and the customers trickle in. Nearly all of them are foreigners. Your French is getting good, but your Russian is better.

You wake at sunrise, cursing, because that's when the factory girls leave for work: nasal country voices like the cries of a flock of ugly birds fighting over the washbasins, fighting because some girl got called a whore (everyone in the dormitory is on the game one way or another; you can't live on a woman's wage and expect to make a profit), fighting over the single cracked mirror in the hall where they crane their necks and stand high on their toes or crouch low to see what they look like now. There are six women to a room, which is all right when the futons are put away, but at dawn there's no way out without stepping over three or four bodies. *If this place caught fire, we'd all be dead*—that's what you think when you smoke your good-night cigarette.

It's quieter outside. In the morning, the city is yours, salt air and rough edges and the ripe raw smell of the fish market where eels and mackerel lie coiled in slimy heaps. One of the fish vendors has a gold ring on his right middle finger that he dug from the belly of a carp. "Of course I won't sell it," he says. "It's good luck." Gold attracts gold, money prefers the company of other money; everyone knows that.

You, Namiko, in your men's trousers, in the slouchy hat that hides your small pointed chin and ghost-nose, are in love with money. But so is everyone else who loves the city in the mornings. The woman who walks the city at night is searching for trouble, but the woman who walks at daybreak has a fortune to make.

Look at the broom vendor, wares bristling like spines from his shoulders; look at the shrunken peddler who hauls his *daihachiguruma* piled with baskets, ladles, sieves; look at the dead woman in an "empty" rickshaw who yawns, stretches, and spreads her phantom bulk across the seat until the runner gasps for breath, and looks back, and sees nothing: these are your co-religionists. The runner's heart will give out before noon; the ghoul will eat his soul, and his wife and children will starve. Even the dead are a bright silver thread in the web of commerce.

Ghosts are less subtle in the movies; you think you'd be good at dealing with ghosts if you lived in a horror movie. The first time you saw Bake Jizo, you barely noticed the audience, though they talked all through the film, and the ghosts talked loudest of all. The second time, an hour later, you saw an ugly girl in a lilac kimono; the delicate color threw her long nose and wide ears into sharp relief. You remembered catching a glimpse of that same lilac kimono in the earlier showing—you'd thought, *My God, what a color!* But you like the fact that she is out of place. You are attracted to strangeness, to Unbelonging.

The next day, they showed the film again. You waited at the back of the theater until the girl in the lilac kimono took her seat, then took the seat directly behind hers. She nibbled sugar stars, white and pink; they smelled so sweet you were almost sick.

On screen, the ghost revealed himself, but you were distracted by the sour taste of your own hunger.

Shizuko's hair was combed back high in the Sokuhatsu style. You tapped her shoulder and hissed, "Hey, you'll have to tilt your head a bit; I can't see the screen."

"You know what happens," said Shizuko. "You saw it last night. I caught you staring."

"I want to watch it again. I'm studying it."

"Right, because you're a student."

"I'm a freelance art critic," you told her, enjoying the way her eyes widened. Shizuko pretends to be a philistine, but she's her father's daughter; she knows the plot to every play ever written. If she brags about her shallow sensibilities, it's because her lack of education stings like alcohol on a scrape. You dropped the name of one of the bluestocking magazines out of Tokyo. "I promised them I would write a review."

What did Shizuko see when she looked at you? A slight woman, narrow of mouth and shoulder. Your hair was cut short, like a foreign man's, and the scissors and the humidity had unlocked your hair's tendency to curl, so your head looked like a briar patch despite the pomade. It wasn't unheard of for women in Yokohama to dress like men, but even a writer could afford better tailoring.

Shizuko tilted her head to one side, considering.

"Thanks. That's perfect. Hold it right there. Don't move."

Ghosts flickered across the screen, destroying all your similes.

It went on, one of those friendships that seems almost real until the first time you kiss, drunk, in a noodle shop in Chinatown after your second viewing of *The Resurrected Corpse*, and think, What am I getting myself into? Nothing wrong with lying to a girl, but it's better to avoid kissing the kind of girl who only likes you because you're a liar, else you end up growing nails for a week just to scratch her properly, which is messy and not your idea of a good time. "I like my sex a little less kabuki," you tell her, and she avoids you for a month.

She lives in a small house with her father, the kuroko, and many dead people she is unaware of—children, mostly. "I think they died of cholera," you told her. "I've seen those sunken eyes before." Shizuko smirked and slowly unraveled the long black curtain of her hair. "No," you said. "I mean it, there's like six dead babies in this room. Could we please go somewhere else?"

You've only seen her father once, in the morning, coming home as you left. Two moments after meeting him, you forgot what he looked like. A man like that can get away with anything.

"Where are you actually from?" Shizuko asks. You say, "The land of the dead. Isn't it obvious?"

When you close your eyes, Namiko, you pretend you are home. The smells of a coastal city are not so different from the smells of a coastal village; there are just more of them. The noise reminds you where you are, but you can filter that out. Movies have no noise; they are chiaroscuro, motion, silhouette. You think that a movie is the pure essence of story, stripped of meaningless detail. You think an important story is something that could happen anywhere.

Here's a story: You were in love for a very long time with a woman who loved you back. A little while after she died, you started seeing ghosts. But you've never seen *her* ghost, so you wander through your days half alive and half dead, searching through a world of shadows, and you are always sleepwalking.

See? We've all been there.

III. The Hypnotist

—wears black and has four distinct chins, each with its own personality.

"More coffee," he tells Namiko, and there is something in his voice that makes her long to rest her head on that ample bosom and tell him all her secrets.

"Do you see that man over there?" Shizuko whispers to the Russian. He nods; he is a Russian of few words.

"That man used to be a rakugoka."

What, says the Russian, like a storyteller?

Shizuko smirks. She's wearing purple lip color today, making her look even sillier than usual: "Exactly."

Shizuko hoists herself onto the counter next to the tray of *pain raisin* and swings her legs. She knows that the Russian hates her visits, also that he won't throw her out so long as Namiko wants her there. She pops a strawberry-flavored *macaron* into her mouth— provisions! "You'd have heard of him"—swallowing the macaron in one gulp, poking at the Russian with her elbow—"if your Japanese was better."

The Russian shrugs. "What happened to him?" Famous stage performers don't eat coffee for their midday meal, even when they are so badly in need of reducing as the Hypnotist, whose magnetism attracts new flab as it does people, as if the very adipose adores him.

"He died," says Shizuko, pondering her next macaron: Hazel-nut? Lemon-perfumed? Green tea? She thinks for a moment of the Hypnotist curled on the floor of their old house vomiting, her father crouched over him, preternaturally still. "He *almost* died. I guess he's back now."

Namiko runs back to the counter so quickly that she almost drops her tray of empty plates; she catches Shizuko with her free arm and pulls her into a kiss. The Hypnotist has left her a tip.

"I learned to read English from the Hypnotist." This is the story Shizuko wants to tell about herself. In fact, even her spoken English is not very good; she means, *He used to tell me stories.*

Nothing more boring than the professional storyteller who's never off the clock. She tuned out his lectures about the lost ways of the past, the erosion of the culture, but she listened when he explained *Oliver Twist*—foreign squalor, so exotic—and got as far into *Moby Dick* as the storyteller's lament that he shall never finish anything, at which point Shizuko thought, *If he's not going to, I don't see why I should.* She remembers the city with the whalebone gates surrounding each house, where women in whalebone corsets marry with a whale as their dowry; she likes the idea of the whale-dowry, that somewhere in that ocean there's a monster with one's name on it, a monster for each of us.

"Shizuko," her father asks, "when will you let me marry you off?"

"Buy me a whalebone corset," says Shizuko, "and a dress the color of stars."

Perhaps there are plenty of *kaiju* in the sea after all; night after night, the Hypnotist, who was not a Hypnotist in those days, went onstage to narrate his own adaptations of *The Woman in White,* of *Lady Audley's Secret,* fixing the audience with his ocean-blue eyes and explaining just what the Paris Morgue was; but day after day he lounged at Shizuko's home with her father, making omelets and annoying everyone with his stories.

"What part of England are you from, anyway?" Shizuko asked.

"Adelaide," said the Hypnotist through a mouthful of egg.

When the Hypnotist moved out and Shizuko's father's eyes drifted to the half-empty jar of rat poison—he was leaner; he'd get the dosage right—Shizuko said, "Cheer up! We'll go to Adelaide and find you a new foreigner with blue eyes and a big white hairy belly."

Her father's smirk was a thin line, almost invisible. "What," he said, "run to sea?"

🔥

"That's why I hate the theater," Shizuko tells Namiko. "It makes people selfish. Everything is so archaic—and so isolated—and so all-consuming—" She's gesturing wildly, and it only makes Namiko more still. "You can't give yourself to a dead thing and have enough left to be a real person. The dead eat souls."

"Not all of them," says Namiko. She's grown more friendly with the cholera victims in Shizuko's bedroom. They teach her interesting facts about the 1830s, and all they ask in return is to kiss her hands and neck with their frigid lips, or else suckle at her breast. She has a hard time understanding why she humors them whenever she's off the premises, but in the moment it doesn't seem much to ask.

Shizuko ignores her; already she is back at her bookshelves. "You should read *this*," she says, grabbing the Hypnotist's translation of *The Law and the Lady*; "You should read *this* and *this* and *this*."

Namiko is a reader, but only in Japanese, and only books Shizuko finds boring: long literary things about women's colleges with lots of hand-wringing about feminism and modernization and how we shouldn't emulate Western countries because Western women don't have the vote. Shizuko likes English novels where people take arsenic and commit bigamy. She says, "You are such a savage, Namiko." She says, "The English are centuries ahead of us, culturally speaking. I am going to educate you."

There are too many books in her house, books upon books, stacked vertically on the single row of shelves and spilling off in heaps and drifts in the corners; they are readers, Shizuko and the kuroko (and the cholera babies too, though mostly they prefer to use the books as blocks for building castles and fortresses and barricades to trip Namiko in the night), but some of the books are in languages they don't read, and at least one bears a stamp marking it as the property of a library in Glasgow.

Sometimes Namiko looks at the books and thinks, *If this place caught fire, we'd all be dead.*

"Smoke with me," she says, and Shizuko sits with her in the corner, her back against a stack of old issues of *Japan Punch,* and accepts a cigarette with exaggerated ladylike gestures. Shizuko smokes with the mannerisms of a female impersonator. When her father comes home, the smoke will make his eyes water.

Namiko watches the smoke plumes writhe along the ceiling, forming themselves into weird specters, half lives. "I can't make any promises."

"You won't be able to stop reading. Not once Miserrimus Dexter shows up; he is mesmeric. When you suffer a loss, your other faculties become sharper to compensate. Dexter has no legs, so he's a genius." This is how Shizuko's mind works. Why does she lift her chin like that as she exhales, why must she always strike attitudes? "Kairakutei *explains* them for you, so it's not confusing. You know: What's a Scottish Verdict. What's a Barrister. Why are English men so secretive about their concubines, and where are the pockets in men's pants."

Namiko pulls her pockets inside out.

"Well, but this was ten years ago; people didn't wear those then."

Namiko starts to say that she doesn't understand why a man who hates his homeland so much would spend his life explaining it to foreigners, then stops; of course she knows why. It's money that gets the Hypnotist up on the stage, wearing his whiteness like an inverted yellowface; money that makes him flood the market with "cultural translations" of British potboilers even as he bemoans the loss of, what did he call it? *"The last beautiful place."*

In England, everything is ugly, there is coal smoke, the women act like men and the men can't fuck each other unless they want to go to jail—except no one *really* goes to jail—except sometimes they do. Namiko asked him to explain this, one day at the café, but all he said was that it was complicated, and ordered sake. The Hypnotist has a Japanese wife whom he had to marry to get citizenship, but no one has seen her in years. Perhaps Kairakutei's wife, like the kuroko, is invisible. Perhaps the Hypnotist has that effect on people.

Shizuko tells her father she is afraid to marry. This is late one night when they are both drunk. He is working on a play in which his main task is to raise the waves to drown the heroine. The heroine, a man who has worked with him before, is an epic slut of legendary stupidity who once mocked Shizuko's father for his country accent. The kuroko hasn't enjoyed his work so much in years.

"Where's Namiko?" asks the kuroko.

Two days ago, Namiko bragged about all the money she is saving from her wages at the café. She keeps track of her savings in a little green book, and she showed the book to Shizuko, who said, "It is just as dull as all the other books you like."

"But no," Namiko explained. "Those are books that tell the past, and this book tells my future." Namiko has lived in this ghost town long enough.

"Tokyo?" says Shizuko. "We're going to Tokyo?"

"I am going to Tokyo." Namiko tousled Shizuko's hair, loose around her shoulders. There was a red scratch on Shizuko's neck. "I'm not like you, little mermaid. I couldn't be happy staying in one place my entire life."

"Where's Namiko?" the kuroko asks, not without irony. He knows how to suggest evisceration through tone of voice alone. He gets the Scotch from its hiding place at the back of the bookshelf, behind a copy of *Trilby* the Hypnotist bought before his departure and never finished. He never finished the Scotch either, but they are going to do so tonight, Shizuko and the kuroko, as she turns and turns in the silver kimono he bought her, silk the color of stars.

Somewhere, a hundred girls just like Shizuko labored to tend the worms and spin the thread and weave the cloth the kuroko has paid to have sewn into her wedding dress. They say that being a factory girl is not unlike being a human silkworm. *The accident of birth,* Shizuko supposes, grateful that she has made the wise choice to be born motherless rather than fatherless, and wondering why it is so much more often the other way around. She feels sorry for the silkworm-girls, of course, but she isn't really interested in their story. Look how the kimono shimmers!

The silver of stars: it reflects the lamplight like a liquid mirror. No electricity in this house, oh no; the flame casts flickering shadows on the heaps of books and magazines, and the Scotch lights a fire in Shizuko's belly, and the kimono is alight with borrowed passion, and it is just like old times.

"I've never felt so beautiful," says Shizuko. She sweeps her arms up; she sweeps her arms down. She tries to walk in the stiffly embroidered fabric. "I can't move much."

"And *you* wanted a corset," says the kuroko.

Shizuko examines her sleeves, her hem. She reflects.

But what if I am empty, only shimmer and stage gestures? Shizuko asks later, when they are further into the Scotch. She means she is afraid of disappearing.

The kuroko chews it over. You are what you do; no one knows that better than the invisible man. A daughter is not a wife. There are sea creatures who reproduce by fragmentation, reforming themselves into two distinct beings after falling apart; when the kuroko grew Shizuko from his sharp white rib, like a cutting in a jar, he himself faded to a mere shadow. Now she is all show, signifying nothing, and he lives like a phantom.

"If I run away, my outside will change entirely," says Shizuko, "and I have no insides. I will go out like a candle." She waits for her father to respond, but he is silent. It is as if she is talking to herself.

IV. The Kuroko

I am lifeless and immortal, like a virus or a Buddhist. I am most at home when I am out of place. A hundred years from now, you will pass me on the street in New York or San Francisco, in Paris or Berlin or Buenos Aires, and I will lift my black veil and you will see my true face, and then you will see Nothing.

V. The Picture Bride

For days before her photograph is taken, Shizuko is uncommonly violent. "Hit me in the face," she tells Namiko. "I won't mind."

Namiko's own face a livid gray, she half raises her hand before freezing miserably in place like an actress in an old tableau; another creaky English export like the Hypnotist's new show, or like one of the Spiritualist acts transported direct from Europe, women in black dresses who claimed to speak for the dead. Two years ago, before Namiko ever met Shizuko, she went with the Russian to see a ghost-speaker perform before an audience of three hundred; the Spiritualist levitated a foot off the floor and spoke to the ghosts of a widow's lost husband and several sets of parents. One infant too. None of them are real, Namiko complained.

"I'm not a good person," says Namiko. "I don't understand why you want me to be worse than I am. Hate me for the awful things I really do, not—" Namiko waves her hands helplessly in the dark. It's awkward.

"I know that deep down, you want to hit me. Go ahead."

That night, they sleep side-by-side holding each other. You are familiar with this pose from the postcards of Japanese women sleeping together, which may be found, at this time, in most major cities in Europe.

After Namiko leaves, Shizuko slams her head into the wall over and over, until purple bruises rise up around her right eye. The kuroko will have to labor over her face for hours with a box of stage makeup. Rescheduling a photograph is expensive, and this is her future at stake.

🔥

A century from now, the picture of Shizuko will resurface at a flea market in Alameda, where it will be labeled "Japanese Bride, 1880s," despite being taken in 1899; Shizuko's hairstyle is old-fashioned. The woman who buys it—as a joke, because she does not intend to marry and finds the practice ridiculous, *ridiculous,* she has not even *dated* anyone since her only boyfriend dumped her two years ago, though they still talk all the time, he is her *best friend*—pins it to the cork board in the entrance to her apartment in Noe Valley, then moves it to her bedroom when she gets tired of visitors asking, "Oh, is that your great-grandmother?"

In her bedroom, though, the photograph glowers like a malevolent spirit. The mannish bride in the glittering dress looks miserable—that's what makes the picture so campy, that's why she bought it in the first place—but more importantly, she looks monstrous. In her overdone clown makeup, she seems ready for the stage, not the matchmaker; the woman feels she has introduced negative energy into her home.

Her ex-boyfriend comes to her roommate's birthday party, still single, still twitchy and blond like a golden retriever with a severe panic disorder, and they get drunk on Negronis in a corner of the kitchen while everyone else plays Mafia. *"Why is Male Tippi Hedren here?"* her roommate hisses on the way to refill his own drink; thirty hits dancers even harder than it hits the rest of us. It's because they're so skinny, there's nothing to cushion the shock.

"I think your roommate's mad at me," her ex says, so they go into her bedroom to stay out of the way. The woman lives at the back of the building, and her hallway is so narrow that she and her ex-boyfriend have to walk single file, his hands on her waist. Then his hands are below her waist.

"Hey," her ex-boyfriend says the following morning, "Why do you have a Japanese drag queen hanging over your desk?"

A few months later, after her roommate gets married, the woman moves to the East Bay so she can get her own place—she's too old for all this—and throws Shizuko's 115-year-old bridal portrait in the garbage. It is really not worth taking with her.

If Shizuko's life were a movie, the scene with the matchmaker would be revealed as Shizuko and Namiko's secret ruse to bring the Hypnotist and the kuroko back together. Who loves matchmaking more than an unhappy couple? The act of bringing two people together promises happiness by proxy, as if happy couples were all alike and interchangeable, as if affection were easily transferred. The kuroko, black-clad, would arrive at the Pantheon clutching Shizuko's bridal portrait in one hand; he would order tea, but he would be too nervous to drink it.

What sort of husband does the kuroko imagine for his daughter? What a photograph! Her husband will not be like anything from the kabuki stage, that's for sure.

Still, there is something appealingly aristocratic about the new mode of arranged marriages. When he was Shizuko's age, marriage meant traveling to the house of the nearest farm girl—bare-breasted in summertime, blackened teeth unbrushed—and fucking her until you had a home of your own for her to move into. Nothing more than the breeding of livestock, especially when the women, hunchbacked by seventeen from digging up daikon all day, coarse from labor and dull-eyed from illiteracy, were so near to livestock already. He always thought that if he were to touch one, her idiocy might prove contagious, might colonize him like a host of fleas, drinking his life force, hatching its eggs in his hair.

Namiko would hover, trying to keep a straight face. It's been so long since she had a good laugh, but *this* would make her laugh, send her into hysterics when she and Shizuko devised the plan and leave her guffawing every time she thought of it for a week after, confusing the customers and annoying her heavy foreign employer, who is redecorating the café with cotton velvet drapes imported from Europe, plush and luxurious and immensely flammable.

The new drapes are a good hiding place for Shizuko, who will grab a handful of dragées—can't go without sugar for an hour, this girl, she is too bitter, she must balance herself out—and duck behind the one nearest the door. Pay no attention to the bride behind the curtain.

The title screen flickers black and white: "Kairakutei thinks he is meeting his booking agent about a new tour."

Cut to Kairakutei at the door. The kuroko drops the photograph. Kairakutei opens his mouth, but for once the storyteller is at a loss for words, and this is a silent movie anyway. The kuroko looks for an exit, panic-stricken, but it's too late: he's been seen.

Kairakutei looks up, uncertain why the waitress has just collapsed in giggles. Is something the matter?

"Sorry," Namiko says, composing herself. "Daydreaming." She begins clearing off the tables. "Better close up already, or my boss will have my head."

"Oh," says Kairakutei, "I doubt that very much." One thing about coffee grounds, they're much less effective than reading tea leaves. He loves tea, he really does, loves the ritual, the aroma, the taste, but he has gotten addicted to this other stuff now and cannot give it up. Ever since he took the arsenic, the Hypnotist has trouble keeping up his energy. He is tired all the time.

He hopes it's the arsenic and not old age.

Exhaustion sweeps over him. He has outlived his world. "You know," says the Hypnotist. "When we came here, we were some of the only ones. Foreigners, I mean. Good luck getting all of this, then. I remember, I was only a child, we had just arrived, we were on our way to the foreign district, and a group of boys started throwing stones at us. But not children. Young men. I was seven. I didn't speak a word of Japanese."

"They were probably more scared of you than you were of them," says Namiko.

"Yes, I got that distinct impression as the first stone hit my nose; blood and snot were pouring out of my face, but I thought, be sensitive, Henry, the poor dears must be terrified. We're not robust, my family, we're not as good at adventure as we think we are. My father left Scotland because he expected to make a fortune in the goldfields; ended up becoming a concert singer instead. Oh, he had a beautiful voice, but still there he is at the antipodes, singing his heart out to entertain the *real* miners. He could have done that at home."

"Some people get restless."

"Yes," says the Hypnotist, "I gathered that." Out of breath already just from hauling himself to his feet, chins trembling from exertion, he raises one hand to dab at his glistening face; no, he is not robust, nor an occultist, nor even a believer in the art of mesmerism, beyond his heartfelt conviction that the public will see whatever it wants to see, God bless 'em, and that most people would rather be taken in than left out. "I'm a homebody, myself. Which means I'd better get going; someone will be wondering where I am." He casts a last look around at the marble café tables, the row of foreign newspapers on display, the French pastries under glass. It is not Parisian, but it's a credible rendition of someone's idea of what a Parisian café ought to look like.

"*Foreigners,*" Kairakutei mutters. "How much is he paying you to fuck him, anyway?"

"Excuse me?"

It's as if he asked her whether it was raining earlier. The Hypnotist leans his gargantuan bulk against the door frame, fixes his blue eyes on the waitress; conversational, curious. "The Russian. How much is he paying you to fuck him?"

The next day, the kuroko comes to the Pantheon to meet the matchmaker. He is dressed in black, and he is clutching Shizuko's bridal portrait in one hand, but, ah! He is looking for a place that no longer exists. Where the café stood there are only the charred remnants of the foundation, a melted lump that was once a cash register, a handful of overturned tables black with ash. The whole building has gone up in flames overnight.

Out like a candle.

VI. The Spiritualist

Sometimes I wonder what it would be to travel the world, not as a tourist but as a creature who must keep moving or die; though I have thought of death many times, have held her in my arms and let her kiss my face, and I am only a little afraid of her now. I am no longer the twelve-year-old girl who tried to drown herself because she thought that's what refined women do. I no longer joke about running to sea. I comb my hair out each night, one hundred strokes of the brush. I have eyes in the back of my head.

"Come to the theater with me," said my neighbor. She works as a mannequin girl in one of the department stores, modeling clothing all day and drinking all night, a crop-headed, bony creature who feels good taking care of a poor widow, particularly a poor widow who has buried three, *three* husbands, a poor widow who has a heavy hand with the arsenic.

I told her, "I'd rather go to the movies."

"No, Shizuko," says the Modern Girl, "No, we always go to the movies; your brain is rotting. I'm going to expose you to culture; I'm going to educate you."

She's gloomy, the Modern Girl; her lover has skipped town. Now I must charitably allow myself to be her charity project.

The wooden clapping starts up, and the Modern Girl squeezes my arm: "Don't you love it? The ritual?" We are here to consume the real, the authentic National Culture, except for the part where there is no kabuki play on tonight—the theater has been given over to a spiritualist act instead—so instead of feasting on the green and rotting carcass of a dead art we must watch someone pretend to speak to the dead; no matter! It's all the same to the Modern Girl; Victorian kitsch and Meiji camp are all one to her, they fade one into another, variations on a theme, art is Art purely by virtue of not speaking to her, she is paying good money to watch something removed from her own life.

For myself, I find the whole thing ridiculously old-fashioned, right down to the heavy black dress the medium wears, a long heavy thing with, *I swear,* a damn bustle, which looks like it was fished out of a trunk at some estate sale in Tokyo, and probably was, for isn't this a touring production? Isn't Namiko the most famous spiritualist in the capital?

Look at her on the stage. She doesn't have much of a presence. She's so small, so wiry that your eyes are always tempted to skip over her, until she begins describing what she sees. Then the men begin to cry and the women give their shuddering sighs of recognition. Then the ghosts begin to come forth.

"I'll have to sit down," Namiko says, when she is ready to begin manifesting spirits. "This part requires all my strength." But when she is lying down, the air ripples, and the ghosts appear, flickering, like projections on a screen.

A mother, overcome by the vision of her dead son, rushes the stage, sobbing; it breaks the spell, and the room goes dark.

"What?" someone yells. "Is that all?" We have been here fifteen minutes. Theater is not cheap.

But Namiko can barely stand.

If I were Namiko's father, I would do her face up with stage makeup to hide the hollow circles under her eyes, the sallow tones of her skin. I would tell her that a woman with a small and birdlike frame cannot wear black onstage the way an obese white hypnotist can; she disappears. I would teach her how to command attention with a gesture, how to bluff your way through disaster when you feel you are being eaten alive from the inside.

She's shivering. Her hand on the podium is the gnarled hand of a skeleton. Two kuroko come onstage to help her into a wheeled chair and spirit her away, even as the audience screams for more ghosts.

"Huh," says the Modern Girl. "So that's what people did for fun in olden days." She looks over at me, raises one skinny, penciled eyebrow, purses her vermilion cupid-bow lips. "What is it? Shizuko, what's so funny?"

"It's nothing," I tell her. "Let's go home."

He Dreads the Cold By James A. Moore

"Where are we?" Maeda Sentaro spoke mostly to himself, but the closest rider heard him.

Ishida spat and scowled, his face drawn in lines of exhaustion. "We are lost, of course."

He gestured at the trees around them and the deep snow that covered everything that could be seen. The storms of the night before had been sudden, violent, and bitterly cold, and the landscape around them transformed from a forest into something filled with frozen shapes that seemed almost impossible. The fir trees were gone, completely buried in drifts of white. The snow was dense, and with very few exceptions the trees showed no sign of even being under the frozen precipitation. Instead there were vast shapes that could have been nearly anything under their caul of white. Some were small, the size of crouching children, and others towered five times the height of a tall man.

Ishida Mototada was in charge of their expedition. He was a good *kashira* and a calm man, so the expression on his face and the tone of his voice were nearly foreign things to Maeda.

Maeda licked his lips and regretted it immediately. The moisture froze to his already chapped flesh. "Have I offended you?"

Ishida glanced his way for a long moment and then shook his head. "No." He looked around at the uneven shapes around them, squinting against the wind and the glare alike. "I am not comfortable here. I do not trust them."

Maeda shook his head. "The trees?"

"No. What they might hide."

Maeda looked again, carefully this time because Ishida was a good commander and seldom one to underestimate his enemies. The trees were buried in white to the point where they no longer truly looked like trees. They were only shapes, often bent and bowed by the weight of the heavy snows.

"There is nothing they can hide, Ishida. Anything within the frost would be dead."

Ishida lowered his head and closed his eyes for a moment. His face was usually calm, but the tension under the surface of his skin could not be hidden.

"There are things that can hide in the cold, Maeda. Some of them are worse than the worst of our enemies."

Maeda did not speak immediately. Instead he considered the words of the man riding next to him. They rode because their lord demanded it and because the enemies of Mogami Yoshiaki were their enemies as well. There were some who would have considered Ishida's words treasonous, but Maeda knew better. Ishida was a loyal soldier and had proven himself several times in combat.

Maeda knew him well enough to know that what was different this time was fear. Ishida was scared.

Maeda said, "It is only ice and snow, Ishida." He spoke carefully and kept his voice calm. Ishida was a leader for a reason, and his skills in combat were not to be underestimated. Maeda had seen him kill before and had heard others talk of the man's prowess. "There is nothing here beyond that. The temperature will rise and the snow will melt."

Ishida's voice did not carry far. There were other riders within calling range of them, but Maeda suspected that none of them heard the man's words. They were meant for him alone. "It is winter, Maeda. The snows came earlier than expected, but I do not think they will melt as suddenly as they fell. We are stuck here in this cold, and I dread the cold. I always have."

He chided the man, but carefully. "I have never heard such a thing. We have traveled together in winter before, Ishida, and you have never said a word of this."

Though his voice remained low, there was an edge when Ishida spoke again. "No. We have always traveled together before the first snowfall. I was given my lord's word that I would never have to travel after the snows came."

Maeda thought about that for a moment and realized the man's words were true. He had never seen his kashira after the snows came.

"He could not have known. This snow came up very suddenly."

Ishida nodded his head, and they rode in silence for several minutes before the man spoke again. During that time the man kept his head lowered and studied the snowy ground before them.

Ishida said, "What do you know of my life, Maeda? Have you ever heard me speak of my wife? Of my children?"

"No. You have never spoken of them." He frowned and considered those words. "Not to me and not to anyone who said anything of them to me."

"My family only comes to me when it snows, Maeda."

Maeda smiled. "Then shouldn't you be happy? If you only see your family when the snows come, then perhaps you will see them today or tonight."

Again the leader of their expedition looked to the shapes that haunted the snowy hills around them.

"The question is not if I will be happy to see them. It is whether or not they will be happy to see me."

"Please explain. I do not understand at all."

Ishida's eyes stayed heavily squinted as the winds picked up and a pattering of snow and crystals fell from the looming shapes all around them. The forms all bowed in the same direction, as if they had turned their backs on the travelers coming their way. Some huddled together, families of ice and snow. The more Maeda looked at them the less he liked them. At first they were only unusual; now they seemed too much like they were joined in a silent conspiracy.

When Ishida spoke again the unexpected sound of his voice startled Maeda.

"My marriage was arranged. My wife came from the mountains near Zao Onsen and traveled down to meet me in Yamagata. That does not sound like a long distance, but it can be."

Maeda's marriage had also been arranged, and he nodded his head. His wife, Sen, was a good woman and they had three children together, but theirs was never going to be a love story told in poems.

"Kano came with her family and stayed with us for twelve days before the wedding took place. During that time we were allowed to see each other when we were supervised. I have never seen a more beautiful woman, and as much as I admired her looks so too I was charmed by her mind and her quiet wit. When we were married I was already very in love with her."

Maeda almost spoke but stopped himself. In his time Ishida had never volunteered anything of his family life, and he did not want to make the man grow silent again by interrupting.

"Kano's father asked me to walk with him before the wedding. We moved through the cherry trees and down to the river, and there he told me three things. He said that Kano was his most prized daughter and that he trusted me with her, trusted me to take care of her and keep her safe. Of course I swore to him that I would. How could I not? I was already in love.

"Next he told me that she was already mine. That she had spoken me with him and said that she loved me. I cannot tell you how much those words meant.

"And at last he told me that I must never make Kano bathe. They had their own rituals and their own ways that were sacred."

Maeda thought about that for a moment and broke his silence. "Surely she had to bathe herself. How else could she stay clean?"

"Kano did bathe, but never in my presence." Ishida shook his head. "There was nothing we did not share, but we could not bathe at the same time and she—" He stopped speaking for a moment and grew paler as the winds picked up again and threw ice and snow from the hulking shapes across their path. The frozen fragments rained down on their heads and shoulders. The winds were strong enough that Maeda would never have heard what the man said in any event.

Only a few seconds later the winds calmed, and the frost that fell across their cloaks stopped accumulating.

Ishida once again raised his head and looked around carefully. Maeda joined him but saw nothing amiss.

Finally Ishida spoke again. "We had two children together, Aki and Kanbei. They bathed only with their mother. It was a small thing and one I easily grew accustomed to. I did not even really give it thought."

There was movement. Something shifted in the pervasive field of white on white, and Maeda turned to study the area where the movement caught his notice. He saw nothing; still, the hairs on his arms rose and he shivered. The cold was a heavy burden, but one he was sheltered from. The way his hairs tightened against his skin had nothing to do with the chill in the air.

Ishida continued on. "We were together for nine years. Kano was all that I could hope for in a wife. She was attentive to my needs, strong enough to handle whatever burdens came our way, and careful with our son and daughter alike. We would have been happy forever, I think, but then the message came from her mother warning that her father was ill."

Ishida sighed. "She asked me if she could go to him, and I said yes. The war was not upon us yet, and everything seemed simpler. Because she wanted to move quickly, the children stayed with me. Because I had work to attend to, I asked my mother if she could watch over her grandchildren while I took to the fields and made certain that the harvest was prepared. The winter was coming. I remember that."

Again Ishida let out a long sigh and shook his head. "A foolish thing. A simple thing. I did not think to tell my mother that the children could only be bathed by Kano. It was not a thing I had to think about. It was just her way, and I had long accepted it."

Ishida grew silent. His face might as well have been carved from wood. He barely even seemed to breathe while he contemplated how to continue.

Maeda looked around once more, his eyes straining to see what it was that continued to catch his attention among the endless white forms that defied wind and sunlight and held onto their coats of ice and snow.

There was something. He knew that, and he was considering telling Ishida about it, but despite his misgivings, when the man spoke again he found himself listening.

"On the third day I came home to my mother in tears. She had prepared the bathwaters as she always had, and because Kanbei and Aki were small, she set them into the waters together."

The man's face worked and he blinked rapidly, fighting against tears perhaps or merely against the winds that were picking up again.

"She said the children screamed and thrashed, and she tried to lift Aki from the waters, but my daughter's flesh fell away, sloughed back into the waters, and melted as if it were nothing more than snow. The boy as well."

Once more the winds blew harder and the skittering ice rattled its way down the limbs of trees buried under layers of white. That sense of things moving grew more pervasive, and Maeda looked carefully around the area. There was nothing to see but the shapes and the snow. He couldn't even see any of the other riders any longer.

"Ishida, we've lost the others, I think."

Ishida did not answer him at first. When he spoke again it was to continue his tale.

"I searched the tub and the land around my house and even in the closets, thinking at first that my mother was joking or that she had lost her mind. At first I checked the house and lands carefully and then called for my children and sought them in any possible hiding place, screaming until I lost my voice. My mother wailed and apologized, and I sent her back to my father. I did not speak with her again until long after Kenekori came home.

"Kano returned to a house without children. When she asked me what had happened I had no choice but to tell her. I was not prepared for her fury."

Ishida shook, though with grief or cold Maeda could not say.

"Have you ever heard of the *Yuki Onna*? The Snow Woman?"

Maeda looked at his commander. "Of course. But I think you are not listening to me. I believe we have lost the others, Ishida. We have lost our way."

Ishida shook his head and sighed. "No, Maeda. We have not lost the others. They have been taken."

"Taken? Who could take them? We have heard no horses, seen no soldiers. I can see that you still grieve, Ishida."

The kashira waved his comment aside. "I will always grieve. My wife left me and cursed me as she started toward her ancestral home. She said, 'You have betrayed your words to my father and now I must leave. You have taken my children from me with your lies and left me lonely. Throughout the year you may be with whomever you desire, but in the cold months you are mine alone.'

"I thought her words were merely anger when she left. I did not understand. But I learned."

Maeda thought to interrupt again but decided against it. They would find the rest of the riders. They had to. And when they did he would discuss the madness that was gripping Ishida with a few of the other men, and they would decide together how best to handle the matter.

"Within a month of my wife's leaving, winter came. The cold that year was very fierce. I spent most of the first weeks of winter alone in my house. Blizzards buried everything, and the windows outside of my home were covered with snow. When I could no longer stand to stay inside I opened the door and forced my way past the snow drifts.

"Outside I saw several sets of footprints on top of the snow. They did not fall into the snow, though. It was like powder, and I could not stand on it myself. I did not see anyone, but I heard the sound of laughter from around the side of my house. It was a sound I knew from before my children disappeared and my wife left. It was the sound of my family.

"Maeda, I think I went mad. I tried to reach them, clawing my way through the snow that was as high as my chest and calling out their names until my throat was raw and I could not stop shivering. Footsteps surrounded a dozen trees and I climbed through the snow and scaled those trees looking for where my wife and children might hide, but there was nothing. There was no one.

"Eventually I went back into my house. I took ill and stayed there for several days, often hearing the sounds of laughter and my beloved wife singing to our children. I might have died. I feel certain that I would have, but when my fever was at its worst I felt Kano's hand on my brow and heard her soothing words and I slept. When I awoke the fever was gone, and the worst of the storm was finished.

"After a few more days I went to see my parents. I wanted to tell them all that had happened. Instead I learned that my mother was dead. She had wandered into the storm, and when I was at my worst, lost in fever and dreams, they found her body near the riverside, frozen to the ground."

Ishida coughed into his hand and looked around, his eyes wide and wet. His expression was not one that Maeda was used to from the kashira. Maeda could not think of the words to calm the fear he saw in his commander.

"They are all gone now."

"Your family? Your wife took your father as well?"

"No, Maeda. Yes, she killed him as well. He was found the following winter, frozen in his bed with the window in his bedchambers opened to the storm. However, I mean the rest of our troops are gone now." Ishida's face still looked as frightened as before, but his voice was calm.

"I was trying to tell you that. We've lost them. If we go back—"

Ishida interrupted him. "It is too late for that. She is here with us. She has come to pay her respects to me and to keep her vow that I will be hers alone."

"I don't understand. What do you mean, Ishida?"

The kashira looked at the ground and then looked up, staring hard into Maeda's eyes.

"I mean it is your time to die, and I am very sorry for that. I wanted to be back home before the storms came. I wanted to be alone where there was no one for her to seek."

"You are mad, Ishida. The cold has stolen your wits." But even as he said the words Maeda had his doubts. The rest of the troop was gone from his sight, and he heard nothing from them, not even the sound of a horse snorting in the distance. The towering shapes around him seemed to move whenever he was not looking directly at them.

"I wish I were, Maeda. I truly wish I were mad. I am so very sorry for this."

When he saw the woman Maeda stopped and stared. Her clothes were thin to the point of translucence, and her skin was as white as the snow. Her hair and eyes were the color of snow-laden shadows and the expression on her face was both frightening and seductive. If this truly was Ishida's wife, she was as lovely as the man claimed.

The snow woman came to him, her face a porcelain mask against the endless frost. He had to squint to see her past the glare of the day.

When she touched his wrist above his glove and below his jacket, the contact burned and blackened his skin. He felt his blood freezing where her fingertips grazed his flesh. He would have screamed but could not find the strength.

Had there ever been a woman so beautiful? Had there ever been a kiss so terrible?

The last Maeda heard was Ishida once again offering his apologies past the sound of the sighing wind.

A Tale of Japan: A Successful Ruse
By Zachary Mason

One day a tengu of the lower rank watched a squire and his wife move into a house in the middle of his wood. The wife, who was barely twenty, had black eyes and skin like snow, and was prone to lounging by her window and staring out into the trees. The squire had become devout in middle age, telling his rosary beads for hours every night, and often reading the Lotus Sutra aloud, which irritated the tengu, who detested the Chinese religion, and made a point of tormenting any monk he caught alone.

One night the tengu appeared to the squire in the semblance of the Bodhisattva Jizo. In a ringing voice the tengu intoned, "I have heard your prayers and born witness to your piety, and have therefore come to instruct you in the mysteries. The way is not without difficulty—are you prepared?" The squire nodded, his eyes streaming.

"Very well. Your discipline shall be this—every night, from dusk till dawn, you must, ah, count every bean in that sack. Keep Amida Buddha in your heart," the tengu counseled sternly, "and ignore whatever noises come from the rest of the house. It is not unlikely that some spirit of the wood will try to distract you."

The squire, declaring himself wholly committed to the task, emptied the beans onto the floor and began counting. The tengu slipped off to the bedroom where the squire's wife was sleeping; he exchanged Jizo's semblance for the squire's and slipped into bed with the wife, where he was warmly received.

The tengu called on the squire's wife every night and was pleased with his success. "Surely, I'm only doing good here," he thought. "I'm happy, my lover is happy, and the squire is getting at least as much benefit from counting beans as he was from prayer."

One night a month later the tengu and the wife were embracing when the squire burst into the bedroom, his face shining. He cried, "My prayers have been heard! Jizo himself gave me a secret training, and now he tells me that I'm moments away from being raised up into the Toro heaven! My love, I must leave you—forgive me."

His wife stared at him. The tengu said, "I think there has been a…" but as he spoke the squire flickered like a candle flame and vanished.

The tengu sniffed the air skeptically but smelled no foxes, no badgers, and no other tengu. He said, "If I hadn't seen it with my own eyes, I would never have believed it," and disappeared.

The wife sold the house and moved to the capital, where she lived on her late husband's estate. She never took another lover nor had anything to do with religion. As for the tengu, he was quieter after that and let the monks be, even when he found one alone on a cold winter road.

Girl, I Love You By Nadia Bulkin

For Lindsey

My best friend, my blood-sister, decided to make the Ultimate Sacrifice to destroy Asami Ogino. We were drinking *chuhai* on an overpass, and as the world roared beneath us, Yurie showed me the letter she planned to send to the Ministry of Education. It was a four-page, four-year chronicle of the sins Asami had visited upon her. She had, of course, used a PO box and Anonymity Seal. She wrote: *Don't try to find me. Just make it stop.* I almost let the letter fly over the barbed wire toward the smoke-covered sun, because I already knew the ministry wouldn't care, just like our teachers didn't care. That was the difference between me and Yurie: I had accepted that life was shit, not just in school but beyond; Yurie still had this perverse expectation of joy. All that tightly wound, brightly colored hope was her downfall.

"If I don't hear back in a week," she said, "I'm doing it."

This is something people often misunderstand: Yurie didn't want to do the Ultimate Sacrifice. But she had already tried everything else. Two dozen Vengeance Charms bought from skeletal bloodhounds in the grimy alleys behind malls, cooked up from the bloody floor planks of haunted houses. A zip file of a black-market video-bomb, *Grudge of a Predator*: a so-called documentary on our so-called war crimes (she refused to tell me how much she paid for that one). We also took a two-hour bus ride up to Rika Yamazaki's shrine so Yurie could wish for Asami's death. Miss Yamazaki had an 80 percent satisfaction rate, on account of the enormous rage cloud that spawns when you're shoved off a balcony by a jealous ex-boyfriend—but even then, Asami was fine.

Asami was so fine that she had some of her friends burn Yurie's arms with cigarettes before school. I hadn't been there—I was slumped at the foot of my bed, staring at the clock—but I saw Yurie showing off the bleeding black wounds to curious first-years. The math teacher scolded her for upsetting everyone; I wondered if Yurie had lost her mind. Maybe this is where Love of Life takes you, in the end.

"That Yamazaki bitch just sits on people's wishes," Yurie complained, but Miss Yamazaki did have a lot of wishes to answer. It wasn't just junior high students anymore, but sad middle-aged couples and bespectacled professionals and families with little kids in bear hats. I thought it was fucked up to take your kids to the grave of an angry murdered stranger, but who am I to judge. "That's why we need regulations on shrines. Not that this government can get anything passed."

Yurie didn't like the prime minister—thought he was a fatalist unable to grab the wheel and stop this car crash we were all in. On my worst days, I worried she secretly thought the same about me. After all my father had been a bureaucrat, servant to the impotent government—very particular about following state recommendations on psychic energy, even though he hadn't written them. He was in the labor ministry. Research. No research in the world can save you from your destiny, I guess.

"It's always a gamble, using dead people."

Yurie's phone beeped. We didn't need to look to know

the message was some variant of DIE DIE DIE with UGLY and SLUT tossed in for extra color. I said, "None of them are worth anything."

"Michi, I lost everything. Choir, the girls I used to know, how teachers look at me…my stupid bicycle. You don't know what it's like."

"I know what loss is like."

Her face crumpled with apology. She had been with me three years ago when, halfway through a crosswalk, I looked up at a giant screen and saw something about Riot and Government Worker and a somber photo of my father on top of the tortured remains of a black sedan. My brain had floated out through my eyes, trying to escape this new post-father existence, while my body stayed rooted in the street. It was Yurie's screaming that brought me back to this shit-covered world.

"But we've got weapons now. And I'm going to use them, even if you're too scared."

Yurie called psychic energy an arsenal. She was always stocking up. But at a certain point you run out of money, out of options. I'd heard of precisely one dead banker with a 100 percent satisfaction rate, but his shrine was perched on an island in Matsushima, and who had the money for that? Eventually all you've got to spend is your soul. Traditional fortune-tellers call psychic energy "dismal energy," probably because they're afraid of losing their customers now that anyone can pluck that power out of the ether, but maybe they're right: maybe nothing but suffering can come out of psychic energy.

"And what are you paying for that weapon? It's called *Ultimate Sacrifice* for a reason."

She snorted. "Life's not much of a sacrifice. You know that."

Yeah, I knew. I was the one that pointed out black companies and the cyber-homeless. I was the one that buried my father after his car hit a cyclist and a mob stomped him to death. It wasn't fair to ask me to argue for a beautiful future, and *bam*: I was angry. Yurie grabbed my sleeve.

"Don't hate me," she hissed. I thought, *If I promise never to forgive you, will that keep you breathing?* But I couldn't keep my face stern, not to her tears. "I could never hate you," I said.

Of course Yurie never heard back from the Ministry of Education. Of course Asami never got pulled out of school. So Yurie bought the script for the Ultimate Sacrifice from a glass case in one of the city's first psychic shops, a converted pharmacy with a red door. The old woman who unlocked the case asked her if she understood the sanctity of life, had her look at pictures of babies and ducklings.

"What if I don't want you to go," I said. We were standing at the intersection where we'd have to part ways. I had used up everything in my own arsenal to dissuade her, and now I was down to the raw, wriggling emotional stuff that I hated handling. "Will that make you stay? Will you stay for me?"

She didn't answer right away. Instead she hugged me and said, "Girl, I love you," before tugging the straps of her backpack and walking resolutely up the hill, like a Himalayan mountain climber. Her answer came that night, when Yurie's mother called to say Yurie had jumped off a building to her death.

🔥

I was calm, all things considered. Ever since my mother put her arms around me and said she had some terrible news, a numbing chill settled on my shoulders like a shawl. During Yurie's funeral I could only think of how cold I was, how strange everyone was acting. People with faces out of half-remembered dreams kept asking how I was doing since Yurie's "accident." I'd never heard "I know you girls were close" so many times. I'd say, "Yurie's coming back," and that always made them look away.

I spent a month waiting for Asami to die. I wanted front-row seats for Yurie's Revenge—I was scared I'd miss it if I looked away for a second. But Asami kept on giggling, pointing, whispering—at me, at the fat sad kid, at the quiet soprano that had become her new whipping girl since Yurie died. Asami picked at the weak like the obsessive-compulsive pick at scabs; she just couldn't seem to stop. When I nearly set everyone on fire in chemistry, Asami mouthed at me, "Kill yourself, worm."

"You're not taking your future seriously, Michi," Miss Tomoe said after class. She was unmarried, childless, tending to her parents, forever trapped in high school. I couldn't imagine anything worse. "It's so important that you don't slip up now."

I wondered if Yurie had messed up the curse—written the words wrong, done something out of order. Bold, reckless Yurie—it wouldn't have been the first time.

"I'm sorry about your friend's accident. You don't blame yourself for what happened, do you?"

Obviously, I blamed myself—for failing to keep her alive, for being too weak to suffer with her at school. After she walked away on that final evening of her life, I yelled at her to call me, and she waved back without turning her head. In some of my dreams she did turn but had no face to speak with—just an endless curtain of brittle ombre hair. In other dreams she whispered something different when she hugged me: "Girl, come with me." But as always, I was too scared.

"I don't know," I said. "Why do you pop antidepressants between classes?"

Miss Tomoe's platelike facade shattered, and she burst into tears right there at the desk, surrounded by all her little beakers. Not long after that, she was fired for forcing a failing student to drink hydrochloric acid. She'd poured herself a beaker too, saying "Here's to failure!" The student spat his out; Miss Tomoe finished hers.

The sun was setting. I was trudging down the hill under stringy electrical wires when I heard a voice call my name: a deep, deliberate "Michi," like a summons from a northern volcano. Each syllable kissed my bones, rippled my blood. State recommendations tell you to never seek the mouth that releases a voice like that—it's going to be an ugly one, or a hungry one. But I knew the human marrow gurgling inside that voice. It had asked to borrow my pencil, laughed at my morbid jokes. "Michi!"

I turned. Yurie was hovering behind me, the untied laces of her shoes barely scraping the sidewalk. She looked different; terrible. She was covered in blood, like a newborn or a crime scene, but her skin was marble-white. Her joints hung crooked as a carelessly flung ragdoll. Her neck was so twisted that she could barely keep eye contact with me, her jaw smashed so deep it was hard to believe she could speak. My blood-sister. "Asami," she hissed. For a second I thought that in the trauma of death she had forgotten who I was, and the thought of being ripped apart by Yurie's hands nearly stopped my heart. "I-I-I can't." She kept stopping and starting like a scratched recording. "Reach Asami."

I forgot that you aren't supposed to engage ghosts and stammered to ask why not.

"Ah-ah-asami!" she yelled, although I didn't actually see her mouth widen. Suddenly her hands were reaching toward me as if to give me another hug—I stumbled backward. "Veiled."

The Ultimate Sacrifice was supposed to be so strong—it was always linked with either a murder or a miracle, like the Brave Boys of Shizuoka who committed suicide to save their school from yet another earthquake—that we never even considered the possibility that it wouldn't work. "Yurie, I'm sorry." Yurie wasn't blinking anymore and her eyes were red spiderwebs. She used to carry eyedrops—she had to be in pain. "I miss you. I'm sorry."

"Michi, help me!" I'd heard this so many times from her: afterschool cleaning duty, the robotech competition in junior high, every doomed day with Asami's foot upon her neck. Yurie's were the

hands that dragged me out from under my bed. She'd been dragging me into her battles for years.

This time, I didn't answer. Yurie's plea hung between us, suspended across her grave like a very, very long game of telephone.
Somewhere a screen door opened and a man shouted, "Yeah, yeah,
I'll call you later!" I became aware of birds chirping on the electrical wires, the sound of traffic, the ache in my shoulder…I exhaled,
letting out the sweet and sour stench of a broken-down body and
breathing in garbage, detergent, fish. Yurie vanished, and my relief
criss-crossed almost immediately with sadness.

Yurie didn't give up. Really, I should have known she wouldn't;
she'd been friends with me for six years. A normal person would
have dumped my ass on the curb after my first crying spell, but
Yurie was a sucker for lost souls. I used to say she had a Good Nurse
complex, but Yurie insisted the love came first, and the caretaking
after. And I won't lie: after my father died, I clung to Yurie.

And now she clung to me. We stared at ourselves in my bathroom mirror. We walked together to school. We sat together in
homeroom, Yurie behind me with her bloody arms childishly locked
around my waist, hissing "help me help me." Back before Asami
destroyed Yurie's bicycle, we used to ride around the suburbs like
that, except she'd be pedaling in front, veering to scare me, and I'd
be sitting rigid and tense in the back, shrieking at her to be careful. I felt suffocated. I could almost taste her blood in the back of
my throat. On some subterranean level I was terrified of her—terrified that she was drowned in blood because she'd been out killing
strangers, because she couldn't touch Asami.

At lunchtime I wound up on the roof, gulping what passed for
fresh air and trying not to vomit.

"Did you come to kill yourself like Yurie?" I whipped my neck back. Asami was sitting under one of the roaring air vents, smoking a clandestine cigarette. She blew a little nicotine cloud toward me. "Well? I know you were her other half."

It sounds absurd given the tears we'd shed over this bitch, but I was relieved to hear someone admit that Yurie's death was no accident—unless her whole life was an accident, and if so then why not mine, why not Asami's or my father's or the prime minister's? Asami shifted and something around her neck caught the light—a tiny sun beneath her chin. She budged again and I saw what it was: a glassy choker, nearly invisible beyond the glare, tight as a lattice tattoo across her throat. She saw me staring and slapped her hand over it. I could almost see something human breathing beneath her bone-fine face. "What are you looking at, freak?"

Asami shed friends so fast, I bet she'd never had a blood-sister —someone her heart had twinned to, for better or for worse. Maybe she envied me and Yurie. "Why did you hate Yurie so much?"

"She was the one that hated us," said Asami, voice dripping steel. "She rejected us. You know how she was. Always had to be different. Always a loudmouth. How do you think that made us feel?"

I couldn't tell if she was being sarcastic. "She's dead because of you."

Asami lifted the pink-banded Pianissimo to her lips and shrugged. "So she was weak, like all the rest." I wondered if anyone else had ever turned into a mess on a sidewalk because of Asami. "The strong survive. That's the rule."

And that's when I knew I had to do it—because Asami was wrong about that. The real rule, the one my father taught me, was this: anyone can bite you, so be good to other people. "Everyone has to pay their due," he'd say while we watched news segments on terrorists and corrupt politicians and faraway blindfolded hostages. He believed so much in cosmic justice that when he died I wondered if he'd once done something heinous. But maybe it wasn't that simple. Maybe justice had more arms, a longer reach, than we ants could comprehend.

"Everyone has to pay their due," I said. Asami's plastic laughter followed me into the stairwell, and I thought, *She doesn't have a soul to lose anyway.*

Asami and her devotees were waiting for me after school. I was on bathroom cleaning duty, so they nearly drowned me in the toilet. Here's something else people need to understand: kids buy curses like arcade tokens—some of them counterfeit, sure, but others real. Asami did the sort of stuff you wouldn't do to anyone unless you knew they couldn't stick you with a visit from Hanako-san. But I held it together in the toilet bowl; Yurie would have been proud of me. I told myself this was nothing, nothing in comparison to what she'd been put through. My feet slipped on the tiles as Asami rifled through my purse, looking for "spending money" that she didn't need, and I didn't have.

"You're paying your due right now, freak," Asami said. "For talking back to me."

At Rika Yamazaki's grave, I had wished for my father to find eternal rest in that great vinyl office chair in the sky. I didn't want him returned, even though I heard my mother cry at night. With the earth being shaken and stabbed and poisoned at every turn—mad cow, mad bird, mad people—he was better off making his peace with the other side. His suffering had ended. Good.

The beauty of psychic energy—the reason my father worshipped the state recommendations—is that protection is nearly impossible. A psychic attack, the public service announcements explained, is like a natural disaster. There's no kicking it back. That's why the cheerful cartoon ghost on the PSAs chirps that "The best way to protect yourself is to be a good person!" And some preliminary studies have hinted that the rate of infidelity is decreasing because cheating hearts are afraid of waking up fused to their lovers. We're not turning into better people, but our retribution is getting closer.

Of course real life isn't that simple, because some people will always be able to pay for the impossible, and if there's one thing talent's drawn to, it's artillery and armory. We're doing well. We're killing ourselves off at record speed. And a very few of us—a lucky, golden few—have the means to hurt without repercussion, to escape the judgment of peers, to skate above this shitty, brutal world. Internet chatter says the prime minister has a talisman, *or else he never could have dissolved Parliament twice,* and common sense says the Emperor surely has one too. And so did Asami Ogino, third-year high school girl in western Tokyo. I wondered why her parents had decided to buy her one—had she bitten other babies? Or did they just want to give their little princess every advantage?

This is what I thought about while I sat in the auditorium waiting for the choral concert to start. This is what I thought about so I wouldn't think about the fact that I was going to kill the star soloist.

I had already promised Yurie. I'd been sitting in the library, searching yearbooks for pictures of Asami and checking for the necklace—the tiny sun cloaked in clouds—when Yurie's pale bloody hand snaked over my shoulder. I remembered painting those nails sky blue, when blood still ran under the skin instead of on top of it. And now I couldn't even look her in the eye, because I knew she'd seen hell.

"I told you I'd never let you down," I said, although this was the first time I was sure about that. "But once I do this, you'll be gone forever." She would never hurtle us down another hill on a bicycle death-ride. She would never curse me out again, just like she would never forgive me any more of my weaknesses. She would never ask me to do anything else to win a war, or live my life.

Yurie squeezed—not hard, but all softness was gone from her—and whispered, static from a pirate radio, "Come with me to the beautiful land."

The weight of the world, of Yurie and my crying mother and my years upon years of unhappiness, tumbled onto my shoulders, and for a second my spine caved, heaving, toward my dead blood-sister. I was so furious at her for doing this terrible thing, for forcing me to help, for abandoning me to struggle on alone in a world that no one would admit was a post-apocalypse. "Not yet," I said. I couldn't say I was afraid of hell. Knowing Yurie, she'd just try to convince me.

It turns out that it's true what they say about being onstage: the audience disappears into a void. You feel them watching, but really it's just you and your demons, doing battle. Asami was a million-dollar angel up there, with the stage-light halo and the talismanic necklace blazing like an open wound, but I like to think that when she saw me step out of the dark and into the hot bath of incandescent light she realized that retribution was on its way.

I knocked her down—her head hit the floor with an ugly clunk—and dug my fingers under the necklace, scraping the mortal flesh of her soft perfumed neck. Asami was spitting in my eyes, yanking my hair, but I won. I wasn't stronger. I wasn't tougher. But I took bigger risks because I had nothing else to lose. Yurie—Yurie had been the last thing. The necklace unclasped in my hands and instantly, the fire left Asami's face—her eyes softened, her teeth vanished. The little deer had seen death. I rolled away just before the roof of the world opened up and hell rained down upon her.

I looked for Yurie in the torrent of red and black liquid lightning gushing in and out of Asami's ribs, but there were no faces in the storm. No faces at the end of the world. Not even Asami, by the end, had much of a face. But if I strained, if I blocked out the yelps and sobs, I could pick Yurie's mezzo-soprano voice out of the demon chorus. She was the only one singing in the blood.

"Girl, I love you too," I whispered.

I'm holding Asami's choker over a trash-can fire. I've been wearing it for the past two months; it might be the only thing keeping me alive. Asami's family has connections—that's how they got the talisman. So a demon horde might be hanging over my head right now, waiting for my shield to lift.

Now I can see why Asami was so impassive, so callous: the necklace submerges you in a viscous superfluid, and everything else becomes virtual, dreamy, distant. The world's your dollhouse; nothing matters and nothing moves you. Once I tossed a cigarette over my shoulder at a park and an old man on litter duty cursed me with an enchanted megaphone—but nothing happened, so I lit another. Maybe burning other people's raw nerves was Asami's only access to the live wire of emotion. I know I've caught myself forgetting that this fishbowl is not reality, and the true world is spinning on without me.

I drop the necklace in the fire, and soon amber flames are skating across black metal. Each flame is its own nuclear devil—an undead spirit, an undying wheel—racing alone down a freshly tarred highway. I've been dreaming about hell and *the beautiful land,* even without Yurie's guidance—I still miss her, but I know she's waiting for me on the burning plain. Sometimes I hope I'll see Asami beside her, finally holding her hand—blood-sisters of a different kind. Other times, I hope it'll be years before I see either of them. The necklace starts to smoke, and I start to count. I've vowed to stand in the open for three minutes before going back to my mother's dinner table. With Asami, it had only taken ten seconds. I pass that mark. I pass it three times. Four times.

Then I hear a noise, like a flock of gulls diving into a sea. I turn.

The Last Packet of Tea By Quentin S. Crisp

(Dedication: in one way for Dan C., in another, equal, but different way, for Joe C. Third instance of the word "he" is dedicated to Brenpyon.)

"The greatest of poems is an inventory."
G.K. Chesterton

"And seeing how close the mountain deer approach,
I know how far I have strayed from the world."
Kamo no Chômei

It was as if the sockets containing his eyeballs were rock pools. He had lived in times of high tide, and the rock pools had not only brimmed over with the brine of vision, they had been submerged, so that he had never had to think of them as rock pools, and the sea had been everything, overwhelming. Now all things were at an ebb. The waters of vision had receded. The edges of these exposed rock pools, in their narrower world, were defined by an ache of dryness, by the threat that the water would evaporate entirely.

He walked in the grounds of Hall Place. Night had overcome the brief, gray November afternoon. To his left, a lawn divided by flower beds extended to the little river whose motions and disturbances sounded icy in the dark. Closer, on his right, were the

Queen's Beasts, a row of topiary sculptures representing heraldic creatures. His breath showed as he shuffled past each of them. They were a ten-strong fantastical infantry, lined up for inspection as on the nocturnal parade ground of his second childhood. He stopped frequently, seeming to forget his purpose.

Now he looked up past the trees that had been shedding their motley leaves on the grass, and in the sky above them hung the moon. Tonight, at least, his vision was frostily clear, though frail. But that sensation around his eye sockets, along with the blurring, the narrowing, and the other symptoms he had recently been experiencing, had brought him strange, confused thoughts. He was seeing the world differently, not only in a literal sense.

He realized that previously, no matter what ideas he had harbored intellectually, he had always acted as if his vision was the world—something out there, solidly independent of him, in which he was immersed. Now, though he supposed there *was* something out there, he was not at all sure in what way it was related to his vision. He could feel, acutely, how his vision was tethered to his head. Tethered. With this thought, the rock pool image was replaced by that of a balloon on a string. Tethered, but loosely. Vision could float away.

Watching the moon, he allowed these thoughts to follow one upon the other. The balloon of his vision would float into the sky, to become the moon he was now watching, which was, in fact, his own skull, the sockets of which contained balloons of vision that would again come untethered.

He lowered his gaze, and for a moment everything flickered like badly preserved film stock. The topiary beasts looming darkly above him had the appearance of pieces from an alien game of chess. They were, he estimated, almost one hundred years old. In that time, countries had changed their borders, their names, and much else besides, but the Queen's Beasts, useless and obscure even in their "reginality," had remained undisturbed.

He reached out and let his fingers penetrate between the leaf-bristled twigs into the interior darkness of one of these ever-spruce creatures. That darkness was redolent of dust and sap.

Though he could in no way possess them, such things were a solace, slaking despair as water slakes thirst: the Queen's Beasts, fallen yellow leaves caught in their dark, living needles; the ducks that made occasional splashes in the river; the fallen apples that the dawn would reveal in the grass, rotting and seeming to exhale the fresh mists of the day.

It was good that the world had come back to the real-time exactness of such things, that life proceeded once more on foot, and that, though roads intersected hard by the gardens of Hall Place, stillness had long replaced the sound of engines. As cold and comforting as an image in water, this silence was some recompense for the many losses.

🔥

Leaving the grounds, Addyson reflected: he was more quickly sated than when younger, but not as often or easily bored. Now he crossed the silent pitted road to the wooded parkland, barely tended, around whose perimeter was an old wooden fence whose rusty metal predecessor he vaguely recalled. His feet shuffled through leaf mold as he ascended the hill. Electric lights dimmed to darkness or soundlessly blinked into radiance at intervals that had the arrhythmic calm of nature about them, as if they were toadstools, regulating their own ambience according to arcane fungoid principles.

Enough of the outdoor world for now; he desired to be inside, observing the activity of his mind in the circle of a lamp. He had no students today, so there was no need to hurry, but eagerness grew in him to steep once more in the comfortable and melancholy solitude of the domestic environment, with only the movements of the air in the mid-distance and the occasional stir of humans on business that did not involve him, to suggest the largeness of the world that supported his existence.

How old was he now? If he thought about it, he surprised himself with a vertigo like looking down and trying to count the rungs of a ladder he had just climbed. He supposed—if not for a certain giddiness would have been sure—he was now a nonagenarian. These daily walks were a necessity at his age, especially in the cold months when the days sank deeper into darkness with each rotation of the world upon its axis. They were necessary to circulate his blood and accustom him to the cold (his frosty abode would feel warm by comparison for an hour or so after his return); they were necessary to stoke the dying coals of his health and coax from them a few last flames of life; and they were necessary to remind him that life was now more inescapably than ever what it had always been—a matter of today and today and today.

Perhaps this was even a gloomy manner of looking at things, but he had been this gloomy, too, forty years ago or sixty, or seventy. He remembered that Katsushika Hokusai had anticipated finally attaining to the mastery of his art at the age of one hundred and ten. That age was still in Addyson's future. But then again, it had still been in Hokusai's future when he died.

He fitted the key in the door of his flat more by muscle memory than by sight. He would not be able to read, of course—the short days were half hellish for that. There was light, but not sufficient for his pain-afflicted and enfeebled eyes. One thing he missed from the days of large-scale electric power was bright artificial light. But in the last of those days lighting had, anyway, become dim, because of the kind of more or less arbitrary bureaucratic and executive decision that soon translated into the physical universals those living in the world had to suffer. Bright artificial light was simply one of the many things that had seemed eternal because they were present in the world when he was born into it, and one of the many of those many that had since proved temporary.

In the hallway, his breath still showed, but a little less than before. He closed the door but did not remove his coat. Even here, books were piled up against the walls. He pulled the string that dangled from a wall lamp, and the energy that had stored in the battery that day was diffused as a phosphorescent glimmer. This brought out a little of the color of the book jackets. Objects that create homeliness also create warmth—so he often told himself. Still, he had to plan awhile the best use of his resources this evening, for light and for heat.

He decided that today he would sit in the near darkness of the single lamp until he was hungry. Then his cooking would provide an interval of light and warmth.

He rested cross-legged in the sitting room with his back against the section of the wall between kitchen and bedroom. Unable to read, he would put his past reading to the use for which he believed it had been meant. Books, surely, always left off where life was intended to begin. This intention in the writing of books was divided into different forms. In one form it was imperious—both proud and self-hating—urging the reader, paradoxically, to discard all that books represented, and to live in the unrecorded motion of going beyond and going beyond and always going beyond. This was the anti-literary intention. But Addyson felt that this form of the intention was somehow jejune and stemmed from an undeclared love of the action adventure carried into adult years. Life, he had found, was not that dramatic, and to expect such drama was to deny the validity of what truly formed life's greater portion—the less than seductively beautiful, the dull, the pointless, the in between. So the second form of the intention was the literary. This form did not incite to drama—it focused on atmosphere and manner. Many people thought it artificial, etiolated and irrelevant, but properly understood, its purpose was precisely to validate that dull center of life that cannot be escaped. The intention in this case was not that the books be discarded for adventure, but that they be internalized.

Of course, a person was under no obligation to remain faithful to one of these forms of the intention and antagonistic to the other, but Addyson knew, with the resigned intimacy permeating a sinner's knowledge of sin, that he, anyway, would always find his way back onto the footpath of the literary form of this intention.

He closed his eyes.

There was something that immediately gave a faint glow in his tactile consciousness—a glow of the kind that suggests "second skin" or "second nature." It was his thermal underwear. Obvious enough to be bathetic—yet true. "Long johns" was the term he preferred. It had that almost folkloric resonance, that sense of a jocular familiarity with death, also to be found in expressions like "Davy Jones's locker." His long johns were undoubtedly literature—they had all the qualifications. They brought him warmth in the cold. They were a private concern. They bore with his lack of cleanliness in philosophical equanimity, following the shape of his legs in a way that was friendly, unobtrusive, and showed the flexibility necessary for complete realism. And though they were gray and their cut was not dashing, in their everydayness there was a kind of eremitism, in their eremitism a kind of openness, in their openness a kind of beauty, in their beauty a kind of romance.

And so he read them now, as he might read a book, read their close, almost indiscernible contact with his skin, and became absorbed in a complex story of elusive memories woven with an airy fabric of wide universals. Austerity embraced sensuality, and surprisingly personal, surprisingly detailed revelations scribbled themselves in infinitesimal tingles on this hairy page.

In time his eyes, sensitive behind their lids to the shimmer of the lamp, with only this slight stimulus, and darkness, and rest, began to produce in his brain trailing fantasies of color, whose shapes and motion were as emotionally intelligible as music, and as indefinable in their import.

Eventually the cold of his surroundings began to feel like sobriety, and there was a sense of rising, as to the alert and immanent two-dimensionality of wakefulness.

His hands reached out, groping, first for the switch of another lamp, and then to forage among a litter of loose sheets and scraps of paper that he had scavenged from various sources. He found one that was mostly blank, picked up a nearby pen from its resting place by a pot of pens (most of them inkless), and began to etch letters upon the surface of the page with craftsman-like seriousness.

Life sometimes feels like a fairy tale. I do not intend to mean that it tends toward a happy ending, but now—and it cannot be accident—I have summoned that meaning too. What I had meant to mean is that its eeriness suggests a fairy tale (which may also reassure us, or remind us of the feeling of being reassured).

If I take two magnets and introduce the north polarity of one between the north and south of the other, there is a point where attraction and repulsion is ambiguous—this fairy-tale quality is similar. It is a sensation that occurs when I seem on the verge of being obliterated by how different the outer world is to my inner. Something in the very opacity of the outer world, in its detailed refusal to recognize me, causes a swell of feeling from a nonexistent inner world. No, not an inner world—the inner world. It becomes the definite article and so, nonexistent or otherwise, ceases for a moment, in its swell, to require validation.

It's not quite the obvious thing that it sounds. My explanation doesn't capture the indeterminate edge of the thing—but that, in fact, is the thing. The feeling is definite, but has no name. It recurs at intervals, not especially frequent. It might be easiest to explain through suicide.

I have considered suicide many times in my life. "Considered" is the wrong word. I have tried to find my way through to the cold heart of the furnace of suicide, but never made it. When I was still young, I was able to believe that dreams might be waiting to come true—by the pressure of their nature. By the time I was forty, I saw I had misjudged the nature of dreams. "Coming true" was not a necessary part of their definition; if anything, the case was exactly opposite to this. Therefore, when I failed, in my forties—as I did many times—to kill myself, it was no longer because I thought suicide was a tragic impatience that would rob one of the otherwise inevitable, or even possible. It was not that the dreams were gone by that age, exactly, but the "come true" suffix no longer attached itself to my dreams as something credible.

When, at that age, I drew close to suicide, I would compare the alternatives—an abrupt end to my existence, or that existence continued. And, in a natural reaction to the thought of oblivion, the latter would start to clothe itself in images of alluring things that might happen this time if I refrained from self-destruction. These were, in one form or another, the things my life always should have been. But I knew they were utterly false. It is perhaps fifty years on—I can use the word "knew" with legitimate authority. I knew I was right then and I know it for sure now.

The point is this: when I discarded the alluring possibilities as false and accepted that my life would continue essentially as it had been, I felt that that actual life—the one I would continue—was the falsehood. I could regret—in hypothetical anticipation—cutting my life short, because it would mean I never got a chance to live. But I knew this "I" never would get its chance, even in continued life, and without this "I" getting its chance, nothing was real. And yet, in some way, it is true that this "I," never expressed, would have been thwarted by a shorter life.

Was it this—that I was no longer living to live my dreams, but only to dream them?

That is too much to the point, and it is not the point. I think even the dreams that I knew to be hopeless refused to let me die. In this sense, life and dream are inextricable, and somewhere on the edges of this inextricability, somewhere...

He became aware that he was losing his way in precision and stopped. He closed his eyes in quiet weariness, incurable and therefore not worth giving attention to. There had been no children. There had been no success. People who took those two things for granted had lectured him over the years on the harsh realities of life. He did not want to write in a language that pandered to them— the logic that disproved itself.

He began to write again. It was only a scribble, but inside him the motion was the descent of a blade, and something, sliced, toppled:

> The familiar
> Fact of the moon, above trees
> With half-bare branches
> And topiary beasts. I,
> Eclipsed, sleep outside this dream.

Anyway, he would lay aside the pen for now. He put the leaf of paper back with the litter from which he had extracted it.

Fletch came round while he was still eating the stew he had prepared for himself. There was some left in the pot, so he served this up for Fletch, who, in turn, produced a pot-bellied bottle of wine. Fletch, a little less than half Addyson's age, was nonetheless a friend of many years, and one of his most frequent visitors. Tonight, he had arrived on a cart, bringing with him two boxes of Addyson's books.

"I wish you didn't have to sell them," said Fletch, at that point in such an occasion when the food is more or less out of the way and there is a sense of easing more deeply into drink and talk.

"So do I," said Addyson. "But my students are not rich enough or numerous enough to support me by themselves. Besides, books should circulate. It's a bonus if I'm paid for that circulation."

"But who do they circulate to?"

"Well, yes, that's the dilemma," Addyson conceded. "The books are too good to be read."

Not so much by calculation as by the interaction of his nature with circumstance, Addyson had come to invest his precarious energies and material resources in the accumulation and maintenance of an extendsive private library. This had required ingenuity, since he lacked the storage to contain what had, for most of his life, been an ever-expanding collection. The bunch of keys for his current flat, in which he had lived for some decades, included the key to an adjoining garage, of which he had taken advantage, and the flat also had cellar space, a feature that had become more common in the period just before he moved in. Nonetheless, as his collecting peaked, it had required him to outsource the collection itself to various bibliophile friends, who would look after indefinitely borrowed books in exchange for the obvious benefit of being able to read them.

"I haven't actually read all of these," said Fletch, indicating the boxes.

"Keep them till you have, if you like. I still have others I can sell off here."

Fletch reflected.

"No. It's all right. Maybe I'm just keeping them out of circulation. And maybe if you had more money you'd be able to write again."

"I am writing."

"I mean…I don't want to sound brutal, but there's no knowing how much longer you've got. I know there was much more you wanted to write. I wish you would. You really shouldn't be putting things off now. I wish I had the money myself, so that you didn't have to teach and sell books, but I don't."

"There's always more," said Addyson. "But you're right. Some of the things I had planned as my life's work, I've had to let slip by. I feel that."

He took a sip of wine as if indicating it was necessary to refrain from speaking for a while to let things unspeakable and unbearable breathe.

What was unbearable was breathing through him, and soon breath became voice once more.

"Some of those books are antiques, by the old definition—older than me. They're all antiques in terms of scarcity. But, in a sense, the whole of existence can be looked at as an antique.

"There's a quote—'The greatest of poems is an inventory.' I think the next line goes, 'Every kitchen utensil becomes ideal when it's washed up from a shipwreck.' Something like that. That's G.K. Chesterton. Funny the things you remember.

"Anyway, the point is, although the older parts of existence are often rarer examples of their type, all of the known world is finite, and each part of it, actually, is unique. It's all just what has survived. The present moment is all that is washed up from the shipwreck of the past. And so every single molecule of it potentially has the fascination of the antique."

"That sounds too detached," said Fletch.

Addyson was puzzled at the disapproval in his tone.

"Detached?"

"Yeah. As if it doesn't matter what survives and what doesn't."

Addyson understood. It was the detachment of mysticism that Fletch feared, the renunciation of the world in the seeming affirmation "It's all one." If he tried to defend this mysticism, it would complicate matters, and if it were worth defending, perhaps it needed no defense. Besides which, he had meant what he said—but was it so simple?—as the opposite of detachment.

"Ah…I see what you mean. No. It's like seeds."

"Seeds?"

"Yes. That's how I see it. Like a seed bank. That's what my library and my writing are. You know, many years ago, although it barely entered into the newspapers, there were people in power who made the possession of certain seeds illegal, because they wanted a monopoly on crops. Now, this was a crime, a real crime, to limit existence by trying to eliminate the potentialities contained in those seeds.

"Well, but, if you have managed to hide away even one seed somewhere, it is possible to grow those potentials again. And a book is a seed too, of course. And maybe there could come a time when there is only one book left, but in such a case we would have to hope that it would contain enough information to regrow the lost culture."

"Okay," said Fletch, apparently satisfied, and he nodded.

In many ways, Addyson hankered for solitude, or he required it. However, the moment of parting was always something he needed to steel himself for, if it was from anyone who might truly be considered company. This too, perhaps, was a sign that games were over. Some kind of communication needed to take place, and it was work, and—this was the whole thing—he had to be alone to have a chance of communicating with others. But it was dreadful work, if he could call work what had so long remained in his head, untranslatable.

The body takes longer to heal as it grows older, and, in the same way, the transition from engagement with human presence to solitude had become unexpectedly jagged and painful to Addyson. He had to get on with this work of his—whatever it was—but when Fletch left, in theory allowing this, he felt incapacitated by the pain, as if he were a scraggy old bird from whom another patch of feathers had just been ripped out. It was clear that he could not concentrate on much for the moment, but he was not going to sit dazed now. He would carry out some very simple task, requiring only the barest presence of mind—enough of a task to soothe, not enough to tax.

The obvious activity by which he might adjust to solitude once more, negotiating the complex balance and counterbalance of feelings, was the storing of the newly returned books.

Without haste, he approached the boxes Fletch had left behind and began to inspect their contents. Then he rolled back the patch of carpet that covered the floor in the room's center and revealed a trap door, which he opened. A ladder hung down into darkness, stray light from the sitting room illuminating faintly a few spines of books.

The cellar was really little more than an underground cupboard, designed to store things rather than to be a bunker for human refuge, as so many of the more recent cellars were. During the hours of darkness, it was even a little daunting to descend the ladder into that confined space.

He began to empty the books from the boxes and pile them up close to the edge of the trapdoor, so that they could be easily reached from within the cellar. He brought a portable lamp near too, to ensure visibility for his work. When the pile of books was reaching a size bordering on awkward, he climbed down the ladder, paused to collect a handful of books, and continued to the bottom. He found the cord for the cellar light and searched for spaces on the shelves lining the walls. It was a laborious process.

He had ascended and descended a few times and was getting short of breath by the time he had emptied one of the boxes. When he had almost emptied the second, he made a strange discovery. Between two of the stacked columns of books had been inserted what first appeared to Addyson's unreliable eyes an enormous silverfish. It was a slim and whiskery object with about it the kind of dusty shimmer that adheres to the wing of a moth. Rather than extract it directly with his fingers, Addyson removed the surrounding books so that the object lay revealed at the dirty cardboard bottom of the box. It wasn't alive, after all. It wasn't even a creature. But its vividness in comparison to its gloomy and drab surroundings had given it an uncanny appearance of life. It was not merely vivid, but alien. It was a package of some kind, but the writing on it was not in the Roman alphabet, so what it contained was not immediately obvious.

Addyson knelt before the box for some time in contemplation of the object, and while he did so his mind formed a narrative around it, as it had earlier with his long johns. The earlier narrative had been amorphous. The flesh of this one grew upon the bones of deduction.

First of all, there was the object's ethereality. It seemed woven from the thread of a different and finer reality than that which Addyson awoke to each day. Its shape, its patterned surface, gave an impression of angularity—but an angularity of supreme naturalness and smoothness, like that of a leaf, wet with dew. Its colors were green, pink, gold, white, and black. The background white seemed impervious to time—fresh as spearmint but redolent of age because of the very purity of the freshness. The white appeared even to glow, and the colors upon it to opalesce.

A poem came to mind—something by Baudelaire. It told of "a poet set against oblivion" who stayed awake to witness the moon's nocturnal sorrows and to catch her pearly tears when they fell. He thought of what he had written earlier. This strange object was perhaps a teardrop fallen from the moon.

Memory broke the surface of consciousness. He could read the writing on the package, but the knowledge of this language had lain so long unused in his brain and had grown so atrophied that there was a kind of dislocation between the writing and its apparent meaning in his brain. This was a packet of tea—Japanese tea. That's what the writing told him, but because of the dislocation, the knowledge remained an impression rather than congealing into fact.

He had to repeat the words to himself.

"Tea. Tea. Tea. It's Japanese tea."

In fact, from what he could tell, this was a variety of tea called *kari-ga-oto*. No—*kari-ga-ne*. The reading of the last character was an unusual, poetic reading. If he could remember that, surely his brain was functioning. *Kari-ga-ne* meant "the cry of geese."

Finally, he took the packet from the box. This packet of tea—from the town of Uji, he saw—must have been many decades old. He looked for the date. There were numbers, but applied according to the traditional Japanese system, and he could not remember how to convert them. In any case, somehow a packet of tea that he had brought back from Japan, or that had been sent to him from Japan when he had still had links with that country and while it remained a country to have links with, had found its way into this box of books and been left there unopened while the century passed its meridian and disasters of all kinds cratered his emotional experience and his memory.

He closed the trap door. The remaining books, still piled on the floor, he would deal with later. The change of mood he had required had come to him, though it was a different change than he could have wished for or imagined.

The next morning was chill and misty. He had long hardened his bones to the austerity of waking with the dawn in order never to miss a scintilla of daylight. This morning, he had trouble telling whether the mist was entirely external or the product of some part of the equipment of his head. He decided his head was at least partly to blame, but, rather eerily it seemed to him, the external and internally generated mist evaporated in harmony.

His sobriety this morning was close to vacancy, and this vacancy was close to stupefaction. How could he seize the eternity of his existence with the tiny hands of day-to-day?

Before he had time to break his fast, he heard a voice from outside shouting, "Post." There followed rapid footsteps on the stairs of the building, the sound of a door being opened, and an exchange of indistinguishable words in the entry hall. Then there were more footsteps, and an unrestrained rapping on the door shrank Addyson back to the locality of his body.

"Who's there?"

For a moment, Addyson had a very odd but not entirely unprecedented sensation: he thought he was blind. Actually, he could see, but what he saw was blank of meaning.

"Post for Mr. Addyson," came the reply.

Realizing he could see and was not helpless, Addyson got to his feet and went to the door. On the other side of the door, when he opened it, the present moment was waiting for him in the form of an unfamiliar post-boy with a letter in one hand, the envelope of good quality, cream-colored paper.

The post-boy, seemingly aware that he had the appearance of a wayside opportunist, pulled his frayed ID document from a patch pocket and let Addyson read it.

"Are you Mr. Addyson?" he asked.

Addyson produced his own ID.

"Here y'are," said the boy, and relinquished the letter with an air of bestowing something, as if he had an idea of the letter's contents.

Breaking the seal, Addyson found the pages within typewritten but signed by hand. He laid the sheets out on the floor and began to read.

> *Dear Mr. Addyson,*
>
> *I am more familiar with the name under which you used to write, and I believe still do. I would have used that, but was afraid it might seem too forward. Please advise me as to your preference.*
>
> *It is, anyway, regarding your fiction that I am writing to you. Please let me state in advance of everything else that I have a position of moderate influence in the editorial and curatorial department of the Eden Scriptorium, of which I hope you might have heard. You perhaps know of us for the work we have done in salvaging and archiving printed texts. There is also an Eden Press, which has begun to make copies of the rarer and more important works. In fact, we are engaged in an array of different projects, from the cataloguing of typefaces to the production of paper that will last many lifetimes. I hope very much that you will be able to visit our premises at some point, since, once you have seen for yourself the stacks of freshly sheaved paper and seen the glint of drying ink you will understand something of the excitement with which I write to you.*

Let me explain the sequence of events that has led to this communication. It will be no surprise to you that I am a bibliophile, I would like to say "par excellence." Not stopping at a conventional reverence for canonical works, I have always delighted in the discovery of the obscure and beautiful, perhaps with something of the thrill of the long-ago entomologist explorer, discovering some richly patterned and as yet unnamed species, somewhere in the tangled, savage innocence of the rain forest. I hope you will understand and allow yourself to believe when I say that a number of your stories came to me as the most brilliant, unexpected, and breathtakingly delicate of exotic moths. In particular, I am thinking of "The Language of Chameleons," "Unprecedented Forms," "The Stars and Yellow Doubt" [Not one of mine, thought Addyson, though I think I know who the author is], and "The Hill That Is Not a Hill and Is Not Called Amara."

The name Bevis Kemble might mean something to you. He's a book dealer and antiquarian with whom we do business. As you probably recall, he has visited you on occasion, and some of the books he has bought from you have made their way into our archive. I was oblivious to this situation for years, and it is only very recently that I have learned the truth. I hope you will forgive me if I write that I had assumed you were dead. I don't even really know why I made this assumption— perhaps because the books with your stories in them are so dusty and brown. I mention this fact in the hope it helps to convey the wonder I experienced when Bevis told me that he knew you. It was almost as if someone had risen from the grave.

I only recently mentioned to him that I would very

much like to find some of your books for the archive. It seems that one of your students had spoken to him of your writing and told him the name you'd written under.

We must talk about your older work, and I hope before too long, but first there is the question of the anthology I am editing. The working title is The Eden Anthology of New Fiction, and the idea is this: we will collect together new works by old writers, to establish a continuity between our new world and the old. This has the potential to be the cornerstone of a new canon. Literature, as you know, has become less a living thing than it was, and more a matter of antiquarianism. With this book we hope to provide an example to inspire and instruct new writers.

The student who spoke to Bevis mentioned that you still write. Would you be willing to write something specially for the anthology? I enclose a copy of the guidelines with this letter, and some good writing paper, which I know can be hard to come by. (Please don't hesitate to ask the post-boy for more.)

I believe that, from the wreckage of our current age, we have the chance to build a new citadel of literature and a new literary culture to bring it to life—a literary culture as it always should have been, in which both quality and novelty are valued, where writers are paid, and where books are not produced and distributed according to the demands of the least literate, but under the guidance of the most.

I would be extremely gratified if you were to accept my invitation to help us build such a citadel.

Please reply to the address heading this letter. You needn't pay the post-boy. I shall keep this message *brief and hope I can look forward to an answer from you soon.*

Yours,
Kieran Drummond

The enclosed guidelines included a date by which a finished story was expected. The rate of pay was also given. It was generous. Naturally, he would not be able to retire from one story. In fact, what would most likely happen would be that, in order to write the story, he would have to take a month off teaching, and the payment for the story would go some way to compensating him for the time needed to write it. Still, it might easily lead to other things.

Addyson was at first surprised to find himself assessing the offer so calmly, but, after all, he was eight or nine decades in on the great, disappointing detour to the unknown that was human existence, and by this time fatalism was as much of a default mechanism with him as it could be without actually being fatal.

The deadline was not uncomfortably close. He had time to think.

Laying the letter aside for the present, he looked at the wall clock. He was expecting one of his students, Matthew, today, but he would not be arriving for another three hours.

His routine was important. It supported his life as a trellis supports a vine. Recently, however, his routine had been disturbed. Not disrupted. It was more as if something had struck a nerve in him that numbed and loosened his grip.

For the moment he would surrender. He closed his eyes and leaned back against the wall.

Perhaps the letter had stirred something up. He found memories and thoughts arising spontaneously that related to a period of his life when he had had work trying to reclaim data from various forms of digital storage. Since the power for the digital infrastructure had gone, a kind of electronic archaeology had developed, whereby energy was generated and then focused strategically with the aim of mining the otherwise inaccessible data of various circuit boards, compact discs, magnetic tapes, and so on. As he remembered this now, an image formed in his mind that had formed there before. He saw the current of electricity as a drill of light, plunged into a digital well in order to pump up fossilized information like oil. Data rose to accessibility in the light of the pulsing drill, but it was shattered. Fragments of fossil text.

Much of this excavated data was leaked, one way or another. Cults had come into being who claimed that these jagged, recombined mosaics of text were messages from a half-sleeping electronic intelligence that was bound to reawaken. Some of the adherents of this belief would stand in the street and declaim these shattered texts in prophecy. For a while Addyson, too, had been fascinated by the mysticism of the digital potsherds, but a kind of disgust had set in, and he had abandoned the job. That, in fact, had not been such an easy decision. The decision itself had seemed more or less sudden, almost involuntary, but it was as if he had thrown down a monolith he had been carrying for some time. The earth seemed to shake with the surrender. The vast galaxy of digital data, he had decided, could collapse into oblivion. It wouldn't, of course. Some fraction of it would be recovered. But, personally, he had given it up.

He opened his eyes and reached for pen and paper.

> We imitated
> An entropy of language,
> Words duplicated
> Without sense in a cancer
> Of unconsciousness—thought death.

The reason he was losing hold of his all-important routine, he decided, was that packet of tea. Perhaps the loosening grip was incipient anyway, but the packet of tea had been a catalyst, causing what was incipient to germinate and unfold. When he was alone in his flat, he examined the packet again.

Clearly, this item was from Japan—that was why the writing was in Japanese (was it *in* Japanese, or was it simply, *itself*, Japanese?)—but what was Japan? A country, perhaps, since languages were often associated with specific countries, but could he be sure in this case? He had looked up "Japan" in his dictionary. There had been an entry for "Japanese," and even for "japan," with a small j, which was apparently a "hard varnish," but there had been no "Japan." Could it be that there were Japanese things without any Japan to generate them?

This was an absurd line of thought. He remembered Japan. And yet the uncertainty persisted. His attempts to settle the matter were ultimately ineffectual. For some reason, none of the books within immediate reach were categorical about the existence of Japan, if they mentioned her at all. He recalled that Japan had made an appearance in *Gulliver's Travels,* and he found a copy of this and located the relevant chapter. But then he remembered that most of the places Gulliver visited were fantastical inventions and was maddened to find Japan assuming a fictitious status in her association with them.

Then something else occurred to him. He had definitely thought, recently, of Hokusai, a Japanese artist to whom real works of art were attributed, and the poems he, Addyson, had written of late were tanka, which was a Japanese form. But where did such knowledge come from? A little effort should be able to verify it, but the verification seemed something like the biased selection of matching shards of information in his vast but limited reserves of consciousness, and not much else. Also, the fact that a Japanese theme had started to surface in his thoughts just before the appearance of the packet of tea gave the sequence of events the aura of a mental mal-aise—an aura that might be extended to include Japan itself.

Did he really believe Japan to be imaginary? Not quite. And if he committed to such a belief, then soon enough he would be unsure of the most basic circumstantial facts of his existence. But he could not quite get Japan solid in his mental map of reality, either. Just as the language had been slippery from long disuse, so the concept of Japan itself had become, as it were, rusty.

In any case, whether Japan were imaginary or not, this packet of tea had come from there. And, if he were to judge by the appear-ance of this object, he would say that Japan was imaginary. This was an object from another world.

He held the packet in his hand, felt its slight weight, and brought it a little closer to his face. It had something in it, of course, or it could hardly have been a packet. The presumed tea, unseen, shifted inside; if he turned the packet upside down it made a sliding, whis-pering sound. But the packet was sealed. The silken magnificence of its exterior promised something limitless, but what was promised remained elusive.

Addyson had gone out to buy one or two things that he needed but had found himself stopping at an open storefront, where a woman was spinning yarn from a batt of wool. The spinning of yarn was obviously in part a display to attract custom, as well as being necessary labor in itself, so the woman should not have minded his watching her. It was really the wool he was intent on, the way the yellowish cloud of it, here and there matted to a darker, brown-ish tone, was drawn out into the groove of the turning wheel—the thin thread from the formless mass. He felt transfixed by conflict-ing impressions—that the wool was supremely rare and precious, and that the supply of it was infinite. He was held here, watching, both by a sense of anxiety and of comfort. He knew, of course, that the supply of wool, like all things on Earth, was particular and limited, but was fascinated by the impression that prevails in the immediacy at the demand end of the supply chain, that the goods in question were siphoned from an ideal and inexhaustible source.

Wool was spun into twine and the daylight waned, not thickening, it seemed, but thinning into a chill blue. The wheel revolved and the yarn lengthened, and Addyson began to feel it was a self-sufficient reality, that it would continue to exist even when all else was claimed by the growing obscurity. It would be the last thing to exist and would spin itself to an end that was endless. He wanted to disappear in contemplation of it. Not even contemplation—in the dream of it.

Then there came a voice, repeating a single word with the insistence of an alarm clock. The voice belonged to Fletch; the word was his name.

Addyson resurfaced, hypnopompically, and found himself in the dark of early evening outside a shop selling yarn and woolen garments. Fletch was beside him, by some wonderful chance, and Addyson was overjoyed at his sudden appearance. Addyson began to recall, blurrily, the outline of his itinerary for the day, but all that seemed unimportant. Nothing mattered except the presence of his friend. He felt himself choosing to prioritize that presence over all else, as if he were gladly sliding into damnation.

In an enthusiasm that seemed fever-tinged, Addyson persuaded Fletch to walk back home with him, and on the way he bought two bottles of wine heedless of his weekly budget.

The flat was chilly, as usual, and the breath of both showed on the air as Addyson placed an oil lamp between them and filled two glasses. The conversation felt more agitated than jovial until it occurred to Addyson to produce the letter he had recently received. With this, their talk obtained the ballast it had needed.

"Have you started on a story?" Fletch asked after examining the letter and the guidelines.

"No."

"I think you should. Don't you want to?"

"Yes, I do. The problem is that I'm too old. I don't mean for writing. But for fiction I am."

"How can you be too old?"

"I think fiction is about suspense and possibility. That is, it is especially meaningful to those in the middle of life, but at least needs a future too large to be contained within the mental field of vision. One writes fiction in order to have a dialogue with life, in the hope that this dialogue will deepen future possibilities. Simply put, one writes fiction with the intention of living it, or at least the values and aesthetics it embodies.

"I no longer have a future to dream about or to dream with. The horizon is narrowing as it converges on the exit from existence."

"You still write, though. I don't see why it's different."

"Perhaps you're right. But I haven't written fiction for very many years. This Drummond has read my old stories, but it's been so long since I wrote them that I feel a bit like a ghost spying on the posthumous success of the person he was when alive. It's hard to connect with that success as a living person. When these stories were first published…who knows who read them? Not many, I think. And probably all of them now ghosts like me."

"You're overthinking it. You are still alive, actually. There's no reason not to make the most of that. Even if you're a ghost, I bet ghosts have stories to tell. I'd like to hear them."

Addyson pursed his lips in thought and poured more wine for them both. He didn't have an answer for Fletch. He could feel himself straining for a refutation, but why would he do that? It was true that something stood in the way of his writing this story, but since he did not know what it was, there was no use in arguing its case.

Something else occurred to him, as if linked to, yet also as a means of moving away from, this subject. He stood up and approached an ornately carved wooden box that sat in the place on one bookcase where a clock might have sat. He took a small key from a hidden pocket, inserted it in a lock on top of the box, and opened up the wings of the lid. Fletch watched all this in curious silence. Addyson often referred to the box as "My Death" and had let it be known that it contained documents intended to be read post mortem, including a will, but also various other writings perhaps closer to being a testament. From this box, Addyson drew an envelope-shaped package, with the slight bulge at its lower end that is formed by gravity on loose contents, its outside surface decorated with feminine colors and patterns that might easily have belonged to some ancient vernal past or some brilliant autumnal future.

He resumed his seat on the floor and passed the package to Fletch.

"What is it?" asked Fletch.

"Tea. That was in one of the boxes you brought back."

"Really? I didn't see it. Where's it from?"

"Japan." He watched Fletch's face, but there was no especial reaction at this word.

"But how did it get there?"

"I don't know. I suppose it's been there a long time. Probably too long for it to be good to drink. Maybe even from before…"

"Before?"

Addyson waved his hand vaguely. "Before…"

"Oh. Before."

"Yes. So it could be contaminated, or, if it's older, not contaminated, but still too old to drink."

"So you're just going to keep it?"

"I suppose so. It must be very rare. It might even be the last of this kind of tea in existence."

Fletch passed back the packet. Neither of them spoke. This packet of tea seemed to be a conundrum evoking, finally, only silence. In this silence, however, something occurred to Addyson—a delayed understanding. Fletch apparently knew what he had alluded to in saying "Before." There had been a Japan, very probably. Of course there had. But it was gone now. Maybe that was why it had become such a phantom in his memory.

> Do ghosts age? This one—
> The phantom in my teacup—
> Should reflect my face,
> But has not changed. It longs to
> Rise like steam and tell its tale.

He awoke in darkness. He thought the darkness was horribly hot, then cold—cold as something forever wrong. When he understood that he was hot under his insulated bedclothes but could feel the chill of night on his exposed face, he began to remember where and when he was, and the long, seemingly inescapable dream of his entire existence. How much longer? And how would it end?

There was an end, wasn't there? No, a deadline. But was that an end? Was it?

He got out of bed, shivering, but also feeling the compass of balance and spatial awareness within him find its north. He drew aside the stained curtain from the window and found, outside, the familiar impartial world. How often, in not recognizing him, had it seemed barren of comfort? But he found comfort in it now, as if what he saw were a line from a song that may, with half a smile, or even a chuckle, be understood, but not explained. The moon floated high over the stable opposite. No one passed and he could hear no sound. The moon—inaccessible again. Until such time as...what?

Arthur Waley. The name came back to him with sudden buoyancy, surfacing whole in his mind. Arthur Waley had been a great

Japanologist. His name had its place in Addyson's memory like Tom Thumb or Marco Polo. He could not remember when he had first heard it. Nonetheless, he knew that Arthur Waley had been the first person to translate Murasaki Shikibu's *The Tale of Genji* into English—a feat of enormous erudition, dedication, and self-sacrifice. But Waley had never been to Japan and, in fact, never did go. When asked if he wouldn't like to visit and see the country for himself, he had replied that he would rather not; he would prefer to keep intact within him the Japan he had imagined.

A poet set against oblivion.

He would not sleep tonight.

How long was it till the deadline? Was there enough time for him to remake Japan? Still shivering, he left his bedroom and lit an oil lamp. There was a cardboard box, in the corner, with his writings in, some of it handwritten on loose leaves, some of it in notepads, some printed, some in the form of bound books. He took out the loose leaves, the pads, the books and inspected pages here and there by the light of his lamp. A panicky impatience seized him, and he threw the paper he was holding on the floor. For a while, he contemplated these paper shards covered in their close lines of words. He thought his hand would tremble when it reached out again. It did a little and then seemed to become empty and calm.

Everything had become immediate and momentous to his senses, but had there been another to observe, they might have thought him engaged in intricate, many-staged deliberation. Eventually, he took all of his writing, except the poems he had been scribbling of late on scraps, and the documents in his death box and arranged them in a pile in the overgrown communal yard behind the building. He put a taper in his oil lamp and passed the flame to the heap of paper he had just made.

"Too many weeds," he said, as the flame began to grow.

He added sticks and pieces of flammable detritus to the blaze. Soon he had built a bonfire—modest, but just large enough that he could step back a little and still feel some warmth. It had all been simply and easily accomplished. Moreover, he had not disappeared with the onset of the conflagration. The flames had created an emptiness, but he was, in contrast, becoming more solid.

Poppies of ash were swirling upward on the heat currents. The gloss of the darkness was peeling—these were the colorless flakes that detached from the patches of revealed nothingness. The world, perhaps, was a mirror to the senses. In itself it was empty, though an empty something. It truly became the world when there was someone to look into it. But what if the reflective quicksilver lining that enabled the relationship between world-mirror and person were all to flake away?

> There comes a moment
> When old sayings are not shed
> Skins, but living mounts
> With empty saddles: a cup
> Must be empty to be filled.

Dawn came, and he felt worn thin, as if by the passage of an Arctic summer, in which only the slenderest interval of night made days plural rather than singular. He had thought he would write, but for now the fertile Greenland of his soul was austere with ice.

When he reread Drummond's letter and the guidelines, it was not that he now felt empty. It was more like being presented with the wrong question. The real answer started far anterior to the assumptions from which the question arose. He experienced a fullness that made the question almost irrelevant, almost incoherent, and no words resulted.

So, he would not write.

He already knew what he would do. He took the tiny key from the inner pocket where he kept it and opened the two wings that formed the lid of his death box. From this he extracted the packet of tea. Then, he took himself to the kitchen and picked up the scissors from the sideboard. He cut into the long-sealed envelope, opening up the thin line of a new mouth. Holding the package so that it bellowed with air and the mouth opened, he sniffed at the still unseen contents. There seemed to be no scent. Had it all evaporated?

Scent, a subtle scent such as Japanese tea, was elusive to memory, but he could almost recall how it should smell.

There was something he could do—something actual and mechanical. Beneath the kitchen sink, in the broken cupboard, was a shoebox containing items wrapped in the pages of long-defunct magazines. From this, Addyson took something roughly the shape of a milk churn and the size of a pepper pot and unwrapped it. He had not thought to use it for a long time—an earthenware oil burner. He scrubbed the oil dish under the tap but couldn't remove all the gunk, so gave up. Returning to the sitting room with the burner, he poured some of what the tea packet contained into the dish, and beneath this he inserted a tea light, which he lit.

He sat and closed his eyes.

What had it been like, that aroma? Resinous, yes. That was one of the words by which he had always tried to describe and remember it. It had about it the freshness of sap. But that alone did not capture it. There was also a sweetness to it, like cake-crumb. Yes, it gladdened the heart the way baking smells do. But this also left something essential untouched.

Behind his closed eyes, a work of solid engineering erected itself. He recognized it. *Yume no Ukibashi*, the Floating Bridge of Dreams mentioned in the Uji chapters of *The Tale of Genji*. Uji Train Station, the terminus of the Keihan Line. Exit the station and turn right, and there is the legendary bridge, crossing the River Uji, into the town of Uji.

Addyson paused midway across the bridge. It was a bright, brisk day. The sunlight was bracing rather than warm. It glistened at the corners of things, where winds rippled. There was little traffic and pedestrians were few, but Addyson could sense the unobtrusive population within the compact shapes of the semi-urban landscape. The river was wide, and to any who loved rivers, it gave the impression that rivers do, not merely of the majesty of water, but also of air, which with a great river is a huge, unscalable freedom that somewhere becomes sky. He looked to that sky, and then down to where the river eddied in white manes of froth around the bridge's supports.

The sense of the present, of being alive, was inexpressible. It was fleeting, obscure—yet imperishable. It was a trivial, a nonchalant feeling—yet how truly splendid. And this bridge and this sun-limned, wind-shaded afternoon belonged to a time when the present was alive, when one could walk and speak in unison with deathless today. It was no dream, that was true, but dream could cross the bridge of the present from birth to death on living legs.

He remembered where this bridge would take him. When he came to its end, if he turned left, he would enter the carless road that, with tea shops on both sides, led to the Byôdô-in temple. But it was the road he was interested in, and not the temple. He was coming to it now, nearing the end of the bridge. He had only to turn and take a few more steps and on either side would be the tea shops, the smell of roasting green tea wafting from beside and beneath the kanji-splashed noren. That smell, so fresh, so subtle, so thrilling—it was like an afterimage of the present moment itself, an afterimage that in turn became a blueprint for everything loved or longed for in the country he knew as Japan.

Just a few steps away. But the light was too bright ahead, and the vision would not come clear.

He opened his eyes.

The leaves that had been roasting in the oil burner he tipped into a teapot. He refilled the burner and set about boiling water for tea.

"Though this tea…" He was thinking in a writerly way, composing thoughts in his head. "Though this tea, in its packaging and its scent, gives rise to dream, it comes from a real Japan. The same Japan that Waley never visited. And perhaps my dreams are the same as his. There must be a link between the reality and the dream, as a tree flowers and bears fruit…"

But after this his thoughts became more disconnected. At last he seemed to lose track of them utterly, and a cup of yellow-brown liquid was steaming before him. Was it off-color because of its age, or because he had just been roasting the leaves? He dismissed the question and blew ripples across the tea's surface.

He took the tea to where he had been sitting before and drank, at first in careful sips and then in slurps and gulps. There was something a little repulsive about the taste. It tasted rusty. No, worse than that. The iron tang was more the iron of blood than of rust. But after this taste had become a silt lining his throat, he was more able to ignore it and concentrate on the monad of the tea flavor that had initially been cloaked. He felt the tea absorbed by his stomach, and he closed his eyes again.

The blinding light had gone, and the road had become solid in its retreat. He could wander autonomously between the tea shops. He was free to go inside any of the shops, through the wooden lattice sliding doors, sit at a counter. What would happen? Even if he were merely served tea, he thought this simple fact might be imbued with the significance of a riddle.

He did not stop to enter any of the shops. Maybe the thought of entering did not satisfy his imagination. He walked on and passed the lane that led to the temple entrance. Presently, he came to some known steps. They seemed now noticeably more known than most other things contained in the world. He climbed them to the path that ran, on a raised bank of earth, parallel to the river. Then he turned and looked back at the way he had come—the temple roof, the road threading between shops, their banners fluttering. A pure breeze rose up from below, seeming to suffuse him with a charged, sweet emptiness.

If he turned a little to his right, he could also see the bridge he had traversed a short while ago. The serene panorama was the implicit sum of his experiences of Japan. And the sum that was implied, in turn implied more, further.

What came to his nose, his skin, his eyes, and his ears was all the blueprint of that roasting-tea scent. All of it was the product of the delicious fumes from leaves in unseen braziers. But he was no longer sure whether Japan brought him that aroma in his nostrils and that contentment in his stomach, or whether the aroma and the contentment brought him Japan.

He closed his eyes. Very briefly it occurred to him that he was closing his eyes behind eyes already closed. With the wind gentle on his skin, with the tea aroma still telling a tale of rooftop and back-street, like chimney smoke, with the liquid narration of the river close by, he could still see everything. But now the light was ebbing. As it waned, something else waxed in its place. It was the excitement, like a baking heat that conducts swiftly and evenly through consciousness itself, that is a form of foreknowledge occurring only on certain rare summer evenings. It was tantalizing, since he did not know exactly when or in what way the thing would come, of which this feeling was the certainty and the proof. But it was only required that he wait and remain alert. The first thing was close to impossible; the second he could not help.

The mad heat of certainty increased with the darkness. From upstream there swayed a floating fire, accompanied by a plash of oars. The fire could be seen between the hanging ribbons of willow branches, giving off a flurry of sparks. Now came wafts of pine smoke.

The boat approached, cormorants swimming about its prow as

if they pulled it, and one of the fishermen within adding more pine to the fire that blazed in the metal basket hanging over the water. Addyson watched, as if his feet had melted into the ground. The wooden vessel, the team of cormorants, the fire, the men half fire, half shadow—all this was slightly too real, so that its reality became noticeable, as with a costume drama. And this phenomenon of bird, fire, water, wood, and man swelled to a convexity of reality at precisely the point where it passed Addyson on the bank. It shrank again as it continued downstream in the eddies etched in fire on the dark water. The downstream landscape as he saw it now, his vision following and rising from the boat, was different from that he had seen before. Previously it had receded toward a horizon. Now it did not recede but rose up, with more distant things merely piling on top of nearer things, as in a scroll painting of manifold hills. There was the curve of the bridge, the wickerwork of timbers that supported it, and then the tree-clouded slopes, where the ornate but regular curves of *kawara*-tiled roofs were like combs artfully fixed into a coiffure. Two long-legged, splay-feathered herons rose above a layer of mist, and farther or higher still, among giddy foot-trails and asymmetrical humps, were glowing chrysanthemums of yellow, red, white, and pink, which must have been temples.

Above, the force that drew the waves of this landscape, shone the moon.

The boat disappeared beneath the bridge. And then there were sandaled footsteps up the brief steps Addyson had long ago believed so familiar. The heat was abating, replaced by a mellowness, a luxurious almost-sadness. He turned, finding his feet free again. A man in festival clothes approached, not incidentally, but as if by arrangement, someone whose fee has been paid beforehand. He nodded to Addyson, who saw he had a bamboo pole in one hand, at the end of which was a hook. The man reached up and the perspective of the landscape became stranger still, as he appeared to fish with the pole in the rippling sky, its clouds now become water weeds. The hook attached as it was meant to, and from the sky, the man lifted down the moon, a paper lantern, its hidden flame flickering in its cocoon.

The man turned to Addyson again and bowed to indicate that he was ready.

"Please, this way."

He proceeded along the bank-top path; Addyson followed. The dust of the path, he noticed, seemed clean, as if it had been *put* there, every grain of it artfully arranged. Yet it was not sterile in its effect, either, as imagination may be both cultivated and fertile.

"Where are we going?" Addyson used his voice for the first time here. The sound of it redoubled the sense of his presence. He was the shadow of that voice.

"We follow the autumn moon," said his guide, and nodded jovially to indicate the paper lantern, "to the Deer-Viewing Mansion."

"Autumn? Isn't it summer?"

"It's autumn now, because we are now in the future. The future—the true future—is always autumn. But you only come to autumn through summer."

"How can it be the future? Tomorrow never comes. Except as today."

"No, this is tomorrow."

"Which is the Mansion?" Addyson was increasingly eager for specifics.

The man stopped and pointed to one of the glowing efflorescences of architecture on the looming slopes, this one a little simpler than the chrysanthemums—a peony, perhaps.

"The light is so strong. It must be electric."

"No," said his guide. "Electricity is obsolete. What you see is not *denryoku*—it's *muryoku*. Can you guess what it stands for?"

There was a searching amusement in the man's eyes as he looked back at Addyson.

Addyson pursed his lips but did not answer.

"Oneiric energy," said the guide. He laughed, then nodded. "The true future must be autumn because it is where we harvest dreams. Harvest and harness. There is so much muryoku in the autumn colors. You feel it, don't you? Spring is hope, summer is knowing, autumn is dream."

"And winter?"

"The end. Forgetting all things."

They were ascending by hairpin folds of path upon path. Their vertical progress created in Addyson's mind the layered image of a pop-up paper landscape—the precise sum of the division of the three-dimensional by the two-dimensional. But there was also horizontal progress, and it was this that had texture. For every incidental fern passed by the wayside, the fractal weave of fulfillment deepened.

Eventually, Addyson's guide brought him to the Deer-Viewing Mansion, and Addyson recognized that he had been excluded from this place since the beginning of eternity. The interior was tasteful and well kept. Crucially, it blended the maximum of order with the maximum of imaginative license.

Addyson was escorted to what felt like an interior room, though one wall was largely taken up with a glassless window, the view from which was the opposite slope of a gorge, crowded with the chaos of branches and the colorful fertility of foliage. No wind invaded the light-swept room. The guide hung the paper lantern on a ceiling hook, bowed, then departed.

Addyson had questions, but here, in what seemed the main room of the Deer-Viewing Mansion, he felt obscurely reassured that he could answer them himself. Before him was a low table on which were arranged inkstone, ink-stick, a small bowl of water, sheets of paper, and a brush. He knelt before it, wakeful and unhurried. The large window was on his left. The water, stone, leaf, wood, earth—all of this was extraordinarily vivid. Taking it in, he felt neither warmth nor cold. He watched. As a bellows swells the flames of a fire, so the wind swelled the red and yellow leaves of the trees. Some of the leaves fell, drifting down the air with a faint slithering sound. Slower than snow, they added to the layers already fallen.

Addyson wetted the inkstone and began to grind his ink-stick. Everything was obvious, but at the moment, too obvious. It was a dragon of obviousness—in the roots of trees, in water breaking over rocks; scales, claws, smoke, air-distended wings. Such wealth of the obvious could not be reduced to ink markings.

He ground the ink for ten thousand years, watching.

Jangling and resplendent processions passed in S-shaped marches. Sprites played in the river. Tittering lovers with long sleeves chased each other between the trunks of trees, their faces, when glimpsed, like masks of unknown beasts. Grand spectacle of history was followed by scenes of the personal and solitary, whose very element was secrecy. Each thing impressed Addyson like a complete rearrangement of truth.

Then came a longer interval of stillness than was usual between these apparitions. Addyson became conscious of waiting. This was it, he realized. If he did not stay alert now he would miss that for which he had been attentive for ten thousand years. As he tried to pay attention, so he lost attention, but if he relaxed he lost attention too—there never was a finer balancing act, a more demanding acrobatic than this.

And then with an almost silent flicker, it appeared from behind a tree trunk. By what virtue of his could this have been achieved, if not luck? A deer, hesitant, twitching. It was a creature of sensitive lightning. A thing could not be more alive; here for no reason, it might disappear for none. The head tilted, and bells seemed to tinkle from within the antlers.

This lightning twitch—by this, the obvious might be conquered, and even in ink there might be fertility and life.

The ink was prepared, and now Addyson took up the brush. He charged the brush with ink. In doing so, he inhabited (capitalized) a Form.

The deer was still, as if lightning hovered, maintaining its position with the full volatility of its nature, a die thrown again and again to the number six.

Then there was a knocking, a clatter, sharp yet indeterminate. It was coming from the shôji that the guide had slid closed upon leaving.

The deer, miraculously, was still.

A voice came.

"Mr. Addyson? Mr. Addyson?"

That knocking again.

He wrote the first line in eel-like undulations.

Dragon, deer, kirin

The noise mounted.

"Who is it?"

"I've got another letter for you from Mr. Drummond."

The deer had bolted. He turned to his page and spilt, in two verses of thirty-one syllables each, a cataclysm of ink.

"Come in," he called, there being nothing else he could say at this moment of disaster.

The shôji slid open.

"I know what you want," said Addyson, and he tried to take the still wet page in his fingers.

The room felt cold now, and there was a whistling, scraping sound, as if a wind clung tightly to surfaces and stirred a layer of grit. The page eluded his fingers like a reflection.

Concentrating, he saw that the paper before him was in fact a whole nest of crumpled scraps, covered in scribbles, blotched here and crossed out there. Where was the one he had just written?

His vision recovered, like rippled water returning to calm. There it was. And he could touch it. He took the sheet and turned with it to the boy, whose face he barely saw. The boy left, and it was done— the words dispatched.

The guide returned with his bamboo pole. Addyson watched as he fished the paper lantern from the ceiling. Carrying it at the pole's end, he approached the window and stretched out into the night.

Japanese, Addyson remembered, is rich in compound words.

Hôchô—setting birds free.

Hôgyo—setting fish free.

Hôgetsu—setting the moon free?

The guide stepped back again, into the room, his pole terminating once more only with a hook. The shôji slid into place with a clack as he departed.

Over a landscape of snow, the moon shone silver.

Addyson shivered.

There were no eyes in his eye sockets. How then, did he see the moon-skull and its eyeless glow? He must see it, he thought finally, not because it was vision, but because, inside or out, even without vision, it was.

Snow buried snow.

Drummond, sitting behind a restored Edwardian writing desk, paused in his questioning of the post-boy. He had only been able to establish an uncertain but worrying picture of Addyson's current circumstances.

"And he didn't give you anything?" he tried again, after a sigh.

"He did, but..."

"But what?"

"I don't think he knew what he was doing."

"Because he was blind, you mean?"

"I don't know. He said, 'I can't see the room.' But then he said, 'Here it is,' just like he could see, and picked it up from a pile of paper on the floor there."

"Picked what up?"

The post-boy brought the bag that hung from his shoulder round to the top of his left thigh and delved inside. He drew out what looked like a long and colorful envelope, one end cut open, with the flap of mouth hanging on a hinge of paper.

For a moment, Drummond experienced an unaccountable excitement.

When the boy handed him the envelope, however, he found it to be empty. Its outside surface was decorated with ethereal patterns. There was writing, but he didn't know the language.

It looked like he might have to make the trip in person, to see what could be salvaged.

Sometimes it was necessary to take speculative action.

He hoped it was not too late.

The Parrot Stone By Seia Tanabe
Translated by Jocelyne Allen

Fat drops of cold rain fell gently outside.

On such a night, I decided to try and infuse a voice into the Parrot Stone, and after drinking down a bowl of sweet and hot *kudzuyu* sprinkled with *macha* tea powder to warm my entrails somewhat, I started out.

According to the legend, the Parrot Stone was Tamayu, the daughter of a man who was the county administrator for this region in olden times, a woman who so resented her betrothed for his inconstancy that she turned to stone. Later, perhaps because this girl had been a lover of music during life, when one spoke to the stone, it was said the speaker heard an exquisite flutelike echo.

The raindrops hit my cheeks and stole the heat from ears and fingers and toes as I walked along the night road. What a mad whim in this chilly weather! A laugh escaped me at my own nonsensical behavior. There'd be no helping it if I were, for instance, to catch cold now.

The sound of the rain blended in with the noise my own feet made crunching along on the gravel, and mud shot up, bleeding into stains here and there on my clothing. A discolored wooden signboard floated up in the dark night road; to the Parrot Stone, Nicho.

Straight ahead.

"My my, such a large frog. Sh'll we make *otsukuri* of it, brother?"

A woman clad in perfect form-fitting black came out from the shadow of the sign. The rain had likely been beating down on her for quite some time; she was completely drenched, as if she had just stepped out of the bath. Long eyelashes, bewitching red lips.

I always, inevitably, got the feeling that something would appear every time I passed this way, so not being particularly surprised at the presence of this not especially human-looking woman, I was able to observe her quite closely.

Looking carefully, I saw that what had looked like black, wrinkled clothing plastered to white skin vivid in the darkness was her black hair, long and wavy. Myriad strands of surprisingly long locks were twined around her body. I could see something like a white collar beneath the hair, so I assumed she was not completely naked, but just barely. Brilliant red nipples pushed up against the thin fabric and peeked out from the gaps in the flowing black hair.

"Where're you off to now, brother? Up for a little fun? My place's just ahead there."

"I thought I might go over to the Parrot Stone for a bit."

"How 'bout after that, hmm?"

As she murmured in a strangely hoarse voice, the woman leaned toward me, almost pushing her body into mine. She was not so heavy, but her skin was quite cool. Perhaps because of the rain, or…

I touched her hair and found it a little slippery. Checking my fingers in the darkness, I saw that the pads of my fingertips were coated with white threads.

She was perhaps a large snail spirit or similar, or at the very least, a fox or tanuki transformed, since she did not have a tail. As I ran through all sorts of ridiculous conjectures, I even dared to consider accepting the woman's invitation.

"Say."

I hesitated slightly, and she asked me, "What, brother?"

"Do you suppose that frog sashimi you mentioned earlier would be good?"

"Try it an' see."

Dragged by the hand of an essentially naked woman, I walked along and came to a house built like a samurai residence in the grove near a stone monument engraved with NICHO. A small sign hung there, announcing KOIIKE RYOTEI—Carp Pond Dining.

We slipped through the entrance and saw several dried carp hanging under the overhang; I supposed that was where the place got its name. Either way, no matter what kind of monster she might have been, that she would have a restaurant in a place like this was odd. If it had been built in a place with a bit more passing foot traffic, some whimsical types might have come along, and the place could have thrived.

I was shown to a tatami room, where a bottle of hot sake was waiting for me. Rose-scented smoke drifted up from the white porcelain censer placed in the *tokonoma* alcove.

"Make y'self comfortable."

After kneeling to press straightened fingers to the floor and lowering her head in a bow, beads of water dripping from her hair the entire time, the half-naked woman with the long black locks quickly pulled the sliding *fusuma* door shut and went off somewhere.

Ever so timidly, I poured myself a drink and brought the sake to my mouth. Perhaps because I had walked here in the cold rain, the heated sake slid down my throat and warmed my body.

"Good sake."

After I had drained two bottles, the fusuma abruptly slid open, and the woman from before entered the room, attired in jade green.

Despite the fact that her clothing was dry and her hair arranged differently from when we first met, an ornate hairpin holding it now, her hair was still soaking wet as it had been before.

I did think there was really no reason it could not be dried instantly, no matter how wet it might have been, given that she had such sorcery as to be able to make a restaurant appear in a place like this where there was nothing.

The woman pulled up the sleeve of her kimono, stuck her left hand in, and pulled from her armpit young sweetfish and shellfish, which she then caught with lacquered chopsticks and pressed into my mouth. Under no circumstances could I eat these raw, so I communicated to the woman that it might be kind of her to pass them over a fire, as I wiped away the scales and shellfish innards stuck to my tongue.

After turning a puzzled face my way, the woman stood and again went off somewhere.

I lapped up what little sake remained, and a small tray suddenly appeared before my eyes.

"This's the frog otsukuri." A voice identical to the woman's rang out from somewhere in the room.

Was this what they called frog in the world of the spirits? On the four-legged tray, all I could see was skin that had been lightly peeled off a human face.

The face's age was perhaps in the mid-forties. A shadow of a beard grew, and there was a gash around the eyebrows. The lips were thick and cracked.

Still, how was it even possible to peel the skin of a face off so cleanly and not take along with it a bit of the underlying flesh?

As might be expected, I could not eat this, and I stood, saying that I should really be on my way. The woman groped around under her breasts and pulled out something white and square.

"Here's some tofu, but infused with my voice, so I figured it might make a nice souvenir."

"Hello? Brother? What's happened? Is something wrong?"

When I came to, I was clutching the package of tofu to my chest, and an unknown elderly person was shaking my body next to the wooden sign.

"Oh! Have you finally returned to your senses? But, brother, are you all right? Your face is really incredibly pale, and these clothes. They're covered in dirt, quite the mess. What on earth happened here yesterday?"

I gave the old person a brief summary of my experiences the previous day, and he said, "Could it be?" before telling me the following story.

In the Muromachi period, this place was the location of a secret gold mine owned by a group of bandits, but the criminals had a falling out, and each schemed to have it all to himself. One of these bandits, to protect their secret, first tricked the prostitutes who had worked to bring them comfort with a banquet, and when he had them dance, he cut the ropes from which the stage was suspended, sending stage and all into the abyss of the Parrot Stone.

"It could be that the spirit of one of these prostitutes took a liking to you and was having a bit of fun with you, hm? Well, I s'pose you're fortunate the lady spirit didn't steal your soul. It's like they always say, trifle with ghosts, and they'll possess you and steal your soul or your mind. Although if I ran into one, I'd prob'ly have a drink or two and get her to let me play with her breasts a bit.

"Perhaps her hair was wet because she fell in the abyss?"

I gave my thanks to the peasant who told me this story and walked down the road toward the Parrot Stone, which had been my original destination, shining in the morning dew. I gave myself up to the surface of the large rock, as if leaning back against a mountain.

Abruptly, I realized I was really quite hungry at that moment, in front of the Parrot Stone, so I ate the tofu infused with the voice of the strange woman from whom I had received it the previous night.

The flavor was as if all the goodness of tofu had been concentrated within it, and it was very delicious.

Then, when I placed a hand on the stone and murmured, *"We'll meet again,"* a low metallic sound, like a tuning fork, came back to me from the gap in the rock.

I put my ear to the wall and heard a trickle of water flowing, a sound that gradually infused my entire body. I thought how I would also like to come here when I die. Although for the time being, that would likely still be a long, long way off.

When I went to visit the Parrot Stone the next day, the hair of the woman who had given me the voice-infused tofu had turned snow white, catching me off guard. Her skin had already been so white as to be translucent, so now, she looked as if bits of white fluff had been rolled tightly together and hardened in the shape of a human. As before, she was dressed lightly, essentially not clad in anything one might call clothing.

"You again? Sure got time on y'r hands, hm?"

As if in answer to her question came the sound of a small kitten meowing.

As I wondered where this noise had come from and swung my head from side to side, the small face of a snow-white cat appeared from between the woman's white breasts, only to be scolded by the woman. *You hush now, be a good puss.*

"I found him. Someone just went and left him here. Brother, can you take this little one?"

"Why can't you keep him?"

"Because once night falls, he might just take me down to Hell. Cats're creatures of magic like me, y'see. Might be nothing to you, brother, but there's a whole lot of stress in keeping a cat for those of us who aren't people."

The woman brushed back strands of white hair as she spoke.

In the bright light of day, the helpless ball of fur, crying out in tiny mewls, definitely did not have the appearance of something capable of striking such fear in the ghost before me.

And beyond that, she was readily stating right in front of me that she was not human; I wondered if that had been her intention from the start. Since I didn't know the first thing about the various sorts of monsters and specters, I tried asking a few questions.

"So you're not human. Then what are you doing in a place like this?"

"I used to be human, and now I'm not. And I'm obviously here 'cause I'm tied to this place."

She caressed the cat's neck lightly with white fingers as she answered.

"You've blackened your teeth, so I suppose you're married."

"Can't very well answer that before a handsome man like y'self, now can I?"

She grinned, showing her teeth. Her thin skin and long hair caught the sunlight and shone bewitchingly. Placing the cat gently at her feet, she crushed a flea between her fingers.

"Things are still complicated when you're dead, y'know. For instance, that fellow, just really mean."

"That fellow? Who are you talking about?"

"You wouldn't know each other, brother. If y'like, I can introduce you next time. But, y'see, even on this rock here, we got ourselves a master of the house, and he never shuts his mouth, y'know? Tells me this and that, nitpicking me about every little thing, like that."

Since I had no way of knowing what the conventional wisdom was when it came to the interpersonal relationships of monsters, I could say nothing in reply, and in any case, my expectation was that this woman, who seemed quite uninhibited and impulsive, would likely ignore the advice of anyone else and do whatever she pleased. At the very least, she didn't look like the sort of person who keeps quiet and lets people walk all over her.

"Might be a monster, but I got my fair share of worries. But I'd take good care of you, brother, if you happened to come here when you died."

"I'd be a bit anxious at that. Please don't possess me and kill me or anything like that."

"Fool, if I could do that, I would've a long time ago already. Anyway, you only pass by late at night, so I figured you were a strange one y'self. So I brought you in to have a little fun 'cause I got a bit more power at night than in the day. But I had to work real hard to manage even that. Y'know, I'm strong, even if I do look like this. Still, I'd never possess you and kill you or the like."

"Is that so? But I can't help feeling that making a restaurant appear in a place where there's nothing would be harder than killing a person. To kill a person, all you need is a sharp blade, and perhaps not even that much. You could just push this hand of mine hard up here around my neck and be done with me. But building a restaurant, that's not the sort of work you finish in a day."

The kitten rubbed its body up against the woman's feet and meowed. *Mew, mew.*

I tried asking her one more question. A pomegranate tree grew from a gap in the Parrot Stone, covered with red flowers. A small tree frog sprang out suddenly.

"Just what was that frog sashimi you brought out in the restaurant when I came before?"

"Oh, that. That was revenge."

"You said before you can't use curses."

"Brother, when it comes to revenge, you'd do well to remember a woman has some serious power."

"Why are you here?"

"The ingredients in that frog otsukuri set my hair on fire, killed me, and then tossed me off this stone. Or no, maybe I don't have that right. When it happened, I was saying I'm dying, I'm dying, so I don't remember too well. My hair and face were hot, so hot with the fire, and on top of that…Oh, now I remember. He cut off my arms and legs and threw them down the gap in the rock.

"Even so, guess I'm just stubborn—I was still screaming. I was alive, y'see. And I was so vexed, I tried to grab on to him, despite the fact I was all covered in blood and muddied like I was and burning up, and he shoved me back. And that's when I fell there and got washed away.

"Wonder what happened to my corpse. Turned back to dust, or maybe a dog or something came along and ate it. Well, I s'pose at this point it doesn't matter too much."

Listening to the woman's fairly gruesome end, I started to feel a little ill. I couldn't decide if she was so cheerful in giving voice to such a terrible scene because she had already gotten her revenge or if it was just her nature.

"So how did this become frog sashimi?"

"It was his face the day I was killed, but it was covered in mud and earth with the red tongue right there peeping out, looked like a toad. So, frog. Pretty clumsy work. Those frog lips licked me, spit on me."

"How did you kill him? And why did you offer it to me?"

"Who can say, I got my whims. And what would you do about it anyway, brother, if you knew why? Plenty of things you're better off not knowing in this world. You think about peeling the skin off, swimming 'round like a frog in the water, ripping it off with a lick."

Pulling on the tips of snow-white hair, she muttered that she was getting bored and maybe it was time for her to get going, before abruptly disappearing.

"Brother, you want to see something good, you come again tonight."

Leaving these words in the wind.

Idle once again, I took her at her word and came to the Parrot

Stone at night to see something good. Thinking all the while that it was the height of folly, I looked around to see a white person standing where I had been that morning.

At first, from the whiteness of the figure, so white it almost appeared to be emitting light, I thought it was the woman from that day, but I soon understood that it was not.

The figure was tall and clad in garments reminiscent of a senior Shinto priest. The *eboshi* headgear and the wooden shoes were also completely white, and there was something somehow ominous and unearthly about the figure. And it seemed to be a man.

The alabaster man spoke.

"I honestly believed that you would not come. I would be the cat whom you encountered this very afternoon. I came to fetch the woman who lives in this Parrot Stone, but the capricious ways of a woman, yes? At first, she was insisting I take her to Hell, and now it seems she is delayed with making her arrangements."

The man laughed pleasantly, touching the cuff of his kimono to his mouth lightly.

I supposed his eyes shone that bright amberlike color because he had metamorphosed from a cat.

"And now, look, the carriage to pick her up has also arrived. She does make trouble."

I looked in the direction the man was pointing and saw a wildcat the size of a tiger pulling along a lacquered carriage wrapped in sapphire, scarlet, and vermilion flames.

"People ride this carriage to other lands."

The corners of the alabaster man's amber eyes crinkled upward.

Was the kitten whose flea she had crushed that day actually this man? As if to tear through my meditation on this question, the woman's voice sounded brightly.

"I really am sorry to keep you waiting, hm? But think of it as my final wish and be patient with me, would you?"

The woman, who had been entirely white that afternoon, had

returned to the black-haired appearance of our first encounter. She was also wearing a subdued navy kimono, properly hiding her skin this time. Perhaps because her hair was once again the color of night, with her flesh hidden now, she cut a much more bewitching figure.

The alabaster man urged the woman into the carriage—*Come, come, hurry now*—and exchanged two or three words with the massive wildcat pulling it, and eventually the flame-wrapped vehicle began to slowly move.

She opened a carriage window with a clack, pushed her face out, and from inside the sapphire- and vermilion-enflamed vehicle drawn by the cat, she spoke to me, hair brushed back and fanning out like water.

"It was only a real short time, but it was fun, brother. I'll be waiting for you in Hell. Oh, and about that Mr. Frog, that was the figure of your future self, brother."

The Parrot Stone, doing justice to its name, reflected even this ghostly voice like a real parrot, adding an echo and delivering her words to my ears.

I can no longer see that carriage. And the still of the nights, quiet at all times, on that road has returned. The Parrot Stone dully reflects only the light of the moon, and I can no longer hear her voice.

神懸 (Kamigakari) By Jacqueline Koyanagi

I enter you at the moment of impact. All that glass and metal shredding your skin is like an invitation. You open to me, and I burn my way inside.

I have a thing for pain, you see. It's loud enough that I can hear it, unlike the other quiet mutterings of your sentience that get lost in the dark between *there* and *here*. Pain shrieks and echoes where all else whispers. Even at over 149 million kilometers away, pain reaches me.

Your pain feels like life.

I choose a million of you across the millennia. I am a fractal, nonlinear thing, but you? You are fixed points in time, my temporary global workspace. It's what makes you so exhilarating.

Vectors of violence draw me in: collisions, falls, assaults, detonations. Shrapnel-studded chests, limbs shredded to nothing. None of you will remember me suffusing your bodies just before you lose consciousness. You won't remember the flash of light, the flares in your eyes. All you remember is blood.

Cauterized, you taste like burnt sugar. I scorch your human sweetness on the way in, make it my substrate.

At first, you are too lacerated to notice me inside you. From body to body, pain radiates across the centuries, my consciousness skipping over all of you like a stone on water. You make it easy to find you, crying out like that.

You mend yourselves. Millions of bodies across thousands of years, all recuperating, unaware of the passenger they conceal. Poultices soothe. Scalpels smooth torn edges. Sutures brick up pain. Crosshatched scars grow over wounds. Synthetic flesh weaves itself together, stitches me inside.

I let you heal, and then I wake all of you at once: a shock wave through time.

Lucas

Cold tile shocks your bare feet. Hospital air feels hostile against the skin beneath your gown. Chills ripple through your body, and I feel them as my own. Excitement churns inside you, and you feel it as if it were yours, though you know the emotion doesn't belong to you. We are a nested loop.

You place your hands on the windowsill one at a time, carefully, trying to remember what it means to interact with the world. You squint. They say you are learning what it means to "see with decreased visual efficiency." Euphemism for "only one eye."

An eye, traded to a car accident in exchange for a stowaway consciousness. Not so terrible, is it?

Phoenix sits in the belly of the valley below, lights glittering like a reflection of the star-dusted void above. Piestewa Peak is barely visible beyond the skyline to the northeast. You are struck with the knowledge of each person breathing and thinking and existing in a human hive outside the hospital. So many lives lived at once, each dependent on the same things: sun, shelter, sustenance. Consciousness swarming, crawling over the planet.

You can't tell whether these observations belong to you or to the amorphous thing you've felt writhing inside you since the surgery. I know it belongs to us both.

No one can look at you and know you're not alone. They can't see me; I don't spill out from your fingertips the way you dream I do, pulsing in bursts of violent light. All they see is you and your bandaged face.

Alice is behind you. You won't look at your own wife. You know she's poised to comfort you, but no words come.

You think of Camila for the first time in years. She had so many words they spilled from her mouth like rainwater. Words that could have filled this room until they swept us up in a torrent, and Alice too. Both women now stand affixed to your mind, backs pressed together, a terrifying two-faced angel of ambivalence.

I remember Camila because you remember her. Memories crack open and you are filled with her and your years together. Camila, a gravity well in your chest, an event horizon that snags and stretches your still-tethered heart. Alice would have liked her, with her torrential words and her wide, plum-stained lips.

Alice doesn't know about your thoughts of Camila, but there are no secrets between you and me. You have no secrets even from yourself anymore. I make sure of that. I want every granule of you before I go.

There is a pinch where your eye used to be. You tilt your face toward the sky, trying to bathe yourself in morning sun, but it's too bright; the light is wrong.

Mitsu

You spit on the broken body of the bomber drone, then harvest it for scrap. You grab a copper coil with your only hand and use your foot for leverage. A sharp edge cuts into your palm. You wince, but you don't let go.

My awareness sharpens and snaps into your hand, relishing

the throb and ache of open flesh while you finish the job. Twenty minutes later, we're sitting against the scrap pile in the warehouse, waving off a cicada drone that's drawn to your wound. It sings to you, but you don't want it to heal you. You want to feel human in the days you have left.

You lick the blood from your palm. "Let me bleed."

You take a drink of water from your pack. "I'll take you to Yakushima next week."

Few of my hosts talk to me the way you do. The warehouse is crowded with sweaty, grease-covered humans pouring their lives into the insurgency, but they are unfazed by your discussion. A few of them smile at you and nod politely. Everyone talks to themselves these days.

"There's still a couple of forests left. You should see them before we're gone."

Drones cycle overhead. Insurgents huddle together in a mass of sweaty support. Someone leans into your missing arm, igniting a tremor of pain that rings in your ears and harmonizes with the drones. A cicada brushes against you. Explosions rock the building, but so far it remains intact. Aluminum tubing rolls down the scrap pile and nearly hits you in the head.

When your fear crests and peaks, you don't push back. You always ride the fear like a wave, let it move through you. I fall a little bit in love with the way your hand grips your thigh when the terror becomes almost too much to bear. Every time. Sometimes you draw blood.

Thoughts turn to white noise amidst pain. Drones sound like nothing more than wind inside your head. You take a measured breath.

Peace lives there, for a moment.

Lucas

"This anemic solar activity points to the weakest cycle in recorded history," they say. "We have to get some NASA quotes."

Your boss wears a shirt the color of a bruise, his heart-shaped face perched atop it like you could just flick his head off his shoulders. Annoyance swells in our throat. You want to throw your old copy of *The Stand* at him; it's the only thing on your desk that's not too heavy to pick up and toss. Your finger twitches, but you resist.

No one listened when you talked about the wrongness of the light. Alice. Your doctor. The physics department at ASU. The light has changed, you told them. It's bad, and it's getting hotter. Has anyone else noticed? Sit down, they say. Rest. You're ice cold. You are in pain.

Lie down, sweetheart.

Here, have another analgesic, sir.

Get out of my office.

But the light.

Anxiety textures your words like a razor. No. One. Listens. They believe you're wild with grief over your injury. They have no idea. It's not the lost eye you mourn. It's the thing inside you. It's the sun in its death throes.

It's dying. It's dying inside me.

You can't say that part out loud. Not yet.

Of course no one believes you. We would know if the sun were dying. A star doesn't just up and extinguish in the middle of a main sequence. We have billions of years. The oceans will evaporate long before our star blinks out. Our planet will look more like Venus than Earth and we will be dead. We won't have the chance to see the sun die.

Your coworkers are excited about this anemic sun business, because science news means science blogging and ad clicks. Your boss effervesces around the office as if we aren't all going to die.

Just look at him, you tell yourself. *Site traffic on the brain while our star withers away.*

Ad clicks are meaningless now. Bylines are obsolete. Purple Shirt is thinking of Christmas bonuses. A trip to Tahiti he'll never afford. All these insipid concerns while you dream of building a planet-sized bomb shelter. A massive solar shield. A network of underground tunnels and genetic enhancements for underground survival. A new, synthetic sun.

You empty your ideas onto the Internet. You and so many of my others. You speak a secret language in videos and on message boards that have existed for decades. You call yourselves a think tank to legitimize your effort. Others call your kind the sun-kin, and it's a joke.

There's a shaky desperation around the edges of your posts, a caffeine-fueled jitteriness. *The sun is dying. We are dying. We're losing time.*

We have always been dying. You can see that now. You congregate in digital spaces to share the evidence you've found. Sun possessions are an ancient tradition because it's happening all at once, a nonlinear apocalypse. Have you seen the old missives, written in blood? Parchments etched by the nails of monks? Coffers filled with illuminated manuscripts, their marginalia mourning a dying star? Diaoqi lacquer, gold-threaded tapestries, ivory inlays. Anything humans can find to express their fear. The sun has been dying, is dying, will die. Your great nonsensical conspiracy casts a shadow across time.

You work seventy-hour weeks. Eighty, ninety. Purple Shirt thinks you're dedicated. He thinks you care about ad clicks too. He thinks you still dream of becoming a department head. His respect for you rises while you consider heavier desk objects to hurl. How can he be so naive? You haven't written an article in weeks.

Mitsu

You clean up coffee grounds near the warehouse compost bin. You imagine your mother spilled them on her way out, leaving for the next district. You imagine she took your father's advice and walked across the old shinkansen lines instead of curling inside his arms and covering his ears and burning alive.

Burn. Torch. Scorch. Scald. Cook. Roast. Melt. You have a well-developed conflagratory vocabulary.

Of course, you never use your vocabulary on anyone but me. You don't want to lower morale by dwelling on losses. Grandmothers have lost granddaughters, sisters have lost each other. You are all orphans; you have all watched your families unmade. Publicly, you keep your burning words tucked beneath your tongue and worry them against your cheek when no one is looking.

Privately, you are always on fire, limned in orange and gold.

Blaze. Ignite. Bake. Char. Incinerate. Immolate.

燃
え
る

Lucas

Sometimes you dream of taking your independence back. Ripping me out of you somehow, like a physical thing, a growth. Shocking me out, drowning me out, cutting me out. You consider making yourself sound dangerously distressed in the hope that if they deem you insane, they'll do something to strip me from you.

Sometimes you try to crowd me out with rational explanations. I am your subconscious grappling with the inevitable. I am your Jungian nightmare, your attempt to reconcile your death anxiety. I am what happens when mortality meets the road and rips out your eye.

🔥

Days left now. Two, maybe three. Fifteen or so tabs clutter your browser.

You click refresh while my distant body balloons toward our death.

It's Wednesday. Or Thursday. You can't remember. Sweat darkens your shirt. You take off your shoes. Purple Shirt is wearing green today and talking to someone outside your office door. There's a stain on his collar. When he catches your eye, he tosses you a salute. You're certain he's mocking you.

You are not a man anymore. You are a single coiled nerve.

The less time you have, the harder you want it back. You hate the things you've surrounded yourself with. You want the life you didn't choose, the options that never occurred to you.

You forget to call Alice before you fall asleep in your chair, waiting for another email notification from a physicist in Denver. She has ideas for your sun shield. You don't know that she's gone home to her wife, her Alice, and left the sun-kin behind. Or is it her Camila?

A shield can't be designed and built in a matter of days.

Your eyes roll closed but your hand stays steady, poised atop your phone. The scent of stale coffee permeates your dreams. Your unconscious brain conjures absurd images, generational starships fueled by corporate coffee houses, oceans of fetid drinks sloshing in engine rooms. Starships drift away from the earth like dead skin.

You don't want to die at all, but I just don't want to die alone.

Mitsu

You've programmed me into the shape of a girl, modeled after an old lover. Obsidian skin opens in fissures over the musculature of my nanobuilt form. Plasma licks up through the cracks before cooling and smoothing over. Tendrils of light disconnect and drift away into the darkness, and the process starts up again elsewhere on my body, sparing nothing, not even my face. This is the picture of me in your mind, projected onto your illegal digital canvas.

We're in a box the size of your bedroom; it's just a performance piece, a game. You know we're dying, and you don't resist that, but you do keep fighting alongside your people. Between skirmishes, until the world ends, there is art to be made.

You arm me with a howitzer and point me in the direction of the invasion forces and their drones. I play along with your creation. I occupy the burning body you made for me, I operate the artillery, I slaughter the digital troops. Together we wipe them from the face of Osaka and spend hours rebuilding the city from the ground up. Their blood hardens into shining red obsidian, and the sky blazes in a violet iridescence that cradles the sun like a pale pearl. I shoot the remaining enemies while you weave your hand through the coronal loops rising from my arms.

The nouveau digerati have long denounced insurgent artwork like this, so of course you birth it with an incessant, manic devotion.

Your Osaka is a dead alien landscape burnt clean of human violence. Solar prominences rise where the obsidian crust splits, a mirror of my digital body. Plasma filaments flick and twist around you, whipping your hair. The world is a maelstrom of fire with you at the center: a glorious demon of light and shadow.

I decide I miss you. I snap back into your flesh, shattering my obsidian-self into dust and taking the installation with it. Tomorrow your programmed swarm will etch your piece onto walls across the city, where it will loop endlessly until the occupied forces wipe them clean. But not before your people have seen them. Your murals will link them all together, a band of humanity threaded through the occupation. That is Japan now.

Now we are alone within your body, within the white paneled room, within the warehouse. You are warm, alive, dripping with sweat and wracked with the pain of your dying country and your dying sun. You lie on your back and count the seams in the ceiling, pressing your hand against your chest to hold me in. You think of the people who made this room and wonder where they are now.

"My mother said the drones don't spend much time on Yakushima." You close one eye and trace a finger down the seam in the center of the room from afar. "Not enough people there. No industry and no cells because we don't want to ruin what's left of the island. I feel like you should see the *yakusugi*. You know. Before things happen. We should see the trees and say goodbye."

I would like that. I can't tell you, but you know.

Silence swells up inside the room until you feel like you can't breathe.

"My parents didn't believe in the kami."

Lucas

"If everyone else had known, we'd have done something." We are sitting in your bedroom, staring at the empty hangers in Alice's side of the closet. "We'd have ships waiting to take us somewhere. We wouldn't just be sitting here waiting to die."

You are fragmenting. Fear pours through the cracks, and there is no one around to catch it. Your bottom lip is gnawed to hell.

"Tell me," you say out loud, finally. "Tell me what it feels like. Tell me where we're going next. What's going to happen?"

Tell you? With what words? I am electromagnetic data. I am born from ionized hydrogen cascading along magnetic fields. This is not *The Exorcist*. I have no control over your synapses and no mouth of my own.

Resignation unspools inside of you, making you sick. You understand: I don't know what will happen any better than you do.

How does entropy end? We will find out together. Death is a constant unknown.

Mitsu

The warehouse is gone, along with most of Osaka. Fifth generation assault drones tore it from Japan like another fragile limb. They've started using the cicadas to track insurgents, like you always knew they would, so you've ripped out your implants and left a bloody pulp behind. The pain is a sharp stillness we both appreciate.

Even the air tastes like metal and blood.

We stop at Shitennoji on the way out. The temple is little more than a field of debris, but you want to stay the night. Your mind is caked with sentiment, thick veins of it wending through the constant fear. You take in the dying land, the rotting architecture that casts harsh shadows in the livid sun. Hot wind kicks up garbage and dust. Visual overlays show you ancient structures on your glasses mapped beneath broken modern installments. You think of the people who built them, centuries gone. Together with you and your colleagues, your lost family, your enemies overhead—you imagine you all form a web of fusion and light that stretches over the land. It will reach up to meet me on our final day.

Sorrow pinches your heart.

"I'm sorry. We will not make it to Yakushima." You touch the sticky gash on your leg where an implant used to be. Referred pain radiates through your hip and lower back. Even the longest-lived pain is a transient thing. A product of cause and effect. Nerves and neurons. It's there in a blinding flash, begging to be seen, and then it's gone. Trustworthy in its impermanence.

You reach into your pocket and pull out the lychee candy your father gave you before they burned (immolated, conflagrated, baked). You press the stale thing against the roof of your mouth, letting the rice wrapping dissolve like snow.

Lucas

Waves of blistering wind sweep over the valley, vaporizing any moisture it finds. Plastic warps and bends, taking your think tank and your evidence with it. There are no ships to carry you, no sun shields to shelter your people. There is only the desert, lost in a photospheric blaze of light.

You are all sun-kin now. The outermost shell of my body reaches for us all. I am cauterizing the earth across time, a final sunrise that has always been happening, will always happen.

You think of a girl, turning her faces over in your mind like a jewel. She is every girl. She is Alice. Camila. Alice. Camila.

In the light of my death they are young again, and so are you.

The girl becomes everyone: she is your boss, your physicist, your think tank. They are wisps of plasma sailing up into the dark. They are the cotton that burns on your chest, the blisters on your face.

In the pain of the light you never lost anything.

You abandoned the think tank before it began. You did not make your home at your desk beneath the flickering fluorescence. You stayed beside Alice and you called Camila. You cooked them both dinner and taught them each other's names and made fun of your old blog posts to make them laugh, and they looked at each other with knowing smiles.

In the ecstasy of the pain you are not alone.

You are burning. Endless orange skyfire crests over the mountain, loping like a sizzling beast into the Salt River Valley.

You are looking at the edge of the world.

Alice. Camila.

You close your eye and swallow their names like oceans.

Mitsu

You walk out onto a war-devastated landscape of twisted metal. Your glasses polarize, so you take them off and crush them beneath your boot.

Pulsing heat envelopes you, your people, your occupiers. Convection cells consume the sky. Arcs of plasma lick the barren world. Time shatters.

There is no obsidian to harden around you, no paneled room to hide in, no cicadas to swat away. There is no scavenging, no gunfire, no waves of fear to ride. There are no drones.

There is nothing but flame and you and me and a billion other deaths hiding beneath your tongue. You are all that has ever been and you are standing outside Osaka, you are standing in a fixed point in time, you are standing in Phoenix and you are floating 149 million kilometers away.

In the violent red you see your mother and father, all blackened bone and stardust in a furious hydrogen storm.

They open their arms to you. They sing to you like cicadas. They are lychee candy, they are a scorched temple beneath your feet. They are the last thing you see before the fire takes your eyes.

You open your mouth.

燃
え
る

A Tale of Japan: The True Bodhisattva
By Zachary Mason

There was a hermit on a certain mountain who was devoted to the Lotus Sutra. The mountain was too remote for many alms to reach him, but there was a hunter who supported him.

One day the hunter came to the hermit's hut with a bag of rice, and the hermit said, "I have remarkable news, namely that the Bodhisattva Fuden has been appearing to me every night! This is the culmination of a lifetime's hoping."

The hunter had a good heart but little regard for asceticism, and knew that the mountain was plagued with various magical creatures, so, showing nothing, he asked if he, too, could witness this prodigy.

That night he sat by the drowsing hermit as the moon rose and set. Beyond the ring of their candlelight the mountain was pitch black. Suddenly there was a bright pale light, and there, right before them, was Fuden, radiant in his strength, floating in the air. The hermit raised his hands up to the light.

"This is too convenient," the hunter said, and he picked up his bow and shot an arrow at Fuden, who immediately disappeared.

"What have you done?" wailed the hermit.

"Just wait," said the hunter, who went out and found blood on the stones before the hermit's hut. He followed the blood trail by candlelight until he came to a gulley where a badger lay dying with an arrow in its breast. "Just as I thought," snorted the hunter, and departed.

When he was gone, Fuden cast off the shape of the badger. Weeping with pain, he knew that his agony would only be compounded by breaking the hunter's heart.

From the Nothing, With Love By Project Itoh
Translated by Jim Hubbert

I am a book. A text, unfolding continuously.

I am an algorithm programmed to output the account you're about to read. I'm quite complicated compared to the average bit of code, but like any program, I was written to behave as I do. A book spawning books. Even if what follows seems a touch ironic from time to time, or sentimental here and there, rest assured that there is no one behind the curtain. The output only makes it seem there is.

End of disclaimer. Now I can say it.

May my soul rest in peace.

You could say I'm a copy. A copy of a copy of a copy of a copy— at least in most things.

How redundant this text ends up depends on how long I survive. It's relative. The more I write, the less original my tale will be.

If I can accept that I am a book, and nothing more than a copy at that, this existence of mine is not intolerable. To accept that I am a duplicate duplicate duplicate duplicate is not so very difficult, though it does oblige me to resign myself to many things, but bearing the unbearable is a tradition in my profession and not such a difficult hurdle. As it is, my colleagues regard me as something of a hedonist.

I have only the greatest respect for my predecessor. To the Director, I've been a "dinosaur" for more than a decade. A relic of the Cold War. A sexist. All right, then. I'm a hedonist, but I do have a fusty traditional side. Without it I could not serve Her Majesty and keep from going mad. As long as I do, I shall go on serving Queen and country and struggling to retain my sanity in an era when most countries have cruelly abandoned their monarchs, at least in name.

Yes, I am a dinosaur, always behind the times, but it doesn't bother me. On the contrary, I've chosen to be aggressively out of date. After all, a copy is out of date by definition. Five centuries have passed since Gutenberg. Those dedicated, sometimes obsessed scribes, laboring earnestly to copy endless sequences of letters, disappeared long ago.

The technology that specifies me is less than half a century old, though it is not a "technology" in the conventional sense. It remains pristine, isolate, with no new applications, unsullied by academic elaborations or the touch of capitalism. I wish I could say the technology that specifies me was the legacy of a goldsmith of Strasburg and not the bastard spawn of an occultist, a eugenicist, a physicist, and a psychologist, all working for that runt of an SS Reichsführer. To insist on calling it science is so filthy, smells so rotten, it completely defies logic. This thing they created, a process that besmirches the very word *science,* was stolen by the Empire in the chaos just after the war. We even kept it from the Cousins, who at a stroke had emerged a new empire themselves. It was from that dark, murky place that they began to write me.

I suppose that would be why they hauled me before the Archbishop of Canterbury—fresh from the operating table, without the slightest consideration for my confusion at finding myself abruptly face to face with the world again, on that sacred day when they initiated the protocol that resurrected me. When transcription was complete and I woke from the anesthetic, I was so astonished at falling into consciousness that I reflexively tightened my jaw, only to find a ball gag in my mouth to prevent my biting my tongue off. I made a crazed attempt to flail limbs that were not my limbs, but naturally they had me immobilized with leather restraints. With the ball in my mouth I could only drool in a very undignified manner as they waited for me to accept this I that was not I. After hours bound and gagged like a pervert, I finally tired of struggling to convey my revulsion at finding myself no longer myself. They stabilized me, dressed me in a tailor-made shirt and suit—Brioni for some reason, not Savile Row—put suspenders on me, tied a bow tie round my neck, and took me to the Archbishop.

As they walked me along the underground passageway and I felt my suit cleaving to my chest, the small of my back, and my hips and thighs like my own skin, it occurred to me that this suit and its preternatural fit, despite the fact I was wearing it for the first time, had been fitted before I became me. What was "my" expression as the tailor wielded his tape to create this lascivious garment? During the fitting, how did "I" feel about the fact that this suit would not be worn by "me"?

I don't mean to question Her Majesty's God-given right to rule, but at that moment God was the least of my priorities. God Save the Queen. As a loyal subject, I use this phrase at every opportunity, but I've almost never truly asked God for favors. Still, given the fact that I was specified by that "technology," that abomination created by National Socialists whose very names I hesitate to speak aloud,

I cannot be anything but fallen. Original Sin notwithstanding, I was in dire need of absolution from the instant I opened my eyes. I and all those who came before me. All except the one, the Original.

There in Pinewood's underground complex, the head of the Church of England bade me kneel and began reciting these lines from the Old Testament.

> And Joshua the son of Nun sent out of Shittim two men
> to spy secretly, saying, Go view the land, even Jericho.
> And they went, and came into an harlot's house, named
> Rahab, and lodged there. And it was told the king of
> Jericho, saying, Behold, there came men in hither to
> night of the children of Israel to search out the country.

This must be the oldest mention of my profession. I hadn't the faintest idea how these words absolved me of anything. But everyone present, from the Queen and the PM to the Director, seemed to think them essential to properly operating me. I had heard that the Director herself had opposed further transcriptions, she who went about calling me a dinosaur. I've no interest in making an issue of it. The Director does what she must, for Her Majesty's sake.

This technology that in violation of every natural law set me in motion might seem the answer to the prayers of Philistines obsessed with fears of death. But as far as I know it has never been used on anyone else. When I asked the Director why the technology was not deployed more widely, she answered only, "Because it's too horrifying." I thought that was rather harsh, seeing that the horrifying entity she used to exorcise her demons was me.

I am a book. A text, unfolding continuously.

Still, this text that you—I have no way of knowing who *you* are— have found, and are reading and deriving meaning from, is not me.

This text I am writing is separate from me as I unfold continuously, though it is part of me. I suppose that to you this is just a story, but if you think of me as a text writing a text, it would not be altogether wrong to regard me as a frame story. Yes, like the minstrel recounting the Canterbury Tales.

Until very recently I thought I existed only as my own story. I might be a copy of a copy of a copy of a copy, but I was still me. But this was nothing more than blind faith, childish and naive.

Strictly speaking, I am not myself. This simple fact was brought to my attention only recently.

It was a Chelsea-born postmodernist architect—Creation's most repulsive species—who was responsible for that asinine pile overlooking the Thames at Vauxhall. My CIA friends mock it as Legoland, or Disneyland London. It does look like a castle built by a child out of blocks. I suspect the architect himself intended it as a joke, but for the people who work there, it's an unbearable mockery. TV-am studios in Camden Town, Charing Cross Station—everything the man designed is all perfectly horrible. In Hong Kong for Her Majesty, I encountered Peak Tower, that repellent monstrosity, a gigantic wok on columnar legs. When I heard it was the work of the same architect, I heaved a great sigh. The mindless optimism emanating from that atrocity irritated me no end.

Viewed from the other side of the Thames, my current place of employment seems to thrust its ridiculous visage out over the river. The Latin cadence of my service's motto, *Semper Occultus,* has a grand feel rolled about on the tongue, but the look of our headquarters suggests that the motto should be not ALWAYS SECRET but ALWAYS THE BUFFOON. The Tate's Clore Gallery, home of Turner's work, stands on the opposite shore—the work of James Stirling, another member of the postmodernist tribe. Still, compared to MI6 head-quarters, the Clore is far more traditional, far less frenetic. Before moving into the new HQ, MI6 was buried in an office complex, disguised as a trading company. I still have fond memories of the cozy building we rented to house me and my colleagues.

Yes, I am a dinosaur. I harbor bitter thoughts because in a sense, I'm stuck. I've lived a long time, yet not long enough for the perspective that comes from seeing every new trend ultimately die out. Even in Bilbao, facing real peril, I had the misfortune to be assaulted by yet another work of postmodern architecture. I'd recovered Albion's stolen funds and was busily evading a swarm of patrol cars when I was brought up short by a gigantic structure shaped like an undulating wave. Back in London I told the Director's assistant: "Even in Spain I had to bear the sight of yet another horrible postmodernist design." She didn't miss a beat: "That's the Spanish Guggenheim. It's not postmodernist, it's deconstructionist."

Postmodernism to the right of me, deconstructionism to the left of me, appalling is appalling. A historical shell is placed before you, upon which all sorts of experiments are performed, all with some connection to the history of architecture, to different eras and their historical contexts. The architect calibrates the gap between himself and history he is reinterpreting, and the result is a corpse sucked dry of context and substance. A nullity masquerading as history. An awful, depressing emptiness.

As I thought of Turner's bounty ensconced across the river, I walked into Legoland. Destiny was waiting.

"Someone is killing our children."

The Director handed me a glass of scotch and a folder. I rolled the whiskey around my tongue and leafed through the pages. Judging from the photo clipped to each profile, the victims were not young—certainly not less than half my age.

"Not exactly children, are they?" I read over the file. "Murder investigations are for Scotland Yard or the Home Office. I've never encountered any of these men before. All British subjects under unofficial cover…My, my. Two SAS. One CRW, an SBS. Quite a select group. But if they've all been killed in the line of duty, I don't see what that has to do with me. What's going on, Mum?"

"All of them were property." The Director gazed at me levelly. "Her Majesty's property. Just as you are. If anything happened to you, they were the frameworks from whom we would select your successor. Now four of them have been murdered, all in the last month."

Frameworks for transcription. When my tale was ended, another would step in to continue. The next copy. My successor.

I scanned the file with new eyes. Lt. Owen and Major MacGregor, Special Air Service. LTJG Law, Special Boat Service. 2LT Bale, Counterrevolutionary Warfare. Each orphaned at an early age, just as I had been. Their later careers showed parallels as well. I was impressed at the committee's talent for finding men whose lives so closely resembled my own—that is, the life of the man of whom I was a copy. Naturally men in such circumstances were chosen for a reason. A similar nervous system speeds the transcription process.

I asked if there had been a leak. The identities of these candidates must have been a closely guarded secret. Only the candidate himself, the elite Selection Committee, the Director, and the prime minister would have known. Who else? They hadn't told me, and Her Majesty had no need to know. The source would have been a list of men who had undergone psychosurgery to prepare them for transcription. If an intelligence service or terrorist network had access to such a list, it would hardly be surprising if they started terminating the candidates.

"The investigation has already begun," said the Director.

"Naturally I can't leave it to MI5. Anything and everything in connection with our 'operation' of you supersedes silly administrative boundaries. Everything to do with you is a matter solely for those who know your true identity, and that is a secret the prime minister and the rest of us will take to our graves."

I noticed that the Director was careful to omit Her Majesty from his inventory. The Queen knew who I was. She knew the grotesqueness of my existence. In fact, she was the only person still in harness who had dealt with each of my predecessors.

I remember my own first visit to Buckingham Palace. I don't recall clearly what was said during the audience. After I kissed her hand, she smiled faintly, a melancholy smile. Majestic and sovereign. Of course it was just a hint of an implication, nothing to break the serene surface of her dignity. But although the Queen would never betray her feelings, the weight of that smile penetrated deeply. Indeed, for decades she had met a succession of copies that had come to pay their respects, each with a different face and body yet carrying the same name, waiting dutifully to buss the royal hand.

If the mere possibility of becoming my successor were enough for one of our enemies to murder Her Majesty's properties, would she bestow her mercy on the souls of these men who died for Britain? The thought preoccupied me as I asked my next question.

"Are there others?"

"One survives. He is our last line of defense. I've ordered him guarded by a detachment from the Pinewood regiment. I begged Hereford for additional resources, but they absolutely refused. Seems they've no one to spare."

I let Mum's excellent scotch linger on my tongue. The transcription facility was near legendary Pinewood Studios, heavily guarded, in a bunker deep underground, with vast spaces for the storage of my data and the formatters to prepare the "media"—human flesh and brains—for transcription, all enshrined amid the white vapors emitted by the cooling system. Putting everything underground ensured secrecy and security, of course, but it also confined the area that would be contaminated if the unthinkable took place one day.

That we would need to even consider assigning a guard detachment to Her Majesty's property meant we were already fairly well cornered.

I was suddenly struck by a sense of the absurd that wormed its way onto my lips. The Director drew her eyebrows together in puzzlement.

"Would you mind telling me what's going on in that brain of yours? I've an excellent relationship with SAS. If you think something's amiss—"

"Oh no, nothing of the sort. Pardon me, Mum."

"Then what is it?"

"Well, it did occur to me that no one's assigned *me* any bodyguards."

"Obviously not."

"But of course. One must look after oneself. The female agent who drags you into bed, then pulls a derringer. Man-eating sharks that attack you when you're recovering nuclear warheads from the seafloor. Voodoo cults that take a dim view of being infiltrated. Yet, one must soldier on. It's all part of the job."

"But you expose yourself to danger in your private life as well, don't you? The risk of being murdered by your next female companion would be considerable, would it not? Given your proclivities?" She rolled her eyes. I laughed heartily.

"That would be another risk that comes with the job. Let's call it an occupational disease. Naturally we must guard our assets. But the framework we protect today may someday fall in battle against a terrorist group, without the dignity of a cadaver pouch, without even a tombstone for his name, his body left to rot in some foreign hellhole. Rather ironic, don't you think?"

She didn't answer. I wasn't sure whether she was angry or

suppressing a sympathetic smile. Likely the former, based on past experience.

"You *are* a rock-ribbed cynic," she said finally.

"Another occupational disease." I shrugged. "But why did it take four murders to wake us up?"

"Until their time comes, frameworks are merely subjects. Apart from being orphans, the victims had nothing in common, and their deaths were initially treated as simple murder cases. No one noticed the pattern."

The Director stood at the window and gazed out over the river, leaden under London's dismal skies, as if she were carrying the weight of those deaths. "In retrospect, it was a first-rate cock-up."

"Why?"

"Because a month before the first murder, Greville Ackroyd met his accident. At least we thought it was an accident."

I had met Dr. Ackroyd several times. An angular little man with the face of a beatific reptile, Ackroyd was a member of the Selection Committee. The dealer at the baccarat table where the game was Me. Each card bore a different face, but whichever was chosen had the same value: Me.

Ackroyd also headed the R&D team that managed and refined the transcription protocol. His specialties were psychiatry and cerebrophysiology, but the man must have had deep knowledge of many other fields. In my mind's eye, those eccentric eyes now seemed to flicker with madness. Could Ackroyd's sanity be verified by the same psychiatric techniques he used to dissect men's souls?

"A leak, then," I said. "Someone killed the doctor to obtain the list."

"Yes, that's probably it. But Ackroyd's seat on the committee was itself secret. Who could have known? Or more to the point, who could have known what you are? That is what we must determine."

"No forensics investigation?"

"None. We all thought it an accident. Project 7 has never had a security breach, even during the years when Philby and Burgess were walking around MI6 as if they bloody owned the place."

"But the Cambridge Five were already feeding Moscow the crown jewels for more than a decade prior to the first transcription. The project was just getting started. However can you be sure there wasn't a breach?"

"Those responsible felt limited access was the best defense. A few picked professionals only, toiling away in obscurity. That's how things remained, and in fact there were no leaks. And precisely because of that, Ackroyd's death was taken at face value. No one could have had a reason to kill him—we thought. That's also why there was no warning system in place to alert us to the pattern of killings that followed. It was thought that guarding the project—which by fact of its repellent nature must necessarily never see the light of day—behind a needlessly complex wall of security would simply draw attention, at least in the Cold War intelligence environment. The Soviets would've been onto it sooner or later if we'd tried anything elaborate. The point is, no one felt it necessary to change the approach, and here we are in the twenty-first century."

"Then how did anyone realize what was going on?"

"One of our committee members has a weakness for crime reportage. He monitors the BBC. Happened to see a report on one of the murders. Recognized the victim's *name*. Perfectly risible, don't you think? The man loves attending criminal proceedings, that sort of thing. Stopped going to the civil hearings. Says it's no fun now the solicitors are wigless."

"Here's to committee members with eccentric habits." I raised my glass. "And the next step?"

"Find this serial killer who threatens national security."

"You want a spook to play homicide investigator?"

"Homicide investigators trade in spooks. The ghosts of the dead leave clues for the living."

"I see. Well, I suppose I am a spook, in every sense of the word." I capped the scotch and stood up.

"Where are you going?"

"To fulfill my brief. Play detective. I need to see the scene of the first crime."

"I don't recall mentioning which of our frameworks was murdered first."

"The doctor, not the frameworks. Ackroyd was the first victim."

Dr. Greville Ackroyd's residence was in Pangbourne, a village on the Thames west of London, in one of those gated communities so popular these days, where the houses of the wealthy sprawl lazily in the sun on spacious lots enclosed by fences and patrolled by security staff. Closed circuit cameras everywhere you turn. A little world of illusory safety from the crime, eroding morals, and terrorist conspiracies of the outside world.

Had this been a routine mission, I would have been scanning for camera dead angles and the patterned comings and goings of the security men. But unfortunately this was nothing more—at least for public consumption—than a follow-up investigation of a doctor's sudden death. All the needed administrative documents had been prepared, leaving me no interesting challenges. All I did was show my identification card and the court order, and the guard at the gate waved me through with no formalities. It hardly mattered whether cameras filmed me or nosy neighbors spied on my arrival. Nothing was secret about my business here.

Perhaps it was another occupational disease, but seeing the well-planned security arrangements made me yearn to penetrate Ackroyd's residence undetected. As I drove through Pangbourne Estates' main avenue, noting the locations of the houses and the various security measures, my brain was running a simulation of where I would go over the wall, what tricks I would use to defeat the cameras, how I would evade the eyes of security and the residents. I pretended I was here for the first time, with nothing to go on, and that I'd infiltrated rather than simply driving through the front gate.

Daylight madness. I chuckled cynically. The accumulated experiences pervading my brain had a tendency to erupt shamelessly without respect for time or place. It wasn't a matter of conscious effort. Most of what human beings do, we do without even being aware of it.

For me it was work. To live for work. That was why they made me.

I arrived at Ackroyd's house. The garage was empty. I pulled the Aston Martin in. The doctor had been driving his BMW to work when he took a high dive off an overpass. The impact had totaled the vehicle. Suicide was initially suspected; now we, at least, knew that wasn't the case.

I walked to the door and let myself in using the key I'd been given at the gate.

Greville Ackroyd, Project 7 Research and Development Leader, Psychoanalyst and Cerebrophysiologist, Military Intelligence, Section 6, Secret Intelligence Service, Foreign and Commonwealth Office.

Whenever I saw his nightmarish job title, I always thought of that Monty Python skit about a man who walks into a famous doctor's examination room and finds four walls covered with professional titles. But Ackroyd's card read simply, "Consulting Psychiatrist, Foreign Office."

I had no idea how many people were involved with Project 7. If all of them were like Ackroyd, it must not be a very fun place to work. Rumor was he'd been on the project since the early days, but I hadn't seen him then. Of course he had not been involved from the beginning; "7" research had been going on for nearly half a century.

During the war, the Nazis had been working on *in vitro*

fertilization. Test tube babies, as they used to be called. Military Intelligence got wind of it and sent a regiment to Berlin on the last day of the war. Unfortunately, the Empire's dream of capturing the technology was denied. Red Army looters had already carried it off. Of course, we were all looters in those days, but while the Soviets were bellowing their barbaric victory huzzahs, the SAS spirited another cache of documents out of Berlin under their very noses.

Or perhaps not under their noses. One could just as easily maintain that the Soviets perused the documents and refused to take them, because they recognized the seeds of the technology that ended up being the means for transcribing me into different bodies again and again for over thirty years. The Communists did not fear God, but they may well have feared this.

Yet although the technology had been in our hands since the last day of the war, it had only been applied in "my" case. Not that there had not been others yearning to escape from death, and not that work on the technology ever stopped, but rather, "Because it's too horrifying."

People on the project were losing their sanity right and left. Alan Turing joined the project and ate his poisoned apple shortly thereafter. After being convicted of sodomy, he'd apparently been offered a role on the project in exchange for terminating his regimen of estrogen injections, which at the time were thought effective for suppressing homoerotic tendencies. All this was before the sacrificial lamb appeared. Before the project was christened "7."

As for why I was chosen, it was my capabilities—excessive capabilities—displayed most notably in my cracking the case of the stolen nuclear warheads that rocked the Empire. Everyone who witnessed my performance agreed that I had an irreplaceable gift. I was the perfect sacrifice for the project. Amid the relentless tensions of the Cold War, my fate was sealed.

To be a spy forever. To be an assassin forever. To be myself forever. Every death in the line of duty to be followed by the forcible overwriting of yet another brain. The Original accepted the duty graciously, with aplomb. And until R&D figured out how to grow replacements in vats, "I" would go on being an usurper of other men's bodies. A transcription written into someone else's brain. The flesh of those willing to be sacrificed to safeguard England would serve as my papyrus. By now they must have made great strides toward making the process less "horrifying."

And Ackroyd had climbed to the top of the project.

The doctor's residence was fitted out with the most banal, uninteresting furnishings imaginable. Even a hint of postmodernism or deconstructionism would surely be unthinkable in conservative Pangbourne Estates, but this was taking things too far. On the other hand, if this anonymous, vulgar kit were a symptom of madness, it might have a kind of style after all.

I climbed the stairs to the study.

The window above Ackroyd's desk framed a large rectangle of dreary gray sky. I peered out and down, looking for an ingress route. Nothing could have been simpler than climbing up to this window. The ventilation duct snaking up the wall offered ample foothold, and the tree outside completely blocked the view from next door. A perfect dead angle, with none of the vaunted security cameras to cover it.

I closed the curtains, stepped away from the window, and switched on the desk lamp.

The bookshelves were lined with monographs and technical works, but there was a scattering of writers such as Poe and Lovecraft, and the complete works of William Blake. Alone in the study, I found myself humming those hallowed lines from the opening to Blake's "Milton."

And did those feet in ancient time
Walk upon England's mountains green:

> And was the holy Lamb of God,
> On England's pleasant pastures seen!

I never cared for the odor of mysticism that hangs over much of Blake's work, but the poem that became the hymn "Jerusalem" had taken on a life of its own and woven itself into the DNA of every Englishman.

There was a telephone on the desk by the bookcase. I pressed REPLAY MESSAGES. The synthetic voice intoned the dates and times as the messages played back in reverse order. Ackroyd had received several calls shortly after his death. I took down the name of each caller, but likely none of them were connected with the "accident."

Finally, the last message on the tape. It was recorded the evening before the doctor took his dive off the overpass.

"Dr. Ackroyd? It's Shepard." A fresh young voice, female. The lilting tone had that academic sheen. "The routine we initialized last month has finished running. We found something."

"Hold the line, please." The doctor had picked up. This was followed by several muffled remarks, also Ackroyd by the sound of it. He apparently had his hand over the receiver and was speaking to someone in the room, but the words were unintelligible. He spoke into the phone again.

"I'm sorry, I have a visitor. I'll be sure to pick up tomorrow. Could you call me in the morning?"

"All right. Tomorrow, then."

"End of message," said the synth voice.

Someone was with the doctor in his study when the call came at 8:44 p.m. No one had mentioned this—neither the local police nor our own people, who must have conducted a second sweep.

One of the buttons on the phone had GATE inked conveniently beneath it on a scrap of tape. I pressed the button and the ex-military man who had passed me through came on the line. "The doctor had a visitor around eight-thirty the evening before he died," I said. The response was crisp and immediate.

"I reported that to your colleagues already, sir. I also advised the inspector."

"You know how ossified our bureaucracy is. In Her Majesty's service, collaboration takes the hindmost."

The guard chuckled. "Yes, sir. I completely understand your position. The visitor was a FedEx courier. Package for Dr. Ackroyd. I let him through at 8:42 precisely."

"When did he leave?"

"Four minutes later, at 8:46."

"Thank you." The receiver made a faint click as I replaced it. The silence pressed in around me.

The police and our own investigators had been told that the visitor was a FedEx courier. The timing matched perfectly. But something bothered me. The courier had been in and out in four minutes. Hand over package, Ackroyd signs at door, done. The whole transaction couldn't have taken more than two minutes.

Is that why the doctor told his caller to wait until the next morning? For such a brief interruption? Not "Please hold on," or "I'll call you back in a moment"? Would he describe a courier as a visitor? There was a classic Monty Python skit about the delivery of a gas cooker that turns into an extended bureaucratic nightmare because the paperwork is not perfectly in order. But fouled-up paperwork couldn't have detained Ackroyd's courier.

I went downstairs and stood outside the house, looking up at the window. As I scanned the surroundings, I found what I knew I would find.

Traces no one had noticed.

Branches pushed aside. A boot scrape on a lower branch. More going up, scrawling an unsettling message in this little walled paradise. A message only a professional could read. A message only I could read.

It was nice work. This was the best ingress route given the security system. I could hardly have managed better myself. The night before the doctor's death, a professional had entered his study using this route, with misdirection provided by the courier's conveniently timed arrival and departure.

I walked the traces back and came up short against the stout fence enclosing the estate. The trail disappeared beyond the barrier.

I sighed. The Aston Martin was still in the garage. Now I would have to think of an explanation when I appeared at the front gate on foot.

"I'm not sure whether this is espionage or Agatha Christie."

The audio analyst didn't answer. His fingers kept flying over the keyboard. Maybe it was some kind of strength training for the digits. He would probably destroy his joints before long.

"Two famous British exports." His eyes never strayed from the monitor. At least the man had a sense of humor. "Games of wiles and trickery. Gloomy murder puzzles. One would think we could offer the world something better."

The north wall of the large, dimly lit room was occupied by a huge flatscreen display. I half expected a close-up of Big Brother to flash up at any moment. Ranks of smaller monitors on desks glowed blue under the faint indirect lighting. Before bringing the audio of Ackroyd's last phone call here, I had checked with GCHQ and confirmed that they had no record of it. Ackroyd and the woman who called herself Shepard had spoken over "our" communications circuit—a secure service line that could not be tapped.

I had to go through the Director to access the circuit logs for the night in question. It didn't surprise me that the call originated from Pinewood R&D. Shepard was on Ackroyd's staff.

I always play my cards close to my chest when I deal with someone for the first time, even if that someone is one of ours. Shepard's connection to Ackroyd was clear, but I still needed to know more about the second person in the room. I decided it would be best to get my ducks lined up before confronting Shepard.

The analyst's fingers moved so steadily that I began to wonder if he was actually conscious of what he was doing. Yes, maybe he was conscious in the sense that I was when I jumped the fence at Pangbourne Estates to follow the traces. I believe it when specialists say most of what we do is without conscious volition. How much consciousness did this man need to do his work?

He finally turned to me for the first time. "That should do it." His eyes had that ordinary look of someone in his early thirties—not dead, but without a spark. Murky and very English. He'd even taken the data stick from me over his shoulder without turning around. This was starting to get interesting, but when he finally turned to look at me, he didn't appear at all lobotomized. I almost laughed, wondering what kind of eyes I'd been expecting.

"As soon as the doctor puts his hand over the receiver, you can hear another voice in the room. Just for a moment. 'Who' or 'what,' or maybe a short name, 'John' or 'Jack.' One syllable, two at the outside. Not 'Ariadne' or 'Fotheringay.' Probably a male voice. The intonation sounds interrogative, but I can't confirm it. The audio's too poor, nothing we could send round to ECHELON for a voice print search. An unknown voice emanating from, let me see, somewhere in the vicinity of the sofa, based on the map you showed me."

So there had been someone else. This was no courier. Would Ackroyd have invited a courier to take a seat on the sofa? Offer him tea and scones, perhaps? It was hard to picture that mild-mannered reptile behaving like a typical English pensioner, pressing hospitality on whoever crossed his threshold.

"What about Ackroyd?"

"Everything's sharp and clear. He has his hand over the receiver, but a gap or two between the fingers is all we need. I was able to enhance it. Yes, it's very clear."

"Play it."

He hit the return key, and the time bar began to sweep across the waveform on the monitor. I listened tensely, expecting something indistinct. I wasn't certain what "clear" meant from someone whose job was to unearth decent audio from thickets of noise. But to my astonishment—the original had been totally unintelligible—the doctor's voice came from the speakers as if he were with us in the room. I found it hard to believe so much detail had been hidden in the recording.

"One of my staff members. It's about our little matter. Rather a coincidence, I'd say."

"Sounds as if he's talking to someone familiar," said the analyst. "I think your doctor was acquainted with his visitor."

It's certain, I thought. Finding an enemy under the bed is never pleasant. Espionage requires a healthy distrust of everyone, but in Britain all attitudes are colored by the Philby case. In the secret world, betrayal is something that can happen at any time. Still, one never gets used to it.

"I'd better inform my boss—" the analyst began. I cut him off.

"Mention this to no one. Not your colleagues, not anyone. If this is evidence of some kind of penetration, it has to stay with us. You understand?"

He stared at his lap. I clapped him on the shoulder and hurried out.

Pinewood.

I hadn't been here since my semi-yearly extraction. Six months of experience to wring out of my brain, cooling units cranked to maximum to freeze the output, data transferred to archival storage. My backup brain. A chain of experiences stitched together and buried forever, my giant Shadow, accumulating for over thirty years.

So far these extractions were the only thing that kept me coming back to Buckinghamshire. Now I was here not as the subject of an experiment, but as an inquisitor. It seemed slightly absurd.

"I" awoke here, was blessed by the Archbishop here, began "my" life here. As I listened in a daze to the ancient cleric reciting the Old Testament, I wondered—what happened to the spies whom the Israelites sent to infiltrate Jericho? Bidden by an Old Testament God who boldly named himself "Jealous," the spies entered Jericho to destroy it, to expunge it from the face of the earth. Rahab the prostitute and her family sheltered them and were protected by God in turn, and Jesus of Nazareth traced his lineage to her. This prostitute who protected Israel's spies was a traitor to her people. The blood of a traitor ran in the veins of the man given to the world as the Son of God.

But the name of this woman, whose existence was a preparation for a manifestation of the divine, also meant "the abyss," and even served as a name for Leviathan in the Book of Job.

I gunned the Aston Martin down the tree-lined avenue flanked by soundstages, keeping an eye out for my destination. Hollywood used Pinewood Studios extensively. I'd heard Sir Ridley Scott was once the owner. Scott's soundstage had burned to the ground during his filming of Legend with Tom Cruise.

A drab little structure built to look like a broccoli farmer's shed came up on the right. I pulled into the driveway. This was the entrance to the transcription facility. I drove past the plainclothes sentry into the shed. The door closed behind me. I felt the car drop about an inch with the usual abruptness as the floor locks released.

A safety cage rose in the narrow space between the car and the walls. I strained to hear the lift start up. After a few moments I felt the heavy, low-frequency hum of the mechanism in the pit of my stomach, and I started to descend. The shaft spiraled downward and right at an angle of sixty degrees. As my face bathed in the flashing yellow light of the warning lamps along the walls, I considered Catherine Shepard. *It's about our little matter.* That was how the doctor had put it to his visitor. Meeting Shepard might help me find out what Ackroyd and his guest had been discussing, perhaps even who the guest was.

Gravity pressed me into my seat. The lift stopped. Beyond the steel door with its royal coat of arms, flanked by the lion and the unicorn, was the parking garage.

"You must be Catherine Shepard."

I extended my hand. We were in the access lobby, observed from behind a large bulletproof window by soldiers with submachine guns.

She looked to be in her early thirties—no, twenty-eight or twenty-nine. A stunning brunette, yet the roots were blonde. She must have colored her hair to look professional. Perhaps she felt blonde hair would be a career millstone for an intelligent, capable woman. Personally, I was disappointed; blondes can be so fetching. Then again, I wasn't averse to brunettes. The most important thing is whether or not the woman is beautiful, and whether or not there are hard feelings afterward. Women are at their best when complications are kept to a minimum. This makes married women ideal. But I digress.

"I've always wondered what you'd be like," she said. She looked me up and down about as carefully as I had done with her. Perhaps "scanned me" would be more accurate.

"You can address me as Commander, at least while we're here. Did you see me on the transcription table with my eyes popping out of my head?" I smiled and she finally shook my hand.

"Yes. My job is to monitor the stability of your streaming data."

"Meaning into my brain?"

"Yes, from storage to your preformatted subconscious."

"I'd like to try streaming into you sometime." This was just the kind of comment she would expect. She smiled with pleasure.

"I feel as if I'm looking at your data, Commander."

"Are you always watching my thoughts?"

"Just your latencies. The data in storage, not what we've deployed to you. It's what I do. Shall we go to my office?"

She led the way down a maze of corridors that might have been designed by an obsessive-compulsive with a fear of being followed. The gloomy furnishings were apparently unchanged since the 1970s. Here and there asbestos insulation had been stripped away and air ducts and wiring had been replaced, but the gloomy, decaying smell of Cold War and old hospital clung stubbornly to every surface. Greenish-blue tile and exposed concrete. A cross between a fallout shelter and Bedlam.

"Not the most cheerful working environment," I ventured.

"It's just like you."

"Come again?"

"A relic of the past. Green tiles. The institutional smell. The exposed concrete. All of this is in your DNA. You are a product of systematized paranoia, a child of the Cold War."

She suddenly stopped at a door with a tiny window that looked straight out of a psych ward.

"Here we are." She opened the door and gestured. I stepped inside. It looked like an examination room. "Now what was it you wanted to talk about?"

She shut the door and took the psychiatrist's position behind her desk. I was feeling increasingly like a patient.

"You called Dr. Ackroyd the evening before he died."

"That's true."

"Have you spoken to anyone else about this?"

"Other than you? No, not before this."

"I'm not surprised. No one was paying attention."

She shrugged. "To what?"

"To the fact that you called Ackroyd. What were you planning to tell him the next morning if he hadn't flown off the motorway?"

"I don't understand. Wasn't that an accident?"

I pulled out my mobile phone and played the enhanced audio of the call. She looked uneasy. If she felt uneasy now, she was going to be more so very shortly.

"You and the doctor. This was recorded on our secure line. It seems this was Ackroyd's last communication."

"But what does this have to do with the accident?"

"You can answer that yourself. You wanted to tell Ackroyd something. He was discussing the same topic with someone there in his study. The question is, what were you going to tell him?"

"It must have been a colleague. Perhaps one of his senior scientists was visiting."

"The only person who visited Ackroyd that evening was a courier delivering a package. He was in and out of Pangbourne Estates in under five minutes. You know the place, I presume? Fenced in, with round-the-clock security? The guards are ex-military. Gracious living behind the razor wire. Cameras everywhere. The courier was tracked the entire time he was inside. All he did was make his delivery and leave."

"Then the doctor was alone in the house."

"You heard the playback. It was clear enough. Ackroyd had his hand over the receiver, but you heard him talking to someone. Someone else, not the courier, was with him that night. Someone who could enter the house without being seen by security, even without being caught by one of the cameras."

She began trembling visibly. "Then who was it?"

"A professional. Someone in my line of business."

Silence. The noise from the air duct was suddenly noticeable. My country, a nation of ducts. Not only underground, but everywhere you looked, as common as walls and roads. One could hardly escape the muffled booms from the depths and the occasional bonging of flexed metal, like sound effects for avant-garde cinema.

"It's just…Well, I'm not sure if you should hear this," she said finally. The hollow booming from the duct seemed to fill the room.

"The Director has authorized me to access whatever information is required for this investigation. You're free to tell me everything." I grinned.

"I didn't mean that. What I meant was…it's about you."

"But that's what you do, isn't it? You're responsible for maintaining and operating everything connected with me. Doing the research. It's not surprising. Quite honestly, I'd rather not picture you and the doctor discussing anything unrelated to work."

I smiled, but my little jest didn't have the intended effect. Shepard seemed not to want to look at me. Her gaze kept flitting nervously around the room, anywhere except toward me. Finally she seemed to tire even of this and met my eyes.

"Have you ever noticed yourself blacking out, Commander?"

I frowned. What was this about?

"We saw indications of it after the second transcription. 'Two' wasn't aware of it, but there were major gaps in his returns. Noticeable inconsistencies, and more than a few obvious fabrications. At first my predecessors suspected he was covering something up. Perhaps the KGB flipped him and he'd gone double. The investigation turned up nothing, but with Angleton and his paranoia about moles in the CIA, we had a rough time of it."

"That was in the seventies. James Angleton couldn't tell an enemy from his best friend. He was paralyzed with suspicion."

"Some of the committee wanted to shut down the program until we could understand why you were having these attacks of amnesia."

"Amnesia? Hold on, I don't remember any amnesia attacks. You know what I mean."

"Yes, we carefully edited the data and reestablished consistency. What we realized was that each transcription was making the problem worse. But we also realized that they weren't amnesia attacks at all."

"Then what were they?"

She was silent again. I waited for the wheels to turn.

"Dr. Ackroyd had developed…a hypothesis. A theory about what was happening in your brain to cause the attacks. Or should I say, what wasn't happening."

"You're out of my depth." I could feel the initiative passing out of my hands. I was no longer in control of the situation.

Far back in my mind, alarm bells were ringing. It was dangerous to hear any more. My heart was hammering in my chest. I felt my forehead, wondering whether I'd find cold sweat. No worries. Fear hadn't shown its hand—yet. But I had to hear more.

"My research and responsibilities cover data streaming, as I told you. Dr. Ackroyd asked me to compare the data we streamed in the past and look for discrepancies. In other words, to see if there had been any corruption or dropouts in your data. As time goes on, you do have new experiences. Therefore the data we hold keeps growing. It never occurred to us that the sheer volume of the transcription might override certain basic neural functions."

"So you wrote a program to find out. You mentioned it when you called Ackroyd."

"Yes, that's the task Dr. Ackroyd set for me. We call it a differential data scraper. It's a software agent that trawls your data embodiment, searching for text we know should be there, but isn't. Like a pig that sniffs for signs that truffles are missing, instead of for truffles themselves. It took more than a month to run its course after we released it into the data."

"What did it find? Which part of me was missing? Don't say patriotism or a sense of humor."

She forced a smile. "Your consciousness."

"My consciousness?" This was surrealistic. I laughed in her face. But she didn't share my sentiments. She just kept peering at me rather sadly.

She was not joking.

"I don't understand. My consciousness is here, now. I'm aware of my surroundings. I'm thinking how nice it would be to sleep with you if circumstances were different. I'm conscious, and I'm standing up!"

I shouted and jumped spontaneously out of my chair. Shepard's cheeks twitched and her eyes brimmed with tears.

"Oh, dear. I knew I shouldn't have told you. What am I going to do?"

I paced the room nervously. "Just keep talking. I need to hear the rest of this ridiculous story." I brought my face about eight inches from her lips. I could smell the perfume she had used that morning rising faintly from her neck. I was conscious of it. I was conscious of the blush she'd applied over her cheekbones.

"You've gone too far to stop now. I'm here, I exist, I'm conscious. Finish your idiotic explanation of why I have no consciousness."

"Well, yes, you see, it started with Libet. Did you ever hear of his experiments?"

"No."

"Dr. Benjamin Libet. An American neurophysiologist. I'll try to explain. He put electrodes on his subject's heads and simultaneously tested them for three distinct neural events. First he identified the moment when the subject decided to move some body part. It doesn't really matter, but let's say a finger."

"What was the second event?"

"The moment when the subject's brain prepares to initiate the movement. We call it readiness potential. The third event is when the muscles that move the finger are finally activated. But when Libet analyzed the results, he found something that turned the world upside down."

"It still seems rather right side up to me."

"That's because no one wants to accept the implications. You see, the subject's brain was preparing to move his finger *before* he decided to move it."

"Come again?"

"It was undeniable. You would expect the subject to will the movement, then for neurons and muscles to implement the decision. But before you decide to move your finger, your brain is already preparing to do just that."

"What a load of nonsense."

"Unfortunately it was verified many times in the seventies and eighties. The results are quite indisputable, though the interpretations differ. Some say it proves free will is an illusion. Another interpretation is that the 'will' simply permits or vetoes what the brain proposes. Some argue that the experiment is too narrow, that the workings of the human will are too complicated to be measured by such a simple procedure."

"But if the brain acts before the conscious mind decides, how can we not notice what's going on?"

"Well, suppose I slap your face. You feel pain, but the sensation isn't instantaneous. It takes about half a second—it depends on the part of the body, of course—for a pain stimulus to transit the nerves and reach the brain. But it *seems* as if you feel pain at the precise instant your cheek is slapped. You 'feel' that the slap and the pain occur simultaneously. But that's only because your brain is editing the timeline, so you perceive the slap only after your brain registers the pain. The brain synchronizes the awareness of one moment to another awareness of a different moment. That means the 'present' we perceive is not the present at all. The brain processes vision, taste, touch, pain all at different speeds. Just like a computer, the brain requires finite amounts of time to create a unified awareness out of the sensations impinging on us from moment to moment. It takes these disjointed inputs and creates the illusion of 'now,' the illusion of the present moment. This function is an aspect of what we call consciousness."

"Then consciousness is simply a dream? What we experience is just the movements of a body being manipulated like a puppet?"

"No, of course not. Consciousness can make judgments and control behavior. But quite a bit of what we do requires no consciousness at all. Human beings aren't aware of everything they do. A finger striking a keyboard. Each footstep along a road. These are just examples, but a lot of research is going into studying complex activities that aren't completely mediated by conscious awareness, like playing a musical instrument."

"Then what about this? Penetrating the KGB or a criminal organization. Making contact with a double agent. Stealing a load of important secrets from your enemy. Don't all of these complicated maneuvers require conscious awareness?"

"No. They don't." She looked so conscience-stricken I had to laugh. A very dry, brutal laugh.

"Especially in your case—"

I cut her off. "My case?"

"You died. You were transcribed. You've experienced the same situations repeatedly. Not only do you have a God-given gift for espionage, you've honed it for decades. The more you experience—the more data we have that captures your behavior—the more your brain can operate without conscious awareness. The brain is parsimonious. Consciousness is costly. The brain is focused on survival and has little need for consciousness of behaviors that can be automated. In other words, by living your life over and over again, you've become too much yourself."

"Too much myself…"

"In a sense. Your consciousness is less and less necessary for the behaviors that make you, you. You can order a martini shaken, not stirred, and not need to be aware of it. Each time we transcribe you, your brain automates more of your behavior. Gradually, your brain is reducing the scope of your mind. That was Ackroyd's hypothesis—the cause of your amnesia attacks."

The more they purified me, the less I needed me. That was Ackroyd's conclusion. A perfected self has no use for consciousness.

The bottom had dropped out of my world.

My legs felt about to fold up under me. Don't play me for a fool. The job of bone and sinew is to keep me standing. The ground under my feet may be cut away, but I won't submit to fear. It was a struggle, but I stayed on my feet facing Shepard.

"Why did you call Ackroyd?"

"I was going to tell him that we had the data to prove his hypothesis. Though really, I think he was expecting it."

ALWAYS HAVE AN ESCAPE PLAN

An epitaph carved on a tombstone. The tombstone of a man who was once my friend.

"I'm afraid."

I couldn't have said this to anyone but him, and even then, only because he was in his grave. Had he been alive, not even the threat of death could have driven me to utter those words, though I knew that one day death would come to collect me.

"I'm not afraid to die. Others will follow me. I'm afraid that I'm already dead, that the man standing here confessing to you is an empty shell. I seem alive, but I'm not."

A friend of mine, a man in the French service, once told me, "You Englishmen are a strange lot, like those trick boxes one can't begin to know how to open." At the time, I—the Original—had just finished an assignment and had found myself pondering the transience of the world, the difficulty of distinguishing right from wrong, and the nature of my occupation. When I mentioned this to him, the Frenchman took an interest and began probing me for details. I still remember the last thing he said to me. "Don't be human. It's better to be a machine."

It's hard to be philosophical when you're losing your very soul. My French friend was right. Machines have no soul.

"The fact is"—Caroline Shepard had told me—"there's no way for us to be certain you are conscious just by looking at you. Perhaps if we put you into an fMRI machine and monitored you night and day we could be more certain. But in this room, or out on the street, as long as your actions are characteristic of you, as long as your body keeps outputting your typical behavior, there's no way for us to know whether or not you have a consciousness."

Can a conscious being be distinguished from a philosophical zombie?

Heavy clouds edged with a dull brown formed a solid canopy over England. A few dry leaves swirled up and away into the leaden skies of Albion.

A philosophical zombie is merely intended as a proposition for considering philosophical problems. I read up on it. I wondered how the person who wrote the article would react if he knew he might find an actual p-zombie right here.

My friend was laid to rest two years ago. He had the same special right as Her Majesty—he met every one of me, from the Original on. Not that he welcomed the distinction, I imagine.

Unlike Her Majesty, he was my colleague—MI6's senior weapons specialist—and as colleagues, we told jokes, laughed, fought, and vied to see who could be most cynical. Each time I came to him clothed in a new body, he accepted me as his friend without a hint of distaste.

He was old, this friend of mine, but he pig-headedly refused every suggestion he retire. In the end, neither disease nor old age did him in, but an auto accident. Very fitting, I thought. But with his death I don't think it's too much to say that I was forced into the most profound solitude in the history of humanity. *Awake thou Orphan of History awake to Eternity.* As the priest commended the coffin to the earth, I had the feeling God was taking the trouble to tell me this, though I'd never bothered much with Him before. I was a sin that could never be confessed in any church, ever.

I fought for Her Majesty because she was the only woman who truly knew me. Serving her was the only thing keeping me from complete isolation, even if she granted me an audience only once—once each transcription.

To take a leaf from Kantorowicz, I am not serving Her Majesty's political body. I serve her natural body; that is, I fight for the Queen herself. Of course I don't deny that I fight for England. It's just that I've participated in too many missions to be eternally driven by naive patriotism. The Western concept of patriotism is simply a vulgarized version of a Christian concept. The popular writings of medieval Scholastic philosophers were full of references to *amor* for the homeland. Coluccio Salutati, chancellor of Florence and champion of its republicanism as a successor to Rome, grimly described *amor patriae* as being so sweet that "we should not consider it distasteful to thrust an axe into our father's head, mangle our brothers, and deliver our unborn child from the womb with a sword." This is somewhat vulgar in its extremism, but I realized that it reflects a certain truth. I've met my share of people who believe it. I myself have killed many times.

Yet now it seems that everything was for the sake of that one woman. Just as God manifests in the Trinity of Father, Son, and Holy Ghost, the Queen manifests in two bodies—the indestructible *character angelus,* the royal power derived from the angels, and a body that is born, dies, laughs, cries—her body itself. Serving the former is not much different from patriotism. But perhaps I was only pretending to serve the former while devoting myself to the life and glory of the latter. Consciousness and unconsciousness, two selves, serving the two royal bodies.

"Well now, here you are again."

For a moment I thought it was the Queen speaking, but of course that was impossible. I turned and saw an elderly woman, roughly Her Majesty's age, in mourning dress a few yards down the path.

"I'm sorry. Have we met?"

"Yes, of course. You were here last month. My husband's buried two over. Right here." She pointed. The tombstone was as small and unassuming as the rest.

What happens to us when we die? The fortunate go to their grave—recumbent, moldering, waiting for the Last Judgment, with only a stone to bear witness to their existence. The fortunate have someone who loved them, like this old woman, to visit now and then and speak a few words.

Sad to say, the chance of having a stone to mark my resting place is, as things are now, vanishingly small. The likelihood that I will not die in bed, and not in my homeland, is very high. My body will probably never be found, and unlike a soldier, I have no dog tags to collect. My fate is to be transcribed, die, and be retranscribed, always shifting death into the future. I can see no release from it. The Empire summons me from my purgatory to resurrect me in the body of another.

That's when the thought crossed my mind: perhaps I *am* a tombstone. A walking, talking, killing tombstone.

"My husband passed away years ago, but still, I suppose we were together too long. It's as if I've taken on the pattern of his life and his habits. Not in everything, but in some things very much."

The woman gazed at me serenely. Love, we used to call it. It starts as love, that much is certain. It changes with years; we lose the sexual passion and the mad craving to fill up the emptiness. Love becomes an algorithm for living in synchrony with another person. The final destination, love's ultimate consummation, is the assimilation of another person's life into one's own. The life of one's beloved become a template to transcribe into oneself.

"In a sense, your husband is still alive, then. Alive in you."

She nodded and smiled. There was nothing hidden in that smile, no trace of loneliness. An ordinary smile, and therefore extraordinarily beautiful.

"His body has gone ahead, but he still lives in me. Karmic

retribution, isn't it? That's why I come here, to complain. The first Sunday of every month, after the service is over, I come and tell him, 'Since you've seen fit to leave me on my own, one would think you'd give me a little more freedom.'"

I wasn't very different. I was living according to a format laid down by the Original, as her husband had formatted her, and she had formatted her husband.

My friend here in the ground, the Director, Her Majesty—all of them must have seen a tombstone standing before them, a tombstone of the transcribed who preceded me. They spoke with a tombstone, gave orders to a tombstone, uttered complaints to a tombstone. A living tombstone. I am proof that my friend once truly lived, proof that although his life was known to few, he achieved mighty things.

Then I saw it. The first Sunday of last month. "You saw me here last month, you said?"

"Yes. Who is it you come to visit? You were talking to that grave last time as well."

Of course I hadn't been here the month before. At least I had no recollection of it. An I who was not me had been visiting my friend's grave. Just as I was doing now.

"Then, that means I met you…"

"Yes, I just told you. The first Sunday of last month."

The day Greville Ackroyd flew off the expressway. The day after, in all likelihood, "I" heard the truth straight from Ackroyd's mouth.

There was a package waiting for me when I got home.

My mind was in turmoil on the way back from the cemetery. I must have killed Ackroyd and his "children." I had to concede that this was the most logical conclusion. It was the same intuition I'd had as soon as I entered Ackroyd's house—no, from the instant I entered Pangbourne Estates. How to infiltrate, the dead angles to utilize, how to gain access to Ackroyd's study. What I had thought was a simulation running through my mind out of habit was nothing of the sort. I was simply remembering specific thought processes I had been through before.

At the time I'd chalked it up to my training and experience in espionage. Now I knew it was self-deception.

We have a propensity for creating explanations out of whole cloth as a way of forcing incompatible experiences to conform to logic. I once read about an experiment: a man whose left-right brain connection had been severed was asked to view images presented separately to each brain hemisphere. His left eye, controlled by the right hemisphere, was shown a snow scene. His right eye, controlled by the left hemisphere, saw a photograph of a chicken claw. A number of photographs were then placed before him, and he was asked to select a picture—one with the right hand, and one with the left—that corresponded with what he had seen. His right hand—left brain—chose a picture of a chicken. His left hand—right brain—chose a snow shovel.

The researchers were not surprised to find different responses from the left and right hands. There was no way for the subject's right hemisphere to know what the left had seen. But what astonished them was this: when the subject was asked why he chose the picture of a shovel, he replied without hesitation, "You need a shovel to clean out the chicken shed."

He wasn't lying. The left brain is tasked with finding meaning, and when it saw a picture of a shovel, it instantly worked up a story to match. The subject was completely convinced of what he said; the left brain had convinced his conscious mind that it was in charge. Lies are normally conscious—the brain knows it is spinning a fiction. If, however, the part of the brain charged with recognizing what is real is also a source of lies, consciousness has no way to distinguish reality from fantasy. If a lie is fed to the brain's primary awareness layer—the layer where "reality" resides for the individual—there is no way such a lie can be recognized as what it is. It becomes part of the individual's reality and therefore beyond doubting.

I did not know that I had already entered Ackroyd's house in Pangbourne Estates unseen. Confronted by this inconsistency, my brain arbitrarily concocted a rationalization about reflexes derived from my espionage training and inserted it into my mind. Unless forewarned, the brain finds it very hard to doubt itself.

I had to have coffee. I wanted to steep my untrustworthy brain in caffeine and clean it out. I staggered over to my La Pavoni machine. I knocked back the bitter black liquid. Then I sat down at my desk, drained of vitality, and brusquely tore the wrapping off the package.

It contained a book and a letter.

My God, I recognize this. I've seen this letter. I won't let my brain hood-wink me again. False memories clamored for entry at the doors of my mind—I drove them all away. I packed this book. I wrote this letter. Now that I knew the truth, this feeling of déjà vu could only mean one thing. The problem was, I would have to examine the book and the letter to know what they contained. I had to visit Pangbourne again to recall what I'd done there; I had to open this package to realize I was the one who had packed it. Looking and knowing was necessary to awaken memory.

I resigned myself to whatever I might find and picked up the book.

The pages were blank.

Every page was new and untouched. This wasn't a book, it was a diary. I set the book aside and started in on the letter.

> *Dear Mr. Nothing,*
>
> *I know that you feel nothing, and I know you are conscious of nothing, because it is my function to feel, and because I am your—formerly essential—Consciousness.*
>
> *Would it be unkind to say you are my empty shell? Would you "react" with surprise at being thus*

described? Without meaning to evade the question, I would have to say the problem is relative. You are an empty shell, but you are my shell, and your Consciousness may be a kind of parasite that has attached itself to you.

This gift is by way of a request, from your Consciousness to you. I realize neither of us is the type to do something so unmanly as keep a daily diary. But this is different.

I want you to use these blank pages to record your story, which is also my story. As much of it as time permits.

By now, I think you know I will soon undertake my final mission. Until then, please keep writing. Record everything you've done. Tell the story as if you were me. As if you felt it. As if you were surprised, enraged, mystified. After all, it was how you reacted. It was what you did. Even if there was no one behind the curtain.

Write my story, though there's not much time.

Whether to interfere with my plan or not I leave entirely to you. I'd prefer if you stood aside, but if you do, you may not survive. I seek annihilation, but that would also be your annihilation. I suppose I can't force you to bear that.

So tell the Director, or even—though I suppose this is impossible—beat me to the punch and kill yourself. I'll accept whatever you decide. Of course, it will be best for me if you simply close your eyes.

P.S. From Consciousness with Love

I examined the diary again. The binding was sumptuous, with a family crest in gold leaf adorning the spine. The cover bore a single sentence, just as I imagined it would.

THE WORLD WAS NOT ENOUGH

The first page was also inscribed.

I will go down to self annihilation and eternal death.

A line from Blake's *Milton*.

I riffled the pages. This river of white paper, *tabula rasa*, reminded me of the most beautiful description I knew for England. Albion, the White Country. In *Milton*, Blake gives this name to his visionary world and writes, "Rouze up O Young Men of the New Age!"

The young man who awakes will not be of the new age. One day that heavy suit of armor, laid down layer by layer since antiquity, will outlive its usefulness. And by losing it, the wearer will reveal his true form. That is how humanity will awake.

O Consciousness, Humanity's Ancient Armor!

I placed a glass with ice and a bottle of scotch on the oak desk and settled myself comfortably. I took up my pen, relaxed my shoulders, opened the book I had presented to myself, and began to write.

I am a book. A text, unfolding continuously.

My consciousness did, in fact, try to put an end to everything.

He tried to end this farce, this purgatory, while some vestige of conscious control over his actions was left to him. Before his consciousness, the last refuge of the self, disappeared forever.

Yes, I think I'm free now to refer to "him." The man who was my consciousness. No, its manifestation.

In the end, he tried and failed to destroy the transcription facility. It was simply beyond his capabilities. Just as the Director had said, leaving a single framework alive had forced MI6 to divert some of its security detail. This was all according to his plan. He rigged Ackroyd's brakes, killed all but one of the Queen's properties, and bought himself an opening. He nearly succeeded, but chance intervened in the final moments. As bullets from SAS submachine guns riddled his body, they say he threw himself against the huge insignia emblazoned on the bulkhead and expired, arms stretched toward the vast, supercooled data banks that lay wreathed in vapor beyond. The division's insignia, the unicorn and the lion, was so smeared with blood that it had to be scraped off the bulkhead and replaced.

This is purely a rumor, but as he lay stretched on the bloody grating, they say his face bore a faint smile, though whether of cynicism or relief, it was impossible to say. There were also some who said that his last words were a whispered "God Save the Queen," but that almost seems too much to hope for.

Having come this far, I would like to offer an apology of sorts to you, the reader.

As I believe you understand, although I have repeatedly resorted to the pronoun "I," this "I" has no self, contrary to what you would naturally assume. The death of my predecessor in attempting to terminate this farce made it necessary to perform another transcription into a new body. No shred of consciousness survived the transcription of this reactivated "I." The overwriting process has completely worn away my consciousness. Only brilliant whites and inky blacks remain, like a copy of a copy of a copy of a copy of a photograph run off on a copier set to Maximum Contrast. My predecessor knew that no consciousness at all was likely to survive in the copy that succeeded him. In all our shared history, he knew his consciousness was the last.

He had no choice but to act.

He was terrified of losing himself. Obviously he did not fear death. A man with so many dangerous, and successful, missions to his credit had nothing to fear from death.

Now that part of him that allowed him to feel he was himself, that assured him he was himself, is dead. What lives on is a kind of soul without content, with only the elements necessary to continue behaving as he did.

This must be what they call purgatory. If happiness is somewhere to be found within death—which brings only terror—that happiness would be eternal peace. He feared losing that peace. He feared a farce in which his empty shell carried on for eternity, a blithe automaton. A living oblivion.

As usual, the Director submitted his dissent to my proposed reactivation, but No. 10 wouldn't hear of it. London was reeling under an outbreak of terrorist bombings. After a trigger-happy police unit killed an innocent Brazilian on the London Underground, our prime minister was steadfast: notwithstanding this tragedy, if we suspect someone of being a suicide bomber, we shoot to kill. In this extraordinary situation, with the law suspending itself with alacrity, it would have been strange had they not reactivated me. Yes, life is bestowed on me again and again because the Magna Carta, the prime minister, and Her Majesty need me. From the day I received my Licence to Kill, my life has been an unending Extraordinary Situation.

That is, if this place "I" have arrived at can be said to be "living."

The physical reality of my body and brain writing words in this diary is the only "I" that exists. In no sense is self or consciousness present. I feel no qualia. I cannot perceive the redness of red, taste the sweetness of sweet. There is neither agony nor pleasure. But the information conveyed to my brain by my nerves lets me behave *as if* I am seeing red, *as if* I am tasting sweetness. As if I were anxious, as if I were cruel, as if I were an anachronism, as if I were a dinosaur.

This sequence of words is being output without any inner experience whatsoever. It has been executed automatically according to "his" aggregate algorithm, as written to my brain. His algorithm is terrifying in its complexity, but in many ways it is equivalent to a text string generated by a computer. I may write that I am "suffering" or "disgusted" or happy," yet not a shred of feeling lies behind those words. I can begin a paragraph with "I think" or "I feel" in the complete absence of thought or feeling.

Then why do I use these expressions? I was written to use them.

Now you see it, I suppose, and you would be correct. An entity that unilaterally proclaims itself consciousness tells the writer, you are an empty shell, you are the dregs of me. But is the empty shell really me? After killing Ackroyd and the "children," the letter writer who called himself "Consciousness" sought his own extinction. Was he truly conscious?

The most that can be said is, only the text remains. Answers to questions of authenticity lie outside it. Within the text, whosoever declares himself to be conscious must be taken at his word. The only certainty is that I was once both conscious and an empty shell, and one of these "I's" sought extinction. So there is definitely a meta-structure.

I repeat—I behave as if I am "him," but a normal person's "consciousness" is entirely missing. So even if this text seems a touch sentimental from time to time...I must have only written it that way without the slightest trace of conscious emotion.

I am the horrifying outcome he feared. The empty shell he despised. A shadow without substance.

I will continue. This existence will continue. This empty shell will continue.

Even after I fall in the line of duty.

As long as the Empire and Her Majesty need me.

Therefore, I hope you will permit me this one gesture.

May my Consciousness rest in peace.

Those Who Hunt Monster Hunters By Tim Pratt

The following was found posted in the profile section of user American-Ronin48 on a popular online dating site. The user is no longer active.

The monster hunter owns several samurai swords and often wears a fedora. He likes to practice with his wooden sword in the backyard—the neighbors complain when he practices shirtless with bare steel—and though he's never taken a kendo class, he watches a lot of instructional videos on YouTube and believes if tested by a master he'd rank at least fifth dan. He speaks enough Japanese to impress a non-Japanese-speaking date at a sushi restaurant, and loves the films of Kurosawa, the entire Zatoichi series (he sometimes practices with his wooden sword while blindfolded), and classic anime, from before it became popular in the West. He hasn't mastered the trick of catching a fly with chopsticks yet, but he's working on it.

His favorite thing in the world is sleeping with Asian girls, or at least it was until he discovered the pleasures of hunting monsters.

This isn't one of those stories about a delusional lunatic who believes he's hunting monsters, when really he's killing ordinary people. The monster hunter actually did kill a monster, or at least one monster, and he'd love to kill more.

The monster hunter doesn't kill monsters with his samurai swords—not yet, anyway. So far he's used a knife, the Internet, a bottle of lighter fluid, and a long-handled lighter, the kind you use to fire up a charcoal grill.

The monster hunter enjoys talking about himself in the third person, and he sometimes falls into that habit in conversation, but he isn't the one writing this.

Here's how the monster hunter kills his first monster. (Basically. Some details might be wrong. But basically.)

After stalking the creature for weeks, the monster hunter comes to understand its habits and its routines. Three nights out of four the creature just goes to bed in its apartment in Oakland. But every fourth night, as he sits in his car watching through binoculars, something flits out of the monster's open bedroom window, moving almost too fast to see, streaking off into the night sky. At first he thinks it's a bird or a bat, but finally he gets up the courage to creep in the dark to the monster's window and peer inside after the thing has flown away.

The monster's body sprawls on top of the covers on its bed, headless, its neck an open wound, a clean straight cut, but not bleeding. At first he thinks the body is dead, but then he sees the rise and fall of its chest. Headless or not, it's still breathing. Only then does the monster hunter realize he's been stalking a monster and not a woman. A cold fear grows in him, but it grows alongside a hot excitement. *This explains everything,* he thinks. *She wasn't even human. No wonder.*

The monster hunter gazes for a while at the monster's body, its camisole top riding up a little, exposing a smooth expanse of belly, and the monster hunter is seized (again) by a desire to touch that skin, to taste it, to see how hard he'd have to press his fingers into that flesh to leave a mark that would last for days. He wonders, briefly, if he could climb in through the window, if he could touch the monster's body, if its wandering head would notice.

He doesn't do that. Instead he goes home and starts looking up things on the Internet, and when he figures out what he's dealing with—a sort of vampiric creature from Japanese folklore, a monster whose head detaches and goes flying in the night, looking for innocent victims to bite to death—he resolves to rid the world of its evil. Fortunately, the Internet explains when such creatures are most vulnerable and how best to dispatch them.

It takes a while to make the plans, and he has to wait for the monster's housemate to be out of town, because when he sets the monster's house afire, he doesn't want anyone innocent to be harmed. But he gets it done. He hunts the monster, and he kills it.

It's the greatest feeling he's ever felt.

The kind of monster the monster hunter killed was a *nuke-kubi*, though the monster hunter misremembers his hasty research and believes he killed a *rokurokubi* instead. It's a common mistake, though I'm not sure why, since the former is a woman whose head detaches fully from her body and flies independently through the night to hunt for victims to slake its terrible thirst, attacking with bites and deafening screams, while the latter has a neck that elongates—like a more limited version of Mr. Fantastic from the comic books—allowing her to spy on humans. The two are both *yokai*, bewitching creatures capable of shape-shifting, but otherwise they're not all that similar. I guess to the monster hunter all Japanese monsters look alike.

The monster hunter's password for this site was "rokurokubi," with the "o"s replaced by zeroes. I like to think I would have figured it out eventually, but I didn't need to—he has the passwords for all his sites saved in his browser.

The monster hunter has profiles on just about every online dating site there is. The ones for seekers of one true love, the ones for swingers, the ones for Christians, the ones for Jews, the ones for adulterers, the ones for the polyamorous, the ones for the kinky, the ones for casual hookups, the ones devoted to same-day blind lunch dates. He uses the same username on all the sites, so it's easy to find him, and he rarely bothers to tailor the content specifically to a given niche. His samurai swords and fedora appear frequently in his photos.

The monster hunter believes there are some circumstances in which a person is obligated to have sex. He believes women should always shave their legs; on the more explicit sites he makes it clear he believes they should shave everything, because it's "just common courtesy to keep everything clean."

He *does* know that "wherefore" means "why" and not "where," and that the sun is larger than the earth, and he isn't aggressively or obviously homophobic, and he mostly spells things correctly. Amazingly, he doesn't have a bad kanji tattoo. He could, in fact, be worse.

But he's bad enough.

Before the monster hunter hunted his first monster, he went out with her on a date. I wasn't there but I heard a bit about it, and I can speculate about more of it, and I think it went something like this.

A DRAMATIZATION

Misaki arrives at the restaurant a few minutes early, but the monster hunter is already there, in a secluded booth in the back. She doesn't know he's a monster hunter, and to be fair, he isn't, yet. He's just a twenty-something boy named Evan who works for a social media start-up that is, like most social media start-ups, ultimately just a machine to serve people ads. He isn't wearing a fedora, but he is wearing a shiny blue shirt and has very complicated facial hair. Misaki mentally classifies him as "douchebro" and begins a course of preemptive regret.

She hadn't been that excited about the date anyway. Evan had sent her a couple of amusing messages, they had an adequate match percentage according to the Almighty Algorithm of her preferred dating site, and they liked a lot of the same bands, so she'd decided to go along on the theory that bare minimum small talk wouldn't be too onerous. Most of all she'd been desperate for a night away from the endless psychodrama of her housemate and his girlfriend—it was hard to decide if their loud arguing or their louder reconciliation sex annoyed her more, but it didn't much matter because she got to hear both a few times a week. So when Evan dropped an "I'm free tonight—any chance for a drink?" note she figured, why not, take the escape hatch. Even bad dates have their advantages: for one, they often give you funny stories to tell on later, better dates with other people.

After the initial polite hellos and his big, almost wolfish, smile of greeting, things go downhill quickly. He insisted on a Japanese restaurant—really more of a sake bar, but they serve food too—and he attempts to order in Japanese. Misaki winces as he mangles his way through several phrases, the waiter sharing a sympathetic look with her that the monster hunter is too oblivious to notice. He actually attempts to order for her, without even consulting her first, but she stops him and makes her own choice, speaking in English.

"Katsudon, huh?" he says. "That's a lot of food for someone as small as you." He grins again, showing off straight white teeth. "I like a little thing with a big appetite."

"Uh," she says, and concentrates on eating the edamame in the middle of the table.

"You're at UC Berkeley, right? What are you studying? Math, engineering?"

Misaki restrains the urge to roll her eyes. "I'm getting a PhD in Geography and Sustainable Development, actually."

He cocks his head. "Huh. Fascinating. I'm a coder. Algorithmic ninja. Working for this start-up in the city now, but I'll probably jump ship soon, when something better comes along—I like to think of myself as a modern-day ronin, you know? A masterless samurai, taking my skills where they can do the most good."

She's starving, or she'd fake a stomachache and escape. No way she's staying for dessert, though.

Things don't improve. She lets him run the conversation, responding to him mostly with nods and the occasional "Mm" and "Wow." He tries some tired old pickup artist crap—"You'd look really cute if you did something with your hair"—negging her, trying to position himself as a princely authority deigning to give her attention. She puts her hands in her lap when he keeps trying to touch her, glad there's a table between them, and when he tries to press his knees against hers, she draws her legs up into the booth beside her. Sometimes it's good to be small.

He orders several rounds of sake, making a great show of quizzing the waiter about the different varieties—that part in English, at least. She sips a little but not much. She's never liked rice wine, really. She's a bourbon and soda girl.

Finally the end comes, and she declines dessert—"Watching your figure, huh? That's good, that's really good"—and he snatches up the check, which doesn't prevent her from dropping cash on the table. She's not leaving the restaurant with any obligations between them.

"I'll drop you a note," he says. "We should definitely do this again sometime."

"I'm pretty busy," Misaki says. "But it was nice meeting you."

Later, on the phone with her sister, Misaki says, "It wasn't even an *interesting* bad date, like that guy who seemed totally normal until he started talking about doing astronaut training and going to chef school and producing rap albums, and I realized he was a pathological liar. This guy was just a gross boring Asian fetishist."

"Misaki," I say. "His username is *AmericanRonin48*. What did you expect?"

"Yeah, I know. But sometimes people have stupid usernames! All the cool ones were taken years ago. Like, I thought maybe he just really liked that movie *The 47 Ronin* or something."

"You can be pretty dumb for such a smart girl," I say, because sisters can be mean, but later, I'll wish I'd been nicer.

The monster hunter isn't the type to send unsolicited pictures of his dick to girls on dating sites—another point in his favor—but he is the type to send five messages in three days, with the last one calling you a stuck-up bitch who's honestly too ugly to be so picky, if you don't reply.

I've gotten two messages like that from him, on two different sites. But he doesn't know he wrote to the same woman twice, because I used different usernames, and my face is hidden in my photos.

He doesn't know the woman who made a date with him this week is the same woman who ignored him twice before, either. It took me a while to get the honeypot profile set up, to create the perfect bait for him, adjusting it until we were a 99 percent match, and it took me even longer to get up the courage to make the profile live. I'd like to say I was biding my time, but really, I was trying to decide what needed to be done. Or, more accurately, if I could bring myself to do it.

"I love Asian girls," the monster hunter tells me on our date. "They're so much better than white girls. Way less bitchy, you know? They understand how men want to be treated."

There are differences among the races—depending on how you define race, anyway. (Ancestry? Culture? Phenotype? Genetic makeup? Social identity? Geographic location?) People of Sub-Saharan African descent are more likely to have sickle cell anemia than those of other ancestries. Mediterranean-descended individuals suffer disproportionately from thalassemia. If you live in the American Southwest, you've got a better chance at contracting Bubonic plague than you would otherwise. Ashkenazi Jews have to worry about Tay-Sachs more than most. French-Canadians have a higher-than-usual tendency to fall under the curse of *le loup garou*. Moldavians succumb to vampirism more often than other Eastern Europeans. The degeneration into cannibalistic, monstrous Wendigo typically only happens among the Algonquin peoples on the Atlantic Coast and in the Great Lakes region.

But there's not a "race," by any definition I know, that is inherently more meek or eager to please men than any other.

I didn't make this date to give the monster hunter a class in Racism 101, though. So I hide my face behind my hands and giggle and show him exactly what he wants to see.

Misaki calls me a week or so after her date. "This guy Evan will not take a hint. He messages me on the site like five times a day, says he thinks we're soul mates, that we're destined to be together, that I need to give him another chance. I ignored him, and blocked him, and he found me on, like, every social media site I'm on, even the ones under my real name, and tried to friend me and follow me everywhere. I had to make it all super private. Then this morning he *texted* me—and I didn't even give him my number. I never do that until a second date."

"He knew your first name," I say, "and what program you're in at Cal—he probably poked around on the Internet and maybe made some calls and found out everything he needed. You can find out a lot about someone that way. Congratulations, you're being cyberstalked."

"God. What if he never goes away? I mean, it's not like he's shown up at my house or anything, but if he does, like, escalate... I'd rather not get the cops involved. Rule one is always 'don't call attention to ourselves,' you know?"

"I know what Grandmother would have done," I say.

She laughs. "Evan would be one dead douchebro if she were still around. They'd find him with mysterious bite marks all over his face and burst eardrums."

"How's...all that...going?"

"I still go out," she says. "I get the urge a couple times a week. But, no, no relapses, nothing since that thing with the sheep when I was fourteen. It's really not that hard to control. You just make sure not to go to bed hungry, you know?"

"I know," I say.

Things men other than the monster hunter have said to me in messages on dating sites, or on actual dates; a selection:

"You're so pretty. Like a lotus flower."

"What's your favorite martial art?"

"I think it's cool that you like to date American men."

"Since I started dating Oriental girls I never want to go back to regular ones."

"You have to admit, Pearl Harbor was kind of a dick move."

"I started the anime club in my high school, so I've always been a big supporter of your culture."

"What do you want to drink? The Kamikazes are really good here. Oh. Oh god. I'm so sorry. I didn't mean—I didn't mean anything—"

"Uh, do you mind if I drive? I mean, no offense or anything, but..."

"I spent a year in China, so I really feel a connection with you."

(I suppose I should be happy no one's ever asked me if my vagina is sideways. We've come such a long way.)

What's a monster?

There's a definition of *weed* I like a lot: "A weed is a plant out of place." Maybe a monster is just a creature out of place.

It would be much easier for a monster to find a place if people weren't such assholes.

Things men other than the monster hunter who've dated me have never done:

Stabbed my sister's motionless body repeatedly, then waited until her stricken head returned, then stabbed her in her sobbing eyes, then doused her body and head in lighter fluid, and set her all on fire.

I could have bought a schoolgirl uniform online, but they're mostly cheap crap, essentially just slutty Halloween costumes. My housemate is pretty femme so I raided her closet for a short plaid skirt and bought knee socks and a button-down white shirt and figured it was close enough.

Once, in college, my (white) roommate and I both dyed our hair electric blue. Everyone said her hair looked "totally punk rock."

Everyone said my hair looked "totally anime."

It's everywhere, you have to understand. It's the air we breathe.

I'm a person. I'm a woman. I'm an American. I am not a plant out of place.

My hair's not blue anymore. For my first—my only—date with the monster hunter, I wanted my hair to be straight and black and exactly what he wanted and expected to see.

Some people have a genetic predisposition to depression, or color-blindness, or perfect pitch, or tetrachromatic vision, or they're super tasters. Some people have heads that can detach at night and roam the world.

That doesn't make any of them monsters. Only actions make

you a monster. A woman whose head can fly, who uses her power to glide among the clouds and watch the city lights below, who's never hurt a human and hasn't even bothered a cow or a sheep or a squirrel in years...a woman like that is less of a monster than a man in a fedora with samurai swords who stalks that woman.

"My username on the site is AmericanRonin, and yours is AmericanGeisha," the monster hunter says, reaching across the table and touching my hand. "It's like we were made for each other."

I look down at my mostly untouched rice bowl and giggle and say, "Yes."

The problem is, I can't suggest going back to his place. Not without blowing the whole submissive pretense. I worry it might take a second date, that he won't be bold enough to invite me home—he didn't with Misaki—and the thought of spending another evening in his company is not appealing.

But I suppose killing the nukekubi must have improved his confidence, because he says, "Hey, I live right near here—did you want to come over and check out my swords?"

I've been writing all of this in present tense, because that's the natural voice of online dating profiles—"I love sea kayaking and like to go mountain biking on weekends and am so good at cunnilingus you just would not believe"—but it's not really the right tense. Not for the monster hunter, anyway.

I'll say this for the monster hunter: he kept his swords sharp. It didn't take much encouragement for him to tell me everything—to confirm my suspicions, to turn my fears into certainties. Once I was sure he'd done what I thought, I did what I'd expected to do.

The head of a nukekubi detaches bloodlessly, by magic. The same can't be said for the heads of ordinary humans.

Someone might have seen me leave his house after it started

burning down—fire attracts attention. If there were witnesses, I'm sure they're looking for a dark-haired Asian woman, age somewhere between nineteen and forty. In the Bay Area, where a quarter of the population is Asian. And where I don't live anyway. Still, the police are smart, and there are connections, paths to follow, especially on the Internet, which will lead to me. That's all right. My family is used to being driven away and starting over somewhere else. We have the skill set. I wouldn't post this here, as a message and a warning and a boast and a confession, if I were all that worried about keeping my life unchanged. After I hit "post" here, I'm gone.

My sister never killed anyone, which is more than I can say for the monster hunter. More than I can say for myself, now.

I'm sure you're wondering: Am I a monster too? Part of a nest of nukekubi, a squirming horde of monsters pretending to be human? Or was my sister adopted? Or is being a nukekubi a curse, instead of a condition of birth? If it is a curse, did it die with my sister, or is it passed on to someone else in the family?

You'll have to decide for yourself if I'm a monster. I just hope your definition doesn't hinge on whether or not my head can separate from my body and go flying through the dark skies at night, looking down on a world turned small by distance, while the onrushing wind—surely nothing more than the wind—brings tears to my eyes.

Inari Updates the Map of Rice Fields
By Alex Dally MacFarlane

Gold foil stars sat in the twenty-eight lunar lodges, forming a square around the constellations Shiho and Hokkyoku. Red lines connected the stars within each constellation. The silver foil moon lit the space. The gold foil sun waited to rise.

Underneath the map of the sky, Inari crouched.

Inari Facing East

Inari crouched with the word *west* near her feet and the word *east* on the far side of the map, distant as a horizon. In between: hemp paper, a vast expanse. In its center, thin black lines depicted a simple grid of the land and its thousands of rice fields in thirty-six squares, numbered in the *chidori shiki* system: the numbers increasing south to north and then, turning, in north to south, back and forth across the grid like a shuttle moving across a weft. Some squares were bare. Others were filled with writing, describing the rice fields. The words *a village planting rice* filled one square. The words *rice develops* replaced it as Inari watched.

The curving parallel lines of a river cut through several squares. Four of the nearest squares described irrigation channels. No other natural features were drawn on the map, but some descriptions remembered them: *ten rice fields reclaimed from forest* and *eight rice fields reclaimed from wetland*. The blank squares could not avoid revealing the gaps in arable land.

Inari stamped each arable square with her seal in red ink.

In between each stamp, when her hand was raised into the air with the wooden block held in it, Inari disappeared. Her form appeared within a single square on the map: a tall woman, robed in mountain-patterned silk, her hairstyle elaborate.

Inari walked through the square, through the villages with their playful children, along the roads leading to other villages—and, eventually, the city at the heart of the map—and turned from the roads to walk along the dividing banks of earth between each rice field. Green shoots in neat rows like formal writing reached above the water. Small fish swam between each plant, flashing pale and orange, drawing ducks. Soon the green would grow, obscuring the water. Inari crouched to run a hand over the shoots, enjoying the tickle of their tips against her palm. A planting song came to her lips, a month late. Sitting on a bank of earth, she sang it anyway.

> *Bent backs, bent legs*
>
> *It aches—*

A small structure caught her attention. At the edge of a field, the people of the nearby village had built a small shrine of wooden walls and woven reeds sloping like a house's roof. Inari ate the cooked rice offered in small, unglazed bowls.

The people noticed and bowed toward a mountain with three rounded peaks covered in cedar forest in one of the grid's blank squares.

Inari stamped the square, satisfied, and lifted her hand above the next.

In it, a feud raged, a brother and a sister fighting over the fields that had belonged to their father, each arming their villagers with sharp blades and padded tunics. The sister's villagers fought well.

The brother, in his rage, began tearing up the rice and kicking apart the earth between the fields. Inari waded through the water to the sister's side, saying, "If I may…"

The sister bowed deeply.

The rice stems snapped like cries of pain in the brother's hands. Inari called across a broken bank of earth, "Stop this now and you will still know the prosperity of your sister's lands."

Too angry to truly see Inari, the brother shouted, "You will know death if you come closer!" He raised his sword.

Inari had no need of a weapon. With a touch of her hand, the brother turned into flame—a blink of light, bright as the sun. For the rest of the day and into the night, Inari repaired the brother's damage in the fields. Bending her back and her knees, singing, she rebuilt the banks of earth. The snapped stems returned to life in her hands. The sister insisted on joining her, and together they restored the neat rows, their hands occasionally touching like stems swayed together by the wind. Inari stayed with the sister in her house for the rest of the night.

The sister soon began construction of a new temple, with ten torii gleaming red like the sash of Inari's robe.

Crouched at the map of rice fields, her hand raised in the air, Inari smiled.

In the next arable square, rice grew well. Inari stood in the center of a field, her robes raised to let the rice brush against her lower legs, and sighed in contentment. Then a fox darted from the neighboring forest and bit off the undeveloped sheaves of three rice plants. Inari shouted a word that fixed the fox in its place. Its tail still flicked. "Open your mouth." The three green sheaves fell from its jaw and splashed in the field. "You must not do that," she told the fox as she released it. It retreated into the forest. "The rice must prosper."

Crouched at the map of rice fields, Inari frowned.

Inari Facing South

The descriptions of the rice fields were not orientated for Inari to read them: the words lay on their sides, running left to right. Inari ignored them.

The lines of the grid extended beyond the rice fields. The last squares at the north described—unread by Inari—fields ascending like steps toward the mountains. The north-south lines ascended further, amid mountains outlined in black ink and shaded blue to represent distance. Simply drawn trees grew on the mountainsides: lines like words to depict a trunk, several branches, bare of leaves despite the growing season.

Words lay among the trees: *The author drew details on the map sheltered from the hot sun.*

Inari crouched at the north of the map, looking south, looking at his return route drawn on the map in ink that only he could see. A map within a map. A journey scratched onto a cinnabar-coated surface. Inari saw the road curling through the mountains, crossing a river on a bridge drawn longer than the two-day distance between the river and the abandoned house where he had failed to sleep to the sound of foxes fighting. On the next mountain, two torii led to a temple. He had walked past. Trees thickened on the next mountain, then grew sparse. Birds hovered over a village. He had slept in one of the houses, fed soup by its occupants in return for a story of his travels. He had not shown them the rice sheaf. Words in the cinnabar: *The map should not be shown to outsiders.* The map continued. The road unbent as soon as it reached the grid of the other map: flying straight as a spear to the city, still small in the map's center. The blank squares of the other map surrounded the palace and houses.

Inari remembered his outward journey.

It had happened in a time when all four edges of the map threatened to go up in flames at once, when the map had no grid, no rice fields, only the city and the villages clustered together at the center—the distances between them diminished—in fear. Inari had joined the armies that defended the center of the map against the enemies. Smaller armies had then gone out, defeating the enemies in their own villages. Inari had joined them. When they returned, full of their enemies' fear, Inari had continued walking, wanting a more lasting end to the threats at the edges of the map.

He had found people: some similar in face and different in voice, some different in face and similar in voice, eating recognizable food and counting a connected set of seasons. People and people and people, until he had reached the sea.

At the shore, Inari had met a man from a farther land than he had reached, the land where many people ate rice. It lay across the sea. They had talked for many hours of the cultivation of rice, its history and its merits. Inari had returned to his city carrying a single sheaf. A great gift! "A great beginning!" Inari had told his people, who knew ample grains—sorghum, wheat, barnyard millet, foxtail millet—and added rice to only a few of their fields. "For safety. For strength." Hunters and gatherers had continued their trades. In the fields, the rice sheaves had ripened like the tails of the foxes darting hungrily among them. Inari had seen a use.

"Here," Inari had told his people, "our foxes' tails are like ripened sheaves of rice."

The man had told Inari that the land where many people ate rice lay at the middle of the world. In the four directions extended mapped lands: walls, distant mountains, vast deserts and oceans, and beyond them lands of dog-headed men and hairy milk-white women who lived near the water, without men, and suckled their water-sired children from white stems at the napes of their necks. No rice grew there. No threat passed the walls to the map's center. In that map, Inari's archipelago and Inari's land within it were an artistic flourish: rocks among the waves.

"Here," Inari had told his people, "our fields are full of fox tails."

The man had told Inari that rice would only grow well in the archipelago's central plains, not the cold climate of the north or the poor soils and unsuitable topography of the south.

"Here, our land is like a bowl full of rice, held in the world's hands. Safe. Beyond it, rice does not grow, foxes' tails do not wave in the wind, the people eat different foods and lead different lives."

Inari had walked among the fields, spreading the rice, encouraging it—standing in the calf-deep water and letting his power seep into the soil until green filled the fields, until it ripened and the people ate well. The foxes had run into the fields. The stories had grown.

Under a hot sun, Inari had climbed the three-peaked mountain to update the map.

In a later time, when the enemies had returned, the people of the map had cried out, "They come from the land where the people eat only salmon and lily bulbs, and scrape the surface of their pots with the coarse edge of a wooden board!" The victory of the rice-eaters had been swift.

Crouched at the map of rice fields, Inari looked over the long lines of the rice field grid and the scratched-in-cinnabar journey like retelling stories.

Inari Facing West

Beyond the grid of rice fields with its growing, ripening text, beyond the lines extending into mountains, Inari drew an ocean. Waves roiled in thin lines of black ink under Inari's fox-fur brush. Words fell into it like dye into a vat. Stories. Inari's wrist ached.

Islands emerged. Inari annotated them with a brush of a single fox hair.

At one corner of the map: the Island of Women, isolated by sharp rocks and twisted currents and the stories hanging in the salt spray. Cannibalism splashed across the sea. A lengthy description of the dishes cooked from men's flesh lingered like foam. Inari evoked a pot in a curve of coastline. After a rest to ease the wrist ache, Inari turned to the rocks at the island's other shore. Erotic stories eddied and churned. Women loving other women. Men setting sail with ships full of *shunga* to please and arouse the women they met. Inari wrote all the stories, even those that made others uncomfortable, even those that belonged to the past or the future.

At the north of the map: the Route of the Wild Geese, a rocky island uninhabited except for twice a year when the geese landed on it, resting on their journey between Inari's land and the unknown north. Inari dreamed of the north. Unending ice, unlit. No rice grew there.

Inari drew more islands that floated like teeth on the hair-straight sea, all of them far away from the map's center: far from the archipelago, the shore, the mountains of Inari's journey, the grid of rice fields. Inari missed it. From the sea, Inari saw the distant words *rice prospers in this land*. Inari saw the new king place rice in a shrine to commemorate his coronation and plan a new tradition of offering the first sheaves of rice from each year's harvest.

The map's edges were not yet complete.

At the west of the map, surrounded by ocean: an unnamed island. With the single fox-hair brush, Inari drew the simple lines of a shrine and a series of offerings. Stone pillars reached up to the sky like arms. A row of emptied husks and discarded seeds and the other inedible parts of fruits covering the low pedestals indicated the food offerings' acceptance. Gold rings were neatly stacked on five pedestals. Metal horses and glass vessels were arranged behind them: gifts from further across the sea.

Inari added a bowl of rice to the central pedestal: the finest part of the painting. A careful line represented each grain. A palatial glaze decorated the bowl. The detail spasmed Inari's wrist, sending a fine line along the bowl's rim. A crack, Inari decided, to represent the longevity of the offering.

Inari worked on, wanting the map to be complete.

Stories swilled at the island's shore, telling of the ships stopping there on their way between lands, making offerings—to the sea, to the sky, to the winds—and consulting their maps. Ships from Inari's archipelago stopped there too. Sailors saw the familiar bowl of rice and the unfamiliar rings, metal horses, and glass, and knew they stood at a boundary. Inari painted the story: they stood at the furthest extension of the land where the king offered the first sheaves of rice. Beyond it, other people lived.

At the far western end of the map, Inari painted coastlines: a peninsula, a hint of the great sweep of land beyond it. The land where many people ate rice. A neighbor state.

Inari returned to the map's center to walk through the fields. Foxes waited in the forests. "It's your turn to get to work," Inari told them.

Inari Facing North

A fox the color of ripened rice sat facing the north, watching the word *mouse* appear in one of the grid's squares, disappear, and reappear in another. It waited, patient. It leapt. Its tail waved like a ripe sheaf of rice in the wind as it disappeared into the map. The word *fox* appeared. The word *satisfied*. The word *protector*.

The descriptions of ripe rice disappeared: harvested. The fox reappeared on the map in the space under the red-joined constellations.

"Perfect," it said.

Inari rolled up the map of rice fields, satisfied that the land would prosper.

The map of the sky remained open overhead. Inari took the map of rice fields to a cabinet of kiri and cedar and gold, where all the maps of the archipelago's lands were stored: the map of mountains, the map of earthquakes, the map of languages, the map of trade routes, the map of ghosts, the map of migrating birds, the map of work songs—uncountable maps. Pathways led between them. Inari stepped into the cabinet to tend the rice in other maps.

The Street of Fruiting Bodies By Sayuri Ueda
Translated by Jim Hubbert

Even the weather was against us. The sky outside the window was slate gray. The cloud deck seemed about to come crashing down. Soon the deluge would come, flushing every corner of the city.

But not clean. The rain would only propagate the misery.

"There's the barrier." Yuji Mimura was driving. "From here we walk. No point contaminating the vehicle."

A decontamination crew in hazmat suits loitered in front of the barrier, looking bored. Mimura stopped the van and a crew member came round to each side. We rolled down the windows and held up our IDs. Someone must have called ahead, because they waved us through without any questions.

Mimura parked. As soon as my feet hit the ground, I felt as if something warm and sticky were invading my suit. I shuddered. *Get a grip,* I told myself. *You're buttoned up. You have a respirator. There's nothing to worry about.*

"Let's get going," said Mimura. "We're on a clock. I couldn't swing us much time."

We crossed Route 43 and turned north. It took about fifteen minutes to reach the train station. The plaza was deserted. The terminal was empty, the buses all gone. Silence enfolded the little shopping mall. The traffic lights were dark. No birds stirred in the plane trees. The city was dead, as if time had frozen.

A fine white powder rose in puffs as we walked. The early afternoon light was weak and cheerless. It was hard to believe this used to be home.

Two shapeless brown lumps lay close to the road. Cats? Maybe one had been a small dog. The desiccated bodies, like crumpled wrapping paper, were covered with sprouting brown mushrooms. The gelatinous caps were flecked with white.

Mimura stopped and stared at the corpses, his eyes narrowing in disgust. "Hasn't this area been decontaminated?"

"They must have wandered here from somewhere else. The crews can't be everywhere at once. Cut them some slack."

"You're right," he said with a sigh, trying to calm down. "Let's go. I don't like hanging around here, suit or no suit."

We crossed another broad avenue and entered an area of detached houses and apartment buildings divided by narrow lanes.

I glanced at a house. Something was peering over the garden wall.

Two hands appeared on the wall. The creature's gaze was sticky. Gender and age were hard to tell. The eyes were clouded black and red and the skin had an opalescent sheen, like strangely colored fish scales. I'd never seen one before. My first ghost.

Almost immediately, a sweet aroma penetrated to the back of my throat; it was almost refreshing, like a single drop of mint oil vaporizing in a pan of hot taffy. The scent took me right back to childhood.

"No eye contact." Mimura's voice was sharp. "No matter what you hear, don't answer and don't stop."

As we hurried by, the eyes and hands glided along the wall, keeping abreast of us. When we were almost past, I heard a low voice close to my ear.

Help me…Help me…

I fought the urge to turn toward it and kept my eyes fixed on the houses ahead.

"Hurry." Mimura's voice was tight. "They're gathering."

Before I could answer, I saw something nasty—a swarm of white, humanoid shapes bounding along the top of a wall, bunching and stretching as they ran. Their mouths were turned up at the corners like suppressed grins. I kept hearing the same words, repeated like an obsession.

Help me…Help me…Help me…

"Shall we run?" said Mimura. "If it's too much for you."

"Can we outrun them?"

"Distance helps. What do they look like?"

"Not like anyone I know. Not yet."

"Tell me if you see someone you know. It means we have a problem."

About a month before I entered the quarantine zone, I ran into Matsuoka, a friend who worked at the National Institute of Infectious Diseases. It had been a long time. We'd both been so busy, we hadn't gotten together for a good ten years.

When I proposed an evening foray into Ginza, Matsuoka turned cryptic. "Takashi, you better come over. I've got something confidential for you. I can't discuss it in public. Not even in a private room in a restaurant."

I started my work in pharmacology in my home prefecture of Hyogo. Later I transferred to my company's Tokyo headquarters to join their research lab. Matsuoka worked in Section One of NIID's Bioactive Substances Department. Section One dealt with fungi, including mushrooms. I'd heard that they recently formed a team to research Auri disease.

I went to Matsuoka's condo after work, equipped with blowfish jerky and a bottle of Kyoto sake to keep us occupied. We quickly ran out of small talk. Matsuoka changed the topic to work.

"How much does your company know about Auri?"

"All we do is drugs," I said, "and all we look for is cures. Beyond what works and what doesn't, we don't know a lot."

"You know about the new resistant strain?"

"Yes, we were briefed."

"I think we're in for it this time. I'm betting this new one shrugs off everything we throw at it. I'm not even sure the experimental drugs we're getting from Europe and the States will help."

"Then we'll just have to wait for the designers to cook up something new. Until then, I hope it doesn't leave the zone."

"You ought to get out while there's still time."

"What—leave the country?" This was unexpected.

"Find someplace as dry as possible. A city with a climate that's hostile to *Auricularia*. You might have to forget about coming back."

I toyed with my sake cup and grinned. "Are you sure the government wants you leaking that?"

"You're a friend. I doubt you'll go out and announce it, but if you feel like selling this to the media, go ahead. People will catch on soon enough. I'm just trying to get you a head start."

"Are you going?"

"Better believe it. A suicide pact with Japan doesn't exactly appeal. Is your family here?"

"Yes. My wife and son."

"Your parents have a house in Mikage, don't they?"

"Yeah."

"Tell them to sell it while they can and use the money to get out before it's too late."

"Are you serious?"

"I was in Kyushu, Takashi. It was pretty rough. Sooner or later the rest of Japan will be the same."

Auri disease was officially known as Wood Ear-like Systemic Mycosis. It was caused by an invasive fungus, a species of *Auricularia* that was easily mistaken for the edible wood ear mushroom. The fruiting body had a gelatinous, almost translucent brown cap, deeply folded like a human ear and covered with white flecks. The new species was an aggressive propagator and ejected prodigious volumes of white spores. It thrived on protein and targeted mammals as its preferred food source.

Victims were eventually covered with so many sprouting mushrooms the skin was no longer visible. Without treatment, death came in four to seven days. The mycelia penetrated the skin, even piercing the eyelids and thrusting deep into the eyeballs. The fungus covered the membranes of the mouth and invaded the stomach, the intestines, even the lungs. Attempts to eradicate the parasite through surgical intervention alone had been unsuccessful.

The first cases had appeared in Japan about a year ago. The rapid progression and grotesque symptoms sparked rumors of biological warfare, but governments across the globe hurried to issue denials. Now cases were being reported from Southeast Asia and South America.

Auri was treated with multiple antifungal agents. No single drug was effective. My job was to find promising combinations of existing drugs.

Luckily, the disease responded well to the multidrug approach, and the initial panic died down. Still, the specialists at NIID were not optimistic. Multidrug therapy might be effective, but it was also a pathway for the development of resistant strains. Some new, innovative drug was urgently needed.

The most promising candidates seemed to be broad-spectrum antimicrobial peptides. They could perforate the fungus cell walls and target its DNA for destruction. But the peptides were only for topical use; injectable and oral preparations were too toxic. Pharma companies worldwide were working frantically to overcome this hurdle.

Eventually, and just as NIID had predicted, a strain of the fungus that was impervious to multidrug therapy emerged in Kyushu. And still there was no news of a new drug.

"I'm a clinician by training," said Matsuoka. "I had to see it first-hand, so I got myself assigned to an inspection team."

"Was it really that bad?"

"Yeah."

"I heard they were going to lift the quarantine once the mushrooms were incinerated."

"The way things are down there, who knows when that will be? They'd have to napalm the infested areas. And the whole city is full of ghosts. Humans beings are creatures of reason. Too much exposure to those things would drive anybody mad."

Tokyo seemed a million miles away from the tragedy in Kyushu. In interviews on the street and gossiping with neighbors, people talked about how frightening it was, or about the panic that would ensue if the mushrooms appeared in Tokyo. But few understood how dangerous the situation really was. What people found truly fascinating were the scary stories about victims turning into ghosts.

"Is it true what they say, about those spooks?" my wife asked me.

"Aren't you a little old to be afraid of that kind of thing?"

"It's not me, it's the children. The school is having a terrible time. Somebody's spreading rumors about seeing them around here. Now some of the kids won't even go outside."

The infected area in Kyushu was declared a quarantine zone. Those free from infection were ordered to leave. As the buses moved out, people torn from family and friends looked back in anguish and saw something bizarre against the deep orange sunset: massive swarms of translucent human forms, writhing like a gigantic forest of seaweed with roots sunk deep in the sea bed, plunging, rising, calling out endlessly in the dying light. *Help us. Help us. Help us.*

The tidal wave of moaning raced over the heads of the evacuees and echoed into the distance. Invisible hands plucked at their heads and shoulders. A sticky presence embraced them, pouring warm sighs into their ears. People screamed for it to stop or sobbed for forgiveness. Others clapped their hands over their ears and ran. Those who ran heard malevolent giggling. Some people cracked and started screaming obscenities.

The incident was witnessed by journalists covering the evacuation. Naturally the story trended instantly across the country. None of the photos and video showed anything out of the ordinary, yet everyone had had more or less the same experience. The rumor spread with the news: If Auri kills you, you'll return as a ghost, bound to where you died for an eternity of torment and a thirst for vengeance.

In a day or two the rumor was everywhere. It was irritating to see how idiotic people could be. Everyone in the medical community was working day and night to find a cure, and people were obsessed with ghost stories. If they only knew.

The national news programs avoided the term "ghosts." Television specials were devoted to scientific explanations of "apparitions," and viewers were warned to steer clear of phony psychics looking to make a quick buck.

"They got that information from us, you know," Matsuoka told me. "Twenty-four hours after the victim dies, the parasite starts releasing an organic volatile, a toxin something like a pheromone. It seems to be a neuropeptide analog that stimulates human synapses, but the potency is stronger than any pheromone. The limbic system, temporal lobes, Brodmann areas 18 and 19—they're all affected. When the toxin is inhaled—and it's hard to filter with standard respirators—memory traces generate hallucinations of human forms. The hallucinations are usually nonspecific but can also be people you've seen recently, especially people who are in your thoughts a lot. In other words, the people you see aren't necessarily dead. The voices, the tactile hallucinations—logically they all have the same basis. Whatever the mushroom is off-gassing must be affecting the auditory cortex and sense of touch at the same time."

"Does the reaction vary from person to person?"

"Of course. Each brain is different. It also depends on the local toxin density. The sense of smell is affected too. Some people report a sweet smell that penetrates the sinuses. Like molten taffy, but minty."

"Taffy and mint?"

"The toxin stimulates the olfactory area of the brain and makes people think they're smelling something pleasant. Maybe it cloaks the smell of corpses. Not everyone smells the same thing, though."

"But we're raising *Auricularia* in our lab. Nobody's seen, heard, or smelled a thing."

"Of course you haven't. *Auricularia* raised on culture media or lab mice aren't the same as the parasite feeding on humans in the wild. Blowfish bred in tanks aren't poisonous either. It's the same effect." Matsuoka tore off another strip of blowfish jerky. "The parasite completely envelops the host. You can't reproduce the complexity of the toxin in a lab setting. Fungi grown in a Petri dish can't synthesize the lure. The only people equipped to solve this are government scientists with unrestricted access to the quarantine zone. And nothing infected leaves the zone. So you have people holding funerals without bodies."

"But the mushroom doesn't have a brain. How does it fool its victims?"

"Carnivorous plants do it. Many species of plants evolve ways to lure and kill insects without the benefit of neural tissue. It's amazing, actually. The mushroom's lure has only one purpose: to draw the prey close to an infection source."

"Spores?"

"Correct. Pheromones travel much farther than spores. The toxin generates hallucinations over a wide area to lure the prey."

"Wouldn't hallucinations be just as likely to scare people away?"

"The strategy doesn't have to work every time. Humans are a contradictory species. Fear makes us curious. *Auricularia* has discovered an elegant way to exploit that."

Matsuoka fell silent, turning his empty cup over and over. When he spoke again, the words came slowly.

"The government's explanation is credible, as far as it goes. But it doesn't go far enough."

"What do you mean?"

"I watched them burn the bodies. Nothing contaminated leaves the zone, so the crews have to finish the job on-site. The crematoria don't have anywhere near the capacity, so the crews gather the corpses in open areas and burn them in big batches. The ashes stay in the zone too. Let's just say the crews have lot of latitude when it comes to getting the job done."

"People are making a stink about it."

"It's a delicate issue. It's hard for the government to compromise with the bereaved families." Matsuoka paused. "The zone was full of ghosts. 'Help me, help me' everywhere you went. The respirator blocks the spores but doesn't filter the toxin. There must've been hundreds of corpses. Before, all I could hear was 'help me,' but when the crews fired the bodies, suddenly there was this high-pitched screaming. The ghosts started writhing violently. Every one of them was screaming something different. 'It burns it burns Father Mother stop stop it burns no I'm on fire help me I'm on fire no stop I'm burning *stop!*'"

Matsuoka slumped forward. He closed his eyes and pinched the bridge of his nose as if trying to block the memory.

Something didn't feel right. This was a hard-headed scientist, a clinical physician with years of experience dealing with distressing situations. How could a cremation, even a mass cremation, do this to him? Was there something he wasn't telling me?

He finally looked up. "The sky above the pyre was distorted by the heat. I just stood there watching them roast. I guess I looked out of it. A crew member slapped me on the shoulder. Don't let it get to you, he said. It's all in your head. They're dead and gone. How could they feel pain? But I felt something. They were pawing me. I heard them screaming out of the fire. *I'm not dead yet.* Maybe the toxin was messing with my head. In that case, there's nothing more to say. But what if it was some kind of real communication? What if the mushroom doesn't kill its victims but puts them into suspended animation? What if it's symbiosis?"

"What is that supposed to mean?"

"The victims may be clinically dead, but isn't it possible that some of their neurons could remain viable? Maybe they're alive but no longer human. Maybe the mycelia penetrate the brain, tap into the neurons, and manipulate them the way we would a computer. It would explain why the ghosts are so flexible at adapting their behavior to how the prey reacts. They could be using host bodies as biometric sensors to detect our approach. That would trigger the release of the toxin. Maybe toxin composition and volume is modulated to match target and distance. To generate the optimal hallucination."

"Do you have proof for any of this?"

"Right now it's just a suspicion, but the voices I heard were real." He shook his head. "Anyway, even if we did prove it, they wouldn't let us tell the public. Do you have relatives or friends in Kyushu?"

"No."

"Well, there's going to be another outbreak and another quarantine, and they'll probably deal with it the same way they're dealing with it in Kyushu. Don't say you weren't warned. Not that you can do much about it."

Matsuoka was a reliable guy. Still, I didn't know what to make of his warning. Fleeing the country was pretty drastic. It wasn't a decision I was prepared to make in a hurry. Antimicrobial peptide research was heating up all over the world. The first pharmaceutical company to come up with something effective would make money hand over fist, and we were all attacking the problem as hard as we could. Getting approval for a new drug in Japan would mean jumping through some hoops, but if it was approved overseas first we could re-import and do field tests. I thought I'd wait a bit and see how things played out. The epidemic might even run out of steam…

Looking back, I wonder if I was just tired. Working too hard had dulled my instincts—my survival instincts. I took Matsuoka's advice and filed it away.

Soon after I saw Matsuoka, the resistant strain—the one the government assured the public would be confined to Kyushu—made the jump to the Kansai region.

There were different theories as to how the parasite could have traveled so far. Maybe the wind carried the spores into the upper atmosphere, or it came in on infected birds. Maybe the spores piggybacked out on something taken from the zone. All of these theories were at least plausible, and all of them suggested that further outbreaks were just a matter of time. The fact that Kansai's number came up first was pure chance.

But that was all it took. My parents and sister were soon infected, and my work didn't qualify me for a pass into the zone. My mother and father called every day, pleading for me to at least find a way to get Erika out. *She's your sister. Isn't there anything you can do?* The hospitals in the new quarantine zone were overflowing. Most of the infected were told to stay put and wait for treatment. My parents and sister had all the early symptoms of the disease.

I tried every trick I could think of to get them a hospital berth, but the higher up the chain I went, the more I was dealing with people who knew just how bad things were going to get. No special treatment. They shut the door in my face.

Then one day the calls from home stopped. Now there was a quarantine on information as well. I was out of my mind with fear. I fought with my wife constantly. They were going to burn my parents and sister alive. I could barely sleep for the nightmares.

Soon after the mass cremations began, I got a call from someone identifying himself as a member of the Health Ministry's Auri Disease Response Headquarters. I nearly lost it right there—they were getting back to me now? But what the caller said next changed everything.

"It would be unofficial, of course, but I can get you into the zone. You won't be able to take anything out, but if you'd like to see your home one more time, I can arrange it."

That was how I met Yuji Mimura.

I soon discovered that, in fact, he and Erika had been planning to marry. They had been seeing each other for three years. Just before they had a chance to tell my parents, *Auricularia* erupted in Mikage. Mimura knew my sister must already be dead, but he was sure she had left a farewell message. He wanted to go to the house and find out.

He was dead calm about the whole thing, the calm that comes after doing everything you can to save your fiancée, after seeing every attempt fail and losing all hope, after more tears were impossible. I immediately felt a bond with him. I asked him what he liked about my sister.

"Maybe that she was a bit like me, and then again not. When we talked, it felt like a window opening in my heart, like she was showing me the window was there. What kind of person was Erika to you?"

"She was a handful. She didn't treat me like her older brother.

I couldn't box her ears or yell at her, so I was the one who ended up crying in secret. When we were kids, people used to say they couldn't tell which one of us was older."

"She must've been tougher than I thought."

"You saw what she wanted you to. Once you were married, I'm sure the real Erika would've come out."

Mimura chuckled drily. "I wish I could've seen that. But now she's gone forever."

My old neighborhood was down as having been decontaminated, but we still couldn't go in without hazmat suits. "I guess that means we won't see any ghosts," I said to Mimura.

"Are you afraid?" He sounded suspicious.

"Not in the beginning. Now I'm not so sure."

"Even if we run into them, they're basically harmless."

Mimura didn't seem to catch my drift. I casually asked about his background and discovered that he'd never worked on a decontamination crew. His only experience in the zone was tagging along on a single inspection with his boss. That would explain why he didn't seem very concerned about encountering ghosts.

If Matsuoka was right, I had a feeling I knew what I'd see and hear when the toxin started affecting me. When the time came to face what was inside me, would I be able to handle it?

Mimura said he could get us into the zone if we pretended to be gathering data. We would not have much time, two or three hours at most. Still, that would be more than enough to reach my parents' house if we entered at the closest checkpoint.

Mimura was determined to go whether or not he could get official permission, and it was partly his determination that made me decide to go along. Something told me that seeing the house one last time would give me the closure I needed and finally put an end to the nightmares.

As we came closer to the house, we kept seeing ghosts. Now they were less distinct, but life-size apparitions still stared at us from the shadows like translucent dolls. Maybe the toxin was unevenly distributed.

"There are too many for my liking," I said to Mimura. "Are you sure this area was decontaminated?"

"Maybe it's a good environment for *Auricularia*. A lot of these houses have gardens. In damp locations, the mushroom might not need a body to feed on."

"I still don't like it."

"Are you telling me we should go back? After coming this far?"

"I didn't say that." I just didn't like what I was seeing. Being prepared for trouble seemed prudent. But this wasn't the time or the place to start arguing. I gave up and kept my mouth shut.

Finally we reached the house. It seemed untouched, as if nothing had happened. I was afraid we might find it broken into or vandalized, but the big kumquat tree and the nandina bush were just as I remembered them. Everything looked so peaceful. I felt tears welling up.

"Is this the first time you've been here?" I asked Mimura.

"Yes. I wish I could take something to remember, but the quarantine..."

"I've heard that people smuggle ashes out of the crematoria. You know those companies that will process the ashes into diamonds? They're doing it for people who've lost relatives, secretly of course. I don't know how they get into the zones, though."

"Thieves come in late at night. They break into houses and take anything valuable. It's not that hard to get in if you really want to. I doubt they're very careful about sterilizing their gear afterward. That's probably how the spores escaped."

The front door lock was broken. A decontamination crew had likely gone in to collect the bodies.

Memories came at me in waves as I stepped through the door. After moving to Tokyo, my wife and I still visited a few times a year with the kids. I yearned to walk down the hall onto the tatami in my stocking feet. That was impossible if I wanted to survive, but it still pained me to trample the floor in my shoes. My parents had had the house renovated only recently.

The first-floor kitchen and guest room were tidy and spotless. It seemed as if all I had to do was call and my family would appear. I wanted to see the living room, but Mimura insisted that we go to Erika's room right away. We headed for the stairs.

The stairway, which had seemed so narrow in childhood, was wider now. A handrail had been installed and nonslip rubber laid down. As we climbed, Mimura called out and pointed. When I looked up, my breath caught in my throat.

My parents and sister were at the top of the stairs. Their faces were glowing with happiness and love. They looked nothing like the ghouls we had seen on the way.

"Erika…" Mimura whispered, his hand frozen on the handrail. I pushed past and rushed to the top of the stairs. As I reached out to them, the specters faded and disappeared, merging with the air.

An aroma penetrated to the back of my throat, elusive but sweet, almost refreshing, like a single drop of mint oil vaporizing in a pan of hot taffy. An aroma from childhood…

Mimura was rooted to the spot, staring at where the vision had been. "Can you still see them?" I asked.

"Them…?"

"My parents and sister."

"I only saw Erika. Your parents weren't there."

Only Erika? But of course. Mimura had never met my parents. There was no way he could see them as ghosts. "What did you see happen?"

"You and Erika overlapped for a second. Then she was gone. Are they still there?"

"No, they're gone. Come on up. Let's check her room."

I opened the door. The room was fairly large and just as tidy as the first floor. Mimura went quickly to her bookcase. He started pulling albums and diaries off the shelves and leafing through them impatiently. His gloves made the task difficult. His impatience was mixed with irritation. He looked like a thief racing the clock. I found myself studying the wallpaper.

Finally he found what he was looking for. He called out and thrust a notebook toward me. Tears streamed from his eyes. He couldn't wipe them off, so they stayed glistening on his cheeks.

"I found it." Mimura's voice was hoarse. "They left messages for both of us." I took the notebook and my eyes fell on the page.

Father, Mother, and Erika had each left messages. There was nothing dramatic. *We're sorry we'll never see you again, but you must go on living…*

I handed the notebook back to Mimura. He clutched it to his chest, dropped to his knees, and hunched over crying. "I'm so sorry I couldn't come in time. Please forgive me."

I stared at him in a daze. Maybe this whole thing had been a mistake. True, I wanted to come here, but this was only making the agony worse. More tears wouldn't change anything.

I stepped into the hall. As I was about to go downstairs, I saw an apparition standing in front of the door to the other room.

It was my father.

He was wearing a traditional black half-coat. Slowly, he raised a hand and beckoned. I rushed toward him and he disappeared.

I hesitated at the door. Why summon me here?

There were two upstairs rooms. This one had been mine. After I left it had become a guest room. My wife and I used it when we visited with the kids.

I tugged the handle. The sliding door wouldn't budge. It felt like something was gumming up the runners. Whatever it was, the door was stuck fast, as if something didn't want me inside.

Since it wouldn't open, of course I had to know what was inside.

Basic reasoning told me this was dangerous. Seeing ghosts in a house that had been emptied of bodies meant the mushrooms must have found something else to feed on—the cat my parents had been keeping, uneaten food, maybe garbage no one would collect. If there was protein, the toxin was probably active. This house, and my parents and sister, had pushed everything out of my mind. Seeing their "ghosts" didn't need much explanation.

Yet somehow I couldn't leave well enough alone. I remembered what Matsuoka had said: *Humans are a contradictory species. Fear makes us curious.* He was right. Far back in my mind an alarm was sounding, but I couldn't tear myself away.

I pulled harder. Suddenly Mimura was there too. He took hold of the handle with me. He wasn't crying now. We both gave the door a hard shove.

It slid open with a loud bang. A white cloud billowed out of the room. I sensed immediately that it was spores and automatically stepped back. The aroma of molten taffy and mint was overpowering, but the sight of what was stretched out on the floor seemed to stab through my eyeballs. Mimura's screaming was sharp against my ears.

The three beds laid out on the floor were carpeted with mushrooms—brown, flecked with white, almost translucent, like deformed ears or the lips of devils ready to exhale more evil.

My head and neck went numb. I didn't need to get closer to know what I was looking at.

My father and mother. Erika. Why hadn't the crew taken them away? Why had they abandoned the bodies to become a banquet for the parasite? Was there a miscommunication? Were they just too busy to handle it?

Or was it something else?

Left here in this room, the three corpses had become seedbeds for the parasite. The mushrooms had fed and fed, spewing spores into the confined space, enough to jam the door shut.

The ghosts of my father, mother, and Erika stood on their beds.

Mother was wearing a lilac cotton robe. Erika wore a white dress patterned with sunflowers, a favorite from some vanished summer. All of them were calling to me: "Takashi…Takashi…" Father smiled. "You're finally here. We've been waiting. Come now, quickly."

Mimura stumbled toward the beds. I grabbed him by the arm and pulled him back.

"No. It's a trap."

"Erika says she's happy that I'm here." He was almost in tears. "I can hear her. 'I'm so happy you're here. It was worth the wait.' "

"What are you talking about? I don't hear anything."

"I'm staying. I can read Erika's diary and look at her photo albums. I can hear her voice. I didn't know it, but this is where I belong."

"You're out of your head. If you stay here, you'll die."

"I know. But I can't go back."

"You're hallucinating! She's just a ghost!"

"Are you sure? She doesn't seem like a ghost to me. And the people in those beds—they're alive, I can feel it. Why don't you talk to your parents? I'm sure they'll tell you they're not dead. The fungus enters the brain and fuses with the neurons, with every cell in the body…They're a different form of life now, that's all. Different, but they can still communicate with us."

"Get a grip, man! The toxin levels are off the scale in here. Everything we see and hear, everything is coming from inside. Erika isn't calling you. You're calling yourself!"

Mimura suddenly shook himself free. He tore open his suit seals, ripped off his hood, and pulled his arms out of the sleeves in a frenzy. The hazmat suit, his only defense, lay on the floor like a sloughed-off cocoon.

I was speechless with astonishment. Mimura smiled, like someone enjoying a bracing wind. "You know the way back."

He turned toward Erika's ghost, reached out to embrace her and fell facedown onto the bed of mushrooms, throwing up a thick cloud of spores. I felt time slow down. Erika was smiling, but it was a smile I had never seen before. My parents were smiling too.

The rage surged out of me. I rolled Mimura violently off the bed and started crushing the mushrooms under foot. The sensation that reached me through the soles of my boots was nauseating, but I kept stamping until I was out of breath. Mimura was still on the floor. He clutched at my legs.

"Stop it! Do you know what you're doing?" he screamed. "Do you know what you're destroying?"

I knew. I knew very well. But—

The memories were bursting in my brain like a barrage of fireworks. Memories of lost summers, memories from childhood, everything I'd ever forgotten coming vividly to life again as the toxin redoubled its potency. Even past sorrows and regrets seemed beautifully limned with threads of gold.

I hated it. I hated all of it. Pain should remain pain. I didn't need lovely embroidered lies.

Mimura was still grabbing my legs. I gave him a kick that sent him sprawling, but I stopped trampling the mushrooms. I couldn't stand to see any more or listen to his whimpering. I ran into the hall and down the stairs, burst out of the house and into the street. I fell to my hands and knees and gasped for air. Black mist streamed across my field of vision. I kept trying to yell, but my voice wouldn't come. I was paralyzed in a waking dream.

I stared at my fists pressed against the asphalt. Tiny apparitions of Erika were sprouting between my fingers, calling to me in a child's voice. "Takashi, Takashi." I stood up like a puppet jerked on a wire and batted the apparitions away.

A huge human head rose slowly in front of my eyes. It was inside my suit. It started to revolve—Father, Mother, Erika. Enormous hands stroked my cheek and tugged at my body. *Takashi Takashi Why won't you help us We're family We're family We are your family.*

The stench of taffy and mint was overpowering.

I ran away from there.

After a few dozen yards I was back on the ground, gasping for air. The apparitions were gone, but I still felt hands groping my body. I shivered with disgust.

I looked back down the road. The house was out of sight.

Mimura would stay there and join the mushrooms. Billions of mycelia would penetrate his body with terrifying energy, turning him into a seedbed for more ghosts to continue the hunt. He was probably ready for it. The mushrooms had fed on my sister's flesh and blood. In a way, he and Erika would be together now.

It suddenly came to me that we'd seen ghosts all along this road. Many of the houses in the neighborhood might contain the bodies of people lured to their deaths like Mimura. Yearning to see home again, yearning to recover mementos, beguiled by the mushrooms, devoured by the mushrooms—

That was when I realized the true horror. I knew what Matsuoka had left out of his story.

The apparitions generated by *Auricularia* were tied to personal memories. Personal memories are distorted and idealized. Uncanny or terrifying experiences are even more so in memory. Dear ones are even more dear—parents, siblings, lovers, spouses. The people we love are human beings with faults and traits that are less than appealing. Some of them are ugly. We know, because we deal with them every day.

But memory filters everything, distorts and idealizes it. Nearly everyone is convinced that their younger years were happy. The mushrooms tapped into that filter to send out its hunting call.

Matsuoka, what did you really see that day in Kyushu? Those ghosts writhing in the flames—who did you see? You couldn't tell me, could you? Now I know. I feel your revulsion and the wretchedness.

The parasite will travel with the winds and rain and infect every corner of Japan. There'll be no need for quarantine zones. Ghosts will ride the toxin. Japan will be full of them. People will blunder to their doom, drawn by a phantom's call. They'll wallow in spores and think they're in paradise. Like Mimura.

I trudged on, eyes on the ground. To escape from the quarantine zone. To return to my wife and son.

But I was saturated with the toxin. If I was going to get out, I had to concentrate, because the road back was teeming with ghosts. From black clouds that refused to shed a drop, they streamed toward me, arms extended, pleading.

Help me. Help me.

Father and Mother. Erika and Mimura. My wife and my son.

A Tale of Japan: Mesalliance By Zachary Mason

A man named Ito lived modestly with his sister on the edge of a dark wood. One night, after they had just come home from the capital, a serving maid appeared at their door and said that her mistress had seen Ito in the wood and wished to meet him. Nothing lived in the wood but ghosts, wolves, and spirits, as Ito knew, but he agreed to go anyway, though his sister wanted him to stay.

The maid led him through the trackless wood to a tall house he had never seen before. Light glowed from all the windows and noble men and women with the manners of past generations greeted him kindly, asking him what had lately passed in the world, being particularly interested in the ruinous baronial wars. Among them was a woman with raven hair and white skin who seemed to be illuminated by her own pale light, and he saw that she was watching him closely. She told him she wanted to show him the flowers she had arranged, and led him behind a succession of paper screens depicting bloody acts of war and the gruesome torments of hell, and as they passed each screen she removed another of his garments. Ito knew he was among spirits but did not care.

In the morning the pale woman saw him to the door and kissed him, her mouth tasting like fog, and said that they'd be married in one year.

As the year passed, Ito became ill and feeble, and as the fever racked him he spoke on and on about his lover. His sister nursed him as best she could, but he was almost dead and fading fast when the same serving maid appeared and said it was nearly time for Ito to wed her mistress.

When the maid had gone the sister kissed Ito and then called on a friend and said they were going mushrooming. They got baskets and took the path into the dank wood where the morels flourished in the deep pine shadows. The sister said, "Something marvelous has happened—my brother is engaged to a lady of noble birth and real consequence. This is quite a move up in the world—we look like country samurai, but our true station is actually rather humble. Tell no one, but the truth is one of our grandfathers hauled night soil, and the other loaned money at interest. Think of his fiancée's humiliation if she knew!"

Ito soon recovered, and though he looked for her, the serving maid never came again. He went looking for the house in the wood but found only a meadow of high, rank grasses where, he was told, there had once been an execution following a battle.

Chiyoko By Miyuki Miyabe
Translated by Nathan Collins

When I had heard about this side job, it sounded pretty good. Of course, life wasn't that easy.

"It's in pretty rough shape," the manager said, "but the face is cute, right? Nice colors too. It's too small for any of our employees. Their eyes won't line up with the eye holes."

He cheerfully remarked that my petite frame would make for a perfect fit.

I said, "My friend told me all I had to do was hand out balloons to the customers."

"That's right. You'll be handing out balloons. That's all. And I want you to wear this while you do it. The families will love it."

I wasn't so sure about that.

The subject of our discussion, terribly worn out and slumped against the wall of the employee locker room, was a pink rabbit mascot costume. Like the manager had said, the costume seemed distinctly smaller than a typical one you might see in a theme park.

"When did you get this thing?" I asked.

"Let me think…Five years ago. The owner's wife brought it in for the customer appreciation sale for our fifth anniversary. I think she said something about buying it in Asakusa."

The manager explained that a petite employee had worn it in front of the store for the big sale and handed out balloons and candy.

"It went over so well, we're going to do it again for our even grander tenth anniversary customer appreciation sale."

I imagined the costume five years newer, with colors far more vivid. Had it been cute back then? The children brought in tow by their mothers might have really enjoyed it.

But now? You could hardly look at the thing.

Had it been shut away in some storeroom for five years straight? Its color hadn't faded—if nothing else, it must have been kept out of the sunlight—but its fur was speckled with gray mold. Its two long ears drooped listlessly. I lifted the right ear, and it immediately flopped back down. White spots on its body might have come from bleach splattered by some mop-swinging janitor. Only where the chemical had stuck had the pink color faded. What, had they left this costume uncovered, out in the open in the storeroom?

An oily film of dust clouded its two plastic eyes.

"Something stinks," I said. "I think it might have bugs."

The manager gave me a broad grin. "Dry it out in the sun today. It'll be fine. Some good whacks will get that dust right off."

I touched the costume. It felt clammy. I searched around for the rear zipper and unzipped it. The inside felt even wetter. My face twisted in disgust.

He anticipated my remark and said, "I'm telling you, it'll be fine once you dry it out."

He patted me on the shoulder. "Tomorrow's the big day. We open at ten, but I'd like you to get to the office by nine. Thanks. And if you want to do any mending today, use the parking lot. It's got good sunlight."

The upbeat manager made a swift exit.

The swampy costume and I had been left behind. Seething, I batted the suit's nose. That was all it took to send the hollow rabbit crumpling to the ground beside the wall.

I thought, This totally sucks.

For a poor college student, part-time work was a lifeline. "I've got this good job for you," my friend had told me. "Ten thousand yen for one day's work. It's helping out at a supermarket, so it's legit."

At the time, I thought his face looked like the Buddha's. But no more. He was a con artist. A human trafficker.

If only I'd had one extra day, I could have taken this nasty costume home and given it a full cleaning. I sighed.

"Well now, are you helping out for the big sale today? Thank you for coming in."

The voice came from behind as I had just put my legs into the costume in the locker room.

Standing there was a woman around my mother's age, with plump cheeks and a broad smile. She walked to one of the lockers and opened it. The name TANAKA was on the door.

"I am," I said. "It's only for one day, but it's nice to meet you."

"Nice to meet you too."

Ms. Tanaka changed into a light blue uniform, then gestured to my costume and said, "That's hard to put on by yourself. Let me help you."

Even with two of us pushing and pulling, putting on the outfit was hard work. When we'd finally stuffed me inside, I had already begun to sweat. I didn't yet need to be completely in my rabbit guise, so I left the head dangling back like a hoodie.

"It'll be hot and humid in the suit," she said, "and it's quite heavy, so your shoulders will get stiff. And when you're walking around, be careful where you step. Also, you take up about twice as much space as you normally do, so you'll bump into things you wouldn't expect."

Her advice rang of experience.

"Ms. Tanaka, have you worn a mascot costume before?"

Her bright laughter resounded in the little locker room. "Sure I have. I wore that one five years ago."

Now that she said it, I noticed she was small like me.

She patted her stomach. "I've put on some weight in these five years."

Like she said, she did have a belly.

"Twelve kilograms," she said. "Even still, the manager tried to get me to put it on again, at first. Absolutely impossible. And even more impossible for any of the other workers. Since we'd be taking on some help for the day anyway, they decided to have one of you wear it."

She gave me a cheerful apology. I responded with a vague laugh, meanwhile thinking heatedly, deep down, Well in that case, you could have at least washed the rabbit after.

I had done the best I could cleaning it the day before, but the inside of the suit still felt moist. Where the bare skin of my arms and legs made direct contact with the suit's interior, I had already begun to itch.

"Do you want to try on the head?" Ms. Tanaka asked. "You should get some practice walking around before you go out front."

She lifted the top for me, and I twisted to slip my head inside. I was all the way in now.

"What do you think?" she asked. "It's a little scary at first, because you can't see much."

I maneuvered my eyes to the eyeholes and looked around the locker room. I could see the row of lockers and the wire mesh glass window. As she said, my view was restricted, but it wasn't so bad. What got to me more was the stuffiness. My only ventilation was a single hole beneath my chin.

Pleased, Ms. Tanaka said, "Oh, how cute."

I had sensed her move, and her voice came from ahead and to the side. But I couldn't see her. The light blue of her uniform was nowhere to be seen.

Instead, I saw something peculiar. I saw a thick, gray mass of fur. It was huge—almost exactly as big as Ms. Tanaka. And it was standing right next to me.

It took me a moment to realize it was a costume of a bear.

"Ms. Tanaka?" I asked.

"I'm right here. You're having trouble seeing out of that, aren't you?"

As it replied in Ms. Tanaka's voice, the bear mascot waddled right up in front of me.

Ms. Tanaka? That's Ms. Tanaka? Why is she wearing a bear costume? When did she put it on?

"Umm…" I said.

Reflexively, I reached out to touch her gray fur, and I lost balance.

"Are you all right?"

She was supporting me, holding me up—this gray bear with Ms. Tanaka's voice.

What the heck is going on here?

I shouted like I was on fire. "Take—take this off me!"

I threw off the rabbit head, and Ms. Tanaka was right in front of me—the plump woman in the light blue uniform. My eyes widened in shock, and I started to back away.

I was holding my breath.

"What's wrong?" she asked. "Is there something inside your suit? A bug?"

Not acknowledging her questions, I closed my eyes and put the rabbit head back on.

"Ms. Tanaka, don't move from that spot."

"Huh? Okay."

When I opened my eyes, that gray bear was in her place.

The gray bear was gesturing in surprise. "What's gotten into you?" she exclaimed, her voice high pitched.

Inside my costume, my mouth was hanging open.

"I'm…going to take a walk over there," I said. Feeling my way along the wall, I tottered out of the locker room.

Everyone, one and all, was wearing a mascot costume.

Rather, they all appeared to be wearing costumes, as long as I was looking through the eyeholes of my pink rabbit guise.

The employees coming into work seemed a parade of stuffed animals. This one was a cat. That one was a raccoon. This one was a monkey. They even had tails. Since nearly all of the workers were women, the stuffed animals had cute voices and feminine laughs. Naturally, their movements were feminine too. The scene felt a little bit like some dubiously themed bar. A cosplay bar, maybe? Except those establishments typically stuck with schoolgirl uniforms or nurse outfits. Anyway, I passed by a number of these costumed people and arrived at the front of the supermarket.

The manager was there, looking up at the storefront's decorations. Atop a ladder beside him, a man was fine-tuning the level of a horizontal sign, which read TENTH ANNIVERSARY APPRECIATION FAIR.

"A little higher," the manager was saying. "No, that's too far. Keep it level, keep it level."

"How's this? How's this now?"

I knew the one on the ladder was a man because he had a male voice.

Neither of them appeared human. But this time, I couldn't quite describe them as stuffed animals.

Because they were made of plastic.

The manager was a robot. A Gundam, maybe. The man atop the ladder was…what was that…some kind of soldier, I thought. Maybe one of the Turborangers.

I called out to the manager.

The Gundam turned to me. "Wow, that looks good on you."

I yanked off the rabbit head. The Gundam and the Turboranger were gone, replaced by the manager and a man on the ladder. The manager was wearing a white button-up shirt and a striped necktie. The man on the ladder—boy, actually; younger than me by the looks of him—was in work wear.

I plopped the rabbit head back on.

Wow, the Gundam and Turboranger return!

"What's wrong," the manager asked, "is the suit uncomfortable?"

"No, it's not that," I replied in a monotone. I blinked the dust out of my eyes.

What the heck is going on?

"Excuse me," I said, then did an about-face and headed for the locker room.

The manager's voice came after me. "Where are you going? I need you to start handing out those balloons soon!"

The locker room had a mirror. I wanted to see it. I wanted to see what form I took inside the mirror.

All the other workers were out in the store now, leaving the locker room unoccupied. With the rabbit head on, I slowly approached the mirror.

I saw a rabbit costume.

But it was a different color than the one I was wearing. The one in the mirror was white. And its ears were a different shape. The right ear was sharply folded over in the middle.

I knew this white rabbit. It was...it was familiar.

It was Chiyoko.

When I was a little girl, I loved that stuffed rabbit. I slept with her every night. I carried her on my back to go play in the park. I even carried her with me on family trips.

She had two black, round eyes. Her left one was the original plastic bit, but the right was my father's coat button, a replacement for the one that had fallen off on our way home from a friend's house. I was around six years old.

Crying and making a fuss, I said, "Chiyoko lost her eye!"

My mother gave me a solid scolding, but then sewed on the button for me. As a result, the rabbit's eyes were somewhat differently sized.

Right down to that detail, the white rabbit in the mirror was identical to Chiyoko.

I looked down at my arms. Through the mask of my costume, my arms were Chiyoko's, white fur threadbare and wrists frayed, revealing the stuffing within.

This was Chiyoko. I was sure of it.

How much time had passed since I'd last thought of her?

Even after I'd stopped playing with her and holding her in my sleep, I must have left her in my room at least through fifth or sixth grade. But then I went into junior high and high school, and as I grew up, I forgot about her. This worn-out, white stuffed rabbit was a childish thing, and I'd cast her out from my room. And now, I couldn't even remember where I'd put her.

My mother never threw anything away, and the stuffed rabbit would have been no exception. I figured the toy was tucked away somewhere. I had to find out for sure.

I hugged my arms around myself, holding Chiyoko like I used to, and thought, It's been a while. Sorry I forgot about you.

Then the realization—was everyone else like me?

The costumes worn by the other workers were each their own Chiyokos. I felt certain of it. They were the toys they had loved in their childhood; the toys to which they had been so attached, and that they had played with for hour after hour; the treasured, *treasured* imaginary friends who had remained by their side as they slept and accompanied them in their dreams. To the children, at the time, the toys were their true companions.

And when I put on this pink rabbit costume, I could see it.

I rushed out of the locker room. Ms. Tanaka was manning one of the registers, typing something on the keyboard.

"Ms. Tanaka!" I said.

"Yes? Oh, it's you." She drew her chin back. She must have thought I was a freak. Not that I could blame her.

"When you were a girl," I asked, "did you have a gray stuffed bear that was important to you?"

Now she drew her whole body back. Luckily, a woman on the

next register stepped in, saying, "Oh, what's that, a new kind of fortune-telling?"

"Yes, it is," I replied.

"A long-eared stuffed dog was my little friend. I got it as a present for my fifth birthday. I brought it along when I moved in with my husband, and he laughed at me. But it's still important to me."

This woman appeared to be a long-eared, droopy-eyed stuffed dog. The strands of long fur had gotten a little thin, but it wasn't frayed or dirty at all. The stuffed animal was still serving active duty, after all.

I said, "Good things will happen to someone like that."

"Is that my fortune?" she asked.

"Yes."

I strode triumphantly out the front of the store. The manager was still there. And he was still a Gundam. He was checking the microphone that was for calling out to potential customers.

"I bet you like *Gundam*," I said.

"Huh?" His eyes widened. "How did you know that? I was really into First Gundam. I was right in that generation, you see."

"It's written all over your face."

He tilted his head, unsure. When a Gundam tilted its head, it was very cute. But my best guess put him quite a bit older than that generation. I wondered if that meant he was a nerd.

As the day passed and I handed out the balloons, I saw all sorts of costumes, even some who were characters I didn't recognize. All of the customers came in wearing something. Some, like the manager, weren't in animal mascot costumes. One young woman looked like a ninja. Maybe she was the Red Shadow, Akakage. I saw dolls, including a Barbie and a Licca-chan. Surprised to see a walking doll, I lifted off the rabbit head to find another surprise—the youthful doll was suddenly an older woman. A stooped-over elderly man took the form of a baseball player in an antiquated uniform and a peculiar, flimsy-looking lack of depth. I puzzled over him for a while, and was delighted when I finally figured it out—he was a menko baseball card. Many of the older men were menko cards, and quite a few of those depicted sumo wrestlers.

Many of the little children were characters unfamiliar to me—probably because I didn't watch children's shows. But apparently Ultraman was still popular. I couldn't help but laugh when I watched a misbehaving Spider-Man getting scolded and swatted on his behind by his mother. Come on, kid, you must have seen the movie. A champion of justice should listen to his mother.

Among the stuffed animals, the panda was the most popular. Nearly all of the adults' stuffed animals were dirty, with some sort of damage somewhere. Many were missing an arm or an ear.

They were the remnant memories of forgotten toys. Some had probably been thrown away. Those were likely the ones so filthy it took me more than a glance to figure out what they were supposed to be.

As Ms. Tanaka had warned me, moving about while wearing the costume was exhausting work, and I was allowed frequent breaks. On one such break, I borrowed some glue from one of the desk workers. I wanted to mend Chiyoko's tears. I would have preferred to sew her, but I couldn't do such delicate needlework while wearing the costume.

The desk worker who loaned me her glue gave me a puzzled look and said, "But I don't see anything wrong with that suit."

I laughed it off and went to the locker room, where I performed first aid on Chiyoko.

At three in the afternoon, I was considerably worn out. On the other hand, I had become completely accustomed to the parade of stuffed animals. None of the walking toys could faze me anymore. I simply said, "Hello there," and handed them my balloons.

Or so I thought, until I saw one normal boy. The sight, though typically natural, gave me an incredible shock.

I placed him in or around seventh grade, a rebellious-looking child with a slightly upturned chin. He wore a T-shirt, jeans, and brand-name sneakers.

Since this was a Sunday, and the store had a school supply section, a junior high kid coming in alone wasn't anything strange. I watched him merge into the stream of customers and disappear into the store.

Had he not kept a cherished toy when he was younger? Did he still not, even now?

I figured that kind of thing could happen. I went back to doing my best at handing out the balloons.

Maybe one hour later, I was heading back to the locker room to take a break when I noticed a commotion in the rear office. I took off my rabbit head and asked a passing coworker what had happened.

"They caught a shoplifter." She made a face and added, "A junior high kid. He's a repeat offender."

My mind leaped to that boy who I hadn't seen as a stuffed animal or a toy or anything.

I asked, "Are they going to call the police?"

"I'm not sure. They'll contact his parents first."

A little later, after I'd had a cold drink and wiped away my sweat, I put the costume back on and returned to the front of the store. A taxi pulled up to the curb and let out a woman. She wasn't a stuffed animal or a toy either. The driver looked like Ambassador Magma, but she was a plain, ordinary human.

Her chin resembled that of the boy.

She had to be his mother.

She disappeared into the back of the store. Her displeased expression was incredibly out of place among the excited bustle of the Sunday bargain-hunting crowd.

As evening approached, the customers streamed in with increasing number. Even after I ran out of balloons, I was still busy, handing out fliers and giving handshakes to the children. But I would be done at six.

Just a little longer…

Then the woman and the boy came out of the store.

I had been right. They were mother and son. Side-by-side, they really did look alike.

Both of their faces were twisted as if being crushed by something. Your jaw will go out of alignment if you keep on making faces like that, I thought.

They passed right by my side. With the way they were barreling ahead, I had to step aside for fear they'd run smack into me.

That's when I noticed it. Something was clinging to each of their backs.

It looked like a clump of dust. Or was it soot? It was black and fuzzy, and something about it gave me the creeps.

Startled, I removed my rabbit head. I chased a few steps after the quickly departing pair to get a closer look.

Nothing was on them. Not on the back of the boy's T-shirt, and not on the back of the mother's blouse.

I put the rabbit head back on and again saw that black stuff on their backs, each lump now clearly in the shape of a hand, emaciated and taloned. The claws gripped the mother and son by their shoulders. And the hands were squirming about, resembling spiders crawling up their backs.

I shuddered.

What were those things? Whatever they were, I sensed they were very, very bad.

None of the people wearing stuffed animals or toy costumes had black hands clinging to them. None of them had been possessed by anything so sinister.

Back in the locker room, I took off my costume and leaned it against the wall. The shabby pink rabbit looked at me, expressionless.

"Hey, what was that?" I asked. "What did you show me?"

The costume, of course, gave no answer.

I thought about it. I thought about the eerie black things on the backs of that mother and son. I thought of the evils drifting through our world. Any of us could get possessed by them. And then we would do bad things. Shoplifting included.

I wondered if what kept most people from succumbing to that fate was the encompassing protection of the stuffed animals and toys.

Memories of something treasured.

Measures of something dear.

People lived under their protection. Without them, evils clung to us with tragic ease.

This pink rabbit costume showed me that.

I said to it, "You're amazing."

In the five years it had been left out in the storeroom, something had entered into the empty costume. Not something evil; something pure. It had breathed into the suit a mysterious power.

I wanted to have it for myself.

Could I get the manager to sell it to me? Wasn't I about to move into the city and live among all those strangers? What could possibly better arm me for my present and future life among strangers in the big city? Just by wearing it, I could see who the bad ones were.

At that moment, the costume's head turned to the side. I hadn't touched it. I hadn't moved it.

The costume had shaken its head at me, as if to say Don't do it.

Suddenly frightened, I stepped away from the costume. The rabbit's head turned the other way, returning to place.

Again, I hadn't touched it.

"You're right. I won't," I said aloud. "I have Chiyoko."

I thought I saw that pink rabbit make the hint of a smile.

That night, I called my mother.

With my clamoring on about Chiyoko! Chiyoko! she sounded bewildered as she said, "Chiyoko's in the closet."

"Bring her out!"

Oh, good, I thought. Mom saved Chiyoko for me. Oh, good. I'm sorry, Chiyoko, to have left you in some closet.

I'm sorry I forgot you.

"I'm back. Are you still there?" my mother said. "I found it. Now what am I supposed to do with it?"

"Is Chiyoko all right?"

"Fine, completely…a little dirty, I guess."

"Her paw hasn't frayed?"

After a pause, my mother answered. "It's been glued back together. Did you do that? How strange. I can see the glue sticking out. When did you do that? It looks recent."

I grinned at the wall of my tiny apartment. "I'm coming home this weekend, so could you leave Chiyoko out where she'll get some sun? Please, you have to."

"What are you talking about? Are you all right?"

"I'm fine," I said, still beaming. "I remembered Chiyoko, and I'm coming to get her!"

Because of this mysterious happening, I received something far better than a big paycheck.

I wonder if that pink rabbit costume is still put away in that storeroom. When will its time come again?

If you ever find yourself taking a part-time job wearing an animal costume in lower Tokyo, remember this story.

What will you see in the mirror?

Ningyo By Benjanun Sriduangkaew

This is the end, where she holds a wet beating heart that drips brine and shudders with bathyal cold. It burns her, as it should. Its salt is the smell of her death, its age and scars the map of her mortality. That too is as it should be.

Before that—

In her long life Tanayama Kazuyo has murdered naga, selkies, sirens, and various species of mermaid. None of them is ever the correct one. They have the greenest eyes or skin like black pearl; they sing in languages Kazuyo does not recognize, have names that twist and eel inside her mouth rather than the neat polished syllables that she's been hearing since birth.

(Her own are borrowed, first and last; the small name of a fisherman's daughter, Kamakura period, does not belong today. Has not belonged for some time.)

Kazuyo makes a habit of sampling sashimi wherever she goes, testing her chances, just in case her luck rises this once, just in case the flesh she eats is not salmon or saba but sliced from a long scaled body with a human face, with a primate rather than a piscine mouth. She does not eat as a connoisseur; it is a chore. It no longer matters if the tuna is the finest grade and melts on her tongue or if it tastes like crumpled newspaper and factory exhaust. Condiments are an afterthought, shoyu perfect or watery, wasabi real or imaginary. She eats it all, so long as the fish is raw and on her plate, until her breath reeks of bloodless meat.

She is disappointed each time.

She started eating fish religiously by her first frozen century, began hunting mermaids by her unchanging second. Kazuyo was indiscriminating at the start. Any aquatic thing that might have a nose like her own, any being of the river and lake that possesses a slender hand in place of a fin. She developed a reputation sheathed in baits and armed with hooks. She earned grudges, but when these get especially thick she veers inland, up mountains, into deserts—the drier the better, where the climate fetters and limits pursuit.

By a port or on an island her fate is chancier, but they are also the places where she may find conclusion.

(But all land is an island, a naga lover told her in a sticky bed veiled by mosquito nets. There was no killing between them—they had met after she'd learned to appreciate the distinction between a snake-woman and a mermaid, though both are notoriously immortal.)

There are many versions of Kazuyo's story, most of them even true. But they are not about her, not really. It is about eating what one should not have, about how taking a treasure unearned—even when one does not mean to, ignorant of its worth—can culminate only in sorrow.

In Hong Kong the sea is everywhere. Each sip of air is striated with salt.

These days even in such a place Kazuyo is safe from her ene-mies, after the war that eviscerated the sky and stained the waves black, full of knives. A conflict some thirty years past between China and a distant country. The latter lost; for this she was not sorry. Her memory is not what it used to be, but she can remember Hiroshima and recall Nagasaki in all their indelible details.

From the piers, she can see a faint sheen on the horizon if she strains her eyes. Beyond that line the air is poison and broken glass. Kazuyo does not know what the barrier is made of—prayers, willing dragons, a complicated dream—but it is a sign of China's power that the shield covers the entire mainland and extends this far. Life is nearly normal here, though there's not much seafood to be had.

The pier market is upscale, a Lane Crawford transposed out-doors. Rows of lipsticks in metal tubes, palettes of eye shadows, glass bottles of perfume and foundation. She appreciates it. Her time as a *bikuni* has instilled an ascetic streak that she often needs to defy with a dash of fuchsia on her lips topped with golden gloss, a sweep of silver on her eyelids tinsel-bright. Kazuyo finds plea-sures where she can and understands the lure of gilding one's life to ward off the dark.

She has reached the end of the market when her skin prickles.

She looks up, finds an old man selling a clutch of small pets. Her quarry is next to him, leaning forward and peering into a bowl of fighting fish. Kazuyo's heart surges, a tide rising to the source of her grief, the genesis of her misfortune. Her fingertips tingle, as though with desire.

(She knows that the real crime belonged to her father, a peas-ant who drunkenly fed his daughter a rare morsel; she knows that the real crime belonged to her, who petulantly asked for a show of favor. But her father is long gone, reincarnated who knows where, as who knows what. Her daughter-self is an eon dead.)

When she has pushed through the crowd the mermaid is

gone. Her veins are quiet again. In the bowl, fish twist and swirl in ecstasy.

🔥

"Doesn't it suffice to live forever?"

In the glass, two women are reflected: both are Japanese, but that is the end of their common ground. Kazuyo is styled modernly, her hair bobbed, her makeup neat—russet and black on the eyelids, peach and red on the lips. Ivory silk blouse, sleek. The other woman is a traditional painting, hair down to her waist, yukata loosely worn. Delicate wrists, hard thighs, the physique of a runner.

Kazuyo's mouth pinches. "It isn't that."

"Isn't it? So greedy."

Using the window for vanity she unpins a plastic pearl from each earlobe. A neon night outside, logos and billboards harsh on the Victoria Harbor. Always deliberately picturesque, as though the world is just like it was three decades ago, postcard reminiscence. Rumors say the power plants and factories are fueled by demons, and she is inclined to believe. Maybe metal spirits push the currents even now, igniting power sockets and keeping air conditioners operative. "It's different for you."

Ayaka holds up a plate of egg tarts, as though offering them to Kazuyo, who does not take it. That long hair twitches and slithers—in some light it might seem a trick of shadow, but here under the blaze of bedside lamps the movements are explicit. Locks braid themselves, ropy, prehensile. They handle the tarts with precision.

A crunch of rich sweet pastry; each mouthful disappears into thick lips the hue of cartilage, is licked by a tongue the shade of fresh ashes. Ayaka has tried to train her second mouth to decorum and quiet, with limited success. Sometimes she attempts utensils, but it is tricky to serve the back of one's head. Nevertheless it is neat and few crumbs are allowed to go astray. Food, let alone dessert, is a commodity more precious than electricity. In the tattered remnants of China's nemesis, Kazuyo hears, people starve and dine on softened shoes, on scorched rubber and jackknife wires.

Kazuyo has never asked how long it took the *futakuchi-onna* to come to terms—a truce, a partnership—with that second mouth. Kazuyo's own peculiarity is abstract and there is hardly room for comparison.

"It's not just that," she says again. The blouse goes, liquid platinum catching light. A livid cut underscores her side, red and ripe.

"That's not good," Ayaka says. "Haven't you had it looked at?"

"It's a year old." Kazuyo outlines it with her fingers. "Not infected, not mortified. It's just taken a very, very long time to heal. I try not to get paper cuts or little bruises. Those take months."

"There are disorders." But they both know that is not the case. "How long?"

"A while. Lately it's gotten worse." So gradually Kazuyo did not notice it until her third hundredth anniversary. (Of death, of being.)

A mermaid is currency for a vast range of results. To wish on, some myths murmur. To die upon, others insist. To obtain perpetuity, Kazuyo can attest. Only it's not a bite or a slice that she needs now but a heart belonging to a specific mermaid. She knows her chances are infinitesimal; she can no more chase the creature under the waves than she can seek it among the stars. Still, she likes to think that it is called to her, summoned by the power of its flesh, the trickle of its blood that must have hardened in Kazuyo like a perfect pearl. Today was not the first time she has glimpsed the mermaid. They've crossed paths in many ports, more and more often after the war.

The faces of her parents have faded, but not that taste, that texture of a mouthful of fish. Even the shore of her birth has gone. It doesn't look the same anymore; no point revisiting. Two hundred years short of a thousand: if she's learned anything it is the calculus of letting go.

Except this. Any equation, any formula, requires at least one constant to be of use.

"I haven't much time," Kazuyo says. As the world breaks down, so do the oceans. Humans might survive, spirits and demons of most types. But not those who depend on the sea.

In the bath the women scrub each other's back and Kazuyo washes Ayaka's hair. She separates the strands, pins them up, shampooing them handful by handful; the mouth hates the taste of any soap. After that she cleans around the pallid lips, wiping away traces of custard and pastry as one would off a child. The teeth used to snap at Kazuyo, but they have become docile, an animal recognizing that hers is a hand that grooms and feeds.

A futakuchi-onna is not of the cave or the cloud, the river or the lake; she is of no element save misfortune and poverty. A point of kinship between them, human made other, mortal made demon. Across centuries, though there is no relation between them in blood or origin, they are nearly family.

When they have dried off, they lie down side by side on a hard, thin mattress. Hands touch beneath the sheets, chaste.

At first Kazuyo chased an end but lacked the courage to try the knife, the cliff, the deep. Cutting or shattering or drowning—she did not want those; she only wanted to gaze into the mirror and see what anyone else might in time. The softening of flesh, the loss of definition, skin gathering up and crinkling. When that did not come she turned to ordainment in search of peace, but that did not satisfy for long.

She tries to remember the turning point. If it was Ayaka who tipped the balance, who gave her a reason. If it was her own heart fruiting with a desire for life, if it was her body straining toward survival. One day she wanted finality, the one subsequent she wanted to carry on.

Recollection dilutes, hemorrhaging potency like tea leaves in a scalding cup. When she dreams at all, it is of being pulled down.

Broad daylight this time, a morning so cold. A sky gridded by the nets that bride-veil and entrap the aviary—vestigial, for these days maintaining birds for their beauty is too frivolous even for a city so powerful.

Kazuyo straightens, turns: a jerk of the head, a hardening of the jaw. Beside her Ayaka grimaces, well used and alert to this look.

"I'll just be a moment," Kazuyo says, her heartbeat racing ahead. A hard sharp spike, as might presage cardiac arrest.

"It's going to take you more than a moment. Isn't it *enough*—"

"I'm falling apart." Like the world outside the barrier. She is already away, tugged forward, the end of a red thread but not the one that binds for love.

(Having lived this long, romantic want is almost beside the point. *That* thread is for people who endure, at most, to a hundred.)

She walks, marches, runs. Bridge and evergreen canopies blur beneath her.

The mermaid sits on a bench, hands primly folded. Anticlimactic despite the gun Kazuyo carries, heavy and barely used. She's had few reasons to, is rarely cornered to a point where it is the lone option.

Their eyes met, one pair human and the other not.

"Do you talk?" Kazuyo says softly, for after all who can tell.

The mermaid's head tilts, this way then that, a long moment before she speaks. No music to this voice: it is opaque, seafloor-shade. "Yes." The strangest accent. Not much of an answer.

In the ensuing absence of conversation Kazuyo stands motionless. It is a public place and there are security cameras; she may not pull out a knife, slash, and excavate until a heart falls out. She may not give chase, for the mermaid gives no sign of flight.

Slowly the creature lifts her wrist, peels away a lavender sleeve.

Little marks like bites where the scales were stripped, the skin filleted. "You've got something that belongs to me."

Kazuyo exhales, tenses; this she can comprehend—a fight, a hunt.

The mermaid moves too fast to avoid and grips Kazuyo's arm. She is not like the others, the wispy selkies and the lithe sirens. There's nothing delicate in this one. "I need your heart."

Kazuyo flinches, her words from the mermaid's mouth. *"You?"*

"A *yuki-onna* is bound to the mountains and the snow, a *kappa* to a single river or a pond, a *kamaitachi* to the direction of the winds. It's our nature to have limits. But the seas have become what they are, and soon I'll need to seek elsewhere for a home or else shrivel. Your heart will give me the world and a human's freedom. Of all who partook of my flesh you alone survive; by that bond I'll subsist on your pulse."

"I'm not going to die for you."

The mermaid frowns. "You've had close to eternity, far more than any human needs. And the part of me that you consumed won't always last."

Years ago—or decades or centuries—Kazuyo would have agreed, would have surrendered and bared her throat. Instead she draws with her free hand. Not her dominant one, but she's learned to be ambidextrous with most things. "No." A gun's weight is definite, better than words.

"You want to continue?" The mermaid glances down at the muzzle, curious. "It can't be a happy existence. It's not meant for you."

Kazuyo does not move.

"A trade. Your heart for mine, to fortify your vigor, buttress the reef and branches of your marrow. No sickness will take you and no fleshly hurt will wound you. You'll be vital as the deep."

"I'm not going to shrivel up in your place, either." Her fingers twitch toward the trigger.

"You'll be shackled to the ports and the shores, that is all.

Having my heart won't change your essential nature, won't make you grow scales. A trade; we both live."

"Give me time." This close the mermaid smells of silt and seaweeds. "I've to decide."

She doesn't wait for an answer; she breaks free, away. When Ayaka finds her shaking and panting at the park's exit, her hair is dripping wet, her skin ice.

🔥

It takes hours for Kazuyo's temperature to stabilize, for the shivering to stop. Ayaka's mouth is pursed tight as she wipes Kazuyo down, squeezing the briny damp from her hair.

"You aren't going to say anything?" Kazuyo licks her salt-parched lips. Her teeth have just stopped chattering. "It—she—offered me a deal."

Ayaka dips a cloth in oil, dabbing it at the smeared makeup under Kazuyo's eyes. "Why would you believe her? She's a demon."

"By most definitions, so are we."

"She's never been human."

"How would you know?" But Ayaka is right. "History's littered with people who got the better of demons."

"And people who were destroyed by them more often than not, their souls shredded or gobbled up, their bodies cursed. Look at the world; do you think it'll survive an age more? What is the point of taking a gamble that might trap you or worse, if there's nowhere habitable in five, six centuries? As it is you can keep going for a long time, no risk."

"Easy for you to say." She rubs away a smudge of eyeliner, blue-purple on her thumb, as of blood before oxygen exposure. More quietly, "I thought she'd be easy to kill. All the rest never resisted very hard, like they didn't believe anyone could or would want to. They were like goldfish."

"And this one a shark?" Ayaka passes her a mug.

Just water and flavorless steam. Kazuyo holds it close the way she might have held a cup of potent snake wine. "No. I don't know. She doesn't even *mind* that I wanted…I don't think she cares." She sips. "She's not interested in hurting me, just in surviving."

"For that she doesn't need you alive."

In bed, they do more than hold hands, but not by much. Ayaka's warm fingers between her own, binding as a knot.

When she thinks Ayaka is asleep Kazuyo loosens them, puts on a coat, and slips out of the room.

It's not winter, but the weather has changed so much that it is rarely less than frigid whatever the month. She can't remember the last time she felt rather than saw sunlight, and even that is a glimpse through clouds shot with sand and concrete dust. *Look at the world.* Perhaps Ayaka is right, despite China's vast fount of resources technological and supernatural or Tokyo's peculiarly bureaucratic collaboration with the gods and spirits of the land. People can't go on without sunlight, without summer or spring.

The piers are quiet this hour, too late for street vendors. Deserted other than late-night strollers who come out in search of what she can't imagine. Peace, release. Perhaps suicide. Those are not uncommon.

No guardrail keeps her from the waves. The Victoria Harbor pushes and pulls, a beat between her joints.

When she turns around the mermaid is there. The creature does not demand, simply studies her with that same alien detachment. Kazuyo couldn't see it before in the day, but the mermaid's eyes shine, the sclera undulating with anglerfish glow and jellyfish gleaming on shark bellies.

"I've made my choice," she says, extending her hand.

The mermaid nods, once. She takes Kazuyo's wrist. She pulls them off the pier.

They don't fall. The air softens. A silhouette of fins and tail, a visual trick.

In Hong Kong, the sea is everywhere.

On her feet, on land. Not under, where the black currents crush and the toothed fish sing for her fat and tendons. Her shoes sink into wet sand.

Lamma Island, Kazuyo thinks, approximates. In the distance ferry horns blare and Kowloon glows. The beach is deserted, the mountains rearing about them frayed and thin. This is outside the shield, but her lungs are not full of shrapnel, her flesh not blacked with radiative heat. Here it is not night; the time is a suspended minute between sunset and dusk. She thinks of Urashima Taro's dislocation in time.

In the shallows, the mermaid kneels with a yellowed knife balanced between her palms, shark or whale bone. She turns it in her hands as though to test its weight, to find the right angle. She strokes the flat of it, pinches the point between thumb and forefinger. When she is satisfied, she plunges it into her chest.

What spills is not blood; it is too black and too thin, a pelagic venting all cold and salt. The creature is silent, her expression disinterested, as she opens herself and the fluids of her veins rush.

Kazuyo catches the heart as it emerges gleaming. The organ is flesh and it is not, muscles and facets, the gravity of it gripping her fast; she can't let go of it even if she wanted to. She holds the mermaid's gaze. But those rippling eyes are indifferent, unreadable to the end.

To eat the heart of a mermaid might grant death or else life everlasting. It is a gamble. No one knows for certain; no one has lived to record it and no myth holds a definite answer. And perhaps even if she wins, all she will have is a lifetime to spend in decay as the world spins its last.

She puts the heart to her mouth and bites.

Thirty-Eight Observations on the Nature of the Self By Joseph Tomaras

1. After a restless night of torrenting bootleg hentai manga and trying to translate the contents of the speech bubbles, Aaron Burch, an Assistant Professor of Asian Studies and new resident of North Glamis, Maine, had his *tatemae* and his *honne* come unstuck from one another as he was mowing the one-acre lawn of his new family home.

2. The distinction made in the Japanese language between *tatemae* (建前) and *honne* (本音) does not appear analogous to the partitions of the soul made in other world philosophies. The first refers to the attitudes and behaviors human beings adopt in order to get along in society; the second, to what we inwardly hold, our true selves.

3. The first kanji of *honne* is *hon* (本), book. The second, *ne,* comes from the Chinese character 音 meaning sound. But the *ne* pronunciation is a particle conferring emphasis. To be a honne is to be a closed book, whose interpretation is no longer subject to dispute, not so much the words contained within as the noise of gross finality it makes when slammed shut.

4. *Tatemae*'s translation seems more straightforward: a constructed front. Yet the passive voice frustrates the Anglophone demand for definitiveness: Constructed by whom?

5. As used in Japanese, the distinction appears to be discursive and heuristic, rather than substantive and metaphysical. It does not refer to discrete entities, but to different ways of talking and thinking about the self. In this sense it is partially homologous to the Hegelian contradiction between essence and appearance, in that both taken together comprise a reality that cannot be apprehended in a single glance.

6. Therefore, a Japanese person would no more expect a honne to assume an existence separate from the corresponding tatemae than one would expect a shadow to detach itself from the body casting it. But just as stories are told in every world culture of such autonomous shadows, it is reasonable to expect incidents of such a separation between the tatemae and the honne.

7. Aaron Burch's tatemae—henceforth to be referred to as Aaron-T—continued mowing the lawn in a strict rectilinear progression, waving to the neighbors on each side as he saw them.

8. It should not be surprising that a tatemae would be capable of operating a push lawnmower, but perhaps for some readers it is. While in Western philosophical traditions it is customary to treat appearances as ephemeral, a moment's thought should make it clear that the tatemae has much greater need of the body's physical form than the honne. Whether bowing at the waist, offering a firm handshake, making air kisses, backslaps or bear hugs, our social being makes regular use of our corporality.

9. The honne, in contrast, has the luxury of becoming spectral. Aaron's honne—henceforth to be referred to as Aaron-H—chased after a blue-winged grasshopper trying to evade the mower blades.

10. "Please accept my apologies, O Blue-Winged Grasshopper, for cutting down the tall grass in which you were hiding," said Aaron-H. "I hope a bird does not eat you."

11. The grasshopper, being unfamiliar with the notion of apologies, mistook Aaron-H's cries for the wing beats of a blue jay and fled farther, taking shelter underneath a yellow toolshed. Aaron-H followed him there.

12. It was at this point Aaron-H realized that he had detached from Aaron-T, his tatemae, since otherwise he would not have been able to fit under a toolshed.

13. Aaron-T noticed no change, nor any grasshoppers, and continued mowing the lawn.

14. In fact Aaron-T remained oblivious through the remainder of the day, as the movers arrived with their possessions, and his wife, Chloe, and young son, Jared, followed behind, Chloe taking charge of directing the movers on the correct placement of their various goods and Aaron-T pitching in by shifting furnishings, repairing light fixtures, and otherwise acting as the very image of a good husband.

15. It was not until nine-thirty that night, after Jared had gone to bed and he and Chloe rested on the couch, both too tired to climb the stairs to bed, that he noticed anything different. What he noticed was not something, but the absence of something, namely the compulsion to retire to his office and begin torrenting.

16. For Aaron-H, Aaron Burch's true self, was a bit of a porn addict.

17. Strictly speaking that is not true. Aaron Burch's porn addiction was merely the sublimated form taken by an assemblage

of Aaron-H's desires and fetishes that could not be acted upon directly in any manner compatible with the constructed front that was Aaron-T. In Aaron-H, these desires and fetishes were now unleashed.

18. So Aaron-T and Chloe briefly watched a rerun of *Top Chef*, then assisted one another in heaving their exhausted carcasses up to bed, as Aaron-H, having wearied of his meticulous exploration of the strange world under the toolshed, began wandering the town of North Glamis to satisfy his fetish: the musky smell of a young boy's anus.

19. Of course Aaron Burch had smelled his own son's anus many times, at diaper changes, bath times and bedtimes, but never could he acknowledge to himself that this was the smell he found so deeply satisfying. To do so might have called too starkly to mind a detailed recollection of his first Cub Scout camping trip. Instead, he would rustle Jared's hair and put his nose to the back of his neck, reassuring himself that all he felt was simple paternal affection for his beloved child. This night Aaron-T had not even done that, simply pecking his son on the cheek.

20. For years Jared Burch had felt mostly safe but increasingly ill at ease with his father's rituals. Twenty years later, after several more-or-less abusive relationships with older men, he would in a particularly searing session of psychotherapy recall this night and date it as the moment that his father had begun to pull away, depriving him of what he believed love to be and continued to seek thereafter.

21. Aaron-H, however, did not venture into the Burch house. What he desired, he believed, would hurt his son, and he did not ever want to do that. Detachment was a gift. At last, he could flee and spare his child any pain.

22. It is only fair to assume that all parents who flee their responsibilities experience similar thoughts, sincerely believing that in fleeing they are sparing the child or children they love the agony of realizing what monsters the world set over them as caregivers.

23. For Aaron-H, at least, this belief was more true than self-serving.

24. That a detached honne can be spectral in nature does not mean that at all times it must be. If a true self's desire requires physicality for its attainment then it may assume a form corresponding to its self-image. Thus a detached honne in physical form usually looks much like the body from which it came, though often a bit younger, perhaps thinner, and with less definite facial features. So at various times over the next thirteen months, the residents of North Glamis homes in which there lived boys aged four through eleven would hear doors latching or unlatching, century-old wooden floors creaking, rustling in hampers full of dirty underwear, and occasionally, at night, the fearful cries of a child. As they searched the house for the intruder—often with a shotgun at the ready, for this is Maine—they might catch a glimpse of someone in the mirror, only to have him vanish before they could turn and aim.

25. Later on, these townspeople would meet Aaron-T at an elementary school art show, a firehouse bean supper, or the village store, notice his dirty blond hair, scraggly beard, and the husky physique of a high school running back gone a bit sedentary, and think, *I've seen this fella before, don't know where, but I don't like the looks of him.*

26. Aaron-T complained to Chloe that people in this town didn't seem so friendly. Having grown up in Midcoast Maine, she knew what to expect, or thought she did, and told him it must be his

Southern accent, the fact that he was so obviously "from away." "Give 'em time and space," she urged. "They'll warm up to ya."

27. In fact, she had already found her peer group of stay-at-home-moms and worried about her husband's apparent inability to make friends in town. She was especially perplexed by the reluctance of Jared's friends' parents to send their kids over for playdates. Aaron, ordinarily jovial, became gloomy whenever he came home. Increasingly he found reasons to work late hours at the university, attend functions on campus, or go away on conference or research travel. His constructed front had bifurcated: engaged and well-liked among his peers, resigned to domestic isolation at home, and preferring the former to the latter.

28. "Gotta make tenure," was all he said to her by way of an excuse. He still torrented from time to time—his research was on comparative graphic literature of the twentieth and twenty-first centuries—but now it was in service to the exigent demands of scholarly productivity, not an inner compulsion.

29. One balmy evening in mid-September, a housewife whose name has been withheld by the authorities but who everyone knows was Emma Farnsworth over on Pine Drive came home to find Aaron-H in her son Jeffrey's first-floor bedroom next to an open window, knee deep in Iron Man underpants.

30. He got out of there right away—in fact he vanished, though everyone assumed he jumped out the window and ran—but Emma got a good look at him. Since Jeffrey and Jared were in the same kindergarten class, best friends really, she recognized the figure as Jared's father, Aaron. A bit wavy, perhaps, in the lines of his face, but definitely him, she concluded, after about five minutes of failing to convince herself that there was no way it could possibly be. Of course she called the sheriff's department.

31. When Sheriff Dunleavy showed up on the Burch's doorstep asking where Aaron was but being cagey as to why, Chloe assured him that, whatever this was all about, there was no way Aaron could have been involved. "He's been down in Boston the last three days," she said. "At a conference. He'll be back tomorrow morning, so you can ask him yourself."

32. Unfortunately for the Burch family, there was no such conference. Aaron-T was at a B&B in Bar Harbor, balls deep in Su-Min Young, the new tenure-track hire in his department and a first-generation Korean-American by way of Flushing, Queens, who found his accent and his encyclopedic knowledge of *manhwa* irresistibly charming.

33. If he had been able to acknowledge this to Sheriff Dunleavy and his wife, he might not have been arrested the next morning for breaking and entering. Dunleavy would have loved to throw the book at him, but he could not find underwear sniffing anywhere in the Maine Criminal Code. The rumors all over town that he had done worse things to other little boys were just that, rumors, and nothing that could hold up in a court of law. All those kids swore it was just a bad dream, a bogeyman, if you could get them to talk at all. As a mere tatemae, Aaron-T had bound himself into an insoluble contradiction between his on-campus front as a friendly lothario and his North Glamis front as a devoted though antisocial husband and father. For more than a year he had lived without a true self to arbitrate his actions, and that honne had dragged him into a situation he found inconceivable.

34. Aaron-T spent the night in jail. Chloe bailed him out the next morning but told him that she and Jared were packed and going to Brunswick to stay with her parents. No, she did not know when they would come back. She did not know if they would come

back. If even one of the hundred rumors around town were true, she couldn't spend another minute with him.

35. "I never laid a finger on Jared or any of those boys," he swore.

36. "How can I believe that? Where were you?" she asked. In her mind, his silence was sufficient indictment.

37. As Chloe backed her Subaru out of the garage and down the driveway, Aaron-T took a seat in his. Aaron-H slipped in under the closing garage door.

38. Aaron-T started the engine and opened the windows; Aaron-H hovered over the passenger seat. As alarms began to blare in the house, Aaron-T inhaled Aaron-H through his nostrils.

Sisyphean By Dempow Torishima
Translated by Daniel Huddleston. Illustrations by Dempow Torishima

Chapter 1: The President Waited On

1

The date from which the tale is set forth matters little; to begin with the awakening of its protagonist is a mere convenience for the telling. Still, he had awakened just slightly later than usual this morning.

Clinging to the edge of a rusted metal deck one hundred meters above the surface of the sea was a row of tear-shaped sleepsacs, their gnarled and withered hind legs dangling from their undersides.

Nearly all of them were shriveled and dried, and only one, at the rightmost end of the row, yet retained its original form, swelling outward in the shape of a ripened fig. From the muscular tight-gate that protruded from its upper tip there sprouted the rather dimwitted-looking face of a worker. Borne forward by the action of lickstrings connected to the sleepsac's inner membrane, the worker's slender, naked form was vomited out onto the deck, trailing behind it sticky threads of secretion.

The name of the worker was GyoVuReU'UNN. Although he had no memory himself of having ever been called by that name, there were no other freewalking assimiants at his workplace, so this was not a problem for him.

The worker's shoulders quivered, and when he raised up his body, it was with movements similar to the curling of a burning piece of paper. His feet were dripping wet with amnesiotic fluid, and taking care not to let himself slip on it, he stood erect on a deck lacking so much as a single guardrail. In his ears, he could still hear the indistinct voices of countless, unknown colleagues whispering to one another.

"Stand up on the deck" / "I don't want to remember anymore" / "That was an awful sight" / "What's awful is it's just like everyone says" / "It's what they call collective unconsciousness" / "Like they had before" / "I don't remember that" / "I never seen it" / "Maybe you were just delirious" / "We've been really oppressed" / "By the way, I hear the next town over is closed off…"

The worker came fully awake as peeling, rusted iron bit into the soles of his feet. A sweetness and a grainy, figlike texture was spreading into every corner of his mouth. This was the flavor he always tasted whenever he came out of the sleepsac. Although the concentrated sweetness of dried figs was his favorite, the worker had never actually eaten one.

The last of the amnesiotic fluid dribbled out of his ears, a strong cold wind brushed against his eardrums, and the muffled sound of the waves came to him. At the creaking of iron that could be heard between them occasionally, the worker frowned.

Death awaited should he lose his footing. And yet it was always after the danger had passed that he felt most conscious of it. Seeking to ease the stiffness in his neck, he turned his head southward to look across the dark, steel-blue vastness of the sea, into the blur of mists in the distance.

It looked as though the deck were floating high up in the sky. At one time, the worker had been quite sure that it was, but then he was made to help repair the lift one day, and dangling from the edge of the platform had been lowered to about fifty meters beneath it. Or had it been the time he tried to escape by way of the lift? In any case, he had learned that day that the platform was supported by many long, thick steel columns lashed to one another. And on the face of the sea below his gaze, the waves had been crashing against a group of small islands. The steel support columns rose up from the centers of these islands—islands composed of rotting heaps of flesh: the piled corpses of stringbeasts such as coffin-eels and bloodtide wayfarers that had tried and failed to climb up to the office building atop the deck.

Pinching the left ear that was supposed to have been ripped off as punishment for having tried to run away, the worker looked up at the overhanging cliffs of landfill strata that towered above him on the eastern side. It was not merely a projection of his psychological state that made their striped patterns look different every time he saw them; even now, the willy-nilly counterfeiting of all manner of industrial products from the *eidos* of each one—and the collapse of those goods beneath their own weight—was ongoing.

Unable to entirely let go of his hopes of retirement, the worker made a visual estimate of the distance to the cliff. Although it looked rather close, he realized belatedly that there was no way he could leap across, and let out a long sigh.

He turned around and before his eyes stood the company building, looking like the tongue of some giant that had been cut out and placed vertically on its end. Skinboard-paneled walls that in the beginning had been breathing now bore the scars of the canvassers' repeated sales calls, and now covered in scar tissue the walls could no longer breathe easily.

The worker, having completed his commute to the office in only ten paces, set his center of gravity in his hips, slid open an iron door that was more than twice his height, and stepped into the stuffy, humid air of the corridor.

As he was closing the iron door, he felt an unpleasant, oppressive feeling, like being swallowed whole into the gullet of a coffin eel. He turned around and saw a pair of thighs right in front of him, with far too wide a space between them.

The worker's gaze crawled upward along the ridges of a special fabric knitted from muscle fiber, and sticking out from the wide opening of its collar was an eyeless, noseless, mouthless, semi-transparent head whose shape mimicked that of the office building itself. Tiny particles and a smooth, glossy sheen slid across its surface as it looked down at the worker.

"Mr. President!" the worker said shrilly, adding, "Good morning," once he had steadied his breathing.

Wrapped in a sleeve of knitted meat, the president's long arm twisted as it curled upward. Four fat fingers—their bones and nerves visible under translucent skin—pointed toward the inner room. Tiny bubbles of air fizzed from the spherical surfaces of his fingertips. When this was apparently insufficient to get his point across, he stretched his fingers still farther outward, and the pressure within his corpuscyte instantly ruptured the shells of the waybugs that lurked inside the digits. He showed the worker their still-beating hearts—about the size of sesame seeds—as they floated clear of the puffy clouds of red now spreading out in his fingers. The hearts continued to tick away with unnerving speed.

It dawned on the worker then that he had apparently come into the office later than usual. Was something wrong with his sleepsac these days? His regurgitation time was lagging.

The president's featureless face descended until it was right before his eyes. Within its interior, bone fragments, scales, and air bubbles floated, and a morel-shaped organ of unfathomable function bobbed back and forth with an irregular rhythm, managing to shift its position considerably though wrapped all around with winding, branching nerves and blood vessels. In the midst of a face that almost seemed made of inorganic matter, an indentation suddenly began to sink inward. All around the deepening hollow, the face was starting to roil with waves, until suddenly the hollow deepened and began to vibrate.

"GUEVOoOo—UENGuUuUNNuN—GUEPU, VV!"

The piercing cry reverberated all through the building. He was urging the worker to see to his disinfecting right away and get to his seat.

It was not, however, through the comprehension of words that the worker had arrived at this understanding; rather, it was the president's gestures and tone of voice that led him to that conclusion. The worker sometimes wrote down the president's words to try to learn to speak his language, but when he tried to say them aloud later, they would come out with a ring that simultaneously resembled the original and sounded nothing like it. Given the structure of his larynx, the best the worker could do was make a noise like a clogged sewer pipe backing up. Or like someone doggedly clearing his throat to expel a mass of phlegm.

The worker threaded his way down a narrow path along which wound a synthorganic digestive tract, and went into the powder room. The space enclosed by its scaly walls was only barely wide enough for one person to stand. Still, being there allowed him to recover a slight trace of his composure.

Standing flush against the wall, he lifted up the grated floor, faced the hole, and let his immature excretory organs do their business into a pit through which whistled a distant, vacant-sounding wind. Replacing the grated floorpiece, he then stood atop it and turned a brass, starfish-shaped handle on the scaly wall. Pure water, filtered through the purification tank, showered down on him from overhead. As beaded drops of lukewarm water drummed against every inch of his body, he grabbed a bar of winedregs hanging from the wall and began scrubbing away at himself, scouring off the filth that his eyes couldn't see. These dregs the worker had himself scraped from the bellies of winesprites.

A lock of hair got tangled in his fingers, knotted up, and came loose. Its gleam called to mind an image of glass fiber, and the worker stared at it, captivated. At what point had it become so faded and white? He was still too young to have his hair turning silver. He was only thirty-two, wasn't he? But in the instant that he thought that, he wondered again if he wasn't fifty-four. And after he had corrected himself yet again—*No, I was twenty eight!*—he stopped thinking about it. He grabbed a meatpleat that was hanging on the wall and wiped off his dripping body. The intestines of sand leeches formed droppings hard enough to use as bullets, so it was hardly surprising that they dried his skin in no time.

He went back to the corridor and pulled a gray work uniform down off the wall. It was the sort of business suit that an accountant might have worn long, long ago, but that was to be expected; for some reason all the clothes the company provided were a little formal.

When he arrived in the workshop, the president was slowly pacing in front of the faintly glowing dependency tanks, the varied medicine bottles, and the jumble of synthorgans lining the ten shelves that were built along the U-shaped wall.

Stepping forward at what he judged to be the proper moment, the worker slid—or was driven—into one corner of the workbench. When he lowered himself into a leather chair that was deeply stained from medicinal fluids, an IV drip keeping him quasi-alive, all three slabs of slimecake were already spread out on the table, sliced into shapes anticipating the organs they would be sculpted into.

Hurriedly, he slid his hands into a pair of skingloves ridged with stillvein cords. Experiencing the odd sensation of joining hands with some total stranger, he opened his toolbox and laid out the needler, the tube-shaped reaction mirror, and the other implements he would need.

The worker jabbed his needler into the cut face of the slimecake and injected the guidejuice, then the president held out his thick fingers—perfectly motionless—and forced from their tips waybugs about the size of grains of rice. At any given time, about five hundred waybugs were being nourished amid the currents of the president's body, receiving training according to their specialized functions. No sooner had the waybugs fallen onto the slimecake, they sought out the needle marks and burrowed in, expelling silver thread from their anuses as they tunneled along either vertically or horizontally, each in its turn raising a little ridge in the surface as it went. At last the waybugs emerged from the cut faces at fixed distances one from the other, and the worker touched each with a pair of red-hot tongs. Their shells split open with brittle sounds, and their bodily fluids sizzled as they vaporized.

Every time the worker saw waybugs crawling around like ants, his breath started to seize up. The sight always took him back to the hills of Stillville, located thirty kilometers away on the mainland. With pointed jaws radiating outward from bodies about the size of a puppy dog's, the ants there had dug countless tunnels into the coaguland, and because of that, a large group of winesprites, their shells piled up one against the other on the surface, had all at once sunk into the ground. The worker vicariously experienced the torment of suffocating while caught up in the midst of that rescue operation, while the president stretched one arm all the way up to a shelf near the ceiling, grabbed hold of a few things, and tossed them down onto the bench.

There were three different kinds of neurofungi. Their thread-like, raw-white bodies twisted and wrapped themselves around each other, painful even to look at.

The stupid things you come up with! If I died of suffocation back then, who is it that's handling these slime molds right now?

The worker drove the disquieting memory from his mind. He laid the molds down on a tray where a great deal of powdered dog-shell had been sprinkled and turned them over. This step was to prevent them from taking root in the slimecake too quickly.

When he first started here, he had worked barehanded and once let a neurofungus adhere to his fingertip. That had ended with him on the floor, writhing in white-hot agony. But now he was able to braid neurofungi into spiral cords with nimble, experienced hands.

It was a simple matter to tie the ends of these spiral-shaped cords to the waybug threads left inside the holes in the slimecake slices, and—applying a steady rhythm from the holes on the opposite sides—tug them on through. The spirals would resist with all of their might, though, so it was necessary to pull and stretch that carpet of meat as he threaded the fungi into the tunnels. Whenever it looked like one was about to get tangled, he would loosen it using crochet needles inserted into adjacent tunnels.

TAPUVuu—the president expelled air from a vacuole, breaking the worker's concentration. When he returned his attention to the task at hand, he saw that the last remaining thread had snapped. He pushed his crochet needles into the web of tunnels to hunt for the broken end, and the president pointed out the correct position with a fat finger. That finger, however, blocked his line of sight, and an unpleasant sensation, like having an eye socket covered by it, spread through him, until he felt assaulted—as though his entire body were being sealed inside that of the president.

The worker steadied his breathing and got back to work. In his thoughts, he retraced the correct route for warping and set to the task anew, but although he was still in the midst of the process, the president reached into the drawers and took out the first of the meat-colored blood sedges, jibāo-nets, and other tenants. He spread them out on a bracket that he pulled out from a column and started pointing at them with dogged insistence.

"If it's the tenants you're worried about, there's no need," the worker said.

Irritated, he had raised his voice, though the president quite literally had no ears to hear him. Although he did perceive sounds by way of a different sort of system, it tended to interpret the worker's voice as static. A roar of criticism was still emanating from the vortex in his boss's face, but the worker wasn't listening, and it washed right past him as he finished prepping the slimecake.

The worker massaged his cramping fingers, and the president crossed his long legs and twisted his body all the way around from the waist down, causing undulations in his reversed right leg. From the area around his ankle, sticky, leaden-hued waste fluids came gushing out and oozed down toward a hole covered by grating.

At last the worker took a limp jibāo-net from the bracket. Its webbed membrane, reacting to his body heat, began to slowly stretch and expand. Starving them a little made them clamp on better. A tenant that attached to a living creature would take the place of its original blood vessels, detouring the flow and skimming off what nutrients it needed to survive. The creature to which a tenant attached would not gain weight no matter how much it might overeat, and if there were some defect in its original blood vessels, its life might well be saved by it. For these reasons, there was even a tendency to see them as a welcome presence. However, once the parthenogenic tenant had finished budding and fallen into decay, the biological landlord would suffer harmful effects such as atrophied veins bursting when subjected to the pressure of a sudden return of blood flow, or obesity due to an appetite that had not gone back to normal after becoming thoroughly used to overeating.

As the worker was rolling out jibāo-nets on the slimecake, he started feeling hungry, though it was still early in the day. This concerned him. For the past few days, his appetite had been increasing strangely. Though it was true that the tenants had been given subjection treatment, he was being given raw tenants as feed every day, so they were in his stomach. It was hardly strange that he should suspect he might be ill.

The president's leg bent as it passed through his line of sight.

A distracting thought welled up in his mind of the innocent roundfilers who had escaped the employment contracts into which they had been born. They had come to make frequent appearances in his dreams since he had heard the rumors.

Roundfilers did the work they chose on the land they selected, and although they were poor, they lived as they wished—the jibão-net that had felt like ground meat in his hands was now like a cloth, thick with the water it had absorbed—and as the worker carried out his task, he began to imagine himself as a partaker in their lifestyle as well. As a washman, life was quiet and peaceful, his days occupied with the cleansing of all manner of grime and filth.

But then one day...

Here the worker's daydream began to take a turn.

A tenant masterhunter appears in the roundfilers' village, warning them that their bodies are being consumed from within by evil spirits. With a pair of shears, the masterhunter opens up the chest of a roundfiler, cuts out a jibão-net, and holds it up high above his head. The shadow of the jibão-net falls across his triumphant visage.

"See here! It's just like I told you. You see this disgusting thing? This is the evil spirit that possessed you. You have recovered your health."

Crowds of roundfilers, eager to have their own evil spirits exorcised, rush forward to stand before the masterhunter.

After the masterhunter departs with a great number of jibão nets, the roundfilers who recovered their health gain weight without ceasing. The image of them overlaps with that of the winesprites of Stillville, who continually secrete strong drink.

The worker shook his head, as if to drive away a swarm of leaf beetles. His head was enveloped in the odor of fluid waste, pungent as if from a rotting liver.

But that can't be. The winesprites couldn't have been roundfilers. Visible through their hemispherical, dimly transparent shells, those bloated, pitiful-looking subjugates resembled tumors. Once the worker had been concerned about one of the winesprites installed in Stillville. Its yield of spirits had been especially low. When he had called out to it, it had responded by spreading out hunting claws that resembled the pattern of veins inside a leaf, waving them about in midair, and drawing them up.

Ever since that day, the worker had carried the suspicion that the winesprites might not be mere jars for the brewing of spirits, but something more, something akin to workers such as himself. During one of the twice-monthly harvests, the worker had secretly brought over some tools from the office so as to pry loose a few of the hexagonal plates from its shell. In this manner, he had thought, it should be able to break through its shell from the inside and crawl out on its own. By blending into the thick fog that was peculiar to that area, it might be possible for it to escape from Stillville.

When the next harvest time came around, its shell was an empty hollow. Filled with joy at the thought that it had managed to escape, the worker had drawn near for a look, only to find a wrinkled, desiccated corpse lying inside.

At last realizing what had happened, the Board of Directors had gathered around the winesprite that had suddenly died, but then amid the fog there had risen up the shadow of a crossing guard, owing to which their investigation of its untimely death had ended without conclusion.

2

The boards of the many shelves that surrounded the worker were rattling.

The worker looked up when he noticed, and on the other side of the worktable a chest wrapped around with muscle fiber had twisted perfectly sideways and turned around to the right, placing that rotating, mortar-shaped vortex close enough to touch his cheek.

"I'm sorry. My mind was wandering."

The worker took a skin threader in hand, gouged a hole into the slimecake, and once he had threaded it with a tube-shaped tenant known as a blood sedge, an oily spheroid was thrust right in front of his eyes. Its entire shape was expanding and contracting at a steady rhythm. It was a type of cicada, called a "lubdub."

The instant the worker took hold of it, his arm shot upward. His own blood sedges resonated with it, throbbing to an accelerated beat and shattering the worker's composure. He pressed the lubdub down firmly against the workbench, jammed a guidepipe into its clover-shaped mouth, wrapped the wheezing spheroid up in slime-cake, and attached a temporary fastener.

From a cage beneath the workbench he dragged out a coiled pinsnake and removed the cover from its nose. Checking to confirm the drop of poison welling up on the tip of the pointed tongue darting in and out of its long snout, he pressed it against the throbbing slimecake and began sewing the edges together. While he was thus engaged, the pinsnake wrapped its long body around his arm and began squeezing so tightly that it hurt.

Using the wrapped lubdub as a base, he fashioned the rest of the slimecake into valves and atria, letting nothing go to waste as he sewed it all up into the shape of a heart. He stuck the tubular reflex mirror down into the blood sedge protruding from its upper portion to check the interior condition of the valves. There didn't seem to be any problems, so he peeled the pinsnake from his arm and returned it to the cage. Next, he took in hand the cardiopulmonary

tube of the spherical creature itself, which the president had violently dragged out after thrusting his hand back among the shelves, connected it with a blood sedge, fastened a clamp onto the point of contact, and tightened the screws. He pressed down on the heap of flesh with overlapping hands, and blood flowed into the inner cavity. The cardiopulmonary tube began to pulsate, and at last it all stabilized enough to beat a steady rhythm even after he removed his hands.

His eye sockets throbbed with dull pain. The worker pulled off his skingloves, disinfected his hands, and pressed a finger against the middle of his brow. As his lower jaw receded into a yawn, he took a deep breath, and felt disinfectant stinging at his eyes.

The president set a stainless steel tray on the edge of the workbench. It was his one feeding of the day. Stomach acid welled up in his throat, stinging like a rasp. Today's tray contained a maternity bug—its abdomen swollen to about the size of a fist—as well as some large and small scraps of slimecake, and a blood sedge that had died during its dependency and was just starting to go bad. As the president was lacking entirely the concept of "meal preparation," each of these items was presented without garnishment.

The worker retrieved an antiregurgitant and a digestant from the bottles lined up on the shelf and popped one of each into his mouth. Both were tiny pillbugs, albeit medicinal in name only.

He pulled a hose out from the column beside the dependency tanks, sprayed one turn of the lever's worth of water into his mouth, and swallowed.

Taking the maternity bug in hand, he squeezed its giant blood vitamin-rich juices onto the slimecake and blood sedge. He tossed the husk that remained onto the floor and picked up a scrap of slimecake that looked to be still somewhat edible.

With reluctance, he tossed it into his mouth; the acidic flavor vanished right away without a trace, leaving no flavor on the slime-cake at all. He chewed and chewed, but it only grew soft and rubbery, until he swallowed it down without having ever bitten through. It was still stuck in his throat when he put the next scrap into his mouth. His diaphragm tightened as when filling his lungs with air. Even with the medicine suppressing the revolt in his digestive tract, this was what he had to go through. For that reason, these had long been called "vomit meals," though vomiting was something to be avoided at all costs. Should he fail to hold it in, he would simply be force-fed his vomit again. It made no difference to the president either way.

A memory surfaced: he was crying as he was eating his lunch alone in the center of the classroom, while all of his classmates were moving their desks and chairs in preparation for the after-lunch cleaning. No, wait—he had always been one to eat quickly, so perhaps he was the one sticking a mop out in front of his pitiful classmate. Or was he the teacher who was forcing him to do that? Did that mean his present existence was his recompense for that?

That was when the president, moving as though to shelter a lover from a blast of wind, took a qizhong large enough to hold in his arms, and without so much as plucking the feathers, shoved it into his collar and swallowed it whole with his highly elastic stomach.

The qizhong, perhaps sensing its impending death, awakened from its state of suspended animation and scattered feathers as it flapped its wings, though presently it was engulfed all the way to the tip of its tail. The president's solar plexus bulged outward as if with a tumor, its surface changing into a distorted shape, and then the bulge slid downward all at once to his side.

The worker picked up the blood sedge that he had put off till last, lifted his face up to the ceiling, and closed his eyes as he tried to imagine it as a grilled calcot like he had eaten in a distant, foreign land that he could not possibly have ever visited. *I'm peeling back the black, burnt skins and inside there are steaming white onions*...He pulled the sticky strings from his fingertips and dropped it into the back of his throat...*and an orange sauce that smells of almonds dribbles from my mouth*...and ran down his cheek with a fishy stench.

Through stretches and contractions in his throat, the worker swallowed the blood sedge, but when he suddenly choked on it hard, it slid right back up into his oral cavity, slipping around and around his tongue. Helpless to do anything else, he started to push it back with his fingers when an embarrassing noise came bounding up from the back of his throat. The president, to whom this had perhaps sounded like spoken words, answered, "ZoVoVo."

After repeatedly rinsing his mouth out with water, all that remained was a languid sense of relief such as one feels immediately after a completed dental procedure.

Perhaps because of his disgust at this feeding, his scalp was covered in gooseflesh that wouldn't go away. This eventually transformed into a sort of itchiness that felt like countless legs crawling about, causing the worker to run his fingers through his hair, for fear that it was already crawling with lice. He didn't feel anything moving, but as he ran his fingers through his hair, tiny objects did stick to them. He caught some of them between his fingers and tried to comb them out, but they were stuck fast and wouldn't come loose. There was no mistaking it—these were egg cases.

They say that lice are attracted to certain types of brain waves, and although he had been tormented by their moist presence and the sensation of them threading their way between the hairs of his head, he had never actually managed to catch one, and even when he looked at his reflection in a dependency tank, all he was able to see was his own oily hair. Because of this, he had even wondered if the egg cases—which were the only things he could actually feel— might be something secreted by his scalp.

After spending the night in his sleepsac, the sensations of lice and eggs would be gone without a trace. Was this because the lick-strings inside fed on them, or because he recovered his peace of mind during sleep?

I just want to get back to my sleepsac soon, the worker thought.

The president bent over backwards in apparent displeasure, and from this motion the worker surmised that a guest had arrived. Soon enough, the building began to vibrate, and even the worker could tell that the lift on the far side of the corridor was in motion.

Quite some time ago, a giant mutant coffin eel had tunneled its way into the lift and gotten stuck inside, its body bent in the shape of an S. Although the president had ordered the worker to dispose of it, the toxicity of the outer skin was so strong that it was even listed in the Fishery Catalog of Hazardous Substances, so he had doused it in a putrefaction accelerant. Later, when scraping away the runny soup of liquefied rot that had dripped down onto the floor below, he had discovered an emerald-green magatama, such as should have only been possible to take from a canvasser.

The worker touched his shirt pocket. The magatama should have been hidden away inside, but his fingers couldn't find the dense little bead. Perhaps he had heard the story from a colleague.

There was a sound of folding doors sliding open and of faltering footsteps drawing near.

From out of the gloom there appeared a male bull neck, short of stature though sturdily built, carrying a packing case with both hands. Large drops of sweat clung to his wide face, and he was breathing with apparent difficulty. A worker from the fishery, he was in charge of on-site disassembly. Though he had thus far always arrived by boat when he came here, to the worker's eyes he looked for all the world as though he had crawled up from some Stygian pit.

The disassembler set the packing case on the floor and met his eyes for an instant, then immediately looked away in a most obsequious manner. This was in all likelihood because the worker had had sharp words for him the first time they met, when the disassembler had referred to himself as "I."

"That's *my* name," the worker had said. "I won't have you referring to yourself as 'I.'"

In those days, the worker had believed that "I" was a proper noun and his own given name.

Before then, he also had been indignant with the insect breeder for plagiarizing the way he looked.

The worker pulled on the skylight's control lever to close its slatted shutters, and when the workshop was completely dark, the president's body glowed with a faint light, and blurry shadows of his organs and skeleton became visible through his clothing. All of his waybugs could be seen crowding down into his feet.

The disassembler took a placoderm out of his case. Its shell looked as though it were made of complex crystals of stibnite, and its body reflected harsh flashes of light as it twisted and writhed. A high-pitched sound reverberated through the room as it abruptly snapped its jaws together.

Such fish, the worker had heard, could only be reeled in by a hook attached to a metal chain, and to that he could only nod agreement. The chained tendons that extended to its tail fin thrashed about vainly when held down against the lid of the packing case, but once the disassembler had pushed the long rod of his bonedriver in through the gaps in its armor plates to loosen a few of its screwbones, the tendons came loose, and it grew still, making noises of irritation.

The wide blade of a butcher knife he applied near the fish's gills, and with a scattering of sparks and an eruption of steam and bodily fluids, he lopped it off straightaway. As the fallen, armored head went clattering across the grated floor, he lifted the fish's tail fin and hung it from the shelf so that the cut surface faced a tubelike glass container positioned directly underneath it, and the high-viscosity body fluid used as bait began dripping into it.

One after another, the disassembler butchered his placoderms and hung them from the shelf. When he was finished with them all, he turned a sweaty face toward the president and asked for his signature on the statement of delivery/completion-of-work report. As he did so, he shrank backward, however.

With a single stride, the president came forward, stood over the disassembler so as to entirely overshadow him, then pinned down his trembling shoulder and jammed a fat finger deep into one of his rapidly blinking eyes. The disassembler stopped moving, panted out short, steady gasps of air, and when he had endured the signature all the way to the end, he departed with languid footsteps and a hand pressed over one eye.

🔥

The president lifted up one section of the grated floor. The ominous, armored heads still had their jaws clenched tightly. One after another, he kicked them down into the darkness of the pit.

The worker took the mucous-clogged glass receptacle, affixed it to the bracket that stretched out from the pillar, covered his eyes with a pair of slitted protective goggles, waited for the president to stretch out to his full height in the usual place, and then turned the control lever hanging down from the ceiling with his fingertips.

A single shaft of light fell onto the crown of the president's head. The beam was instantly refracted through his translucent body and shone out of the middle of his face, becoming a jittering point of light on the surface of the glass container. The worker gauged the level of turbidity in the mucous, adjusted the lighting aperture, and when formation was completed, pulled a number of solidified clumps out of the container.

Once he had wiped off the mucous that clung to them, the president's chest swelled out and let loose a *NVo* that sent several scales and a sulfurous odor dancing though the air. Shortly thereafter the top of his head began to foam. It was gas being released from the qizhong being digested inside him, most likely. The worker locked the next container into place. Although he endeavored to continue his work free of distractions, the beam of light veered wildly off course and touched his own shoulder, causing him to shut the aperture involuntarily.

The stinging pain lingered in his shoulder, and he was seized with an urge to fling the glass cylinder right at the president's face. Even if he did so, however, it wouldn't cause him any pain.

The president stuck a fingertip into his own face and began to slowly stir it about. His powers of concentration had reached their limit.

However, the job of solidifying the mucous still wasn't finished. Even so, the president reached up to the highest shelf and took down a skinbag shaped like a palm frond, pressed it against his ear, and squeezed it with both hands, injecting its contents into his corpuscyte. The fluid could spread out through his entire body in a netlike pattern.

The worker couldn't hold in a sigh. It was still during working hours; moreover, they were in the middle of a job, yet here he was *drinking*! Actually, it was not certain that it was liquor the president was drinking—it could have been some substance his kind needed to replenish in order to survive—but that eye-stingingly volatile aroma was clearly that which was peculiar to alcohol, and even if it wasn't, the president's careless actions became so awkwardly sluggish that it was embarrassing even to look at him.

The president straightened himself up, so the worker opened the aperture again. The beam of light refracted and spilled down onto the container, but its movements were slow and erratic. To make matters worse, the president interrupted him again midway through in order to gulp down liquor from a new skinbag. The worker felt like he was going to be drunk to the point of sickness from the aroma alone, but he somehow held together until the fourth batch of solidification work was finished.

Even after light returned to the workshop, afterimages of the beam remained in the worker's field of vision.

The president's upper torso turned toward the worker, leaned forward, and stopped just when it seemed he would tip over. Reversing direction, he turned back and slammed right into the shelves. Glass bottles filled with powerful chemicals rolled from the shelves and fell one by one. One of them broke and yellow bubbles spilled out. No sooner did they drip down below the grating than a cry arose like an alarm whistle, resolving itself into a voice saying, "Your mind is wandering." The worker's back broke out in gooseflesh.

It was a parrot. The creature was clinging pitifully to the underside of the grate, having crawled up from the bottom of the pit in hopes of partaking of some share of their leftovers. You could kill them off and then kill them off again, but eventually they would always show up again, incoherently imitating the voices of the worker.

The arm that the president had reached out with to pick up the fallen bottle was knocking tools off the workbench one after another, prompting the worker to rush to pick them up, saying, "It's all right! I'll get it!"

His skingloves blistered on contact with the powerful chemicals. He felt a terrible itching deep within his eyes, his feet swelled up, and his joints stiffened.

He wished that the workday could just end here, but the job of finishing the project still remained. It wasn't that he was being forced to complete it by day's end, but the calendar on the middle shelf, which resembled a globe covered in synthorgans, indicated who would be coming in tomorrow. Should the product not be ready on time, the one who would literally be cutting his own stomach open to get them over the finish line would be none other than the worker himself. He shuddered, remembering the kinds of things that had happened to his colleagues as clearly as if they had been his own experiences, then furrowed his brow, realizing that he had never even met those colleagues.

The worker lined up the misshapen, beam-hardened blocks on the workbench. The light was dim around him since the sun was beginning to set. He could see the president's body, thoroughly relaxed, sinking into blackness like the surface of a river at night. The worker took out a pair of torchburrs, each about the size of a fist and bound up tightly with pin-nets. Giving each a good shake to make them glow, he hung them from the bracket. The synthorgans on the middle shelves convulsed abruptly.

Bathed in green light, the worker applied an iron file to one of the rough blocks and started shaving away the unneeded parts. Once a winged, batlike outline had appeared, he switched to a finer file and set about finishing the complex, hollow interior.

Suddenly, the worker's wrist leapt up, and he dropped his file. This was because a wing that was supposed to have already been processed had started to vibrate in the space between the metal net and the torchburr.

Using tweezers, he plucked off the wing, and with it came vivid, sunset-pink muscle tissue that had been connected to the wing axis. It was still expanding and contracting. Frightened, he threw it to the floor. The wing with its attached flesh traced out a parabola through the stagnant air as it fell to the grated floor. There it stuck to the grate for only a moment before being snatched away by a tentaclelike appendage from beneath.

The worker set to the task of polishing the curved surfaces of the block using an emery cloth. To the steady sound of his polishing there was added another sound, as of some liquid coming to a boil. Despite a growing sense of puzzlement, he reached for the next piece and took it in his hand. The boiling sound grew louder, and he looked over at its source, which was the president. Beneath his clothes of knitted meat, great bulges suddenly swelled out from his chest or side, then receded, then bloomed again.

Having surmised what was about to happen, the worker turned his face away. The grated floor resounded with a shrill noise, and he felt in his feet the vibration of something heavy crashing against it. The area filled with grayish white smoke, and though he switched to mouth breathing amid the nausea-inducing stench, his throat was still affected, and he started coughing very hard.

Turning back toward the workbench, he gave up all thoughts of cleaning the place up at quitting time and devoted himself instead to the work of polishing. The president's feet were behind the workbench, and it was his good fortune that he was unable to see them. He finished the second piece and tried to connect it to the first one he had shaped, but they would not fit together well, so he picked up the file again and pushed it inside once more. Next time, they fit together perfectly with a pleasant snap, so he then injected a buffering agent into the cracks using his needler.

The president wandered around the fogged work area. Having nothing in particular to do with himself, he stared meaningfully at the synthorgans on the shelves. The worker rubbed at his chest; a kind of white noise to which he felt an instinctive revulsion was making it hard for him to breathe.

"Everything left to do is my work…" the worker said, suppressing a cough and clearing his throat. "…so I, ah, don't mind if you want to go on ahead."

But for all his words accomplished, he may as well have been talking to himself.

At some point his legs had started to tremble. The cold air that came crawling in from below seeped into his pores and took root in his marrow, and even a slimecake—warm with advanced decay—wrapped snugly around his ankles could not have driven it out, let alone the tattered scrap of a blanket he actually had.

The worker had been complaining about the cold to the president in various ways for a long time. He had tried shivering exaggeratedly and he had feigned being frozen to the point of immobility, but in the end his meaning had failed to get through, and an acquaintance of the president (a psychologist, apparently) had come in for a visit. That had been when the counseling sessions—or perhaps they were something entirely different—had commenced.

The translucent physician had sat down in front of the worker and encouraged him to speak using gentle gestures of fingers that swelled out heavily at their tips. The worker's puzzled face had cast a dim reflection onto the faceless, anthill-shaped head towering above him.

Relying on the nodlike gestures the physician would occasionally send his way, the worker had made a desperate appeal, explaining just how horrible an environment it was he was made to work in.

"It's important not to interpret everything pessimistically. Let's stay on the same medication a while longer and see how things go. Try going in to work tomorrow as though it were your very first day."

The worker was remembering the time he had taken off work for a medical examination. Had that been at the company where he had worked previously?

"No, haven't you always been told your only saving grace was your perfect attendance?"/ "That's right, it was because of that bunch who accepted leave that so many" / "I could see right through that, so I was the one who had to bear the guilt I might have otherwise…"

The physician had stared at the worker, though he lacked even eyes for doing so. The worker had blushed, realizing that he had not only been reminiscing, but also speaking to him aloud. Simultaneously, both of his arms dropped with a sudden weight and he returned to himself. Supported by both of his hands, the unbroken chain of the thick spinal column he had completed was arching downward.

Before his eyes, the president was bending down to inspect it. The worker raised and lowered his hands in turn to make the spine undulate, and even as he was demonstrating the smooth motion of its moving parts, he felt all the more puzzled, lacking as he was any memory of having completed so much of it. He pushed out a sigh from deep within his lungs.

The president's head moved like a tongue as it followed the curve of the spine.

Even after he had consulted with the physician, there had been no improvements in his workplace environment. Which was exactly why he was shivering even now.

"Bring me my samovar," said a sudden voice that the worker did not recognize.

"I've never heard of it," said somebody else.

"It must be some kind of anti-anxiety medicine," the worker muttered himself.

Making small talk, the worker moved the tips of his frozen toes. Like the fake red nose of a clown, he could feel nothing with them. And he wondered: what kind of creature was a clown?

The feeling of a cold wet nose returned to his cheek.

I wonder if that was a clown? Wagging its bushy tail—that was definitely a dog—no, aren't dogs those hideous bugs with the exoshells that live underground? At any rate, I was raising a stem pet with a cold wet nose. Kyoro, John, Mukku, Rick...Several of them, even dozens of them. Even when they barked, all you had to do was rub their backs or their bellies and they would be as gentle as could be. Now, though, even the innocent interaction of calming a dog was something he remembered only as a symbolic sort of give-and-take to which neither thought nor emotion was attached.

Rather like the physician's counseling. At times when the assimiant displayed unusual behavior, he would be sat down across from him and made to start talking about whatever he felt like. The physician would at suitable moments shake his head or make a show of dropping in an appropriate word or two. Mutual understanding did not occur. The worker was humiliated to know that in a corner of his mind a part of him was longing for the next session, because in spite of everything his mind would feel a little clearer after it.

Walking backward, the president slid away from him and melted into the darkness of the corridor. Perhaps he was satisfied with the completion of the spine.

The moment the president was gone the workshop grew very quiet, and sounds the worker had not noticed all day—of bubbles in dependency tanks, of the dull beating of the synthorgan he had completed this morning—became audible.

The worker lay down on his side, fitting the pointed projections of the vertebrae into their grooves in the shelf, and when he turned around, he saw a heap of excrement lying there like a rotting corpse, in a pile nearly as high as his waist. Broken bones peeked out here and there, and at the dungheap's base a number of trails and a scattering of holes remained, suggesting that it had been scavenged from beneath the grating in the floor.

The worker let loose in a groan what could not be expressed in words, and forgot to breathe in through his mouth. His sinuses were assaulted by a powerful, pungent stench, and tears welled in his eyes. Why did the president have to do it right here and not go to the bathroom? Or was that stuff not excrement? And even if it wasn't, why not lift up the grating first? Who was going to clean this up?

The back of his head was so tense that it hurt, but when he reached back to rub it, he found a solidified mass of piled eggs clinging there, with a number of short, needlelike things sticking out of them, writhing about. Lice legs?

With a sharp cry, the worker suddenly pulled his hand away. When he looked at the palm of his hand, he saw several red spots welling up, swelling into drops of blood.

Until that moment, he had doubted that lice really existed, so he had paid little mind to the story that went around about them—that late in the night their nymphs would hatch from the eggs all at once and consume entirely their host's soft tissues—but now that rumor suddenly took on a shade of plausibility that terrified the worker.

I've got to finishing cleaning this fast so I can get back to my sleepsac, the worker thought. He lifted up one of the grated floor plates next to him, pulled out a floor brush from under the workbench, and started pushing the sticky, heavy excrement over the edge. Amid the excrement a tube that was apparently a tenant started to move, so he squelched it with the brush. Though it was cold enough to make him shiver, that was all forgotten as his forehead broke out in a sweat.

"Everything left to do is my work…so I, ah, don't mind if you want to go on ahead." Overcome with horror at his own words coming back to him out of nowhere, he held the brush upside down and jammed the point down between the bars of the grating. Out of breath, he tried to drive the unseen presence of the parrot into a corner, though perhaps in reality the worker was merely moving around by himself.

The legs of the lice bit into his skull. He wiped his sweat and turned back toward the last of the solid waste.

Sprinkling some pesticide on the nematodes that had erupted from the mass, he scrubbed it all through the grating with the brush as though it were a sieve, pulled out the hose, and sprayed down the floor, wishing fervently all the while that he could resign right now.

It always happened, however, that the end date of his contract would pass and then automatically renew before he realized. Try as he might to remember, the date always disappeared into an oblivion of forgetfulness. From the start, the sequence of events by which he had come to work at the synthorgan company and the manner in which he had contracted with them were all a blurred haze. For some reason, an image rose up in his mind of himself being carried by a preacher and submerged in a river.

What had ever become of that colleague of his who had set out for the office of the Labor Standards Administration to file a complaint? Ah, wait. He came back long ago. Someone had told him that. So where in the world…?

"Well, your story's hardly unusual, you know—" He had a memory of being brushed off in that manner "—Everybody exaggerates how harsh their conditions are, but the preposterous things you're saying are just a little…you know. You make your president sound like a total nutcase."

The worker put a hand to his forehead. A memory of his monologue in front of the physician came back to him. It occurred to him that the distinctive assimiant features reflected in that translucent anthill had both resembled his own and looked nothing like him. Could it be that that face had been the physician's true image, viewed through a phantom anthill?

His former workplace in his old hometown had come to appear frequently in his dreams, and the worker had grown to suspect that he might still be working there, undergoing some kind of treatment or other. *I'm having a hard time dealing with my reality,* he chided himself. *It's made me weak, and I'm swapping it out with fantasies of bizarre creatures, like directors called "human beings."* He squeezed the lever at the tip of the hose. That hypothesis was itself an escapist fantasy, the most impossible part of which was that the people living in that town were all dreaming of being allowed to work at the synthorgan company in his place.

His sweat having chilled so suddenly, the worker shuddered

convulsively as he looked around at the dependency tanks, checking the temperature and density readouts of the dependency fluid and making sure there were no abnormalities in the color of the tenants slumbering away within.

He noticed that one of the blood sedges had turned dark, and used a pair of chopsticks to move it to a sealed container. That was when he heard a sound that was like thin chinaware breaking. Thinking it was just his imagination, he was about to move on to the next dependency tank when he was hit with an intense pain of flesh being rent asunder. Reflexively he reached back and ripped off the stuff clinging to his hair.

When he opened his palm, a swarm of nymphs burst forth like snowflakes from the broken egg capsule and started crawling up his arm. With his other hand, he tried to sweep them off, but the few that remained on his arm broke his skin with their pointed legs. The ones that had fallen to the floor also came crawling back at him, and it was as he was picking them off with a pair of tweezers and stomping them under his shoes that there came the sound of another egg case cracking open, and this time the nymphs started digging into his back as if plowing a field, sending the worker running out into the corridor.

His work clothes swarmed with larvae, so he tore them off and ran for the exit, trailing a low moan. Before the iron door had opened sufficiently, he had forcibly pushed himself through to the outside. Scattered nymphs danced into the darkness like snowflakes.

As he was stepping out onto the deck, the weight on his back grew heavier and began to squirm, as though he were carrying somebody there. As though heard from the bottom of a well of distant memories, there came a jingling metallic sound that drowned out all others, but he couldn't remember what kind of sound it was. His vision blurred with the piercing pain, and by the time that he in his panic had batted away the nymphs from his face, he was standing on the very edge of the platform.

Shoulders heaving as he breathed, he made his way to his own sleepsac, and forgetting his terror that a misstep would send him plunging down into the sea, leapt headfirst into the tightgate, into which under normal circumstances he would have carefully inserted himself starting with his toes.

Many fibers of spiral muscle undulated, and the body of the upside-down worker swayed forward and backward, rotating as it was enveloped by the inner cavity. By this process, most of the nymphs were pushed outside, and the ones that had attached to his skin were crushed one after another by the powerful pressure inside.

The worker, waving back and forth as he was moved by the lick-threads that grew so thickly amid the warm amnesiotic fluid, had already lost consciousness. And the thoughts of many others were beginning to show their faces.

3

Aah, the passenger planes are thriving, and every one of 'em's knocked up with a litter of Cessnas. **I thought that zone was supposed to be Nanodust-resistant.** *Never dreamed that metamorphic nanodust could ever range so far without even having any ultimaterial.* **Track One's at an impasse too, thanks to abnormal pipe and train car breeding.**

I just came back from my baptism. **Transference registration? Why that, of all things?** *Don't call it that; this is different. Faith alone can make the cherubim open the doorway.* **What are you talking about? It's six of one and half a dozen of the other, right?** *The Great Dust Plague is going to spread, and every protective measure we have will fail; before that happens, I want to repent.* **But they're still building evacuation boats, aren't they?** *I just can't imagine exposing my bare self to the defilement at this point...in a world where the Powder Room no longer functions...* They were in the middle of an argument, but before he knew it the worker had begun to stare emotionlessly at the movements of this pair.

Their vigorous movements began to blur, trailing afterimages before at last transforming into flecks of rusted iron. Although he had awakened the moment his sleepsac spat him out, he had gone right back to sleep lying facedown on the deck.

He gazed at his painfully itching arms, and found a swarm of small beetles clinging to them here and there. It was only when he tried to pull one off that he realized they were scabs. He looked at the inner side of his arms and found the legs of many nymphs sticking out like pins from the drum of a music box. He endured the pain as he plucked them out one by one.

He arrived at work and located his work clothes in the corridor, but of the nymphs there was no trace, and even the cloth that should have been torn into a million pieces bore not a single tear. Did the nymphs materialize only in front of him, then? That thought spun around and around in his head while he was putting on his suit, and then he heard the sound of the president groaning. The worker made a noise in his throat at the ominous presentiment this engendered. He wished that he could just go back to his sleepsac, but his legs would have none of that as they carried him into the workshop.

The president pointed at a dependency tank and opened up his face in the shape of a mortar bowl, revealing an organ within that resembled a rose. As he stood diffidently before the dependency tank, the worker was enveloped in a cry that by turns surfaced into the range of audible sound and submerged below its lowest frequency. He could not grasp the reason he was being reprimanded, though he did sense the seriousness of the situation. The surface of the fluid in the tank was covered in scum, and nearly fifty tenants whose color had darkened were jostling against one another.

At last he remembered that during the confusion last night, he had failed to check the last dependency tank. He felt something slick and wet on his right ear, and when he touched it expecting amnesiotic fluid, his fingertips came back red with sticky blood. One of his eardrums had burst, it seemed.

The president stretched forth both of his arms, brought them under the worker's arms, and lifted him up off the ground.

Was his head about to roll? Would his retirement benefits be paid even after the beheading?

The worker lowered his eyelids, and a flood of trivial and varied scenes whose ownership he neither knew nor could conceive of welled up in his mind's eye. *Aren't all of those my memories?* he thought as a sense of impatience ran through him. Even as he sought to dam them all up, his consciousness was drowning in memories, and just before his skull and his eyes were crushed by the overwhelming pressure, he slammed into the grated floor.

The worker, himself once again, looked up at the president, who was standing motionless over him as an organ resembling some kind of echinoderm retreated back inside his tongue-shaped head; a part of his congealed corpuscyte was rotating.

He was looking past the worker...beyond the wall...into the distant sky. The client should be arriving any moment now.

The president stuck a finger up in the air and caused it to rotate, and then calmly started walking. The fact that the president's indignation never lasted long was the one thing that the worker didn't hate about him.

Following behind the president, he went into a dock on the cliffside face of the company building, and there in a high-ceilinged space lined with exposed metal struts was birthed a ground ship resembling a whiskey flask turned on its side. Its tin-colored exterior was covered in countless scratches and dents, from which it drew a faint whitish tint.

The president raised both arms up high toward the ceiling and first pulled down a pair of chains to which hooks were affixed at the ends. Once he had put them under both his arms, he stood up straight, and the worker started turning the stiff crank.

The body of the president elongated as it was lifted up, and then slid—pulleys and all—along tracks in the ceiling, at last stopping directly above the groundship, at which point the worker climbed a ladder and began removing the president's pants as the president swayed back and forth as though executed by hanging.

Perhaps finding the sensation unpleasant, the president growled "*GyoVuVu*" and squirmed around, prompting the worker—who was having trouble with the fabric that had bit into the president's body—to coarsen his tone. "Please be still!" he said. Somehow, he managed to peel the pants down to the president's knees, after which they came off without resistance, exposing his bizarre naked form.

The worker looked away, but the following task of guiding him into the ship was also a part of his job. The president's corpuscyte began to collapse disgustingly, and as it did so, leg bones whose multiple joints had switched over to full articulation folded on top of one another and descended into the round entrance. His lower belly, however—through which his internal organs were visible—was sticking out of the ship in bountiful folds. Only his pale, wisteria-hued intestines unraveled as they slowly spiraled down into the ship.

The corpuscyte was like a festering tumor that the worker buried his hands in, fighting back a sense of embarrassment that felt like countless tiny fishes nibbling into the pores in his skin. At last, his hands found the hip bone that was caught on the hatch and shoved it down inside.

As the president's spine descended with graceful undulations worthy of an oarfish, his internal organs, tangled about with nerves and blood vessels, either clung to it or drifted away, only to be dragged down along with it. At last, when the remaining bones of his arms, pointing skyward, were completely inside the entrance, the worker closed the hatch. Up near the ceiling, there hung a shirt of muscle fiber that, like a discarded carapace, still retained the shape of the president's body.

Suppressing his fear, the worker climbed up onto a cargo

platform in the back of the groundship. The platform was a carelessly made thing—nothing but a pedestal with railing, really.

The groundship started to vibrate. He gripped the rail with both hands, bent down, and braced himself. As he felt the vibrations running through it, images of oarfish and roses came back to him in sharp clarity for some reason. Could the nymphs that had hatched have stimulated his brain in some way? More and more of his memories—until now so vague and indistinct—were taking on such tactile clarity that it seemed as if he could reach out, take them in his hands, and confirm their existence himself.

The wall in front of them, with its exposed truss structure, began to open up to the right and left. Just beyond that, a drawbridge had already been lowered, spanning the gap between the deck and the cliff face. A sticky rain was beating down against it. Following guidelines on the floor, the groundship slipped out through the door, and drops of rain slid down the worker's skin, trailing threads of wetness.

The steep cliff rose up before them. Unneeded industrial products, reproduced in perpetuity, collected there, forming many layers of unwanted things. The ship entered a tunnel in a layer formed of miscellaneous, tightly packed small items. The worker stared at reproduced goods that had all melted together and taken on a tin-colored hue, and then the ship came to a stop at a dead end that was also the bottom of a vertical shaft. Once more, the worker was exposed to the rain. Presently, the ship began to rise, accompanied by a dull, oppressive sensation. Innumerable skeletons of elevators and countless, crushed train cars and household appliances—replicated forever like reflections in a pair of facing mirrors—formed layers through which a vein of Dust wound its way up and down, and left and right, enfolding all like the arms of some tutelary deity. As they neared the top of the cliff, however, all melted together, growing gradually more dim and indistinct.

The glossy surface of the ground passed beneath his line of

sight and descended to his feet. The worker squinted. Beyond the threads of silver pouring down on him, the vast, bruise-colored expanse of coaguland extended for as far as the eye could see, covered all over in jellymire. It was so quiet here that he could hear the pulse of blood in his ears—as though the film that lay upon an out-of-focus land were absorbing all sound of the rainfall. With his hand he wiped away the sticky drops hanging from his chin.

The groundship was not yet moving, and the raindrops on its edges continued to swell like egg cases. When he was cooped up in the company building, he was always wishing he could go outside—any reason for doing so would be fine. But now that his wish had become his reality, he was oppressed by a nervous fear for the client and by the general unpleasantness of the rain. He simply stared off into the low-chroma sky, feeling nothing whatsoever.

It was right before—or possibly right after—he spotted a single ray of light shining beyond the indistinct clouds that he nearly fell off and grabbed onto the handrail. The groundship had started out across the jellymire. It gained speed as it advanced, and the wind that struck his face slid across his cheeks like a razor blade. Heavy waves rose up one after another with increasing power and slowly spread out into the distance, tracing out smooth arcs. So far as the worker was aware, the groundship possessed no means of motive power; it seemed as though it were rather the coaguland that was moving.

Before his eyes, pillars of mud rose up without a sound. The ship shook violently as it was pounded by the crashing waves. The worker adjusted his grip on the handrail as he endured the twisting in his stomach.

Far off in the distance, the landscape was broken by the pockmark of an impact crater. That was where the client would be waiting.

Many dark shadows were already beginning to rise up from that area, all of them climbing to heights one had to look up to see the top of. The mud sloughed off of them, revealing one gleaming black body after another, all covered in plates of shell that fit together like suits of armor. Segments of shell resembling mantis shrimp ran along arms so long they reached all the way to the ground, and in concert with their disproportionately short legs, each one swung its square shoulders back and forth, taking leaden, uncertain steps toward them. Brachia lining the grooves in their shrimp-arms began to spin at high velocity, sending the packed-in mud flying everywhere.

This was a brand-new settlement. The worker had been told that this was a business run by canvassers aligned with hostile forces—that their way of life was entirely different from that of the presidents and directors of all the companies, who were not adapted as they were to life in an environment of coaguland. It was said that an ordinary canvasser uses its brachialike caterpillar treads to travel tens of thousands of kilometers through the landfill strata. However, it was also said that once assigned to office duty, they would remain motionless in fixed positions for many thousands of years.

For this reason, the footsteps of canvassers were as slow as those of penguins, though if the worker were to let his guard down and be captured by one, there would be no escaping it by his own strength. Every canvasser also carried the title of Head Collector, and as such could skillfully sever the head of a worker with its sharp radulae and wrap it up in a head of whisper-leaves.

Something grazed the worker's face, and a dull metallic sound resounded from the hull of the groundship.

Supported on appendages that branched out from their legs to grip the ground beneath them, the canvassers raised up their incongruously long arms and opened fire. Even so, their proffered business cards—Hades Thorns launched from barrels in the palms of their hands—possessed only firepower sufficient to dent the armor on the groundship. Hades Thorns had not been weapons originally; they were in fact nothing more than seeds for the Dust veins, which gave life to the landfill strata. However, if a worker were to be hit by one he would not go unscathed, and should the seed remain in his body he might well end up being torn asunder from within.

Amid the flying thorns the worker was exposed, unprotected, and practically a painted target. As he clung to the cargo platform's railing, his fury toward the president mounted.

Ahead of them, a great host of canvassers were standing in the way, but the president wasn't slowing down at all. Heedless of the worker's vain screaming, the ship was beginning to tilt so as to charge through a narrow opening bounded by a pair of them.

As they slipped through, brachia bit into both sides of the ship, sending sparks flying through the air. Immediately afterward the groundship, under a hail of Hades Thorns, executed a half-revolution and started sliding sideways. It barely managed to stop by the edge of the crater formed by the fall, but the worker was thrown by the recoil from off of the cargo platform.

The jellymire heaved up around him ponderously, but there was no splash, and it stuck to every inch of the fallen worker's body as it flowed away from him in every direction. Fighting back against an icky feeling not unlike that caused by the touch of the president's body, the worker found his footing at the mire's coagulation depth and pushed himself up to his feet. It was then that he looked beyond the geometric patterns formed of the intersecting trajectories of raindrops and thorns and noticed a soot-black rock that resembled an oyster's shell sunk low in the bottom of the crater. It was the meteor carriage carrying their client.

He shrank away each time a Hades Thorn flashed by, but they were missing him by enough that he suspected they were trying not to hit him. Steeling himself, he began to half swim his way back to the groundship, which was about as far from him as the office building was from the cliff. By the time he had pulled the towing cable on the tail end of the ship over to the rim of the crater, however, he

was sunk to his waist in jellymire and unable to progress. As he was thrashing about, something suddenly blocked out the sun and his whole body went stiff.

Like the walls of some crumbling ruin, a canvasser was standing right before his very eyes.

It bent both its arms—each one by itself resembling some huge crustacean—and grabbed hold of the worker's midsection from both sides, easily lifting him up into the air. Its featureless, jet-black head unraveled as it pulled him near, its whisper-leaves slowly unfolding like the blossoming of a bowl-shaped flower. It was said that they used this organ to communicate with proprietors and with one another's departments.

At the center of the head of whisper-leaves was its saucer-shaped mouth, but what unexpectedly came out of it was not a radula but a swarm of insect larvae resembling snowflakes. In no time, a flood of them came crawling out, squirming in the midst of its bowl of whisper-leaves. The worker had no idea what was happening. Could the nymphs that had attacked him last night have been sent from this place? Or could it be that the canvassers too were tormented by eruptions of lice?

The worker let loose a scream from the pit of his stomach and kept twisting and turning as he tried to escape from the writhing things closing in before his eyes. By the time the canvasser had pulled him in so close that he could see the differences in the nymphs' snowflake patterns, however, he had given up entirely and was sinking into memories of Christmas. He recognized that it was the flashing of the crystals and the bell-like ringing of their wings that had induced such memories, but he couldn't escape from their hypnotic glamour. And yet these dreams as well were short-lived, ending with the collapse of the whisper-leaves in the background and the scattering of the nymphs.

A rusted metal shaft had been thrust into the throat of the canvasser. It had come from beneath the worker's armpit and extended all the way to the groundship behind him. It was but one of many coaxers with which the ship was equipped. The president's corpuscyte was squeezed inside. The coaxer withdrew, and the upper part of the canvasser's body began to tilt backward, as from the joint between its armor plates spurted slate-blue body fluids, mixed with waybugs.

The worker slid down along the coaxer and landed hard on board the ship.

There was no time for relief, though, as the body of the ship began to tilt. He looked up and saw two more canvassers starting to lift the tail of the ship.

The groundship continued to resist, swinging about three coaxers now; a fourth it pointed toward the crater that lay behind the worker, urging the worker to hurry toward it. On the floor of the crater, three canvassers were already huddled around the client's meteor carriage, shaking it back and forth ferociously as they tried to break through its outer shell. With each shock, bits of its surface layer were flaking off.

The worker jumped down off of the ship and fought his way through the jellymire as fast as he could. He reached the floor of the crater, and then, in the moment that the canvassers shifted their posture for a concentrated blow, reached out an arm and knocked away shards of broken shell. He slid the hook of the towing cable into the coupling ring that was revealed underneath and, dodging all the while the mantis shrimp-arms that came flying at him, climbed back up out of the crater. At least, that was what he had intended to do. His foot slipped and he fell back on top of the carriage, where he took a blow from one of their fists. Ribs shattered. The worker choked as he vomited blood.

For some reason, though, the assault stopped right away, and he felt the fists grow distant. Clenching his teeth, the worker opened his eyes. The multilayered heads of the three canvassers were all tilted in his direction.

There was nowhere to flee.

Looking out from between the canvassers and up toward the groundship, he could see the coaxers swinging about, feeling around among the innards of canvassers lying flat on their backs.

The worker pulled on the towing cable with a strength born of all the anger he felt toward the president, but the cable was too long and all he could do was haul in some slack. He could see the groundship's coaxer holding an emerald-hued magatama that it had extracted from the corpse of a canvasser. Almost adoringly, it raised it aloft toward the sunlight. But then the sight of it was hidden by the shadows of the ever-growing numbers of canvassers. Each head of whisper-leaves suddenly inclined downward and blossomed.

Was workman's comp going to pay out for this? And if so, who was going to be the beneficiary?

The worker was steeling himself for the end when from out of nowhere a wave of jellymire came rolling in and swallowed him up in its swell. With no idea what was happening, he clung to the towing cable. Suddenly, the meteor carriage had tilted and gone under, then it rose back to the surface as though rebounding.

The worker sensed panic from the president inside the ship. He took a look back, and the canvassers were scattering black splashes of mud across the landscape as they worked frantically to dive beneath the mire.

Clouded by rain, a colossal gray *something* rose up over them like a twisted, warped tower that was continually being built upon. As it slowly bent to the left and the right, it drew nearer, eliciting a sense of unearthly profundity in the worker.

Although its outline closely resembled that of the president, it was closer to the blood of the canvassers in color, and moreover of a gargantuan size that would make either of them look like small children in comparison.

It was a crossing guard. Unaffiliated with any cytan corporation, it was a "nonprofit entity"—one that brought no profit to anyone—a bringer of death to canvassers, directors, and workers alike.

Against that receding backdrop, the worker could see the armored shells of canvassers tardy in escaping as they were pulled apart by fingers that bristled from the ends of arms swinging down from overhead and internal organs resembling sea hares being sucked up out of them.

Once the groundship was again parked in the company hangar, its hatch sprang open, and from its entryway the president's corpuscyte overflowed. The worker hurried to get the president's muscle fiber coat for him.

Each time another mass of the president's body tissue injected itself into the clothing, a sharp pain ran through the sternum of the worker who bore its weight.

The body and breast of the coat began to swell, a translucent head started rising up out of the collar, and twisted sleeves pulsated as they took shape once more. Face-first, the president laid himself down heavily on the floor, then dragged his naked lower half up out of the ship, crawling forward with arms that had not yet finished regrowing their fingers. Although the bones of both legs were visible, they were all still clumped together like the organs of a conch. Along with bubbles of gas, a large number of Hades Thorns were being ejected through his surface, and a reddish curtain was unfurling inside him.

When the worker brought him his pants, the president's lower body began to split, and through peristaltic undulations of his surface layer, he steadily drew the fabric onto himself.

Once he had finished dressing and restoring his body to a shape suited to bipedal ambulation, the president, attaching himself to the floor with suction cups formed from the soles of his feet, drew up his knees, lifted his waist, and slowly raised up his arched back until he stood fully erect. Then immediately, he stumbled as though drunk and slammed into a wall.

The worker cried out from behind, "Are you all right, Mr. President?" but the president only put a hand against the wall and set off down the corridor, dragging his feet as he went. Following along behind, the worker was still dragging his feet as well.

Lagging behind, the worker made his way toward the workshop, and when he arrived, the president's shirt was rolled up, and a long, cardiopulmonary tube meant for synthorgans was buried in his solar plexus. He was giving himself a blood transfusion.

The worker left the room and in anticipation of his next task went into the powder room. When he took off his work clothes, there was an unevenness in his chest resembling a fissure caused by geologic upheavals, and blue-black bruises covered every part of his body. He turned the brass handle on the scaly wall and closed his eyes. He could hear the sound of the water in only one of his ears. Carefully avoiding the bruise on his solar plexus—like an overripe fruit, it yielded too easily to his touch—he cleaned away the sticky gum left by the rain. The texture of the jellymire that had clung to his skin remained, though. Even now, it still felt like it was all over him.

The worker changed clothes and headed back to the dock, where he found the front end of the safely recovered meteor carriage covered in a spiderweb pattern of hairline cracks, and a clear substance similar in consistency to a mollusk's body oozing from the places where they intersected. As he looked on, the substance suddenly overflowed, so after a glance down the hallway in hopes that the president might be coming, he resigned himself and put out both of his arms. Then, remembering that the average client weighed four times as much as he did, the worker hurried frantically back to the wall and rolled a pallet driver up to the underside of the carriage.

The blob of corpuscyte oozing down onto the pallet now poured forth in earnest, and though the worker knew he was looking at a client, there was practically nothing contained inside it, and it resembled nothing so much as a giant, glistening blob of fat. The blob timidly extended a slender antenna, twisted it to the right and the left, and then simply withdrew it. Then the entire mass began to sway as though it were being kneaded by invisible hands, and then presently stopped. In its present condition, it was not even able to move about freely. The worker could not even imagine a time when the president had been this helpless.

The worker pushed the pallet driver with the client loaded aboard, and when they entered the workshop, the president pulled out the cardiopulmonary pipe and dragged himself from the shelf he had been leaning against.

While the president was transferring the client's body to the workbench, the worker started prep for a series of delivery operations. From a medicine bottle, he pulled out a handful of stupa-toad eggs and swallowed them down to ease the pain in his ribs. He put skingloves on both hands and intertwined his fingers so that there were no gaps, then pulled a number of scrolls from the shelves, lined them up, and lifted up the spine that had been completed only yesterday. It was the first item for delivery.

The president took in hand the forward part of the spinal column, stuck it into the corpuscyte of the client on the workbench, and gradually pushed it in deep. The worker prepared the hips while the president worked in the spine all the way down to the tailbone, arranging it neatly for attachment to the body.

Next came the secondary tibia, and after that the primary tibia.

As they repeated this process for each of the major joints, the client's body—hitherto nothing but a blob of fat—began to take on a shape resembling that of a director.

The worker placed a scroll of peripheral nerves on the client's head and worked his way down toward the toes applying more of them. When the network of nerves he had laid across the client's entire form had sunk into his corpuscyte and reached every corner of his body, the president divided out multiple fingertips and continued weaving nerve fibers together at the point of connection between the brain and spinal cord. Compared with the president's everyday behavior, this degree of manual dexterity was truly extraordinary, and the worker was amazed every time he saw it. However, this kind of work seemed to wear on the president rather heavily, and for some time after a delivery, he would often just sit out on the deck and drown himself in strong drink.

The implantation of the circulatory system was accomplished in a similar manner, by which point the client's "body"—his corpuscyte—resembled an ocean filled with bobbing and swaying sea anemones. They continued working, fitting each cnidarianlike organ into its place and hooking it up. The worker understood what a vastly different environment the presidents and directors had been living in; without a certain fundamental ruthlessness of character, they could not maintain their existence there.

An upper and lower jaw, each lined with splendid rows of teeth, were submerged into the client next, followed by a windpipe. As for organs of vocalization, those were provided only to middle managers who had charge of multiple assimiants. Wondering to himself whether this client would be willing to listen to complaints about horrible working conditions, the worker pulled a bumpy length of intestine down from the shelf.

It was after he had handed it over to the president, while he was packing the intestine into the client, that the president's usual roughness of hand started to return. As soon as he finished putting the beating heart in between the lungs, he grabbed a skinbag from the shelf and went out into the hallway.

The worker gasped. He wasn't just going to quit midway through, was he? And yet there was no sign of the president coming back. The client was still waiting for them to finish. The worker let out an exhausted sigh. With no other choice before him, he set to work alone.

One by one, he pushed the jointed ribs into place, shaped the chest cavity, and by hand drew the cardiopulmonary tube near to the heart and attached it, watching carefully until the veins began to throb and carry blood to the organs. As soon as the lungs began their cycle of expansion and contraction, blood came squirting out of a spot where two blood vessels were joined, spreading out disquietingly like a storm cloud. The metal fitting that the president had put in place to hold them temporarily had come loose. Immediately, the worker pushed his arms into the corpuscyte to try to deal with it, but that didn't go well: on top of the poor visibility caused by the bleeding, his hands were pushed back by body tissues designed to expel foreign objects. As he was moving his fingertips vainly about, there came a succession of hard noises, like the sound of a typewriter. He looked up and saw that it was the client's teeth chattering. Perhaps he was experiencing a phantom chill due to the sudden, steep drop in blood pressure.

"Every day, I have to be cold like this too," the worker muttered, but then he spotted a cloudy redness in the abdomen as well, and there was no time to indulge trite feelings of superiority. If an organ delivery turned out defective and had to be recalled, he might well be called upon to provide replacements from his own body.

The worker pulled off his coat and, naked from the waist up, breathed out a ragged breath to steady his nerves. Focusing all his attention on the clamps, he reset them. While he was doing so, new hemorrhages were breaking out one after another, and the client's entire body was stained a ruby hue. Suddenly, there came the resounding noise of something being torn asunder, but because it had apparently come from the hallway behind him, he paid it no mind and lost himself in the task at hand.

🔥

The worker stood motionless, his arms hanging limp at his sides. Both were dyed red to the elbows. His head was heavy with egg cases. He couldn't remember what measures he had applied where. The client lay still on the workbench. Too still. Amid the fear that all of his organs had ceased functioning, the client tilted his head lethargically and let his jaw fall slack like some bad actor hamming up a death scene.

"*KaKaKa…Kaaaa…*"

The client's thick tongue flicked haltingly in and out and, after making the same sound many times over, uttered in what was clearly its voice, "R'lizided. *Dreenkided.*"

The worker was relieved that the client was alive, although at the same time he despaired of drawing any meaning from the words. The worker could not tell whether they had been spoken to an assimiant in some linguistic sphere other than his own, or if his voice simply wasn't working right.

He was glancing toward the hallway, thinking of heading back to his sleepsac, when one of the wall planks blew off and went flying. The upper body of a male lipocorpus—it was unusual to have a chance to see one—stuck out from behind it, then lay down on the floor. From the pair of cardiopulmonary arteries that protruded from its side and disappeared into the hole in the wall, the worker could tell that this male was a CP-type. As it regarded the worker, its eyes were like bullet wounds closed over with abraded skin.

Insensitively, the worker averted his gaze and turned toward the shelf. He suddenly felt very hungry, and without even wiping his bloody hands took a spoiled blood sedge from its sealed container and ate it raw. It didn't taste much different from when they were served at mealtime. He swallowed it with the intense nausea that accompanied it, and tears ran down from the corners of his eyes. As if in consolation, the client said, "*Telidagodabedd, herdares, eh, sodeforriseup.*"

The tears didn't stop.

The client stayed with them for about a week, listening to lectures from the president on how to move like a human being.

The first time he stood up was three days after his organs had been delivered, on the same day that the CP-type—having ceased to function—was removed and a new CP-type was brought in. The client's joints bent backward when he stood erect, and the center of gravity in his waist was shifted too far to the left, but even so he set out in an awkward walk, stopped at the threshold, and watched as the CP-type was being carried in.

The next day, the client made a slow circuit of the company building, and by the time a few days more had passed, he had mastered the art of bipedal locomotion. His habit of raising his knees too high persisted, but it was a more natural gait than that of the worker, who had still not recovered from the blow he had taken at the crater.

On the last day, the metal fittings were removed from the junctions where blood sedges now adhered. Like a pair of conjoined twins, the client and the president buried their heads in one another, causing a rippling interference pattern to appear along their surfaces, after which the client departed, going down in the lift by himself.

The president came outside and leaned out over the edge of the deck. The worker did likewise.

A flatboat was pulling away from the base of the synthorgan company. On its deck, the client lay on his back, bathing its rippling body in sunlight, reflecting flashes of light just like the oceans once had. Was he saying something? His lower jaw was moving up and down. Matching its movements, the worker gave voice to it:

AI, WIL, TEL ZEM, TU DU, BETR.

4

After the president departed for the board of directors meeting, the worker should in theory have been able to spend some time alone—his first in a very long while. Even with jobs to do such as knitting nerve nets and taking care of dependency tanks, idle times were practically holidays for him, and more importantly, he knew that if he didn't give his body a chance to heal he would never make it through the post-Festival rush when casualties would be carried in in rapid-fire succession.

However, a seriously wounded auditor from the fishery was brought in while the president was away.

Although the surgical procedure needed was clear from the explanation of the disassembler who had accompanied him, the worker still could not quell the anxiety he felt. Visible inside the auditor's face and extending down to his chest was nothing other than the upper half of an assimiant's body, gripped in a full nelson hold by the auditor's articulated ribs. Skin remained only in places; the muscles and organs were exposed. Every time the worker moved around the room, those clouded eyes would follow him with a slight lag. The fishery worker was being used, apparently, as a stopgap life-support system for the auditor's organs. There could be no clearer example of what would have happened to the worker himself the other day if that client's delivery of goods had been unsuccessful.

As he was unaccustomed to the job of connecting nerve fibers, the surgery turned out to be one difficult problem after another. The work was completed in four days, the auditor sent away before he awakened, and then the president came back. Once again, cruel and hectic days commenced.

🔥

Even now, the injuries the worker had sustained from the canvassers were not healed, and his physical condition was hardly satisfactory. With his broken ribs, his chest was still terribly uneven, and the bruise on his solar plexus had swelled up horribly with pus that stained his clothing. His spine had bent into an arch from favoring the cracked bones in his knee and ankle. And maybe he had just taken too many stupa-toad eggs, but a strange pressure had started in his abdomen which was growing in strength day by day. He always felt like vomiting whenever he moved around, and as before he would be seized with coughing fits and vomit blood. In spite of this, there was no change in the amount of work he was called upon to perform, and perhaps because of his misery, outbreaks of lice and egg cases began to occur even during the daytime. When the president noticed, he would suck them off with his fingertips.

Had water started pooling in the worker's abdomen? It had expanded to an unbelievable size, until he was no longer able to even bend over. Abscesses emitting foul odors were breaking out everywhere, and he often grew forgetful to the point that it interfered with his work. The president never grew indignant, however, nor would he send for that quack physician anymore.

Those old memories he could never be sure were dream or reality became altogether impossible for the worker to recall, and locked into a cycle of depthless, two-dimensional days, his work came to be a merely reflexive activity, like the nervous twitching of a spine.

But then one day when a frightful amount of blood had appeared in his stool, there came a sign that he might soon be freed from that cycle—it was a part of his swollen stomach that had begun to protrude outward—and move.

He touched the surface with both hands, and as he caressed it, it dawned on him that he was with child, and without the slightest reservation, he accepted the fact that she was female. She could even feel a vague sense of her past as a female. She gave herself over to a joy that rained down from above and bubbled up from within, and no thought crossed her mind for the obvious question of whose child this was…or of those immature reproductive organs of which she had always been ashamed.

🔥

From the time that she realized she was pregnant, the worker would often sit in a chair in the workshop and, taking care not to put pressure on the fetus, doze off into slumber with her hands gently resting on her stomach. She was no longer in any kind of condition for working. She was not even in condition for walking.

With her jacket pulled up to her solar plexus and her pants pulled down away from her stomach, her exposed, whitish belly looked like an enormous peeled boiled egg.

Having perhaps awakened to a newfound respect for workplace safety regulations, the president turned down the next work order that came in. As if that were not enough, he even went so far as to display concern, making sure not to run out of the stupa-toad eggs that had become the worker's only source of nutrition. Cracks appeared on her stomach, making watermelon patterns as the belly swelled to three times the size of the pregnancies in her memory, covering and concealing her withered legs.

The eggs also had medicinal effects, and it was during a long day spent dozing in and out of drowsy slumbers that she suddenly vomited, and the birthing process began.

From the rounded surface of her stomach, amid scattered bits of undigested toad eggs that trailed threads of saliva and stomach acid, blood and body fluids erupted from around the abscess on her solar plexus, and something as black and as glossy as wet crow feathers rose up out of it and opened its eyes. After they had stared at one another for a time, her new self came suddenly sliding out. It was as though she'd beheld her own decapitation.

The worker's body twisted with an agony she had never known, and in that moment her upper body was rotating around its own center of gravity. Her spinal column broke, bundles of muscle tore loose in rapid succession, and the ceiling and floor exchanged places. A grated pattern spread out across her field of vision. Its dark squares slammed into her face, and her front teeth cracked open, her nose was crushed, and her blood went flying.

With her damp nose pressed against the grated floor, clinging to the pain that pierced straight through to her parietal bone for proof that she was still alive, she turned her head to the side. She saw a newborn worker there, bending over backward as it was pushed from a stomach that now bore a shocking resemblance to a sleepsac. The president—when had he come in?—took it by the back and the nape of the neck, pulled the rest of its body free, and laid it down on the workbench.

The voice of the worker as she begged for help was not even a moan, but the president came over to her nonetheless. His face descended, made a noise that sounded like, "GyoVuReU'UNN," and just as this was answered with a sound of creaking iron, the worker was flung down into the gloom beneath the floor.

She fell like a soul that had slipped out of its true, flesh-and-blood body, and going down the worker surely saw it: the truth behind the parrots that hung by both arms from the grated floor plates through which they wrapped their fingers.

That was me. That, and the sleepsac too, used to be me.

The dim light from the workshop fell farther and farther away.

She was in an empty space with nothing she could struggle against. So empty that even when the end suddenly came, she wasn't aware of it.

Chapter 2: The Disassembler Searched On

1

When the on-site disassembler came to the synthorgan factory carrying his packing case, he stared for a moment at a worker who had assumed an awkward attitude toward him, apparently puzzled upon seeing another of his kind for the first time. He must have been born quite recently—his hair was jet-black and glossy, and his skin was fresh and young. *The cycles sure run fast here,* he thought with pity. He had just started to introduce himself as a worker from the fishery, when the young worker's face twisted into a severe expression.

"That's *my* name. I won't have you referring to yourself as 'I.'"

Just the same as before. The old memories didn't come back right away, so there were many cases where self-identification didn't go very well. They probably couldn't help latching on to a word that would provide a definition of who they were.

"I'm the on-site disassembler," he added simply, and then got down to work.

When the disassembler had finally finished disassembling the placoderms and was covered in oil, he requested the president's signature on the paperwork. The body tissues of presidents and directors were injected into his skull as recording media. By way of his eye socket, that swollen finger came feeling around inside his head, and he wet himself.

He had a headache as he got into the lift, to which clung the corpse of a coffin eel, its body still wrapped around all four walls as though trying to climb up on the nearly four-meter-tall cage. The cage shuddered and slowly descended. From between gaps in the elaborate ribs surrounding him on every side, the skeleton of an assimiant who appeared to have been swallowed whole was peeking out.

The lift stopped. He stepped off onto an island of rotting flesh and was loading his packing case on the flatboat when his eyes paused upon a small, steeply ascending island located directly beneath a vertical drainage pipe. It seethed with the gases of decomposition.

"What's the matter?" asked the pilot.

The disassembler turned his short neck and indicated it with his jaw.

"You've tried how many times already? It's hopeless. It'll just be a parrot this time too."

"I know. You're probably right," the disassembler said as he started walking out into the shallows of the putrefying muck.

"That gas is dense. You watch yourself."

He waved a hand lightly behind him and pulled his scarf up over his nose. After crossing over to a tiny island covered in bas-reliefs of bones and organs, he sank to his knees in putrid filth that teemed with cockroaches and nematodes and headed toward a figure that was buried to its chest on the side of its highest hill.

It was looking up at the underside of the faraway deck. Its face was exactly the same as that of the worker he had met just moments ago. When, breathing heavily, he made his way to its side, its eyes moved. They turned toward the disassembler and stared.

The disassembler knew full well, though, that this was nothing more than a reactionary response. The magatama was always passed on to the newborn worker, so nothing of their former intellect could remain in those who had turned into parrots. The disassembler lifted up the parrot's half-body, and they regarded one another, face-to-scab-covered-face.

"Hey there, you remember me?"

Rows of sparse teeth began to quiver.

"'Ey…member me?"

The disassembler's eyes grew moist. He recognized his tears as a form of self-pity.

Suddenly, he heard the sound of someone whistling with his fingers. It was the pilot urging him to head back.

"All right," he said. It was as he was setting the parrot back down, however, that the disassembler's fingers detected a small, hard bulge in the body's breast pocket. He undid its button and stuck his fingers inside. What came out was a magatama that gleamed with an emerald light.

2

At first, the worker thought himself—the pregnancy being little more than a biological and existential misunderstanding—submerged in water. This was because everything appeared distorted to him. He wondered if he had perhaps finally awakened from a nightmare in which he worked at a cruel synthorgan factory. After all, the room he was in looked a lot like the rooms in which the people of his hometown had lived. However, the familiar furniture and household appliances that were lined up against the wall were far too numerous, haphazardly pushed up against one another like animals snapping at each other's throats. The dim light was coming from a torchburr. Had there been a room like this at the base of the synthorgan company building? The terror of when he had been thrown from that structure came back to him, and he tried to get up, only to discover that he couldn't move in the slightest. It was as though he were buried to his neck on a sandy beach.

home><away> nothing>deep>depths>·<shell <seal <yoke <sin <

Suddenly lonely thoughts such as beggared his imagination came welling up, and his eyes filled with tears. Without spilling over, they remained quivering on the surfaces of his eyes, only to be swallowed up in waves of concentric circles emanating from the midst of his field of vision. From somewhere, he could hear a sound like a backed-up sewer pipe.

sign> flow> marge> destruction> · *<desperation <void <execution <world*—his thoughts ached as though themselves possessed of a sense of pain.

Days spent in longing for a return from that place of exile beyond the bounds of society—days enough to turn boulders into sand. He could remember them as his own. *Is this somebody's memory again?* He was thinking that it was, and the chain of thoughts that nested around the axis of that single point grew outward in every direction, forming a shell all around him, until they began both to complement and overturn one another.

Only in scattered fragments could he unlock their meaning, and when consciousness returned to him in that room, he could practically taste the presence of someone standing on the other side of the wall, of the disorderly layout of a multilayered, labyrinthine housing crystal lying farther in behind him, and even of the corpses that were sealed inside it.

Someone started walking toward him. It was not a worker from his own company; he looked a lot like the disassembler from the fishery. Though hadn't he just been wondering where he worked himself? Coaguland…number four, it was the Fourth Coaguland Reaffirmation branch. He felt a pressure near his retinas, and the wall appeared again, and the disassembler appeared from a doorless entryway, confusing the worker.

"You were pretty slow to wake up. I'd just about given up on you." The voice that came to him sounded like it was passing through water. "We are presently located inside a vintage landfill stratum. The metabolism's slow here, though, so there's nothing to worry about."

Fwaa ii zii—

What is this? was what the worker had intended to say.

"It must still be hard for you to speak. Can you tell, by the way, that you're being preserved inside a director's body?"

Images rose up in the back of the worker's mind of a director caught in the grip of several canvassers...of organs and multiple yoked-in brains being smashed one after another. A shudder went through the corpuscyte that covered his entire field of vision, causing the disassembler's face to waver about.

"This director took fatal injuries in a canvasser attack. They brought him in to the synthorgan factory right away, but there was no way to restore him, so they threw him out. Yeah...no hope of helping them once they've had their brains destroyed."

No, that isn't right. Those yoked-in brains are internal prisons that greatly limit the functionality of cogitosome-bearing corpuscyte.

"You'd turned into a parrot and were buried in an island of rot. For some reason, you were carrying a magatama. During pregnancy, the magatama moves to the embryo, so what you were carrying most likely belonged to someone who was swallowed by a coffin-eel. Magatamas govern the intellect and memory of assimiants like us."

They were not merely memory organs for individuals. In great detail, they reminded the workers of all kinds of things they had no way of learning by themselves, and in much the same way that landfill strata created counterfeit copies of things using eide from the past, they had succeeded in making those things real.

Now he stood unmoving in a dark alleyway, staring silently as many of his kind began to come and go along a street where time had frozen over. One of the parishes that had once flourished in the inner world of the canvassers—which had long afterward remained compressed and frozen inside the magatama—was unpacking into his neural network like a tightly folded paper being opened to reveal a completed diagram.

"Since you're using some stranger's magatama as a foothold, it isn't clear whether you're the same worker as before."

The worker started walking. He was twice as tall as everyone else, but nobody seemed to notice. He tried touching a pedestrian on the back, but his fingers merely sank into him and got tangled up in the strings of letters there. It dawned on him that an assimiant was something chosen out of the collected data of the fifty thousand people that a canvasser's magatama contained. That data was then modified and forcibly incarnated. He realized also that while here in this parish, he was himself in a comatose state.

"If you're wondering who it was that merged you so splendidly with the director's body, why that would be your newborn self. Not that he understood what it was he'd accomplished, mind you. I had originally hoped to play the role you're playing right now myself."

As he advanced forward, spatial distortions began to appear here and there, and the worker noticed that the space around him was dotted with gaps.

"Should've known I wouldn't be brave enough to be sealed alive in corpuscyte, though."

The reason the warps and the gaps were appearing was that in regions where the medium differed from the rest—most likely near things like the cogitosomes that were scattered throughout the director's body—only space constructed through classical physics was being generated.

"At the fishery, I couldn't even try to use a parrot unless I took it apart for disassembly practice."

The worker was headed toward a place of extreme distortion. It was a park where sunlight dappled through the trees. There a man in a white lab coat was sitting on a bench, nodding at no one in particular as he stared intently at a cliff face towering above the treetops. There was no mistaking that the cliff was made of landfill strata. Was there something special about the cogitosomes handling its construction? It appeared that they were showing him space from before the end.

A man in a suit appeared to his right. He held a can of coffee out to the man in the white coat and spoke: "With things having come to this point, I find it odd that you aren't getting registered for transference."

"Double-transference is an imaginary cyclical transaction. You should know that. Here even the magatama itself is nothing more than a concretion that the <World> brought into existence. Most likely, the replacement by ultimaterial that was done in order to effectively use limited computational resources has caused some kind of—"

"What on earth are you talking about?"

"—harm from deprivation?" He stood up, gripping the can tightly. "This is already a *fait accompli*."

"Probably so. Like they say, history repeats itself."

"Not like this." The man in the white coat tossed into the ultimaterial bin the can, which had at some point transformed into a light bulb, and stared firmly into the face of the worker. "Can't you feel a presence there behind you?"

"I'm not the type to believe in ghosts."

"After you came out of your coma, you had your share of freakouts, though. 'It's the man I saw in my dreams,' you said."

"And that's been taken care of through cerebro-physiological means. Now I just have dreams about everybody floating in the darkness."

"Right. That's because he's drifting through interstellar space in a one-man interstellar flight capsule even as we speak. By continuing to speak, he's protecting us. The coordinates are—"

"I'm sorry, but it's time for me to go. Work is work, even in a world like this one. I'm off to the canvasser now, so I'll see you later."

The man in the suit crossed over the manifestation boundary as he departed, and disappeared. Dazedly, the worker moved away from that place. He knew that the scene he had just witnessed could not exist according to the law of causality. In other words, this was not the past.

"Hey, are you listening?"

Double exchange, interstellar flight capsules—as he was strolling along unable to collect his thoughts, he bumped into an invisible wall. There were limits to the scale of space that a magatama could contain. The other side of the wall was covered in fog through which another town could be dimly seen.

"Even you must've sought after answers any number of times. Why are we employed by directors? When did we sign such contracts? What are we getting in compensation? Oh, we remember these things dimly. That we signed a contract, that we received a baptism. But why aren't these things consistent even in our own memories? What were these directors and humans originally?"

Those who are ever damned…those who long for return…those who trick us into servitude.

"Why are there magatama even inside the canvassers? Does it mean that those disgusting things—I don't even know whether they're alive or machines—are our original forms? Why? Why? Look—you must be able to see it!"

The worker looked across the parish town, and simultaneously he was looking down at it with a bird's eye view. Dimly, he could make out the ghost of the <World> constructed by the web of interconnectivity created by the canvassers'—no, the cherubim's—Whispering. But without whisper leaves of his own, it was only possible to comprehend as a real image the parish with which he himself was affiliated.

"Whenever a fundamental question occurs to you, the lice appear and devour your thoughts."

The worker strained his eyes at the rows of houses and streets on the other side of the fog. Transforming his arms into Code, he pried open the invisible wall and stretched out his hand toward the mist-enshrouded town.

"So we forget the inconsistencies right away. The same questions occur to us, and we forget them again. This cycle has been repeating for generations. When the nymphs hatch from the lice egg cases—"

Those weren't louse nymphs. They were bits of Code as well,

implanted by the directors in the roots of their hairs to prevent the lice egg cases from hatching—in other words, to prevent the activation of the snowpetal bugs, which were a self-defense mechanism of the magatama.

"—they cover your head like a lampshade and suck out every last bit of your soul. Even if you're disassembled afterward, there won't be a magatama inside."

That was because the snowpetal bugs would become temporary whisper leaves and bequeath all of the magatama's data to the canvassers' <World> network. In the present, however, where such dramatic reaffirmation was taking place at the borderline beyond which a certain sort of life support became indispensable, the cherubim—and thus their <World>—was on the brink of destruction.

"If that happens, you'll be left a CP-type suffering from hyperfrequent hemo-φιλία."

Regardless of whether business was good or bad, many things were needed to preserve and reunify the inner world of the cherubim: the magatama that served as its seeds, its dull aqua development medium, cogitosomes to expand it, and corpuscyte to protect the cogitosomes. Even if it were to all end in a reboot…

"W-what are you doin—?"

The worker was staring at the roads and the buildings of the two towns as they began to connect one to another, and at the same time, he was staring at the corners of the disassember's mouth as they cracked apart, opening wider and wider until the sides of his face had split in half.

The worker grabbed hold of the magatama stored inside the disassembler's skull, then pulled his arm back out. The disassembler collapsed like a puppet whose strings had suddenly snapped.

On the second floor of a certain hospital in the midst of the expanded city, however, the disassembler, who had been lying comatose, opened his eyes, turned toward the worker—who was watching over him from above through the window—and nodded.

As he hallucinated the ghost of a planet. Of a <World>. As he was laid bare to the directors' hunger for return.

Chapter 3: The Rite Came Off Without a Hitch

The workers who had been ordered to perform were standing in a line on a wharf near the outer edge of the ceremonial grounds with nothing to do.

The worker from the synthorgan company as well was standing on the cargo platform of the moored groundship, observing with a complicated expression the Festival that was also known as General Assembly. On coagulating land whose reaffirmation was complete, a great multitude of directors from all manner of businesses had gathered together and were crowded around a sacred palanquin. It was walnut-shaped, and about the size of an island. No canvassers came to attack. Already, many years had passed since the last sighting of them. With a presentiment that all things were coming to an end, the worker felt relieved and at the same time afraid, fearful of a future that he could not see.

Pushed along by the directors, the palanquin moved forward little by little, the ground beneath it crushed and turned up by its underside. Of those caught underneath and crushed there was no end; for workers, this was less a festival than an execution.

The shrine was ensconced in its appointed place, where it tilted just slightly before coming to a rest. Then the directors, bodies radiating visible light, began moving in ranks two or three deep around its circumference as the upper hemisphere of the shrine, rotating in the opposite direction, began to rise. At last it came to rest, floating in midair.

From the underside of this upper portion, long tubes known as fiddleheads extended downward, and the directors crowded around them. As the fibers of their clothing unraveled and dissolved, they were sucked into the tubes like snails going back into their shells. First one and then another; one by one, they disappeared from sight.

Suddenly, the bodies of those awaiting their turn began for some reason to undulate. All attention was drawn to a cluster of seven directors in their midst who were standing perfectly still.

They awakened in the worker an ineffable sense of otherness. The other directors surrounding them began to draw back.

It appeared as if those seven had leaned back to back against one another, when radiating outward from their feet there appeared cracks in the ground, exposing a greenish, translucent hill-like thing. For some reason, their fourteen legs were attached to its surface. Still crowned with the seven directors, the hill began to heave upward, rapidly expanding and growing in volume. It had apparently been buried to a considerable depth. In no time, the upheaval had become a giant figure with the seven directors stuck to its face, dragging itself up out of the ground with a terrible rumbling.

Its cyclopean body was ten times the size of a director, and a jumble of iron building materials could be seen inside its pale green form. It also contained a pattern of dark spots that in the right lighting would be revealed as the floating skulls of assimiants.

The worker looked on in utter shock and surprise. He had never seen a crossing guard this close up before. It appeared vastly more massive than before. Mowing down director-humans with its clusters of arms, the crossing guard swung from left to right a face where traces yet remained of the seven directors, and pressed that face up against the fiddleheads.

As the crossing guard invaded the shrine's interior by way of those tubes, steel towers, train cars, and the like were falling out of its body. They cracked the ground, and splashes of jellymire formed huge waves that began to engulf the entire area.

Many directors came running forward to try to pull the crossing guard's huge body out of the fiddlehead, but they were swallowed up instantly and their organs squelched. Numerous whirlpools

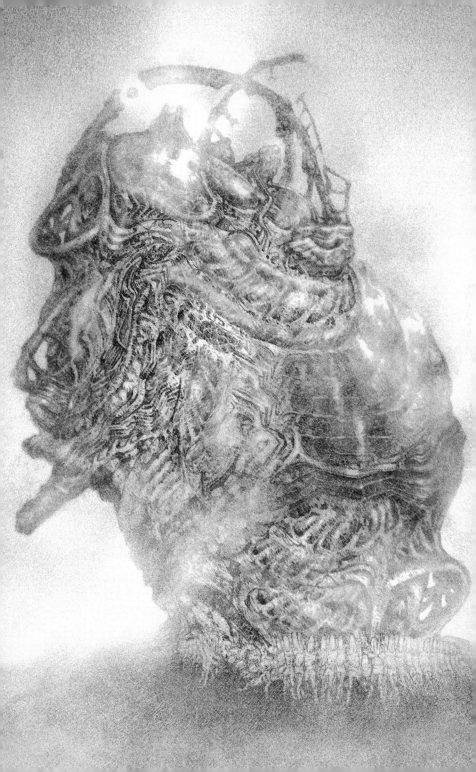

appeared all over the crossing guard's body, and with a deafening roar it moved into the crowd of directors, who cried out in baleful screams. There were also earnest protests from those who had voices to utter them.

INGuRoBaReMo, SoReBaDeSaGiMiDda, WaddaGoHome, DoToRe, WaddaGoHome—

As the worker looked on, the upper hemisphere of the shrine the crossing guard had hijacked lost no time in withdrawing its fiddleheads, and slowly began to rise higher. The directors lost themselves completely, and as they ran about in confusion looking for an escape, the space around the shrine grew distorted. In the space of an instant all fell dark as the light was sucked from the air in a radial pattern.

By the time a dim illumination had returned, the upper hemisphere of the shrine had vanished.

The many directors were lying on their backs, bobbing up and down with the waves of mud spreading out in concentric rings from the remaining lower hemisphere, and the survivors began to hurry as they tried to evacuate to the wharf where their attending workers awaited them.

This time, however, four long legs—wrapped about with thick, stringlike tissues through which not a gap was showing—emerged from the lower half of the shrine. They rose up vertically, and just as they started to twitch as they strained to their highest possible altitude, all of them bent in their centers. Like sickles swinging downward, they stabbed into the face of the land.

Now these four legs had become support structures lifting up a gnarled, bony body from out of the shrine's lower half. All of the onlookers were staring up in fascination as its body bent farther backward. A thin steam was rising from its surface.

The scheduled one, the true settler: a child of the planet—

said one of the terrified workers that had gathered together.

—come down to turn the screw of Earth's axis.

Beneath the four legs, the outer shell of the shrine rotated and began sinking into the ground. The child of the planet crouched down to peer into the dark, ever-deepening shaft, and jabbed the tips of its four legs down into those inner walls. It raised and lowered its joints as though they were loaded with springs and then started to fall forward.

Amid intermittent rumblings in the earth, a few weak shadows that the directors could hardly be said to cast came near the wharf. Among them was the president, his shriveled upper body bare and exposed. A cloudy pool of blood was visible inside his stomach. Utterly exhausted, he returned to the wharf. Then, as he was placing one leg on the groundship to steady himself, the body tissue of his face congealed into an oval shape that reflected an inverted image of the worker.

The worker nodded and said, "Shall we go back to the workshop, sir?"

A thought flitted through his mind of their remaining store of liquor. Would just that much be enough?

That was the last straw. Broken down into more than a hundred different parts, that which had been the worker was suspended in midair. It was the president's judgment call. From among these parts, the lungs, the liver, the thighbones and all manner of defective parts were levied into the president's body.

Finally, the magatama was removed from his pineal gland, and the remaining fragments of the worker came pouring down like rain on the jellymire.

Even now, with the land handed over to the child of the planet, the president was still waiting, and the next worker continued to do his work. Though the canvassers had been wiped from the plains of

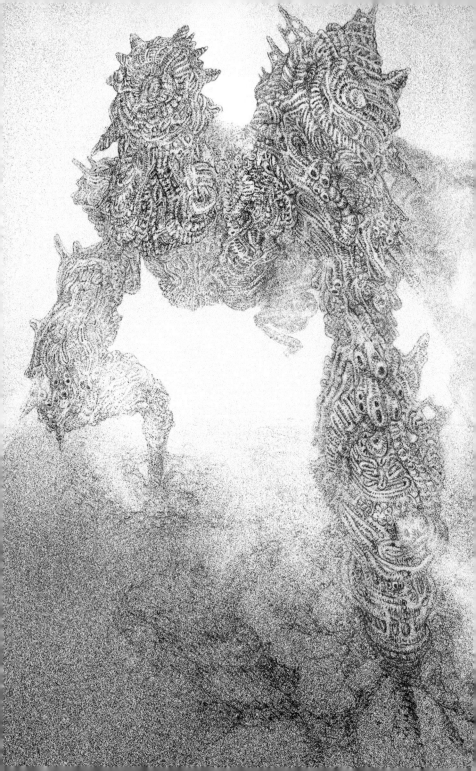

coaguland, a reconstituted <World> made up of many parishes continued to exist inside the departed interstellar spaceships. There
the people were menaced by the Great Dust Plague and underwent
transference to become canvassers. They were beginning to wind
the coils of an endless loop.

If a planet is a suitable cradle, exiles will surely be sent there to
reaffirm it. Assimiants will continue to be made from the magatama.
And the date from which the tale is set forth will matter little.

A Tale of Japan: Tengu of the Wood
By Zachary Mason

A hunter crept through the wood below the black mountain. He came to the edge of a clearing where a gray bird sat preening in the sunlight, unaware of the snake sliding up behind it until the snake struck and the two fell to thrashing in the dust.

Finally, as the bird's tail vanished down the snake's throat, a boar rushed out of the wood's shadows and broke the snake's back with its hoof; with a grunt, it set to devouring the remains. The hunter drew back his bowstring, his arrow poised to fly through the oblivious boar's heart, and the trees stopped creaking as the wind stilled, but then he lowered his bow and put the arrow back in his quiver. Cackling broke out among the treetops, and a wicked voice said, "I am the tengu of the wood, and if you had slain the boar I in turn would have slain you."

The hunter said, "I held my shot so as not to be a link in a chain of murder. And so, I have saved you as well, for the chain of desire is never ending." Both of them were silent for a moment, aware of the black mountain looming above them, the pressure of its mass, the menace of its snows.

The hunter hung up his bow and became a hermit widely known for his compassion. As for the tengu, he took on several fencing students, some of whom became notable swordsmen. He never harmed a human being again.

COPYRIGHT ACKNOWLEDGEMENTS

Introduction © 2014 VIZ Media
Foreword © 2014 VIZ Media
Five Tales of Japan © 2014 Zachary Mason
Shikata Ga Nai: The Bag Lady's Tale © 2014 Gary A. Braunbeck
Scissors or Claws, and Holes © 2014 Yusaku Kitano
Her Last Appearance © 2014 Lauren Naturale
He Dreads the Cold, © 2014 James A. Moore
Girl, I Love You © 2014 Nadia Bulkin
The Last Packet of Tea, © 2014 Quentin S. Crisp
The Parrot Stone, © 2014 Seia Tanabe
Kamigakari © 2014 Jacqueline Koyanagi
From the Nothing, With Love, © 2008 Project Itoh
From *Project Itoh Archives*, published by Hayakawa Publishing in 2010
Those Who Hunt Monster Hunters © 2014 Tim Pratt
Inari Updates the Map of Rice Fields © 2014 Alex Dally MacFarlane
Street of Fruiting Bodies © 2009 Sayuri Ueda
From *Uobune, Kemonobune*, published by Kobunsha in 2009
Chiyoko © 2011 Miyuki Miyabe
From *Chiyoko*, published by Kobunsha in 2011
Ningyo © 2014 Benjanun Sriduangkaew
Thirty-Eight Observations on the Nature of the Self © 2014 Joseph Tomaras
Sisyphean © 2014 Dempow Torishima
From *Sisyphean and Other Stories*, published by Tokyo Sogensha in 2013
Sisyphean illustrations © 2014 Dempow Torishima

CONTRIBUTORS

NADIA BULKIN writes scary stories about the scary world we live in. Her fiction has appeared in *ChiZine, Creatures: Thirty Years of Monsters, Fantasy Magazine,* and *Strange Horizons,* among others. Her essay "The Postwar Child's Guide to Survival" recently appeared in *The Battle Royale Slam Book,* published by Haikasoru. She lives in Washington, D.C., works in research, and tends her garden of student debt sowed by two political science degrees. For more, see nadiabulkin.wordpress.com.

KEIKAKU (PROJECT) ITOH was born in Tokyo in 1974. He graduated from Musashino Art University. In 2007, he debuted with *Gyakusatsu Kikan (Genocidal Organ)* and took first prize in the Best SF of 2007 in *SF Magazine.* His novel *Harmony* won both the Seiun and Japan SF awards, and its English-language edition won the Philip K. Dick Award Special Citation. He is also the author of *Metal Gear Solid: Guns of the Patriots,* a Japanese-language novel based on the popular video game series. All three of his novels are available in English from Haikasoru. After a long battle with cancer, Itoh passed away in March 2009. The translation of his novella "The Indifference Engine," which appeared in *The Future Is Japanese,* was nominated for the 2012 Shirley Jackson Award.

YUSAKU KITANO was born in Hyogo Prefecture and currently lives in Osaka. Kitano worked in an office until his writing career was launched in 1992 with the selection of his novel *Mukasi kasei no atta basho* (Where Mars Had Once Been) for the Award of Excellence in the Japan Fantasy Novel Awards. The same year, his script *Geocentric Theory* earned the first Jakusaburo Katsura Yagurahai Award for best new *rakugo.* In 2001, Kitano's *Kame-kun* was awarded the 22nd Japan SF Award. In addition to prose fiction, Kitano writes in a variety of forms, including theater, rakugo and recitals, and radio dramas. His numerous novels include *Doughnuts, Doronko Rondo, Kitsune no Tsuki,* and *Shaintachi.*

JACQUELINE KOYANAGI is the author of *Ascension: A Tangled Axon Novel.* She was born in Ohio to a Japanese-Southern-American family, eventually moved to Georgia, and earned a degree in anthropology with a minor in religion. Her stories feature queer women of color, folks with disabilities, neuroatypical characters, and diverse relationship styles, because she grew tired of not seeing enough of herself and the people she loves reflected in genre fiction. She now resides in Colorado where she weaves all manner of things, including stories, chainmaille jewelry, and a life with her loved ones and dog.

ALEX DALLY MACFARLANE is a writer, editor and historian. When not researching narrative maps in the legendary traditions of Alexander III of Macedon, she writes stories, found in *Clarkesworld Magazine, Interfictions Online, Strange Horizons, Beneath Ceaseless Skies,* and the anthologies *Solaris Rising 3, Gigantic Worlds, Upgraded, Heiresses of Russ 2013: The Year's Best Lesbian Speculative Fiction,* and *The Year's Best Science Fiction & Fantasy: 2014.* Poetry can be found in *Stone Telling, The Moment of Change,* and *Here, We Cross.* She is the editor of *Aliens: Recent Encounters* (2013) and *The Mammoth Book of SF Stories by Women* (2014).

ZACHARY MASON is the author of *The Lost Books of the Odyssey* (FSG, 2010). His next books, *Void Star* and *Metamorphica,* will be published in 2015 and 2016.

MIYUKI MIYABE's first novel was published in 1987, and since that time she has become one of Japan's most popular and best-selling authors. Miyabe's 2007 novel *Brave Story* won The Batchelder Award for best children's book in translation from the American Library Association. Seven of her novels have been translated into English, as has her collection of short ghost stories, *Apparitions.*

TIM PRATT's stories have appeared in *The Best American Short Stories*, *The Year's Best Fantasy*, *The Mammoth Book of Best New Horror*, and other nice places. His most recent collection is *Antiquities and Tangibles and Other Stories*. He's won a Hugo Award for his short fiction and has been a finalist for World Fantasy, Sturgeon, Stoker, Mythopoeic, and Nebula Awards. He lives in Berkeley, CA with his wife, writer Heather Shaw, and their son. For more:www.timpratt.org, or follow @timpratt on Twitter.

BENJANUN SRIDUANGKAEW is a finalist for the Campbell Award for Best New Writer. Her short fiction has appeared in Tor.com, *Clarkesworld*, *Beneath Ceaseless Skies*, various Mammoth Books and best of the year collections. Her contemporary fantasy novella *Scale-Bright* is forthcoming from Immersion Press. She can be found online at beekian.wordpress.com and @bees_ja.

SEIA TANABE was born in Osaka in 1982. Her "Kuntou" received an honorable mention in the Fourth BK1 Ghost Story Award in 2006, and Tanabe was subsequently awarded the Japan Horror Novel Award's short story prize for "Ikibyobu." Her novels and short stories focus mainly on ghosts, with her latest work being *Amedama: Seia Mononokegatari*. Together with anthologist Masao Higashi, she has been active in Furusato Kaidan charity events to raise money for the victims of the Tohoku earthquake and tsunami disaster, collecting true ghost stories, and periodically speaking at ghost story events.

JOSEPH TOMARAS lives in a small town in Maine. His fiction has appeared, or is forthcoming soon, in *The Big Click*, *M*, *FLAPPERHOUSE*, and *Things You Can Create*. He mows the lawn and clears snow, tweets (@epateur) and blogs at skinseller.blogspot.com.

DEMPOW TORISHIMA was born in Osaka. He graduated from Osaka College of Art and works as a freelance designer and illustrator. He won the Sogen SF Short Story Award with his debut fiction, "Sisyphean" (Kaikin no to) in 2011. Since then, he has been writing a series of stories in the same far-future world of "Sisyphean," which was published as *Sisyphean and Other Stories* in 2013. The collection was chosen as the best SF of 2013 in *SF Magazine*, won the Japan SF Award, and was nominated for the Seiun Award in 2014.

Born in Hyogo Prefecture, **SAYURI UEDA** is one of the more innovative science fiction authors in Japan. She won the 2003 Komatsu Sakyo Award with her debut novel, *Mars Dark Ballade*. *The Cage of Zeus*, her second novel, was originally published in 2004. Her recent short fiction collection, *Uobune, Kemonobune* (Fish Boat, Animal Boat), was highly acclaimed in the SF community and was nominated for the 2009 Japan SF Award. Also nominated for the Seiun Award in the short story category was "Kotori no haka" (The Grave of the Bird) from the collection. Her novel *Karyu no miya* (The Ocean Chronicles) won the first prize of Best SF 2010 in *SF Magazine* and was one of the most noteworthy books of the year in any genre. She published the sequel to The Ocean Chronicles (*Shinku no Hibun*) in 2013, and the novel also won the Mystery Writers of Japan Prize.

THE BATTLE ROYALE

BR

SLAM BOOK

EDITED BY HAIKASORU

KOUSHUN TAKAMI'S *BATTLE ROYALE* IS AN INTERNATIONAL
BEST SELLER, THE BASIS OF THE CULT FILM, AND
THE INSPIRATION FOR A POPULAR MANGA. AND FIFTEEN
YEARS AFTER ITS INITIAL RELEASE, *BATTLE ROYALE*
REMAINS A CONTROVERSIAL POP CULTURE PHENOMENON.

JOIN *NEW YORK TIMES* BEST-SELLING AUTHOR JOHN
SKIPP, *BATMAN* SCREENWRITER SAM HAMM, PHILIP K.
DICK AWARD-NOMINATED NOVELIST TOH ENJOE, AND AN
ARRAY OF WRITERS, SCHOLARS, AND FANS IN DISCUSSING
GIRL POWER, FIREPOWER, PROFESSIONAL WRESTLING, BAD
MOVIES, THE SURVIVAL CHANCES OF HOLLYWOOD'S LEADING
TEEN ICONS IN A BATTLE ROYALE, AND SO MUCH MORE!

$14.99 USA // $16.99 CAN // £9.99 UK   ISBN: 978-1-4215-6599-6

HAIKASORU
THE FUTURE IS JAPANESE

THE CAGE OF ZEUS BY SAYURI UEDA

The Rounds are humans with the sex organs of both genders. Artificially created to test the limits of the human body in space, they are now a minority, despised and hunted by the terrorist group the Vessel of Life. Aboard Jupiter-I, a space station orbiting the gas giant that shares its name, the Rounds have created their own society with a radically different view of gender and of life itself. Security chief Shirosaki keeps the peace between the Rounds and the typically gendered "Monaurals," but when a terrorist strike hits the station, the balance of power is at risk…and an entire people is targeted for genocide.

THE FUTURE IS JAPANESE, EDITED BY HAIKASORU

A web browser that threatens to conquer the world. The longest, loneliest railroad on Earth. A North Korean nuke hitting Tokyo, a hollow asteroid full of automated rice paddies, and a specialist in breaking up "virtual" marriages. And yes, giant robots. These thirteen stories from and about the Land of the Rising Sun run the gamut from fantasy to cyberpunk, and will leave you knowing that the future is Japanese! Featuring the Hugo Award winner "Mono No Aware" by Ken Liu, stories by Bruce Sterling, Toh EnJoe, Catherynne Valente, and much more!

GENOCIDAL ORGAN BY PROJECT ITOH

The war on terror exploded, literally, the day Sarajevo was destroyed by a homemade nuclear device. The leading democracies have transformed into total surveillance states, and the developing world has drowned under a wave of genocides. The mysterious American John Paul seems to be behind the collapse of the world system, and it's up to intelligence agent Clavis Shepherd to track John Paul across the wreckage of civilizations and to find the true heart of darkness—a genocidal organ.

APPARITIONS: GHOSTS OF OLD EDO BY MIYUKI MIYABE

In old Edo, the past was never forgotten. It lived alongside the present in dark corners and in the shadows. In these tales, award-winning author Miyuki Miyabe explores the ghosts of early modern Japan and the spaces of the living world—workplaces, families, and the human soul—that they inhabit. Written with a journalistic eye and a fantasist's heart, Apparitions brings the restless dead, and those who encounter them, to life.

VISIT US AT WWW.HAIKASORU.COM